Home at Last

Suncoast Society

Book 40

Tymber Dalton

Lesli Richardson

Home at Last?

Ben didn't know his Master and boyfriend would leave him homeless and in the lurch. Throw in identity theft to add insult to injury. When his best friend and co-worker, Jake, invites him to move into his spare bedroom, it's the answer to a prayer. Ben knows Jake's straight, but it doesn't stop him from fantasizing about the handsome Dom.

The last thing Jake wants is to take advantage of Ben and come off looking like a douche. That's why, for now, he keeps his carefully guarded secret—that he's bi, not straight.

As Jake realizes Ben is perfect for him, Jake's forced to confront the realities of life. The choice to be with Ben means facing down his homophobic parents and confronting darker, more dangerous realities that he never experienced before.

But can he admit his feelings before someone else steals Ben's heart?

Home at Last

Suncoast Society Series Book 40

Copyright © June 2024, by Lesli Richardson

First Publication: December 2016

Author's Note

This book was first published in 2016. It was lightly edited for this version but there are no significant changes to the story. It was also written before Covid.

The events referenced in regards to June happened in *Vicious Carousel*. Some characters appear or are featured in other books in the Suncoast Society series.

Most books in the Suncoast Society series are standalone works and may be read independently. To avoid spoilers and to not miss any backstory, you can visit my website for a full series listing at:

http://www.SuncoastSociety.com

You can sign up for my newsletter on my website at:

http://www.TymberDalton.com

Dedication

For Hubby and Sir. Also, special shout-out to Rosie M., one of my readers in the Trybe whose generosity and kind words came at the perfectly needed time. And a shout-out to Saya, for letting me bounce grammar off her. Thank you!

Chapter One

Ben

Y*ou've gotta be shitting me.*

Ben struggled not to say it out loud to the woman on the other end of the phone.

Unfortunately, she wasn't giving him much of a chance to get a word in edgewise.

"You need to understand the serious ramifications if this obligation isn't satisfied, Mr. Hodges. We've made several attempts to contact you in writing, and they've been returned to us marked undeliverable."

Ben rubbed his forehead and jumped in when she finally took a breath. "If you'll take a look at the special notes section of the account file, you'll see where I spoke to your supervisor last week. He noted receipt of the certified letter I sent, along with the copies of the police reports, social security statement, and bank records, all noting that several of my credit cards were stolen, along with my identity. You'll also note that I've put both a lock and an alert service on my credit report. So I don't understand why you're the *fifth* person from your company to call me—*today*—about this since I got to work at eight this morning. In case you didn't know, it's not even noon here yet in Sarasota. Do the math."

He heard a keyboard tapping. She didn't say anything for a moment. "Oh."

"Yeah, *oh.* So, lady, whatever you have to do to flag my file so you people stop calling me here at work, I'd really appreciate it. Before you cost me my job, which means I *can't* pay the part of the balance that I have never denied that I owe, and which I *have* been paying on. The information you need on pursuing the guy who stole my freaking identity is all in the police reports that—once again—I *know* you damn well have. Once they track his worthless ass down and lock him up, I'll be happy to forward his prisoner number to you so you can harass him to your heart's content. But until that happens, the next call I get from your company better be an apology and a report back that they're going to remove this from my credit report and reinstate my account minus the fraudulent charges."

More tapping. "I'm really sorry, Mr. Hodges. I don't understand why this wasn't flagged, and—"

"That's *exactly* what the last four people who called this morning told me. Are you all reading from the same script? If you people don't stop calling me here, you're going to get me fired. Look at my payment history. You'll see I've never even been so much as late on a payment in the past seven years I've had this damn card. Then I report it—to the cops—that my identity was stolen, and suddenly you're treating me like *I'm* the one who's the criminal."

He belatedly realized his voice had gone up in volume. Through the opening of his cubicle, he spotted that several people near him had stuck their heads up over their cubicle walls like meerkats and were looking his way.

He toned it down a few notches. "Now, do you need to pass me up the food chain to a supervisor to insure these calls will stop, or are you going to make sure whatever voodoo you have to do sticks this time? Or will my attorney have to handle it with you all?"

"I am *so* sorry, Mr. Hodges. I'll pass this case up to my manager to handle from this point on. It should have been done earlier. I apologize again, and we do appreciate you being our customer—"

He hung up on her. That was nearly verbatim what the other callers had said.

Needless to say, he held little hope of the calls stopping any time soon. So far, three of his four credit cards were frozen. The fourth, he'd managed to call them before the asshole had used it, and had gotten the card canceled and changed.

He was having the replacement delivered to Ed's office for him to pick up there, since he didn't want it delivered to the hotel he was currently calling home. One of those long-stay efficiency suites which was absolutely packed to the gills with most of his crap, the stuff that wasn't wedged into an overflowing storage unit holding furniture and other items he'd taken from the house when he'd moved.

The identity theft portion of the festivities had been round two of the bullshit, with him finding out about *that* last week.

Round one had happened two weeks before that, when Mort up and disappeared just hours before their landlord showed up to collect the several months of rent Mort owed him—rent that Ben thought Mort was paying, because Ben had been paying his half to Mort.

A situation Ben thought was bad to start with and had only gotten worse once he'd moved out and started checking things online.

Especially when a credit card he knew had nothing on it was declined, and it turned out Mort had apparently copied the numbers and purchased stuff with it.

Then, Ben checked his bank account and discovered there was over a thousand dollars missing due to fraudulent charges using his debit card number for online orders.

That'll teach me to move in with a hot guy and let him sucker me into sleeping with him.

Worse, Mort had been his Dominant, not just his lover, making the betrayal of trust that much worse, in Ben's mind.

"You okay?"

Ben started at the voice behind him. He turned to find his best friend and co-worker, Jake, standing there in the opening to his cubicle.

He deflated. With Jake, he could be completely honest and open. He dropped his voice. "No, I'm not."

Jake stepped closer. "That crap with Mort?" Jake was one of the few people who knew all the details about what happened.

Well, most of them. Certainly more than any other person in their office.

Jake also knew more about Ben's personal life than anyone else in their office, since they had some shared…interests, as well as friends in common.

"Yeah." Ben leaned back and scrubbed at his face with his hands. "I'm sick of this bullshit."

"What'd the police say?"

"They're still trying to track him down. They went to the address he was using to take receipt of the stuff he ordered online, and he'd already booked it from there. And—spoiler alert—it turns out he stole one of that guy's cards, too."

"Nothing else you can do, huh?"

"The lease was in his name. So were the utilities. I never dreamed the asshole would fuck me over this badly. I honestly had no clue he wasn't paying the rent the past couple of months."

Ben realized where he was and dropped his voice as he glanced around. "Serves me right for not vetting him better before I moved in. But I lived with him for two years before he pulled this shit. We weren't even sleeping together when I moved in with him. I *trusted* him."

When Ben had spotted the text on Mort's phone from their

landlord, saying that he was on his way over that afternoon, Ben asked him about it. Mort said it was just to check out the AC system, and then sent Ben to the grocery store.

When Ben returned home, Mort—and a lot of Mort's clothes and other belongings—were gone, and that's when the landlord arrived and dropped the truth bomb on Ben about Mort's failure to pay rent.

Thus began Ben's rapid descent into hell.

"Are you still living at that hotel?" Jake asked.

"Yeah. Can't afford to stay there for much longer, though. It'll chew through what I have left in my bank account. It was my immediate option and once I found out about the identity theft, I didn't have time to try to find a cheaper place."

"Can't the bank do anything?"

"They were able to reverse some of the charges immediately. The rest they'll have to research and dispute, and it might take a while. Meanwhile, I'm stuck in legal limbo with my credit in the shitter since he's opened several cards in my name. And that makes renting an apartment impossible right now."

"Even with the police paperwork?"

"Yep. Believe me, I've tried. Everyone runs credit checks." He leaned back in his chair. "And screw me, I damn sure don't want to ask my parents if I can move home."

"Why not? You get along well with them."

"Yes, I do. That's exactly why I don't want to move home. My dad will non-stop tell me he told me so about Mort, and that I can do a lot better. My mom will start trying to fix me up with every single guy she knows regardless of his age or whether or not he's gay."

Ben loved his mom and dad. When he'd come out to them in high school, he couldn't have asked for more supportive parents. He had dinner with them usually one night a week, although he had avoided telling them the full truth about what he was going through now. He was their only child, and they'd definitely vowed to stand by his side, no matter what.

The thing was, he felt embarrassed to admit to them their initial dislike of Mort had been right on the money. He hinted to them that he'd moved out because he'd had a fight with Mort, who wanted to move to a different city for a job, so he broke up with the guy. Not outright lied, exactly, but…

Okay, so they were huge lies of omission and just nodding in the right places when they filled in the blanks with loving parental outrage and leaps in logic.

He hated keeping the truth to himself like that but knew if he told them the truth they'd insist he move back home. And that meant uncomfortable conversations with them about his kinky personal life if he decided to date anytime soon.

Still, he couldn't imagine life without them.

Jake chuckled. "Well, at least they're supportive."

Ben dropped his voice even lower. "I think the phrase you meant was 'borderline codependent.' Also, I move in with them, it's bye-bye what little of a sex life I might have, much less doing any kinky stuff."

"Uh, but I thought you're out to them?"

"I am, but do you want to have sex in the same house as *your* parents? Much less have them hear you doing kinky stuff?"

"Oh. True."

"I'm also not ashamed to admit if I move back in, I might not want to move out again. It'd be too easy to settle in and end up twenty years from now still single and a crazy cat guy."

Not that he'd had much of a sex life in the months leading up to Mort's sudden departure. In retrospect, the "stress" Mort had claimed he was under made perfect sense. The jerk had been juggling a dual deception, both at home and at work.

At least he didn't cheat on me.

That Ben was aware of. One of the first things he'd done after moving out was get a full round of testing done. They'd only gone bareback for oral, though, so that reduced the chances of Ben contracting HIV from Mort, if he was pos.

Still, once he had another round of tests in a few months and those came back neg, he'd rest a lot easier. One of the few things he could count on was that Mort had been paranoid to the extreme about precautions regarding his health. They'd been sleeping together for over four months and completed two testing rounds before Mort would even do oral unwrapped.

Ben leaned forward again and reached for his mouse to wake up his terminal before it went into sleep mode. He was currently working on plans for a client, the CAD representation of what they'd send to the automated CNC machine to produce whatever this thing was supposed to be.

Ben didn't care what they were making, as long as it was made to the customer's specifications and they were happy with the final product. These particular widgets would be produced out of aluminum, some sort of intake fuel valve component for an after-market automotive part.

"Have you thought about moving in with someone as a room-mate?" Jake asked.

"I've been too busy putting out Dumpster fires in my financials, filing the police reports, all of that. Then I was looking around and trying to get a place on my own. Even a little studio or efficiency or something. But it seems like that's not going to be an option right now. Anyplace that would rent to me right now and is within my budget is likely a place I would never want to live."

"Maybe ask around at the munch on Sunday," Jake suggested. "Someone there might be looking for a roommate, or know of someone who is."

"I don't think it'll be in my budget to go. Which sucks, because I was really looking forward to going."

It absolutely wasn't in his budget right now, but he wouldn't admit that, even to his best friend.

"I'll buy you dinner. Allison has to work and can't go." Jake grinned. "You can be my date." He blew Ben a kiss.

"Do I have to blow you, or is this a platonic date?" Ben joked, his voice low enough it wouldn't carry.

"I'll let you off easy this time. Won't even spank your ass."

"Well, *that's* disappointing. I could use a good spanking." Ben played with his pen. "Next time I fall for a jerk without pulling a full credit report on him first, you have standing permission to beat *my* ass in the bad way, dude. Promise me."

"I'll hold you to that. Never give a sadist blanket permissions." Jake patted Ben on the shoulder and returned to his own cubicle.

Ben struggled to pull his mind back into focus on the job before him. He couldn't afford to mess this up. The owner of the company was patient, but this was a big job, an expensive one. If it was screwed up, or time-delayed, it could cost them a lot of money.

He damn sure couldn't afford to lose his job now.

BEN HAD RESORTED to eating ramen noodles and hot dogs for dinner in his room at the hotel. Cheap, filling, and easy to prepare in the limited space.

For lunch, he was bringing cans of generic store-brand soup to work and nuking the contents in a plastic bowl in their break room. Again, cheap, easy—and, oh yeah, cheap.

Jake stopped Ben on his way to the break room. "Want to grab a sub with me?" He grinned at the familiar joke.

Ben stared at the can of soup in his hand—generic store-brand cream of tomato—and sighed. "Where are you going?"

"I'll drive. Subway, of course." Jake's grin widened.

Ben rolled his eyes. "They have foot-longs pretty cheap."

"Giggity."

They could get away with joking like that around each other.

Besides being best friends, they'd known each other for over ten years, most of that time with both of them members of Venture and attending the Suncoast Society munches. Ben was a sub, and Jake a Dom. But since Ben was gay and Jake wasn't, their friendship hadn't led to more between them.

"The thought of soup turns my stomach today," Ben admitted. "Let me go dump this in my desk and I'll go with you." Ben returned to his cubicle and dropped the unopened can of soup and his bowl and spoon into the drawer.

Jake stood waiting in the lobby, keys in his hand, and led the way when Ben returned.

Once they were in Jake's car and safely away from curious ears, Ben threw his head back against the seat rest. "Seriously, you have permission to beat my ass in the bad way."

"Don't be so hard on yourself, dude. People get screwed over. Not trusting anyone isn't an option if you don't want to live a miserable life. Any more details on what all led up to this? I mean, everything boiled over fairly recent, right? This wasn't a long-term thing?"

Jake had taken several days of vacation time right around the weekend that the situation went to shit. Ben hadn't wanted to call and ruin his friend's well-deserved time off. In the interim, Ben had been too busy trying to handle everything to really sit down with Jake and catch him up.

And going out with his friends to Venture hadn't been in his budget the past couple of weeks, either.

"The detective said they think Mort embezzled money from where he worked because of a gambling addiction. Online poker or something like that. The IT department where he worked found visited sites in his history on his work computer despite him trying to hide his activity. So he probably ripped me off hoping to pay that back before they figured out what he'd done. Unfortunately for him, that's not what happened. Their bank flagged one of his transactions before it cleared and that tripped the domino chain.”

“*Wow.*”

“Yeah, wow.”

“Did you get all your stuff out?”

“All of my stuff, and some of his, too. Furniture, dishes, things like that. Shit I can actually use. I put his clothes and other crap that he left behind out at the curb. I don’t want any of it, and I’m not taking responsibility for it. Everything else is crammed into the largest storage unit I could afford, and in my room at the hotel.”

“I wish you’d called me to help you move.”

“I appreciate that, but I paid the guy next door some cash and he helped me move the heavy stuff. I didn’t want to bother you.”

“We’re friends. That’s *not* bothering me. So what are you doing this weekend?”

Ben knew it would have bothered Allison, though, had he called Jake for help and taken Jake’s time and attention away from her. “I’m going to work late tonight.”

“It’s Friday.”

“I know, but not like I’m doing anything else. Maybe come in tomorrow to finish this job, in case I can’t get it done today. That way they can start production on the test unit first thing Monday morning. That’ll put us a week ahead of schedule and make McMannis really happy.”

Carl McMannis was seventy, and had been running a machine shop well before the era of computers and computerized CNC machines. He’d resisted his son’s attempts to get him to retire and turn the business over to him, which had resulted in his son finally throwing his hands up in frustration the year before and leaving to go to work for another, larger manufacturing company up in Tampa.

Which had pissed the old man off. He’d seen it as akin to an act of treason.

If you kept Carl McMannis happy—which wasn't complicated or even difficult to do—you could almost guarantee you had a job for life.

If you did something to royally fuck up when it could have been avoided...

You might as well be dead to him.

Being a week ahead of schedule would allow them to make any tweaks to the programming without creating a stress-inducing panic.

It might also mean that Carl would be forgiving if word of Ben's personal situation and the annoying calls from creditors reached his office.

At the restaurant, Ben ordered the least expensive foot-long sub he could and a cup of water to go with it. When they received their sandwiches and sat down to eat, Jake stared at him for a moment.

"You know, the more I think about it, I have that back bedroom. The one with the en suite bath. If you can't find another option, let me know. I'll rent it to you. I wouldn't mind the extra money. I've been wanting to buy a new car, and renting to you would help me a lot without me having to worry about a car payment on top of my budget."

Ben arched an eyebrow at him. "Allison going to be okay with that? I thought she wasn't fond of me."

Jake frowned. "Allison's not fond of many people, but that's not the point. It's *my* house. She doesn't live with me and gets zero say in anything relating to that."

Ben suspected Jake and Allison were having problems as of late, but no one had witnessed anything directly. It was more the chilly, Arctic frost that seemed to surround the two with increasing frequency when they attended events together.

"Yeah, but that's the room you use as your playroom, isn't it?" Ben asked.

Jake shrugged. "I can move the stuff into the other bedroom.

It's not like I have guests over other than Allison, and she sleeps in my bedroom when she does. There's room in the smaller bedroom with the futon if someone needs to sleep over."

Ben wasn't sure he wanted to hang his hopes on that option yet, although it would be a perfect answer. "Seriously? You mean it?"

"Seriously. Give it some thought. It's not like we haven't known each other for years. Hell, we can take turns carpooling to work and save gas money. I wouldn't mind you having guests over, either. We're both kinky, so not like that's a shocker."

Ben slowly nodded. "Thanks. Let me make sure I run out all my other options first. I still have three apartment complexes I haven't heard back from. If they turn me down, I'll come talk to you."

"Good. It's not a pity offer, either. I'm serious. You're my friend. I want to help."

"I appreciate that. It wouldn't be forever, though. Just a few months, until I can get everything straightened out and fix my credit so I can rent a place on my own."

"No problem. Even if you needed longer than a few months, I'm good with that."

One thing Ben did know, Jake wasn't a bullshitter. He didn't offer something if he didn't really mean it. "Thanks."

"Hey, it's the least I can do, since you didn't call me to help you move, you stubborn subby."

Ben smiled. "Pushy Dom." That was a common exchange between the two of them.

"You'd better believe it." He grinned before taking a bite of his sandwich.

Chapter Two

Jake

After lunch, Jake drove them back to the office. He felt bad for Ben, and guilty that his friend hadn't thought he could call him to help him move. He'd known the guy for over ten years and considered Ben one of his closest friends, if not his best friend.

It didn't hurt that they both had interests and friends in common outside of work.

Not just vanilla interests, but kinky interests, as well. Ben had started working at McMannis Manufacturing of Sarasota ten years earlier, when he was only twenty-five. At forty-one, Jake was six years older than Ben, and had been the one to mentor and train Ben when he was first hired in.

Although Jake hadn't talked with anyone, not even Ben, about his situation with Allison, he knew the two of them had started the long, bumpy slide into breaking up. They'd been seeing each other for three years, and he loved her, but he wasn't ready to marry her, much less spend the rest of his life with her. Sure, he'd enjoyed having her as a girlfriend and play partner at first. They had fun in bed and out of it.

Unfortunately, Allison was pushing for more despite being pretty self-centered and childish in ways that told Jake getting married to her was not a good idea. She was thirty-one, ten years younger than him, and in some ways that really showed. Over the past six months, she'd been increasingly reluctant to play, to the point that Jake couldn't remember exactly how long it'd been since they'd had a good, hard scene.

Then, two months ago, Allison had tried to use reverse psychology on him and threatened to start playing with other Tops if he didn't at least formally collar her. He'd told her okay, if that was what she wanted, he was fine with it and he'd start playing with bottoms who actually wanted to play with him. She'd frozen in her tracks, the shocked expression on her face priceless.

Would have been funny had it not been the final nail in the coffin for him.

He'd called her bluff. Totally.

She'd backpedaled at the speed of light. Still, that little stunt had told Jake more than anything there was no way he'd collar, much less marry, someone so immature and manipulative.

He just hadn't gotten around to breaking up with her yet. He didn't want to give up all hope for their relationship, because he did love her.

Sort of.

Hell, despite not having formally collared her, he'd invested three years of his life in her. He didn't want to overreact and walk away if there was a chance she might straighten up. Still, he didn't love her enough to be legally tied to her in such a way that it'd be literally masochistic to separate their assets later. Plus, he made more than her. He damn sure didn't want to get tied into paying alimony to her.

Also, he wasn't *in* love with her anymore, something that made him a little sad to realize.

If Jake had a choice between taking in a roommate and making extra money he could use to buy a new ride, as opposed to a bedroom sitting there that, honestly, he wasn't even using anymore with Allison...he'd pick renting to his best friend so he could stop dumping money into his crappy car.

Every time.

Plus it meant helping a friend in need.

At least he didn't have a mortgage payment. He'd inherited the house two years earlier from his dad's parents after his grandmother died. But it was a nearly forty-year-old house needing repairs and improvements, in addition to things like homeowner's insurance, flood insurance, and property taxes.

Having a roommate he could count on would take some of the pressure off him. There'd be the added bonus of having someone help with chores and maintenance.

He liked Ben. He trusted Ben. He knew from the man's work ethic, and from having been over to Ben's place countless times, that Ben wasn't a slob.

Ben was someone he could easily share a house with. It didn't bother him that Ben was gay. When Jake was honest with himself, he considered himself bi, even though he'd never dated or slept with a guy before.

He'd never been attracted enough to a guy to take that step. There were also plenty of women he'd never been attracted to enough to take that step with.

To him, it was more about the person as a whole package, not a set of genitals. And since he was a hard-core monogamist, it wasn't like he would go splashing around in the kinky dating pool to see who else caught his interest while he was still tied to Allison.

Plus he never talked about that side of himself around his parents, who definitely would not understand, much less approve.

Why call down trouble when he didn't need to? Let them think what they wanted, that their son was straight.

Life would be much more peaceful with them in that way.

Before he headed out at the end of the day, Jake stopped by Ben's cubicle. The other man sat staring at his computer monitor, but he wore a dark glare that Jake suspected had nothing to do with the project on his screen.

"You all right, buddy?"

"Nope. I heard back from the other three places." Ben leaned back in his chair and stared up at Jake. "They were all sympathetic to my plight, but they declined to rent to me. Once my credit situation has stabilized, they'll be happy to re-evaluate things."

"Okay, seriously. Come by my place tonight and let's talk about the room."

Ben seemed to be considering it. "I might be working here a while."

"I don't care. Call me when you're ready to leave. I'll be home. Quit arguing with me, stubborn."

Ben ran a hand through his brown hair before swiveling his chair to face him. "How much you thinking a month?"

"You look at it first. I mean, I know you've been over before, but really look at it. Work through your budget. Then we'll talk. I guarantee you it'll be a lot less than you're paying at that stupid hotel."

"I don't want this to screw up our friendship."

"It won't. I'll even draw up a written lease. I wouldn't invite you to do this if I thought it'd cause problems."

Ben seemed to deflate as Jake cut through all of his excuses. "I hate putting you in this position."

"You're not putting me in any position, buddy. I told you, I'm good with this. I can buy a new car if you move in, because I could afford it then. The repairs are killing me now, and a monthly car payment would be a little too much of a stretch on my current budget."

"Okay. Thank you. I'll stop by when I finish here."

"See you in a couple of hours."

Jake headed out to his car, feeling a little lighter. The spare room didn't need to be tidied up much, but he had tossed a few things in there to get them out of sight. He could spend the time before Ben arrived straightening up and moving things into the other bedroom.

He hadn't known Mort very well, but he'd never really held a high opinion of the guy.

Then again, he hadn't been sleeping with Mort, or had a reason to have anything other than social interactions with him, so it was easy to not know a person very well or be able to form a better opinion of them to overcome one's initial impressions.

At least his gut instincts were still dead on. From the time Ben had moved in with Mort, it'd seemed like the man had completely monopolized Ben's time, not wanting people to come over to the house if he was there, other isolating behaviors.

After Mort collared Ben, the restrictions on Ben's free time had tightened even further, to the point Jake rarely got to see Ben alone except at work.

Once Jake returned home, he ate dinner, surveyed the bedroom in question, and started moving stuff into the third and smallest bedroom that was more a catch-all space and rarely used for guests. He got so busy tidying up and clearing things out that he missed hearing his phone ring, at first.

When he retrieved it and looked at the missed call log, it turned out to be Allison. They weren't supposed to get together tonight because she was working until nine. Suppressing irritation that she'd interrupted his chore, he called her back. "Hey, what's up?"

"Whatcha doin'?" He knew that syrupy tone all too well.

He swallowed back the growing impatience he increasingly felt over every interaction they had. "Cleaning."

"Oh." She sounded a little more subdued. Cleaning was

supposed to be one of her tasks when she was over at his place. While she'd eagerly agreed to do it early on when they'd started dating and she'd asked him to consider collaring her, she'd been less eager to actually follow through with it, to the point that he'd quit asking her.

And he'd quit considering formally collaring her, although he hadn't told her that.

"Did you want to get together tonight?" she asked.

"I thought you had to work until close?"

"I was able to get out early."

"Well, then you can come over here and help me clean. Otherwise, no."

"Oh." A long pause that he wasn't about to break, uncomfortably long for her, apparently, as she struggled for something to say. "I thought maybe we could go out to eat and catch a movie or something."

"I can't. I need to get this done. Besides, I already ate."

Not to mention he tired of paying for everything. She was more than happy to let him pay for their meals or movies or outings, while not bothering to hold up her end of the bargain.

"Then... I guess I'll let you get back to it." Snippiness in her tone sliced through the connection.

"Thanks. Talk to you later." He hung up without bothering to wait and see if she had something else to say.

He honestly didn't care what she had to say.

Not anymore.

And isn't that the bottom line?

It saddened him to realize he was acting like a cold-hearted bastard, but she'd pretty much drained him dry emotionally. It was only a matter of time before he finally broke up with her, if she didn't do it first.

It'd have to happen, because he didn't want to be alone, and his personal moral code wouldn't let him date anyone before he officially ended things with Allison. Nothing against poly people, because he had friends who were poly. It just wasn't his thing. He didn't share, and since he didn't share, he didn't think it was right to ask his partner to share him.

End of story.

By the time Ben called him a little before eight, Jake had actually cleaned the en suite bathroom and tidied the bedroom to the point it'd take two people very little time to finish emptying it and moving Ben's things in. What wouldn't fit in the third bedroom, he could stash in his garage. And hopefully whatever Ben had in storage could fit in the garage, as well, unless he wanted to keep his storage unit.

The more Jake thought about it, the more he liked the idea of having Ben living there, and not just short-term. Wasn't like Ben would interfere with his love life.

It'd be nice to have someone else around, even if only a friend. He'd felt bad for Ben after the whole shitstorm he went through with Mort.

This was something he could do to help. That it'd be helping himself at the same time was a bonus. And hell, he'd have someone to help him with chores, too.

When Ben arrived, Jake had the door open for him before he even made it all the way up the walk. "Hey!" Jake hugged him.

The other man managed a smile. "Hey. Thanks for this. I really appreciate it."

"No worries. Come on in." Jake led the way down to the back bedroom. He flipped on the overhead light, which was part of the ceiling fan fixture.

It was nearly as large as the master bedroom, but the attached bathroom was smaller and only had a shower, not a full bathtub.

Ben's gaze widened. "*Wow*, you moved everything already!"

"Wanted you to be able to get a good look at the size. The futon is a two-person job, though."

"This is great, really," Ben said. "How much do you want a month?"

"Including utilities, I was thinking seven hundred a month. Plus you buy your own food, or we split shared groceries, and you pitch in with chores. We can take turns mowing, that kind of thing."

* * *

Ben

Ben tried not to look too relieved. He would have easily paid double that to stay here and not have to deal with the bullshit of trying to get utilities put in his name, security deposits, all of that. Not to mention it wasn't even two weeks' worth of what he was paying now at the long-stay hotel.

Jake looked at him. "But if you can't afford that—"

"I'll take it." Ben stuck his hand out and shook with Jake. "I want a written lease, though. To protect you and me." He hadn't had one with Mort, unfortunately.

Hard lesson learned, not that it would have helped him much in the end.

Jake smiled. "I already downloaded forms from the Internet."

"Cool."

"You remember I have a pool, too, right? And a hot tub." Jake led him back down the hall, switching off the lights behind them.

"You sold me already." Ben got the feeling Jake was just as eager to have him move in as he was to get moved in.

"Just saying." He led Ben to the eat-in counter in the kitchen, where the printed forms lay. "The kitchen isn't the greatest, but it's on my to-do list to eventually renovate."

"It's fine, believe me. You saw where I used to live. Not a bad place, but the seventies retro vibe definitely had outlived its usefulness." He quickly skimmed through the paperwork and didn't see anything that concerned him or read any differently than leases he'd signed in the past.

Hell, Mort had insisted they didn't need a lease, so this was a nice change.

"You want to move in tomorrow?" Jake asked. "I insist on helping you move. I'm not doing anything. You can use my garage for storage, too. Save more money that way. I know you said you might want to work tomorrow, but this way we can get you moved, you won't have to pay for extra days at the hotel, and I can help you do it. Please?"

No, Ben knew he'd be stupid to rebuff his friend's help. Especially when he realized how much Mort had cut him off from not just Jake during their relationship, but from all of his friends.

"That would be amazing, thanks." Ben wished Jake was gay, or at least bi. He'd gladly offer to drop to his knees and give the guy a blowjob over how nice he was being.

Not that he was bad to look at, either.

Before Jake could change his mind, Ben signed the lease papers. "I can't tell you how much I appreciate this."

"You're helping *me* out. Seriously."

Ben watched while Jake reached into his pocket and handed him two keys. "Front door, and the side door on the garage. The deadbolt and knob are keyed alike on the front door. I'll find the other garage door opener and put fresh batteries in it for you, and get you an alarm code." He picked up his copies of the lease. "So what time do you want to move?"

This was happening so fast, Ben couldn't even think straight. "What time works for you?"

"The sooner we get it done, the sooner we can relax. We're still going to the munch Sunday, right? I'm buying."

"You don't need to buy. I'll buy you dinner for helping me move."

"Nope." Jake grinned, his brown eyes full of friendly mirth. "Listen, you stubborn sub, I told you *I* was buying. I don't go back on my word. You want to cook me dinner or something tomorrow night, sure."

The unexpected kindness threatened to make Ben cry, and he didn't want to do that in front of his friend. Instead, he tightened his grip around the two new keys in his hand, letting them dig into his flesh to help stave back the prickle of tears.

Sooo different than his experience with Mort. "You have a deal, you pushy Dom." He started to slip the keys onto his keyring.

"If you ever want to bring someone over as a date or whatever, as long as you're not swinging from the living room ceiling fan, no problem. I'll give you the same courtesy if I bring someone home."

That piqued Ben's curiosity. "What about Allison?"

Jake shrugged. "I suspect she won't be around much longer." He tapped the lease papers on the counter. "Just one of those things. Time for some changes."

"Oh. Sorry."

"Nothing for you to be sorry about." Jake started to turn, then hesitated. "Hey, did you eat dinner yet?"

"No. I'll grab something on the way home." Which was a fib. He'd suck down ramen noodles and hot dogs, but didn't want to admit that to Jake.

"That's silly. I'll feed you. I've got plenty of leftovers. They'll just go to waste."

Jake set the papers aside and walked over to the fridge. Reaching into it, he pulled out a couple of containers and started plating food without even asking Ben if he liked whatever it was.

At that point, Ben didn't *care* what it was, he'd eat it without hesitation.

It'd sure as hell beat what he had waiting for him back at his room.

"Grab yourself something to drink," Jake told him while carrying the plate to the microwave. He pointed at a cabinet. "You know where the glasses are. Ice is in the freezer, and there's soda and tea and stuff in the fridge."

Ben moved to do it, hoping to quickly memorize the kitchen's layout. He'd make sure to cook frequently for Jake, in addition to helping with chores. He loved to cook, and it was the least he could do to help repay the kindness his friend was showing him.

Jake stood leaning against the other side of the counter while Ben sat on a barstool and ate. Meat loaf, not the best he'd had, but far from the worst, and it was better than fast food or ramen noodles.

"We still didn't settle on a time tomorrow," Jake said while wearing a smirk that Ben knew he'd have a hard time not getting hard over.

"I'll start packing the stuff in my room tonight," Ben said. "Really, I can get by as long as we move my bed and the dressers out of storage tomorrow. Those are the two worst, because I can't manhandle them by myself and I'll need them. I don't have a truck to borrow, though."

"No problem. I'll take care of that."

Ben assumed Jake had a friend he could borrow a pick-up truck from. "Then I'll try to be ready to start unloading my room by nine. What I have there are my clothes and some important stuff like photo albums, along with small items I could jam in there. It's probably three carloads in my car. I rented a small moving truck when I grabbed everything."

He hated to think of the garbage bags he'd dumped his clothes into when he'd hurriedly moved out.

Far different than when he'd moved in with Mort, when it'd been planned and he'd had friends help him, and he hadn't been in too much of a hurry or too ashamed to ask his friends for help the way he was now.

Except back then he hadn't known he was moving into a kind of trap. Slow-motion quicksand.

This time, at least, he'd be moving in the right direction and regaining his life.

"Text me the address and your room number, please."

Ben picked up his phone to do it. "This isn't going to complicate your life, is it?"

Another smile from Jake, one Ben couldn't interpret. "Only in good ways, buddy. Trust me."

Chapter Three

Ben

When Ben drove to the hotel a little before ten, he realized how stupid it was to ever think of it as "home."

The hotel was merely a waystation in the shitshow of his meandering personal life. The physical manifestation of a series of increasingly bad choices over the years. Mort had been the worst choice, though. Before that, he'd lived on his own and managed to date several guys who'd cheated on him or thought Dominant meant controlling, abusive asshole.

He'd thought Mort was different. They'd started out as friends when Ben had moved in with him to save money, and then it'd morphed into more. Mort had expertly picked up on Ben's every emotional weak spot, just like the predator he turned out to be, and manipulated Ben until Ben had felt dependent upon Mort in a way he'd never felt before.

Not a good way, either.

Yeah, he owned responsibility for choosing to move in with

Mort. Every bit of it. Not for Mort's actions, but for putting up with the crap as long as he did and not backing the guy down.

Looking back, Ben could see a lot of warning flags that he didn't pay any attention to at the time. He'd lived thirty-five years without climbing into a crappy free-candy van...or so he'd thought.

Mort had held out the candy and led him inside before slamming the door shut after him.

Now Ben was left to pick up the pieces of his life.

It wasn't even the emotional betrayals that hurt so much as the monetary ones. A guy cheating, okay, yeah, sucky, but he'd dealt with that before. People could be shitty in relationships but still have a *line*, be honest in other ways.

Possess at least a modicum of integrity.

Mort apparently didn't have that line. Or if he did, it lay closer to the sociopathic end of the spectrum than the plain-ass shitty person one.

Ben had saved the garbage bags that had transported his clothes during the hurried move, since he'd used the dresser and closet in the hotel room to store things. Grabbing one of the bags now, Ben isolated his dirty clothes and bagged them, dumping that bag into a laundry basket so he'd be able to easily tell which ones needed laundering. He'd add the clothes he was currently wearing after he grabbed a shower just before bed.

Working methodically, he started bagging all his clothes, trying to keep them folded neatly and not think how different this process was than the last time. No frantic, desperate race against the clock while struggling against both his anger and shame over Mort's betrayal. At least the landlord had felt sorry for him and gave him enough time to get his stuff out before changing the locks. Ben had also left the place empty and reasonably clean, not needing more than a quick vacuuming and cleaning to be ready for someone else to move in. That wasn't his responsibility, but he didn't want the landlord to regret giving Ben the extra time to move.

Just because Ben had been fucked over, he didn't want to fuck someone over in return. His parents had raised him better than that.

Ben had dumped Mort's crap out at the curb, the stuff he didn't take with him or give to the neighbor guy who'd helped him move.

Considering Mort's next permanent address would likely be someplace owned by the Florida Department of Corrections, the asshole wouldn't need most of it anyway.

In addition, there was the fact that Mort had cost him money, aggravation, and time, as well as peace of mind.

The last hurt worst of all.

If he could recoup a little money by keeping what he could use, he had no problem doing that. At some point in the future, once he'd rebuilt his life, he'd replace everything that had been Mort's with new items that weren't tainted by memories of the jerk.

For now, he couldn't afford to do that.

By the time Ben finished packing and was ready to take his shower, it was almost midnight and he'd pretty much gathered everything together. He'd have to empty the bathroom after his shower, and then the fridge in the morning. Finally, when he set his alarm and lay down to try to sleep, he closed his eyes and envisioned Jake's handsome brown gaze.

If Jake was breaking up with Allison, whoever the guy dated next would have to really make a good impression for Ben to like her. He was already feeling protective of his friend. Maybe that was stupid, but the guy was nice.

The last thing he wanted was to see someone use Jake, take advantage of the guy.

The way Mort had taken advantage of *him*.

Ben knew it'd be a while before he could trust enough to get involved with anyone. Play partners? Sure. But dating would take a while. Going out as friends—whatever.

This had been a valuable lesson in protecting not just his freaking heart, but his wallet. No telling how long it'd take him to get this mess straightened out, and even then, he didn't know what future aggravations Mort's betrayal would cost him in terms of financing to buy a home of his own or a new car.

He could jerk off if he was horny. His own hand wouldn't ruin his credit rating.

At least Jake had given him breathing room. The money Ben would save every month by living there meant he'd be able to build up his savings.

It also meant he wouldn't have to worry about Jake having ulterior motives beyond wanting to help a friend. In the years he'd known Jake, he'd never known the man to be mean or petty or anything other than a straight-shooter.

Plus, he was straight. No chance of the guy hitting on him and taking advantage of him that way.

After what he'd just been through, Ben knew it'd be a relief to be able to close his eyes at night and relax, sleep, not need to be on his guard. With Mort no longer able to access his bank account or credit cards, that was one worry off his plate. The credit monitoring service he'd paid for would stop any additional attempts Mort might make to open new credit cards in Ben's name, although it might not stop him from doing stuff like trying to commit income tax return fraud, if he wasn't caught and prosecuted soon.

For now, Ben would be happy to have a dependable roof over his head and time to sort out his emotional life. He'd gladly pitch in at Jake's, helping out, doing chores, anything he could to contribute and make Jake's life easier so the man didn't regret renting the room to him.

It'd also allow Ben a harmless way to get his subby fix in a manner Jake would appreciate without any strings attached.

And it would allow Ben a chance to figure out how the fuck he'd let himself be so fucking stupid in the first place to put up with Mort's bullshit.

Jake

The alarm blaring in Jake's ear Saturday morning confused him at first, until he realized why he'd set it.

Ben.

He was going to help the guy move in.

That got him moving.

Did he think Allison would act pissy when he told her about Ben moving in?

Absolutely.

It wasn't that she didn't like Ben. She didn't like anyone who made demands on Jake's time when she was around, or took his focus off her.

Shit.

That thought slammed into him as he stood in the kitchen while waiting for the coffee to brew.

He'd let her get away with it, thinking it was cute at first, in her way, and growing so used to it that he really didn't notice it much. It just…was.

The new normal.

Who the fuck is the Dom in this relationship, anyway?

Not him, that was for sure.

It was too easy to draw uncomfortable parallels to what Ben endured with Mort.

That only finalized the realization that he didn't want to be in a relationship with her anymore. Not like that. Not for sex. He couldn't be just play partners with her, either, because he knew exactly where that would lead. She would do her level best to sabotage him at every turn, to the point he'd have to avoid attending events where she'd be if he was playing with anyone else.

Thank god I didn't officially collar her.

After Ben had left the night before, Jake had gone online and reserved a small moving truck for the day. He couldn't imagine Ben would have so much that it wouldn't meet their needs in one or two trips. After fixing his coffee in a travel mug, he returned to the bedroom to get dressed. He wouldn't even bother showering this morning since he'd be getting sweaty anyway.

Twenty minutes later, he was on his way to the truck rental place. He could leave his car parked there and he'd pick it up when he returned the truck. Fifteen minutes before nine, he was pulling into the hotel parking lot and driving around to Ben's room. When he knocked, Ben looked shocked to see the truck parked outside.

"*Wow!* Dude…I…I don't know what to say. Thank you! I'll pay you back. I thought you meant you were borrowing someone's truck."

Jake grinned. It felt good—yes, he'd admit it was selfish—to play the white knight. "No, you won't. Consider it a housewarming gift from me. Hey, the faster we get you moved, the faster we can chill out. Where do you want to start?"

It took them less than an hour to empty his room and go through it one final time, checking all the drawers and under the bed to make sure nothing was forgotten. Jake waited in the rental truck while Ben went to the hotel office to check out and settle up. Then he followed Ben to the storage unit, which they emptied and Ben was able to cancel, saving him even more money.

Three hours after he'd left the house, Jake was backing the moving truck up to his garage door, the truck full and only needing one trip total.

"Let me go in through the side and open it," he told Ben as he got out. "My remote for the door is in my car." He went in and shut the alarm off, making a mental reminder to add a code for Ben.

Allison didn't even have a key, much less her own alarm code.

Another point Jake was glad he'd stalled her about. He wouldn't have to worry about changing the locks.

Unloading the truck went easier and faster. After moving the futon out of the bedroom, and moving in Ben's bed and two dressers in, Jake headed out to return the truck and pick up his car. On the way home, he stopped by the grocery store close by and grabbed sandwich fixings and beer for lunch. He wouldn't hold Ben to cooking for him tonight, but the least he could do was offer the guy lunch.

I'm a sucker for a sob story.

Not that Ben was a sob story, per se. He was a nice guy caught in a bad situation.

Ben had made a remarkable amount of progress by the time Jake returned. He uncapped two beers, carrying one down to Ben. As he leaned against the doorway of what was now officially Ben's room, he looked around. Ben was methodically putting things away, even the chaos seeming to have an order to it.

Hell, Allison could barely cook a frozen pizza for dinner without the kitchen looking like a bomb went off. And when she spent nights over, one small bag looked like a clothing and makeup store exploded.

"Not even two o'clock yet," Jake said. "Good day's work."

Ben sat on the corner of his bed after taking a pull from the bottle of beer. "You have no idea how much all this means to me. Do you want a check or cash for the rent?"

"Check's fine. If I can't trust you to write me a good check, I have no business asking you to move in with me."

"As soon as I find my checkbook, I'll write it for you." He looked around. "It's a temporary check, though. My permanent ones haven't come in yet. I had to close the old bank account and get a new one."

"Oh, you can change your address to here, too," Jake told him.

"Right now, everything goes to the PO box I got near work. I did that first thing after I moved out." Ben stared at the bottle of beer in his hand. "Good thing I did, too. Even the police told me to use a PO box to help protect me, once I found out what happened. God, I really feel like an idiot. How could I be so stupid?"

"Hey, people can be assholes. We don't expect them to be assholes. You'll feel better once you get your mental feet back under you. It happens to the best of us. We've all been there."

"Not like this."

"Well, no, not necessarily like what you're going through, I'll admit. That was on the extreme end of the scale. But anyone can be a victim of identity theft by a stranger. Click on the wrong e-mail link and *bam*." Jake took another swallow of his beer. "I'm going to take a swim. You need any help?"

"No, I'm good, thanks." Ben stood and walked over, holding out his hand. "Thanks again, man."

Jake offered him a smile as they shook, then Jake pulled him in for a one-armed hug. "Friends take care of friends. That's kind of a big part of the deal. I'm glad I could help. You're helping me out, too. This works out perfectly for us both. Make sure you grab a sandwich. Get something to eat. I bought fixings on the way home."

"Did you eat yet?"

"No, I'll make one in a little bit."

"Let me make one for you." Ben started to edge past him. "Seriously." He paused as he slid past, looking up at Jake.

They stood nose to nose in the doorway.

Damn, he's got cute blue eyes.

How Jake had never noticed that before, he didn't know. "Okay," Jake said. "Sure. Thanks. Stubborn subby."

Ben smiled, and it took every ounce of reserve Jake had not to just lean in and see what it'd feel like to brush a kiss across the guy's lips.

"Pushy Dom."

Okay, then. Guess I've found the first guy to flip my switch from "theoretically bi" to "definitely bi."

Ben

Ben forced himself to stop staring into Jake's eyes and make his way down the hall to the kitchen.

Holy crap.

He'd have to be careful to not wig Jake out by letting him know he was attracted to him.

But I can show him in other ways. Like making the man a sammich.

Jake disappeared into his bedroom for a moment and returned wearing swim trunks. He'd drained his bottle of beer, too. "The recycling bin's in the garage," he told Ben as he rinsed the bottle out in the kitchen sink before he grabbed another bottle from the fridge. "Trash goes out Mondays and Thursdays. Plus, yard waste is picked up on Mondays, recycling on Thursdays."

"Okay. I'll make sure that gets taken care of." Ben had already washed his hands and was making them both sandwiches.

"I didn't mean you had to do it. It was just an FYI."

"I don't mind doing it. I'll carry my weight around here. Believe me, it's no trouble, especially considering how nice you've been." He offered his friend a smile. "Go on out to the lanai. I'll bring it to you."

Jake grinned. "Be careful, buddy. I could get used to this, having a resident subby."

Ben had to return the smile. He couldn't help it. "Yeah, well, maybe I could get used to being the resident subby."

Yes, he snuck a glance at the man's ass as Jake crossed the living room and headed for the sliders.

The guy was *hot.*

Allison's a lucky bitch.

If Jake wasn't straight, Ben might be tempted to see if he could seduce the man away from her.

He'd watched Jake play before, and it always left him hard. He could tell Jake held back in a lot of ways when he played with Allison, because the woman wasn't exactly a masochist. Brat? Definitely. And he'd seen Jake play with others, too, before he'd met Allison. Men and women. Ben had wanted to play with him, but Mort never would have allowed it, even if Jake did play with others while dating Allison.

I wasted too many years and too much time on that asshole. I need to stop thinking about him.

When Ben finished making their lunch, he carried the plates out to the lanai, where Jake was already swimming. Ben set Jake's plate on the edge of the pool, next to where he'd left his bottle of beer.

"Thanks, buddy." Ben sat on the edge of the pool with his feet dangling in the water while Jake swam over. "I appreciate it."

Ben paused, his sandwich halfway up to his mouth. "You're welcome." Mort had never, not once, uttered those words to him.

How fucked up am I that I put up with that for so long?

Sure, he'd been single before meeting and moving in with Mort. When looking back, he saw Mort had sabotaged every single potential relationship Ben had tried to have before Mort talked him into being collared to him. At the time, he hadn't seen it that way, he'd seen Mort as being a caring friend.

That was no excuse for the level of sheer stupidity he'd exhibited by allowing Mort to drag him down into depths of hell that would have made Dante envious.

"You all right?" Jake asked.

Ben nodded. "I'm fine now. Thank you. Seriously. I *really* want to pull my weight around here. Leave me a list of chores to do, if you want to."

Jake patted him on the leg. Friendly, not sexy. He held up his sandwich with the other hand. "Dude, you already are pulling your weight."

Chapter Four

Jake

Jake meant it, too. Ben hadn't been living under his roof for twelve hours yet, and already Jake was wishing he'd moved the man in days earlier when he'd first heard the start of Ben's tale.

Hell, when was the last time Allison had fixed him a sandwich, much less a whole meal?

I'm an idiot.

Jake knew it was just a matter of time before he needed to have "that" conversation with Allison.

The one where he told her it'd been real, and it'd been fun, but it wasn't real fun any longer.

Not for a while. A *long* while.

He wasn't *in* love with her any longer. On the contrary, he felt increasing resentment toward her for everything she wasn't doing lately.

Including holding up her end of their relationship, and not even in the D/s ways, but the "normal" ways.

He and Ben chatted while eating, and it didn't escape Jake's notice that Ben waited until Jake was done to get up and return to the house, taking Jake's plate with him.

After Jake finished his swim, he headed into his bedroom and showered, opting not to shave today. Fuck it, he wanted to chill out.

He knew he should be doing the yard work he'd planned to do, but he could put it off until tomorrow morning, when it would be cooler. It meant instead of having most of Sunday to laze around, he'd spend half of it doing chores before they went to the munch.

Worth it.

After his shower, he headed out to the kitchen, rinsed his empty beer bottle, grabbed his third from the fridge, then went to the living room to chill in front of the TV and catch up on a Netflix series he'd been meaning to watch. He knew Ben was still unpacking and arranging stuff in his room, but he'd leave him alone unless Ben asked for help.

It was too tempting to stare into Ben's blue eyes.

He replayed the brief encounter in Ben's bedroom doorway as the guy moved past him.

Even his cock tried to stiffen.

Yep, definitely attraction he felt for Ben.

He'd just settled in on the couch when his phone rang over on the kitchen counter.

Allison's custom tone.

Ugh.

While tempted to let it go to voice mail that would only delay the inevitable. He stood and managed to answer it before it cut to voice mail. "Hey."

"Hey. I'm on break right now. I was wondering if I could come over after work tonight? Maybe we could go out to dinner. Or do you have more 'chores' to do?"

He'd thought about taking her out to dinner to break the news to her, meeting her somewhere so he could pay the tab and walk away if she went nuts, but the snippiness in her tone slammed into him.

How many times in the past had she taken exactly that kind of tone with him and he'd let her get away with it?

Too many times.

"You can come over if you want, but Ben's already offered to cook me dinner, so I'm not going out. And frankly, I'm not in the mood for company. I doubt he is, either."

He could almost see the calculating expression on her face when she didn't reply at first, processing that new and unusual—and totally unexpected—information.

"*Ben?*"

"Yeah, Ben."

"Why's he cooking you dinner?"

Jake could deny he was enjoying dragging this out, but that'd make him a liar.

Especially now that he'd really started putting things together in his mind and saw her pattern of negative behavior. How she'd tried to isolate him. How she'd promised a shit-ton of things and yet never followed through once it was obvious she had what she needed from Jake.

How she'd been increasingly mooching off him financially as of late. "Because I helped him move today."

"Oh. You didn't tell me you were going to do that."

Jake dropped fully into Dom-mode. "I didn't need to. Besides, you didn't ask."

Another pregnant pause from her. "Where'd he move to?"

Yes, the evil smile felt *good.* So did the struggle not to laugh. "Into my back bedroom."

Three…two—

"*What?*"

"What?" All innocence. His smile turned into a grin. Maybe it was a little mean, but *worth* it. Especially after the last several months of growing friction and frustration between them, and after his countless attempts to address it with her had repeatedly fallen on her willfully deaf ears.

She'd had no interest in changing.

She'd wanted *him* to do all the changing.

So now, he was *done*. When they'd first met, she'd claimed to love this Dom side of him.

If she didn't like it now, because she couldn't manipulate him any longer, that was her problem and not his.

"You let him move into the back bedroom? But that's our playroom!"

"No, it's *my* playroom, because it's *my* house."

"You didn't think to *ask* me first?"

"Why? It's *my* house. And he's my friend. He's paying me rent and helping with chores."

"I—" Another pause. "Well, it would have been nice if you'd asked me if I minded first."

"Considering you don't pay rent or do chores around here, it's not really an issue, is it?"

Yes, that was a cheap shot, but he didn't freaking care. Time for Allison to move on along.

"What the hell is *that* supposed to mean?"

"It means exactly what it means. You don't live here. You don't pay bills or contribute to my household, monetarily or physically. Therefore, you don't get a say."

"But I'm your girlfriend!"

"Do you honestly think I should have a say in who your roommate is?"

"I—" Yet another pause. She knew damn well he hated her roommate, Ann, but the women were best friends, had been since high school.

Jake hated Ann, and the feeling was mutual. Jake had always found the woman to be petty and conniving, a constant source of friction between him and Allison.

"You know how I feel about him," Allison eventually said. "I don't like him. I never have."

Jake suspected it was because Allison couldn't manipulate Ben with her feminine charms. "Doesn't really matter how you feel about him. You know how I feel about Ann, yet I've never done anything to interfere with your friendship with her."

She sidestepped that comment. "So what are we supposed to do for a playroom?"

"We're not. It's been months since we've scened, so not like it'll be missed."

"Are you saying you don't want to play with me anymore?"

From her tone, he could tell she was winding up into passive-aggressive threat mode.

Something else that made him sad, that he could predict her negative patterns of behavior.

He'd save her the trouble. "To be honest, I've been doing some thinking. I don't think I'm the right Dominant for you. I need a heavy masochist who's very submissive, and you're more a brat who enjoys sensual play on your own terms. You were the one who mentioned it a while ago, that you wanted to play with others. That's not a bad idea."

She didn't respond at first.

"Allison?"

"Then why don't we just break up, if you feel that way?"

Bingo. "Well, I was going to suggest we play with others, but now that you mention it, it would be for the best to break up now, while we're still friends. I don't want there to be any resentment later, and breaking up would be fairest to you."

She didn't reply.

When he looked at the phone, he realized she'd hung up on him.

Shrugging, he carried the phone over to the couch, anticipating she'd probably call him back in a few minutes when she realized he wasn't trying to call her. If she was on break, though, she wouldn't be able to talk to him for much longer.

Five minutes later, she called back.

He answered on the first ring as he hit *pause* on the remote so he wouldn't miss any of his show. "Yes?"

"Why didn't you call me back?" she demanded.

Called that one right. "I figured you hung up on me."

"I di—I mean, you should have called me back."

He'd really rattled her if she was slipping that badly. "When did you want to come by and get your stuff?" He didn't have anything at her place that he could recall. She'd left assorted odds and ends at his house, mostly bathroom stuff and a couple of changes of clothes. Usually, they spent time at his place, so they could be alone and he didn't have to put up with Ann's antagonistic bullshit.

"This is really shitty of you, to break up with me over the phone."

"You mentioned breaking up first. I only suggested playing with others. I simply agreed with your counteroffer to break up. I mean, it makes the most sense."

She didn't have an argument to counter that fact, either. "*Why* did you move Ben in without asking me first?"

"I told you, because I didn't *need* to ask you."

"As your girlfriend, it's common courtesy."

"No, common courtesy would have been mentioning if I moved another woman in here."

"You know what I mean, Jake. I deserved to know."

"We already covered that. I'll gather your stuff up. Let me know when you want to come get it. If I won't be home, I'll leave it on the front porch for you."

This time when the connection went quiet, she didn't hang up.

He didn't break the silence, either.

Finally…"I didn't mean we had to break up," she said, her voice sounding more subdued. "I don't *really* want to break up."

Fuck. Here he'd thought this would go easily. "Allison, let's be honest with each other. You aren't happy with me as a Dom. Otherwise, you'd be sticking to our agreement and working toward me collaring you. And I'm not happy with you as a submissive. I've tried talking with you about this in the past, multiple times, and every single time you got defensive. You tried to manipulate me a couple of months back—"

"I thought you loved me!"

"I do love you, but I'm not going to marry you. Period. There are too many differences between us. To be blunt, I think breaking up is a good idea. You're obviously not happy, and neither am I. I want you to be happy. If breaking up hadn't on your mind, you wouldn't have said it. If you were using it as a manipulative tactic on me, then it's backfired on you. You need to find someone more compatible with you than I am, because this isn't working for me."

There. It was out.

That time she did hang up on him.

Jake set his phone on the table and hit *play* on the remote. Chances were she wouldn't call him back soon. He might get a series of snarky and snippy texts from her, snuck in while her manager wasn't looking, but probably no phone calls until she got off work at nine.

He expected she might have calmed down enough by then to try a tearful, pleading approach to get him to not break up with her. Negotiating, offering whatever he wanted in exchange for giving her another chance.

He was done playing her games. They'd been here before and he was tired of it.

To be bluntly honest with himself, after his earlier reaction to Ben, he wanted to ponder on that some more. It wasn't common knowledge that he was bi. He'd never mentioned it to Allison. Since he was dating her, he didn't consider it a salient point because he was monogamous and it wouldn't be an issue. He didn't have it on his FetLife profile, either.

There was also the fact that Ben likely wasn't looking for a new relationship any time soon.

Although the thought of having the guy not only as a play partner, but perhaps as his collared submissive—or maybe even more at some future point—definitely intrigued Jake.

Hmm.

***

Ben

Ben hadn't meant to eavesdrop but he couldn't help overhearing parts of Jake's end of his phone conversation with someone Ben presumed was Allison.

Shit.

Yes, Jake had told Ben it was likely he'd be breaking up with Allison soon, but Ben hadn't wanted to be the reason for that breakup.

Finally, he had to go back out to the garage for another load of stuff. He paused in the living room as he passed through. "Are you okay?"

Jake hit *pause* on the remote, a smirk on his face. "Guess who's single?" He held up his bottle of beer. "Party at my place! Wait, we're already here." He shrugged as he took a swallow of beer. "Time to celebrate!"

Ben thought he was adorable. "How many of those have you had?"

"This is my third and last, don't worry. So what's for dinner?"

"Sorry."

Jake looked confused. "Sorry, you're not cooking me dinner?"

"No, sorry that I'm the reason you guys broke up."

"Nope. You have nothing to apologize for. Unless you're not cooking me dinner?"

He knew from Jake's smirk the guy was teasing. "I'm still cooking you dinner."

"Cool. Then we're copacetic."

Ben stepped into the room. "I know you said things were winding down with her, but I didn't mean to speed them along."

"You didn't. It's fine."

"No offense, but it sure sounds like I caused it."

Jake arched an eyebrow at him, borderline Dom tone in his voice. "When I say something, I mean it. You don't need to second-guess me. Honestly? I was at the point I was looking for the least contentious way out with her. Things have not been good for a long while between us and it was only a matter of time before this happened. This was perfect timing all around."

Ben decided to break the ice. "Well, if it means anything, feel free to offer to beat my ass. Maybe it'd do us both some good."

Jake's smirk turned into a grin and he tipped his beer bottle in Ben's direction. "Be careful what kind of invitations you give to a sadist. I might just take you up on that."

"I mean it. It'd be nice having a sadist beat me who I wasn't worried about ripping me off or screwing me over."

Jake's brown gaze bored straight through him. "I mean it, too. It'd be nice having a subby whose ass I can beat who I knew was actually interested in getting beat and not just having me buy them things."

Ben hoped his cock wasn't hardening in his shorts. Frankly, he was too numb to know for sure if it was.

Jake playfully tipped the beer bottle at him again before he took another pull from it.

Fuuuck.

"Y-yeah," Ben managed. "I'd like that."

"Don't tempt me too hard, buddy."

Ben didn't have a reply that wouldn't sound stupid or betray what he thought he might be feeling for Jake. He opted instead to smile back and turn toward the garage while hoping Jake didn't spot the chub sprouting in his shorts.

Jake

Jake fought the urge to cackle with amused sadistic glee as he watched Ben retreat to the garage. He hit *play* on the remote to resume his show.

Topping Ben in a scene was a dang good idea. He wouldn't mind that at all. Although, as he thought about that, he realized Ben might have thought he was joking and maybe a little tipsy and not serious.

Because Ben didn't know he was bi.

Hmm.

Jake didn't want Ben to get creeped out and think he was hitting on him. Especially considering everything Ben had just been through with Mort. The last thing Jake wanted to do was make his friend uncomfortable or think that he'd moved him in with ulterior motives.

For now, however, Jake would enjoy any little incidental sadistic tweaks he could sneak in.

As long as it didn't hurt their friendship.

Chapter Five

Ben

Ben had all his clothes put away and his room mostly organized by six that evening. He still had to organize what he'd stored out in the garage, but he could do that at his leisure over the next couple of days.

He took a shower. While standing under the spray he couldn't help but think about Jake.

Maybe it wasn't the best idea to start fantasizing about his roommate and coworker, but the guy was hot.

A hot Dom.

Now a single hot Dom.

Who, teasing or not, had managed to reach inside Ben's brain and pull on exactly the right nerve to get a rise out of his cock, when in the ten years they'd known each other, Ben hadn't seriously fantasized about him like that before.

He fisted his cock and slowly started stroking. If he wanted to get through cooking dinner without a woody popping up at an inopportune time, he needed to release a little pressure.

Closing his eyes, he thought about Jake's hands, how it'd feel to have the taller man topping him, bending him over a bench—

—or over the end of his bed—

Oooh, yeah. There was full wood.

Jake was six two to his five eleven, meaning if he was stretched out in bed under him…

Fuck, yeah…

He damn sure could fantasize. Nothing wrong with that. Right?

Right.

As he stroked his cock harder, faster, Ben thought about what it'd be like to be on his knees on the floor in front of the man, sucking on his cock.

Bet I could do a better job than Allison.

How it might feel to have Jake's fingers buried in his hair, holding on, taking control of him…

Yes!

He threw his head back, stifling his moans as his cock exploded in his hand, ropes of cum slicking his fingers and quickly washed away by the shower spray.

He leaned back against the shower wall for a moment to recover, his softening cock in his hand.

Something told him he'd be spending a lot of time doing exactly that in here. Releasing pent up energy while fantasizing about Jake.

There are worse things in the world.

* * *

FORTUNATELY, there was a Publix less than a mile away from the house. Despite Jake insisting he'd be okay with leftovers, Ben wanted the first meal he cooked for Jake to be a decent one. After Ben returned with fixings for chicken breasts, homemade pesto sauce with pasta, and salad, Jake wandered into the kitchen and perched on one of the barstools at the counter to watch.

"You know, you're going to spoil me, buddy."

Ben hoped his face didn't heat to much and betray his feelings. "Maybe that's my evil subby plan. I don't want you to regret letting me move in. Oh, I left the rent check on the counter there, under your phone charger."

Jake glanced that way but didn't even pick it up. "Thanks, I appreciate that. You do realize I'm still serious about you going to the munch with me tomorrow night, right?"

"Yeah, and knowing you, it'd be pointless for me to argue. Pushy Dom."

"Damn straight." Ben caught a glimpse of a handsome grin from the other man. "Especially now that I'm single. Not that I'm in a hurry to find someone else."

"Amen," Ben muttered, realizing after the fact that he'd said it aloud. "Sorry. I meant that about me, not about Allison."

Jake had switched to drinking iced tea and took a sip from his glass. "No worries. I feel the same way. Seriously, it was a long time coming. It was more comfortable to just let things go on for a while. I probably should have ended it between us the last time she tried to manipulate me. She needs someone who isn't as sadistic as I am."

"I still feel a little guilty that me moving in pushed things to a head."

"Don't feel that way. It's nice not living alone anymore, even if we're just friends. And all joking aside, don't let me fall into a pattern of bossing you around, either. Feel free to call me out on that."

Ben's face heated even more, to the point he gave thanks he was standing over a hot stove as a ready excuse. "Maybe I like you bossing me around."

Jake laughed one of *those* laughs, playful and not unkind. "Don't tempt me. A Dominant and a sub living in the same house with a power vacuum for both?" He let out a sigh. "I don't want to bork our friendship."

"But I wouldn't mind. Seriously. It'd give me some of what I need and give you some of what you need, too." He finally glanced Jake's way and spotted the thoughtful expression in Jake's eyes.

Handsome brown eyes, and brown hair he'd love to run his fingers through…

Fuuuck me.

There went his cock again.

When Jake next spoke, his voice sounded low and serious. "What, exactly, are you proposing?"

Ben's pulse throbbed. "I'm just saying that you getting a little Dommy with me and me being somewhat subby with you, around here, wouldn't be the worst thing in the world. Think of me as your private butler or live-in housekeeper, if you want."

Pleaseohpleaseohpleaseohplease!

Jake

Jake's mouth went dry at the thought of having Ben running around all day long, wearing *his* collar and nothing else.

And he was damn glad he was sitting at the counter, which hid his sudden, aching erection from the other man.

To buy himself a little time, he took another sip of tea and prayed Ben was far enough away he couldn't spot the way Jake's hand trembled. "I don't want to take advantage of you."

"I agreed to do my share of chores when I moved in. I'd have to do chores anywhere I lived. Doing those chores for someone who appreciates my efforts is a sweet bonus. You wouldn't be taking advantage of me."

Now Jake knew he couldn't reveal to Ben that he was bi. Not right now, anyway. And he definitely couldn't tell Ben he thought he was hot.

There'd be too much weirdness all at once, too much piled

onto Ben on top of everything he was currently going through to sort out the mess Mort had pulled him into.

But…

"So you're saying something…informal," Jake finally managed.

"Yeah. If you don't mind. I mean, if you're comfortable with that. I'm a free-range submissive now. I *like* serving. It makes me feel good, as long as you don't mind it."

Jake slowly nodded, forcing himself not to look like a bobble-head doll. "If *you're* comfortable with it."

"Absolutely. I promise if I feel something's wrong I'll speak up."

Jake knew he couldn't ask for a better plan than that. "Okay. Let's give it a shot."

The grin Ben sent him made Jake's cock throb even harder. "Thank you. I trust you. I know you're not going to take advantage of me the way Mort did. We're friends. I won't let it get weird, I promise. And the reverse is true, that if you don't feel comfortable, say something."

"Deal."

Ben focused on the stove again. "And my offer about you beating my ass still stands. You ever feel like topping someone, I'm willing to bottom for you. I'd be honored to."

Holy…fuuuck.

Jake didn't dare move for fear of rubbing his cock exactly the right—wrong?—way and exploding right there in his shorts.

"O-okay," Jake managed.

Ben glanced his way again. Those blue eyes of his…Jake could imagine them looking up at him from down on his knees, his cock in Ben's mouth…

Jake closed his eyes and breathed through it for a moment.

"You all right?" Ben asked.

"Yeah." Jake opened his eyes and forced a smile. "Just fine."

What he wanted to do was walk over to Ben, fist his hair, and put him on his knees right that moment.

Too soon. Too fucking soon.

Ben smiled. "I promise, if I meet a guy, I'll make sure they get your seal of approval before I get serious with them so I don't fuck up again."

Who says I'm going to let you see a guy seriously?

But that's not what Jake said. He said the adult thing.

The *safe* thing. "Ditto. I think *both* of us need to take things really slow before we get into a new relationship."

AFTER DINNER, which was absolutely delicious, Ben refused to let Jake help him with the dishes.

"Nope," Ben said. "My pleasure. Seriously." He made shooing gestures with his hands. "Go relax."

"If you insist."

"I do."

Jake headed into the living room. He'd already packed Allison's things while Ben was at the store. They now sat in a box in the entryway, next to the front door.

Jake retrieved his laptop and logged on to FetLife. He needed to do this sooner rather than later, in case Allison decided to try round two of begging him to take her back after work.

He deleted her from his profile as his submissive, himself from her profile as her Dominant, changed his status to single, and then unfriended her.

That would likely piss her off, but even though she wasn't very active on the site in the first place, he didn't want to make it easy on her to track his movements there. If she became a problem he'd block her, but he hoped to avoid that.

He thought about changing his sexual orientation status from unlisted to bisexual, then decided to leave it unlisted. If Allison decided to perv his profile, he didn't want her and Ann possibly going after Ben and causing trouble for him. Ben was dealing with enough as it was with Mort's bullshit.

At two minutes after nine, Allison tried calling him again. Jake was sitting on one end of the couch, Ben on the other, the two of them watching a movie.

Jake answered the call as he stood and headed for his room. "Hello?" He shut the bedroom door behind him.

"Can we talk like rational adults now?" Allison asked by way of greeting.

Fuck. You.

That's not what he said, though. "I *was* talking rationally earlier."

"Listen, I know you weren't serious about breaking up, but—"

"Actually, yes, I was."

A moment of silence, but she hadn't hung up on him this time. "What?"

"I *was* serious," he repeated. "We are broken up. We are no longer a couple. If you want it stated formally, then fine. I release you, and you're free to roam about the country and date or fuck or play with whoever you want. I wish you well in your future endeavors, and hope for nothing but the best for you and that you find someone who's a better fit for you."

"What?"

"The way things were wasn't fair to either one of us. Now we can go our separate ways and be happy."

"But I love you!"

Funny way of showing it. "I love you, too, but I'm not *in* love with you. That's another good reason for us to break up. I haven't been 'in love' with you. Never was. Not in a way that would make a successful relationship. You need to find someone who can both love and be *in* love with you."

"Well, what's wrong with just loving each other?"

He refused to let her drag him down that road. "We are two incompatible people. This has been brewing for a while, but the recent events proved it to me."

"Can I please come over to talk to you?"

"You can come over to get your things, but there's nothing to talk about. We're done."

"What if I don't want it to be over between us?"

He couldn't hold back his laugh. *"What?"*

"I say it's *not* over. What do you say about *that?*"

"I say you're delusional and you're only reinforcing why breaking up is the right choice. Anyone who claims to be a submissive and really *is* one damn sure wouldn't take *that* approach under these circumstances."

She switched to desperation. "What do I have to do to get you to take me back? I'll change! I'll do anything you want me to!"

Aaaand here we go. Honestly? He'd expected this to be her first response.

He thought about the man now occupying his back bedroom, a man whom he'd known over three times longer than he'd known Allison, and who in less than one day had already shown more submission, without any kind of formal agreement between them, than Allison had in the three *years* of their relationship.

"It doesn't work like that. If three years together wasn't enough for us to find a comfortable, compatible rhythm, you forcing yourself to change won't help. We're done."

"You're saying you're willing to just throw away three years?"

"I don't look at it like that. I look at it as discovering that we aren't compatible. I now know I need a heavy masochist, and someone willing to be a submissive all the time, not just when they want to be. You should realize from this that you need someone who's playful and sensual and who doesn't need a full-time submissive. If you want to be friends, we can be friends, but it's been weeks since we had sex anyway. Not like we're losing anything there."

She ignored that jab. "If you want a full-time submissive, I'd have to move in with you. Otherwise, I need a job. But you won't even give me a key to your damn place."

Somehow, he managed not to let out a frustrated groan. "We.

Are. Not. A. Couple. Are you dropping by to get your stuff tonight or not?"

"Fuck you."

That time, she did hang up on him.

Okay, then.

When he returned to the living room, he realized Ben had paused the movie. "Oh, sorry, buddy. Didn't mean for you to do that."

"No, it's okay." Ben didn't look okay, though.

Jake knew he had to say it. "It's *not* your fault I broke up with her. Don't second-guess what I'm saying, because I promise I won't play games with you. She's ten years younger than me and I was her first serious D/s relationship. It was never going to work out. Honestly? I'm not sad it's ended, which is telling." He pointed at the TV. "Let's keep watching."

Ben hit *play* and set the remote on the couch between them.

Ben

Ben couldn't help but feel a little guilty that it all came about on the same day he moved in.

I need to take him at his word.

He jumped when someone pounded on the door at twenty minutes 'til ten. Jake, however, let out a weary sigh and stood to answer it.

Ben hit pause on the remote again but didn't get up. If he did, he'd be visible when Jake opened the door. The living room sat off to one side, so you couldn't see into it from the front door.

Ben heard Jake open the door. "I didn't think you were stopping by tonight."

Allison's voice echoed off the entryway's tiled floor. "Are you going to let me in, or are you going to keep being an ass?"

Even Ben knew the testy snark in her voice was the exact opposite tone she should be using if she wanted a snowball's chance of talking to Jake. He was not a man to tolerate 'tude like that, not at work nor in his personal life.

Sad when I know more about him than she does.

"Your stuff is in that box," Jake said, maintaining a remarkably cool tone. "If I find anything else, I'll send it to you."

She switched to pleading, but too far across the spectrum, well past calm and collected and deep into whiny and needy territory. "Come on, Jake. *Talk* to me. *Please?*"

"Allison. There is nothing *to* talk about. We can be friends. There's a remote chance we might even be able to be play partners again one day. But right now, this is what's best."

"Are you seeing someone else already? Be honest with me."

"No, I'm not seeing anyone else. You want honesty? Fine, here it is. You've worn me out mentally and emotionally and I'm *done.* You refuse to live up to the conditions you agreed to when you said you wanted to be my submissive. I don't see any reason to continue seeing each other romantically when we're obviously so incompatible. You have no desire to change, and I'm tired of paying for everything and getting nothing in return."

The quiet lay there long enough that Ben thought maybe she'd picked up her box of things and walked away.

Then he heard her teary voice. "How can you be so cold to me?"

"I'm not being cold. I'm being honest in a way I've been reluctant to for a while for this very reason. I kept hoping my hints to you about your behavior would help you turn things around, but they didn't. Do you need me to carry the box to your car for you?"

Wow. He had to hand it to Jake, the guy was keeping his cool.

Ben was more than a little ashamed to realize he was sporting wood again.

Mort had been a fly-off-the-handle kind of guy. There were no rational discussions with him. It was his way or no way. And if you questioned his way, he'd damn sure browbeat you into submission.

"No! I'll carry it." He heard a noise, like cardboard rattling. "I can't believe you're willing to throw three years away."

"I don't consider our time spent together a waste. I'm sorry you feel that way. That's even more proof that this is the right call."

Holy cow.

"I didn't mean it like that!" she protested.

"There is a perfect guy out there for you," Jake told her. "You'll find him. That guy isn't me, though. Let's add in the fact that you want kids, and I've said all along that I don't."

"You're bringing that up *now?*"

"Yes, as one more reason this is the best decision. I don't hate you. I don't wish you bad karma or anything like that. I *want* you to find someone who will be a better fit for you and make you happy, because I'm *not* that guy. I don't know how to make that any more clear to you. I want you to be happy, but we don't make each other happy. Maybe we never did make each other happy. Not in the ways that really matter."

A moment later, Ben heard the front door close and knew she must have left. As a car started outside, Jake walked into the living room.

"You know, I think I'm going to head for bed. I want to get an early start on the yard tomorrow so I have time to relax before the munch."

"Are you all right?" Ben asked.

Jake smiled, but he looked tired. "Yeah. I just wish I'd done this sooner. I should have, but I kept hoping I was wrong. I don't blame her for being mad at me, but it doesn't mean I'm a bad guy for ending it, either. The TV won't disturb me if you want to keep watching it. I'll see you in the morning."

"See you in the morning."

Jake retreated to his bedroom and Ben hit *play* on the remote again.

Then he remembered his load of clothes in the dryer out in the garage. They were probably done. He waited for the next commercial, then went to get them and bring them in to fold while he watched TV. He wasn't even close to being ready to sleep yet despite the day's events.

After folding his clothes and putting them away, he went through the kitchen and cleaned, setting up the coffee maker for in the morning and mopping the floor last so it could dry overnight.

There.

Maybe he couldn't "fix" the way Jake felt, but the guy could wake up to a spotless kitchen in the morning.

That might help him feel a little better, at least.

Finally, Ben headed for bed after turning the living room TV off.

Chapter Six

Jake

Sleep was difficult to achieve despite Jake's mental and physical exhaustion. He hated the pained look in Allison's eyes and the hurt tone in her voice when he'd settled the matter between them.

Almost hated it enough to make him take it back, but he knew that wouldn't be healthy for either of them.

Delaying the inevitable wouldn't make it any easier. He hated playing games and didn't want a relationship where he had to walk on eggshells. Besides, taking her back would only reinforce to her that all she'd have to do to get her way was cry and make promises they both knew she wouldn't keep.

He could say that because it wasn't the first time she'd made empty promises.

Damn. I should have ended things with her a long time ago.

But back then, they'd still had an active, healthy sex life. As that had fallen off and he felt like she was using him for little more than free laundry services and buying her dinners, the other short-falls in their relationship became far too clear.

When Jake awakened the next morning, he used the bathroom, pulled on shorts and a T-shirt to do yard work in, and headed to the kitchen.

He pulled up short in the doorway. No, the kitchen wasn't "dirty" before, exactly.

But…

It looked like maybe Ben had cleaned it overnight. Everything had been tidied up on the counters, which had been wiped down, there were no dishes in the sink, the dishwasher had been run, and even the floor looked spotless.

He opened the cabinet where he kept the coffee and paused after he popped open the top of the coffeemaker.

Ben had preset it.

Huh.

He'd quit asking Allison to make coffee because it either came out brown water or undrinkable mud.

He put the coffee away and hit the power button on the coffeemaker.

If this was what he could expect having Ben as his roommate, he might not ever let the guy move out.

* * *

Ben

Ben awoke to the smell of coffee brewing and realized Jake must be awake. He dressed and headed out to the kitchen, where he found Jake sipping a cup of coffee and browsing his e-mail on his phone.

"Good morning." He fought the urge to tack a "sir" onto the end of that comment. "Did I make the coffee okay?"

"It's perfect, buddy." Jake flashed him a winning smile. "I appreciate it."

Another wave of those dangerous warm fuzzies rolled through him. "What can I do to help you today?"

"I'm going to mow and run the weed trimmer. Hey, thanks for cleaning the kitchen last night."

More warm fuzzies. Fortunately, Ben was standing at the counter and fixing himself a mug of coffee, so Jake wouldn't be able to spot the chub trying to make itself known in his shorts. "I told you I'd help with chores."

"As long as you don't pull an Allison on me and stop pitching in after a few weeks, we'll be great. Seriously, I appreciate it."

Ben slowly stirred his coffee. "I pull my weight. So give me something to do, or write up a list of stuff you want me to do."

"Well, if you want, you can use the pool brush and clean it, and scrub the hot tub. I had one of those automatic pool sweepers, but it broke and I didn't feel like spending the money to replace it."

"Sure, but you'll have to teach me how to do the chemicals."

"I can take care of that. That's the easy part. The brush is hanging out on the lanai, up under the roofline. Just go over the whole pool with it, sides and bottom, and use the hand brush out there on the table to get the nooks and crannies in the pool along the steps and stuff, and the hot tub."

"I can do that. Did you want me to make you breakfast first?"

Jake turned, a funny smile on his face. "I know you said you wanted an unofficial Dom and sub thing, but I don't expect you to be my servant."

"I like to help."

"I appreciate that. Since I'm buying us dinner, I was actually planning on eating light today." He patted his stomach, which was flat. Ben forced himself not to imagine running his tongue over it. "I want to fill up on prime rib tonight."

"Okay. I'll go put on my swimsuit and get started on that then." He picked up his coffee and took a sip. "Do you have a preference what swimsuit I wear?"

Jake coughed as he laughed, setting his coffee mug down while he tried to recover. "What?"

"I mean, I have regular swim trunks or a Speedo."

"Buddy, seriously. Why would I care what swimsuit you wear?"

"I didn't know if you'd be weirded out if I wore the Speedo or something."

"I honestly don't care if you run around out there naked. I have a privacy fence. Doesn't bother me what you wear. Yesterday was the first time I've worn a swimsuit to swim out there in months. I didn't want to assume you'd be okay with that after what you just went through."

Ben fought the urge to reach down and adjust his shorts at the thought of Jake running around naked. "Okay."

"I appreciate the consideration, but seriously, you're not going to weird me out. Please, relax. We're good."

"If you want to swim naked, that doesn't bother me, either." Seeing Jake naked?

Yes, please!

Jake picked up his coffee to take another sip. "See? We're perfect as roommates."

* * *

Jake

If it wasn't for what Ben had just gone through with Mort, Jake would have told Ben not only was he to clean the pool and hot tub naked, but to stay that way anytime they were home together.

He would have then also admitted he was bi and that he was now more than curious to see if anything developed between them.

All reasons Jake *knew* he couldn't rush things. Hell, he didn't even know for sure if Ben was attracted to him, although that sure appeared to be a chub in the guy's shorts after Jake deliberately baited him.

After Ben left to go change, Jake went out to the garage to open the large door and get the mower out. After checking the gas and oil and topping it off, he got it started and began mowing the front yard. This time of year, it was a weekly task. Come the drier winter it might be once a month, if that often.

He lost himself in the chore, wanting it out of the way before the summer day really heated up. Even though he had several shade trees in the front and back yards, the last thing he wanted to do was push around a mower in muggy ninety-degree heat.

By the time he made his way to the back yard, Ben was out on the lanai and…

Holy cow, that *was* a Speedo, a tiny, snug one, electric blue, that showed off every line and curve and—

Jake focused on mowing so he didn't accidentally run over any plants.

Or his own foot.

Now his cock ached. He knew Ben had a nice ass, but the glimpse he'd gotten of the guy's package outlined by the snug suit made Jake's mouth water.

Somehow, Jake managed to calm his stubborn cock by the time he'd finished mowing and trimming. After putting the equipment up and closing the garage door, he walked around the house and entered the lanai through the side door there. Ben was still working on scrubbing the hot tub, his back to Jake.

After kicking off his shoes and pulling off his shirt, Jake only hesitated for a moment before dropping his shorts and briefs and jumping into the deep end of the pool. Contrasted against the growing heat of the day, the cool water felt great. When he broke the surface, he spotted Ben staring at him, frozen.

His not-so-inner sadist giggled with glee. "You done yet?"

"A-almost."

"Feel free to join me." He dove under the water and started

doing laps. Other than mowing and yard work, this was his primary form of exercise. He didn't like going to the gym and hated running, but he knew he needed to do something to keep moving and stay reasonably in shape.

Okay, dude, don't push him any harder.

It'd be too tempting to see where exactly the line lay with Ben. He'd rather not do that this soon. If something organically developed between them at some point, yes, he'd welcome a chance to explore. The groundwork was already there, with them being good friends and knowing about each other's kinky sides.

Ben

Ben hoped his jaw hadn't hit the concrete. He'd caught the glimpse of a very nice cock before Jake dove into the water.

He's. Not. Gay.

Sidling sideways, so his back was to the pool, Ben continued scrubbing the hot tub. At this point, it was now to hide the raging erection he sported rather than to do a good job. Hell, he was almost finished with the hot tub, but the bathing suit—which he'd cockily decided to wear—didn't allow him any chance to conceal his interest in his friend's body.

Jake was obviously being nice and trying to show him he didn't have a problem with him being gay. Trying to make him feel at home, or…something.

Gulp.

Once he finished scrubbing the hot tub and knew he could make it to the pool and slip into it while Jake was swimming away from him, he managed to get in there without revealing to Jake exactly how into him he was.

The pool was large, at least eight feet deep at the far end, extending the entire length of the lanai and boringly rectangular in shape. But its size meant, unlike many modern home pools, you could actually swim laps in it and get some exercise. If it wasn't twenty-five meters long, it was darn close. The home sat in an older subdivision of ranch style homes, single stories and long, on wide lots that were a little deeper than they were wide.

Jake slowly stroked back up to the pool's edge, the playful smile on his face not helping Ben's situation any. "Water's perfect, huh?"

"Yeah."

"I love this pool. So damn glad my grandparents had it put in when they built the house. I can't tell you how many hours I spent in it when I was growing up. I learned how to swim in this pool."

"Really?"

"Yeah. The room you're in was actually my bedroom. It was their official guest room, but since I was their most frequent guest they referred to it as my room."

"Oh. I didn't know that. That's kind of cool."

"I know, right?" Jake stopped a few feet away from him and it took every ounce of strength Ben had not to stare down into the water to get another look at Jake's cock. "Good news is, at least tonight you and I don't have to worry about our exes showing up at the munch."

It was a left-field comment that took Ben a moment to process. "Guess you're right about that."

"And while I know guys don't usually have the same problem women do, feel free to refer any jerks to me if they won't leave you alone. Not meaning just tonight, but like on FetLife."

"Thanks. I appreciate that."

"I feel bad that I didn't say more to you early on. I should have. We've known each other long enough I should have spoken up and said what I thought about Mort."

Ben felt his heart pounding. "That wasn't your fault."

"Still, you're my friend. I should have done more." He met Ben's gaze. "I promise next time I'll speak up."

Ben nodded. "Thank you. I'm sorry I didn't realize things were so bad between you and Allison."

"The fact that she didn't like any of my friends should have been a clue." That handsome smirk curved his lips again. "We'll be gatekeepers for each other. Deal?" He held out his hand to shake.

Ben shook with him. "Deal."

"Now, I think I'm going to grab a shower and vegetate for a while." He swam down to the deep end of the pool and got out via the ladder there, giving Ben a perfectly unobstructed view of his firm ass.

Yum.

Jake grabbed his clothes and the way he had them held in front of him, Ben couldn't get another good look at his friend's cock.

But he also didn't miss the playful gleam in the other man's eyes as he glanced over his shoulder before heading inside through the sliders.

Hell, if Jake was gay, Ben would assume he was being flirted with. But…

Jake wasn't.

Sigh.

Then again, the guy *was* a sadist, and over the years did have a habit of trying to make him laugh. Maybe he was simply teasing him. Two good friends, just screwing around.

If only that could be literally.

Chapter Seven

Jake

Tilly sat with her chin propped in her left palm, her elbow resting on the table, as she listened to Ben. "Oh, this is getting better," she dryly snarked. "Keep going."

Jake fought the urge to not giggle with sadistic glee as Ben retold the recent events to Tilly. He felt horrible for his friend's circumstances, but watching Ben spinning on the end of Tilly's hook was what had him nearly giddy.

She was the one person who'd had the balls—ironically—to pull Ben aside early on after he'd first moved in with Mort, and who told him she thought Mort was an asshole, and that Ben could do a lot better.

Ben took a deep breath. "You were right. I should have listened to you."

"*There* you go, sport." She leaned in and hugged him. "*That's* the magic phrase I was looking for. Remember that next time." She pointed to Jake. "And you, asshole. About time you got rid of that sandspur."

"Sandspur?"

"No, correction. Sandspurs are more cuddly than Allison was."

Jake wasn't sure how he'd suddenly found himself impaled by Tilly's ire. "Glad you're our friend." Jake didn't know why he would have avoided crossing Tilly's radar once she heard of the happenings. He should have expected it, but still, it stung.

Mostly because she was right.

Tilly had not been fond of Allison. While she hadn't been quite as blunt to Jake in stating that opinion, she had made it known before.

Tilly smiled. "I am your friend, for which you're both very lucky." She held up her right hand, which was currently in a cast from when she broke it punching Paul a few weeks earlier. "At least I don't have to hit you to knock some sense into you."

"That would break your other hand," Ben pointed out.

"No, I'd punch you with the one in the cast. Let it do the work for me. Work smarter, not harder, duh." She pulled out her phone and called up a contact, then Ben's phone buzzed. He pulled it out.

He frowned as he read the screen. "Who is this?"

"Friend of mine who owes me a favor for doing him a few favors. I texted him earlier when Jake gave me the 411 when you two first got here. I told him that you'll be calling him. *Tomorrow.* He's a PI."

"Private investigator?" Jake asked.

She slowly tilted her head, a full-on eye roll in progress. "No, genius. A personal instigator. Of *course* a private investigator. He'll send me the bill. I've got two weeks out of him. He also knows Ed and can coordinate with him."

"Um, thank you," Ben said. "I don't know what to say."

"Just say *that*—thank you. He's good. He can devote resources to finding that slimeball that the cops might not be able to." She stood, lightly slapping him on the shoulder before pointing at Jake. "You two stick together. Making future dates pass the bestie test is a good plan. Unless you want them to go through Tilly torture first." She arched an eyebrow at them.

"No, ma'am," they both said.

She grinned. "Damn, you're cute together." She sighed as she returned her attention to Ben. "You going to start trolling online dating sites for vanilla guys?" She pointed at Jake again. "Because, frankly, I like the plan of you two playing together for now and keeping the kinky confined to that until you both get your feet under you again."

Jake fought the urge to laugh as he faked a teenager's voice. "Yer not my mom!"

"Yeah, but either one of you do something so stupid again, and I'll appoint myself as your Domme, and then you'll *wish* you'd listened to common sense. Neither one of you can afford to fuck up your lives with stupid decisions. You have great jobs, guys, come on. Both of you can do better, and you damn well know it. Although, Ben, I know the dating pool for single gay guys is a little slim around Venture. But Jake, for chrissake, she was a fucking brat, and not even a fun one with winning personality traits beyond being a bratty bitch. I wanted to smack her, and not in the funtime kind of way. It wasn't just me, either."

Jake felt his face heat. "Did everyone think like that about her?"

"Yes," Landry and Cris chimed in from where they were sitting across the table.

"She was...different," Landry drawled.

Tilly glanced his way. "That's Landry being a polite guy. Me? I'm not so polite. I've gotten too used to dealing with pushy Holly-weird execs who need bluntness. She was a total bitch."

She dropped her voice. "There's a reason you haven't received invites to private parties lately. She pissed off Loren, Leah, and Shayla the last three times she came. That's like the hat trick of fucking up in this group, and those three are pretty damn laid back."

She grinned. "That reminds me." Tilly pulled out her phone

again and a moment later, Jake felt his phone buzz from an incoming e-mail. "Two weeks. Expect to see both of you there. Together, thank you very much."

She stepped in close and dropped her voice even further. They were sitting at a table back in the corner, so no one else could hear. "It's at our house, so the invite is for *you*"—she pointed at Jake—"and *you*"—she pointed at Ben. "No plus-ones this time, for either of you." Her expression softened again. "We're just looking forward to having both of you back among friends without assholes in tow. *Capisce?*"

They nodded. *"Capisce,"* they echoed.

Cris snorted. "Damn. They learn fast."

***

Ben

They had a great dinner, even though Ben felt more than humbled when Jake urged him to order something besides an appetizer salad for dinner and playfully threatened to order for him if he didn't get what he really wanted.

Humbled and…well, semi-chub, definitely.

Less than forty-eight hours living under the same roof, and Ben realized how natural it felt letting Jake take the lead.

I wonder if he feels it, too?

Not exactly a conversation he felt comfortable having with him right now, though. What they'd sort of half-seriously agreed upon, resident Dom/sub status at home, was probably already pushing the barrier farther than was safe. Time to let things settle so they could fall into some semblance of a routine.

But…yeah. Even without a sexual or romantic relationship between them, Ben absolutely would let Jake be his Dom in all ways, if Jake wanted to.

He trusted his friend, knew he'd never fuck him over. That

quiet certainty was built upon their decade of friendship and watching the man's actions. Jake had never fucked anyone over before, never cheated on his girlfriends, and everything he did was always honorable and up front.

Whereas looking back at Mort, Ben could clearly see every damn last red flag that had been there from the start, even when they were "just" roommates. Mort had groomed Ben to sub to him, be collared to him, be a fucktoy for him.

It was embarrassing in retrospect to finally see what everyone else had clearly seen.

Embarrassing and humbling.

Tilly was older, wiser, and had been through her own crucibles. Yes, he'd fucking listen to every word she uttered as if she spouted the gospel straight from heaven.

Even more importantly, he'd follow her advice.

As they rode home in a comfortable silence, it was Jake who finally spoke. "So how about Tilly, huh?"

"Yeah," Ben quietly said. "She nailed us good."

Jake didn't respond at first. "I don't know about you, but I think she nailed me pretty accurately."

"Yeah, me, too."

"Do you want to go to the party?"

"I think she made it pretty clear we aren't to bring anyone with us."

"I know." They stopped at a red light. Jake glanced over at him, his face illuminated by the instrument lights. "I'm okay with that, if you are."

Something invisible and yet heavy, dense, hung between them. Still, it wasn't…uncomfortable. As if waiting in the wings for one of them to make a move.

"I'm okay with that."

The light changed. Jake nodded as he faced forward and they continued on. "I guess if we wanted to play that night, we'd need to play with each other." He let out a nervous laugh. "I mean, you know, if you felt like playing. Totally your call."

Ben bit back his eager *yes, please!* for something more measured and…not desperate-sounding. "If you don't mind topping me, I don't mind bottoming to you." He knew Jake would pick up the subtleties of the exact words he'd used. "I know how you play and I trust you. I could use a good hard beating from someone I trust."

"Okay, then." They turned onto their street and as Jake slowed for their driveway, he added, "Let's talk about it more over the next couple of weeks. No pressure, no stress. If it feels right, we can. If not, we don't have to. Either way, I'm going to enjoy us being able to get together with our friends and not worry if our partners are enjoying themselves, or we're doing something that will get us sniped at later."

Ben looked at him in surprise. "She did that to you?"

"Passive-aggressively, yeah. I'll need to talk to Leah, Loren, and Shayla personally, find out exactly what Allison did, and make my apologies for it. I didn't realize she'd pissed people off. I wonder how many other people she pissed off."

"I know Mort was jealous. I guess that was part of the larger pattern. Isolate me from my friends."

Jake shut the car off. "Buddy," he gently said, "Mort was abusive. If you'd been a woman, I'd have been asking some of the other women in the group to hold an intervention for you. The way he used to talk to you made me sick to my stomach. You were a totally different person around him, and not for the better."

That simultaneously made Ben feel worse while also warming his heart that Jake had noticed. "Really?"

"Yeah. You were a completely different person at work, like the old Ben I knew."

Jake

Jake had to bite back the natural ending to that statement that tried to banzai itself out of his mouth and into Ben's ear—*...and loved.*

Shit.

Where the fuck did that *come from?*

A heavy sigh escaped his friend. Yeah, he did love Ben as a friend, for sure. But now that neither of them were attached, and they were circling in such close proximity...Jake would be lying if he said he had nothing more than just friendly feelings for the guy.

Slow. Down.

Hell, he could use Tilly as an excuse, her sage advice logical and easy to follow. If something were to develop between the two of them, it could do so organically with them both single and playing with each other.

He could *show* Ben how he felt over the next several months, coax him into not moving out, and work his way into more if he felt Ben was reciprocating.

"Promise me something, please?" Ben said.

"Sure, buddy. Anything."

His blue gaze nailed Jake right in the feels, which was apparently a shortcut to his cock. "Always be honest with me, even about someone I'm dating. I don't trust myself to make good decisions right now. I'll be honest with you, too."

Jake slowly nodded, realizing he was already skating the edges of falsehoods by not being fully honest with Ben right now. "I promise, buddy. And that goes for me, too." He held his arms open for a hug, which Ben returned. Jake fought the urge to lengthen it, to kiss the top of the man's head. His hair smelled like mangoes or something, but...it was perfect.

He was perfect.

Now I just need to show him how perfect.

After leaning back, Jake got his keys ready as they both got out.

He hit the button on the garage door opener before closing his door, hitting the lock on the key fob as they walked inside so he could disarm the alarm.

Home. He tested out a phrase in his mind.

With *his* guy.

It didn't escape Jake's notice that he'd never really thought about Allison in those terms before.

Maybe Ben wasn't the only one who'd made some pretty bad choices in partners the last go-round.

Chapter Eight

Jake

The next morning, Jake awoke a few minutes before his alarm and realized he smelled…coffee.

Wow.

All joking aside regarding the Dom and sub stuff, just for that alone Jake knew he'd enjoy having Ben around.

When he finally stumbled his way out to the kitchen, he found not only was the coffee brewed, but Ben had showered—guessing by his damp hair—and had already set out the Deadpool coffee mug Jake had used the morning before.

The one he used nearly every morning. One that—ironically—Ben had given him a couple of years earlier for his birthday.

And Ben stood at the stove, cooking something. He flashed a smile at Jake over his shoulder. "Oh, good, you're up."

Jake walked over and started pouring himself a mug of coffee. Hell, Ben had even left a clean spoon out on the counter for him next to the mug, lying on a clean piece of paper towel.

"What are you doing?" He realized the stove was off and Ben was using an electric skillet, which sat on top of the stove.

"Pancakes."

"I didn't think I owned an electric skillet."

"You didn't. This one's mine. How many do you want?"

"Um…" He had to struggle to remember how many spoons of sugar he liked to add to his coffee. "Four's fine. I didn't mean you had to make me breakfast every morning."

"No worries. I enjoy cooking. Really."

Ben

Poor guy looked like he was still asleep. But Ben had hated seeing Jake show up every morning at work with little more than an energy bar and a banana. Maybe Jake wouldn't want him to cook for him every morning, and that was fine.

But for today, their first workday "together," he wanted to put on a good impression for the guy.

Ben also paid close attention to how much sugar and cream Jake put in his coffee. He'd used about the same amount yesterday, so now Ben knew. He'd start making sure he prepped Jake's coffee as soon as he heard him up and about, so it'd be ready for him.

Ben wasn't exactly a morning person, but he didn't consider this a "chore." Getting up to take care of Jake was more like a bonus. He wanted to show his friend how much he appreciated what he'd done for him.

The best way he knew to do that was by taking care of Jake.

Once Jake had a couple of sips of his coffee, he spoke. "Did you want to ride in with me today?"

"If you don't mind, that'd be great, thanks."

"Of course I don't mind. That was one of the bonus points I mentioned about you living here, remember?"

"Oh, yeah. Thanks."

"We can take turns. Don't have to do it every day. I need to go car shopping soon, too." He frowned. "It's got over a hundred thousand miles on it, and it's starting to run a little rough again. I've had it in three times for the same problem. It's nickel-and-diming me to death at this point."

Ben plated four pancakes and handed them over to Jake. "There you go."

"What about you?"

"Mine will be done shortly."

"You're going to spoil me. You realize that, right?"

He grinned. "Is that a bad thing?"

Jake walked over to the counter to sit and eat. "Yeah, for the next person who thinks about dating me. Can you imagine that conversation? 'My best friend cooks me breakfast every morning. Top *that.*'"

Ben knew he could take the route of more playful bantering, but with Jake still closer to asleep than awake, it might come out wrong. "It can be our secret, if you prefer."

"Screw that." Jake buttered his pancakes and poured out syrup. "I want them to know the high bar they have to live up to from the get-go. Not to mention they have to have your seal of approval."

Alrighty, then… "Well, it's only fair. Next guy who wants to get serious with me has to pass muster with both you and Tilly. I'd say we both have high bars."

Maybe I should just shut up now.

Jake grinned. "You know, we keep doing this, maybe you and I should just get married. Save ourselves some trouble."

"Don't tempt me too hard," Ben replied.

Jake

Okay, then.

Jake hadn't meant to go there. Really, he hadn't.

But the opportunity presented was just too…perfect. Start small, salt little clues here and there, settle in, and wait.

He loved his friend. He'd be lying if he said he didn't. He'd "loved" him for years.

What he hadn't counted on was *falling* in love with his friend.

It seemed like the harder he tried to put the brakes on his feelings, the faster he was rolling down that hill.

Out of control.

Ben plated his pancakes, turned off the skillet, and joined him at the counter.

Maybe I need to dial it back to eleven…

"Sorry I'm not awake yet," Jake said. "I usually need a shower to become reasonably human. This is great, thank you."

"How pitiful am I that this is the most relaxed I've felt living with someone else in too damn long?" Ben softly asked. "I was at the point where I dreaded mornings with Mort. I could have done everything perfectly and he'd go out of his way to pick something to find fault with."

"Go easy on yourself, buddy. We all make mistakes." He wanted to pull the other man into his arms and hug him, but that might expose his morning woody that was now more a Ben-woody.

Ben swallowed down a forkful of pancakes. "It was like he did everything in his power to keep me off-guard. Never let me relax. Like nothing was ever good enough, but he'd manage to make me feel guilty for it, like he was disappointed. The clues were there all along, I just never picked up on them before. For example, he might praise me for something, but then pick out one minor thing to talk about that I didn't get right. As time went on, the negatives grew and the positives shrank, until I was driving myself crazy trying to earn his praise."

Jake wished Mort was there so he could punch him in the nose.

Or turn Tilly loose on him. "Typical abuser. Considering what he did to you, it's not surprising."

"Like cleaning the kitchen for you. You appreciated it. I was almost waiting for the drawback, and you didn't say one. He would have praised me for cleaning the kitchen and tacked on something like, 'Next time, make sure to organize the spice rack.' Or something like that. Breakfast today would have been, 'Good pancakes, but next time, maybe some fruit topping or something.'" He jabbed his fork at his food. "God, I'm a fucking idiot."

Jake set his fork down and reached over, laying his hand on his friend's shoulder. "Buddy," he softly said. "Look at me."

Ben finally did, the sorrow in his blue eyes nearly breaking Jake's heart. "I appreciate everything you've done so far. Promise me that any time I do something like that, even accidentally, you *must* call me out on it. Okay?"

"But you've never—"

He squeezed Ben's shoulder to silence him. "House Dom to house sub," he firmly said. "That's a standing rule. Deal?"

It was like a weight lifted from Ben's shoulders. He finally blew out a long breath before nodding. "Deal."

"Thank you." He reluctantly pulled his hand from Ben's shoulder and started eating again. "These pancakes are great, by the way. But I don't want you killing yourself for me every morning, okay? Let's limit it to once or twice a week." He smiled. "Otherwise, I'm going to freaking gain weight and have to start exercising. And I hate that."

"Is this a bad time to tell you I made us both lunches already?"

Jake couldn't help it. He was in the process of swallowing a bite of pancakes when Ben said it, and the adorable look on his face started Jake laughing, which nearly choked him. He managed to get the food down and sip some coffee.

"If you're trying to spoil me, it's working, okay?"

That finally won him a smile from Ben. "Good. I don't want you to regret letting me move in."

"Fat chance of that, buddy."

When he finished eating, Ben insisted Jake leave the plate in the sink for him to wash while Jake went to take his shower and get dressed. As Jake stood under the spray, he tried to drag his mind back to a place of common sense and couldn't.

I need to be careful.

It'd be too damn easy to accidentally pressure Ben into a relationship with him. In the man's emotionally vulnerable state, and with him so eager to seek Jake's approval—not even adding a D/s dynamic into the mix—Jake knew he could likely have the guy in his bed in a few days.

But that might nuke their friendship in the long run. And the last thing he wanted to do was lose Ben as a friend, much less hurt him.

Settle down, cowboy. If anything's meant to be, it'll happen. For now, he needed to back the fuck off and take it slow. Starting with talking about *maybe* playing at the party in two weeks.

Again, he sensed Ben might possibly agree to that just to seek Jake's approval. He'd have to figure out a way to approach it so that Ben called the shots, whether the subby wanted to or not.

Because even if something did develop between the two of them, Jake knew he needed to make sure it was because Ben wanted it to happen, and not because he accidentally steered things that way and Ben agreed because he was eager to please him.

Ben

Ben had the kitchen cleaned up and was ready to leave when Jake emerged from his bedroom thirty minutes later.

"Can we stop for groceries on the way home?" Ben asked. "I've got a list already of meals I want to make. It'll give us leftovers for lunch, too."

Jake arched an eyebrow at him. "You're really taking this 'house subby' thing to heart, huh?"

"I love to cook. Seriously. I enjoy it. I don't mind that being one of my chores."

"Then shouldn't I get to help clean up the kitchen?" Jake asked.

"Why?"

"That's only fair, right?"

"I don't mind cleaning the kitchen. I have a system. I clean up as I go."

Jake sighed. "If I argue with you, it'll just hurt your feelings, won't it?"

"I promise that if I feel like things aren't equitable, I'll speak up. How's that?"

He headed for the kitchen. "Probably the best I can ask for."

"I set your travel mug by the sink."

Jake stopped and turned. "How did you know that's what I was going to do?"

"Because you bring it to work every morning."

"But how did you know which one? There's several of them in the cabinet."

"Because you always use the same one. You like it because it doesn't drip. You told me that after you bought it and used it a couple of times. It's your favorite travel mug. You used it Saturday, too."

Jake

Ben was making this damned hard for Jake to take things slow with him. Jake couldn't even think of a single time Allison had ever anticipated something he did like this, much less had paid attention to things he already did, and prepared in advance for it.

"Thank you, buddy," Jake said, honestly moved by the gesture. "I appreciate it."

Ben smiled. Beamed. "You're welcome. I *like* being helpful. I get off on it. Seriously."

"Okay, then. We'll sit down tonight after dinner and go over a chore list, and you *will* let me do some of them. Right?"

Ben's smile widened. "Right. Deal."

Although he suspected Ben would do his level best to try to do as many of them as possible.

Once they were on their way to work, they'd started talking about work projects when Ben's cell phone rang. He frowned when he looked at it, but Jake went quiet and turned down the radio as Ben answered.

"Hello? ...Oh, yes, Detective Jacobs...um, sure. Can you e-mail me what you need? I'm in the car right now...sure. I'll call my bank and pick the papers up and get them to you...yes, I can bring them tomorrow. Thanks."

Jake turned the radio back up once Ben ended the call, but he didn't speak, knowing from the look on Ben's face that he needed a moment.

And he was in such a good mood, too.

"More forms and stuff they need for the investigation." Ben stared out the passenger window for a moment. "You know, I was having a really good morning not thinking about that part of shit until then."

Jake hated that Ben sounded depressed now, whereas Jake had seen glimpses of his happy old friend earlier. "If you need to borrow my car and do it this afternoon, that's okay with me. I don't mind, you can take it."

"No, I need to call the bank's legal department and talk to the case manager there who's handling my file. It'll probably take them a day to get what I need. I'll drive myself tomorrow and take the morning off. I want to get that project finished today and sent to the shop for the test run. That'll make Carl happy and he won't give me a hassle about the time off. I have a couple other errands I need to run tomorrow anyway. That'll work out."

"Don't forget to talk to that PI Tilly referred you to."

"Oh, thank you." Ben swiped through something on his phone. "I'll call him today. Maybe I can go see him tomorrow, too."

Ben

After dinner, Ben settled on one end of the couch while Jake took the other. He was going over something on his phone.

"Okay," Jake finally said. "You're claiming kitchen chores, am I correct?"

Ben nodded. "Yep. I'm not much of a griller, so if you want to cook on the grill, you'll have to take charge of that, or teach me how to do it."

"Not a problem. I can do grilling." He made a notation. "I'll clean bathrooms."

Ben started to protest, but Jake overruled him. "Don't make me go Dom on your ass."

"Okay, fine." Although the thought of letting Jake go Dom on his ass wasn't exactly a threat. More like a really fun promise.

"We do our own laundry," Jake said. "That's pretty easy. Since you want the kitchen, I don't mind mowing and trimming. I would like some help once or twice a month with weeding."

"Then give me dusting. You have allergies."

Jake looked up, an undecipherable expression on his face. "How do you remember that?"

"It's a subby blessing and a curse. Yes to me dusting? And I mean the whole house, including your room. Allergy meds make you sleepy and cranky."

Jake noted something. "I can't argue with you there."

They went through the basic list of chores, Jake taking more than Ben thought he should, but knowing if he tried to argue the points with his friend the Dom would just dig his heels in.

And he calls me *stubborn.*

Jake e-mailed him the list. "Check it over. If it's good, I'll print it out."

"It's good." And the good thing was, Ben knew he could sneak in extra chores so Jake wouldn't have to do them, like cleaning the bathrooms himself. Hell, he already kept his bathroom clean, and Jake wasn't a pig, either.

If he was sneaky and used excuses like needing to do a full load of laundry so he didn't waste water, he could probably start washing Jake's clothes, too.

Jake arched an eyebrow at him. "What are you thinking?"

Ben hoped he didn't blush. "What?"

"You look like you're calculating. You trying to figure out how to do more of the chores?"

Ben didn't want to lie and opted to divert. "Why would I do that?"

"Because you're stubborn."

"And you're pushy."

That seemed to steer Jake onto a related track for a train of thought. "While we're talking stubborn and pushy…"

"Yes?"

Jake set his phone down. "Tilly's party."

Now Ben really hoped his cheeks weren't flaming red. "Yes?"

"I don't want to be pushy. So I'll leave it up to you whether or not we play, or how we play, all of that. Totally up to you."

"What if you don't want to play?"

"Obviously, if either of us decide at the last-minute that it's a no, then we don't. But assume that I do want to play, unless I tell you otherwise, all right?"

Ben's mouth had gone dry, so he nodded.

"I'm putting the responsibility of this on you. You need to negotiate your hard limits with me, make sure my implement bag is packed with what you want me to use and is ready to go, all of that."

"Me?" Again he had to bite back the urge to add a "sir" to the end of that.

"You. Because then I'll feel confident that it's what you want, and not what you think I want, if that makes sense?"

If Jake was trying to shake his equilibrium, he'd done a great job of it. With Mort, it was straight orders, period. While Mort hadn't ever technically violated a safeword, Ben knew if he'd told the guy he didn't feel like playing, Mort would have pouted and generally made life difficult for him until Ben gave in. The expectation was always that they would play, unless Mort decided they weren't going to play.

This was…different.

Different in a *good* way.

"So you're okay with me organizing your implement bag?"

"Knock yourself out, buddy. I'll warn you that if it's in the bag at the party, I'm guessing you don't mind it being used on you unless you specifically safeword for it. So if there are things you don't want me to use on you, seriously, leave them out."

"Would you mind if I organized that whole room?"

"Mind?"

"Well, I mean, it's your house."

Jake chuckled. "Again, knock yourself out, but please don't kill yourself doing it. I rarely use that room for much."

"Okay. Thanks."

Jake picked up his phone and headed over to the desk in the corner to turn the printer on. "Remember, you need to schedule a time for us closer to the party to sit down and discuss limits. I want it to be next week, so you have time to really think about them. They need to be *your* limits, not what you think *I* want. Okay?"

"Are you really okay playing with me?" Ben asked.

"We wouldn't be having this discussion if I wasn't." Jake switched on the printer and did something on his phone. "Remind me to give you the info for the printer. It's networked, but you can e-mail documents right to it." Sure enough, it spit out two copies of the chore list.

Jake walked them back to the couch, handing Ben one. "There you go. And this is flexible, too. If we need to change it, just say so." He let out a yawn. "Now I think I'm going to hit the hot tub. Feel free to join me, if you want."

"Thanks." Ben knew if he did that, he'd be exposing how hard he was right now just thinking about playing with Jake. "I need to work some more out in the garage organizing my stuff. But thanks."

"Not a problem."

* * *

Jake

Twenty minutes later, Jake was out on the lanai, enjoying a soak in the hot tub, naked.

Maybe it's better Ben isn't with me. It'd be too tempting to tease him and try to talk him into doing…something.

Anything.

Jake had wrapped a towel around his hips for the walk from his bedroom and out to the lanai, but he hadn't bumped into Ben, who was busy out in the garage. Jake left all the outside lights off, the lanai and hot tub cloaked in darkness broken only by the stars above and lamp light filtering out through the horizontal blinds over the window in his bedroom. He'd turned off the living room lights, too, the light in the hallway barely visible from the hot tub, and all Ben would need to walk back and forth to the garage.

Jake leaned back and closed his eyes, the jet he was sitting against perfectly hitting a sore knot in his back.

The only thing better would be not being alone out there.

Fuck it.

The jets stirred the water, making it impossible in the dark to tell what Jake was doing. Stretched out in the molded lounger seat, he closed his eyes and fisted his cock as he thought about Ben.

Slowly stroking, he imagined it was the other man's hand on his cock, picturing Ben's blue eyes gazing into his. Just the fact that he could get so hard over fantasies of the guy instead of past fantasies of women—or men—was even more proof to Jake that this wasn't merely a passing crush.

With his other hand, he cupped his balls and stroked them, lightly tugging on them even as he jacked his cock. Maybe there'd be nights like this for them together in the future.

He damned sure hoped so.

Ben

Ben hadn't meant to spy on Jake. He'd intended to step out onto the lanai and ask him a quick question about some stuff in the garage, until he recognized what the movements of Jake's upper arm signified, just visible above the water.

Heart racing, he stepped to the side, deeply cloaked in shadows, and peered through the vertical blinds covering the living room sliders as he watched his friend jerk off.

Go. Help. Him.

No, that might freak Jake out.

But now his own cock was hard, aching, and he slid his hand

inside his shorts and briefs and cupped it, his thumb rubbing over the slit and the drops of pre-cum there.

Fuck.

Jake was facing away from the living room. The other man tipped his head back against the edge of the hot tub, his motions growing faster as Ben bit his own lower lip and watched, now jacking his own cock as he stood there.

He could easily envision himself kneeling between the Dom's legs, his hands coaxing an orgasm out of Jake, how it'd feel leaning in to take Jake's cock into his mouth and wrap his lips around it, swallowing as he—

The orgasm caught him by surprise, nearly taking his knees out. He had to brace himself against the wall with his left hand as he came all over his right, his briefs now filled with hot, sticky cum.

Jake had come, too, his movements stilled.

Ben stood there for a moment, staring out into the dark at his friend and then suddenly realizing...*fuck!*

He quickly darted back down the hall and to his room, closing —and locking—the door behind him.

Okay, you cannot *do shit like that!*

It was one thing to fantasize about the guy while rubbing one out in the shower.

Totally another to secretly perv on him like that.

Then again, Jake *had* invited him to join him in the hot tub.

Yeah, and then you turned him down and he thought *he was alone, you perv!*

Trembling, he stripped and stepped into the shower to rinse off. Never before in his life had he done something like that. Torn between guilt and lust, he turned the water temperature down to cool himself off, literally and figuratively.

If he didn't want to fuck up his friendship and get himself thrown out, he'd need to control himself a lot better than that.

Maybe he shouldn't let Jake play with him. He'd be begging the

Dom to let him blow him at the private party, where full-on sex was allowed, unlike at Venture.

All he knew was that he'd have to be careful. Now he got why Jake wanted to move slowly, cautiously.

Was I this fucked up all along and everyone could see it but me?

Chapter Nine

Ben

Tuesday morning, after fixing Jake's coffee and making him a breakfast sandwich while Jake was in the shower and couldn't protest, Ben left the house, driving himself.

He also didn't want to have to face Jake any longer than necessary that soon. He'd started his morning by rubbing another one out in the shower while thinking about the view he'd had of Jake's sexy ass while getting out of the pool on Sunday.

Obviously, there'd be a lot of morning—and nighttime—masturbation in his immediate future until he got this out of his system.

He needed to hit the bank to pick up the paperwork, deliver it, and he wanted to get an in-person status update from the lead detective on the case. Since Ben was still waiting for his new ATM card to arrive, he also cashed a check while at the bank. That way, after his initial consultation with the PI, he could drop by the mall and pay his cell phone bill in person at the store there.

Monday afternoon, Carl McMannis had gladly approved Ben

coming in late after he'd finished the project and the prototype was run and already approved by the client.

A very happy client who was already promising to send more lucrative work their way for a job done not only well, but ahead of schedule.

He was actually done with those four errands by ten thirty. The PI had looked at the paperwork Ben gave him, copies of stuff from the bank as well as from the sheriff's detective on the case, and had promised to e-mail Ben a questionnaire later that afternoon for him to fill out regarding Mort. He didn't promise he could find the man, but he certainly sounded more confident and eager than the detective had.

Then again, Ben was realistic. The detective was probably handling dozens of active cases for the sheriff's office, many of them likely far more serious than Ben's. The PI surely had a much smaller—and more lucrative—caseload.

It was something, though. A little progress. He didn't feel nearly as helpless and hopeless as he had in the beginning. Plus, the rep at the bank said he'd have most of the remaining money returned to his account by close of day Wednesday.

That was a huge win, as far as Ben was concerned.

While still a little early, he opted to go to the food court at the mall and eat lunch before heading to work, since he was already there to pay his cell bill. One of the things he loved about that food court were the planters spaced at irregular angles throughout the seating area, making some almost private-feeling alcoves. Being a work day, it wasn't very crowded.

As he sat down at a table with his tray, he heard a familiar woman's voice speaking on the other side of the plant divider behind him.

"I still can*not* believe he broke up with me like that! Fucking asshole."

Allison.

Shit. Could my luck be any worse if I tried? She worked at one of the department stores in that mall, where her roommate also worked.

He thought about moving somewhere else before she spotted him, until he heard another woman reply. "Well, not like you were really that into him."

"We dated for three damn years! Of course I was into him."

"Yeah, and you were cheating on him for the past two months. What difference does it make if he broke up with you? Doesn't that make your life easier? Now you don't have to worry about it."

Ben froze, not quite sure he heard her correctly. He assumed the other woman was Allison's roommate and friend, even though he'd never met her in person.

"No! I had to keep my options open. If Jake hadn't been a dick now, I would have ditched Brian and stuck with Jake. Three fucking *years*, and he won't even give me a key to his house?"

"And—again—you were *cheating* on him."

"Not *technically*." Allison sounded pouty. "We haven't slept together yet. It's just online. That's not cheating."

"It's not just online. You've been chatting to that guy online for two months and leading him on. You've been talking to him on the phone. I've overheard some of what you said. You know damn well Jake would have considered that cheating. If you don't think so, then you call him right now and ask him yourself."

Allison sounded even more petulant. "It's not cheating if you don't sleep with someone. Haven't even met him in person yet. I never slept with anyone but Jake while we were together. That means I wasn't cheating. Besides, Jake moved Ben into the house without asking me."

"So? It's his house. They're just roommates. I don't know why you're so pissed off about that. They've been friends for years. He's known Ben three times as long as he's known you."

"Whose side are you on, anyway?" Now Allison sounded downright childish.

"I'm just saying that maybe Jake sensed what you were up to.

Maybe this is karma biting you in the ass for playing games with him. I warned you not to fuck around, and look what happened."

Accusation entered Allison's tone. "You didn't tell him, did you?"

"No, I said I wouldn't. I haven't even talked to him in weeks."

It sounded like the women were getting up. Ben hunkered down over his tray and, thankfully, they must have exited the food court area in the other direction, because they didn't pass him.

Anger and indignation flowed through him.

Damn right Jake would consider what she'd done cheating.

Do I tell him?

Jake was his best friend. Even though they'd sort of made a pact to warn each other in the future, he wasn't sure what useful purpose it'd serve by telling him something like this. If Allison hadn't slept with someone, that meant she hadn't put Jake at risk.

He'd have to stew on it for a while, maybe ask someone else for advice.

Like Tilly.

Meanwhile, he forced down his lunch, his appetite now greatly diminished, so he could get to work.

Jake

Tuesday afternoon, Jake was head-down over his computer and working on a project when his cell phone rang. He glanced at it and almost let it go to voice mail before remembering delaying these conversations never went well.

It was always easier to face them head-on and get them over with.

"Hey, Mom. What's up?"

"You father and I would like to see you more than once a year, you know."

Cue emotional blackmail…check. That was record time, even for her. "We had dinner together three weeks ago. I'm sorry, but I've been busy."

"Can you fit us into your busy schedule this weekend?"

If sarcasm were a bodily fluid, she'd be dripping in it. Positively oozing out of every pore.

Infecting a bite with fangs.

Pointing out to his mom that she was doing the same exact thing to him that she used to accuse her in-laws of doing to her would be pointless.

He knew that, because he'd tried it before.

"Sure, but I'll probably bring Ben with me."

"Ben?"

"Yeah, Ben. You know who he is."

"Why would you bring him with you?"

"Because he moved in last weekend, he's my best friend, and I don't want to be rude and not invite him."

Countermove: emotional blackmail blocked by unavoidable social etiquette…check.

She seemed to need a moment to formulate an adequate response to that. "What?"

"He needed a place to live, and I could use the extra money in my budget. I'm looking to replace my car."

"You could go to work for your father, you know. He's asked you enough times."

"Yeah, and I've told you both that's *not* going to happen." *Not in this lifetime, or any other, either.*

He loved his parents, but working for his father would be the fastest way to completely remove his parents from his life, in addition to the fact that he had zero interest in taking over his dad's business.

Besides the fact that his dad wouldn't pay him nearly as much as he was currently making, and the health insurance plan wouldn't be as good, either.

"Who is he supposed to leave the business to?"

"I don't know, Mom. He's over eighty and should sell it. Find a good buyer instead of just closing down. Then you two can retire and enjoy yourselves, relax, spend the money."

"If we spend it, how are we supposed to leave any of it for you?"

"I'd rather you enjoy it while you're alive. I'm fine, but you two aren't getting any younger."

"Why aren't you bringing Allison with you?" *One logic point side-stepped to avoid the uncomfortable truth…check.*

"I broke up with her last weekend."

"Because you moved that guy into your grandparents' house?"

"*My* house, and no. I was already planning on breaking up with her. It was coincidental timing."

In the early days when he'd moved into the house, after probate went through and he'd been transferred the deed, his mother and father had both tried to outright tell him what and how to do things there, including him coming home from work one day to find his mother rearranging the kitchen.

He'd changed the locks the next afternoon, buying some on his way home.

No, they didn't have a key to his house. The only person with a spare key—besides Ben—was Ed, his attorney.

Times like this I wish I weren't an only child. Then they'd have an alternate target to focus on besides him.

"I don't understand why you can't understand your father's point of view. You should be able to take over his business easily. You know computer stuff."

"Because I hated every second he made me work there in high school. He was a dictator. I'm honestly shocked he has four print shops and can keep anyone working for him."

"He was just hard on you because he wanted you to do well."

"Yeah, well, I did well in college so I wouldn't have to rely on working for him when I graduated." It couldn't even be considered a low blow, because he'd said as much to his father's face.

Multiple times.

He'd been an unexpected child of older parents, his mom thirty-six and his dad forty-two when Jake was born. Doctors had actually told his mom they didn't think she could get pregnant.

Of course, that's when she did get pregnant.

His parents were a completely expected product of their upbringing, conservative and inflexible, and would flip out if they knew what their son did in his free time.

He'd also carefully guarded the fact that he was bi from them. His father's older brother—and only sibling—had been cut off from the family just out of high school for being gay. When he was killed in a car wreck a decade earlier, only Jake had gone to the funeral, mourning the uncle he'd never really had a chance to know.

So he knew he'd receive at least a little pushback from them when they found out about Ben living there, since they knew Ben was gay.

"How long is that guy going to be staying with you? Not long, I hope?"

Wasn't his first rodeo with the woman, which was why he was used to her darting around from topic to topic in an attempt to catch him off-guard with a guilt bomb. "As long as he wants. He's a nice guy and we've been friends for years. Frankly, it's nice not living alone."

"You wouldn't *be* alone if you hadn't broken up with your girl-friend. What was wrong with her? She was quite lovely. You were with her for three years. You should have married her."

"She was an immature pain in the ass and all I ever heard from you before right now was how much you couldn't stand her. Listen, Mom, I'm sorry, but I'm really busy. Text me a time and place you were thinking about dinner and I'll let you know if we can make it, okay? Saturday night won't be good for me, though. So either Friday night or Sunday. Love you."

He hung up before she could start protesting that she didn't know how to text.

Not for lack of trying on his part to teach her. She could manage to text him when she wanted something from him, but not when it meant it'd be convenient for him.

He set his phone to silent and tried to get back to work. He loved his parents and hated feeling like a shitty son, but he had nothing in common with them other than DNA.

He'd also long ago accepted the fact that, one day, he might end up falling out with them, or at least with his father. Just because his grandfather had guilt-tripped Jake's dad into taking over the family business didn't mean Jake was going to follow in their ink-stained footprints.

The years he'd spent during high school working for his father insured Jake would *never* work for him again.

No way in hell.

His father *literally* couldn't pay Jake enough to work for him.

He'd had one blow-up with his parents when he'd stopped going to church in high school. He didn't care that it was their thing, but they were conservative Baptists from a long line of conservative Baptists.

In all honesty, Jake had been shocked when his grandmother had left the house to him. Jake's grandfather had been an only child, and Jake's father had worked hard to build the business Jake's grandfather had started and leave a "legacy" to hand down to Jake.

With his father having no other living siblings, Jake had assumed everything would be left to his father, which was fine with Jake.

His parents had apparently thought so, too. Jake got the distinct feeling they thought he should have to wait his "turn" to inherit stuff.

What they didn't seem to get was he didn't *care*. They couldn't put themselves in his shoes and process that little factoid. When his grandmother died, Jake had been doing fine. He was renting an apartment and had owned outright the car he was driving now. Not new, but not in bad shape then, either. His debt was low, just some student loans from college, and he'd been building a nest egg for retirement.

Careful money management skills were something helpful he'd learned from his father and grandfather, all due credit given there.

The house had been an unexpected bonus he planned to hold on to.

Needing a quick break to clear his mind following the mental sparring with his mom, Jake got up to head to the bathroom and spotted Ben at his desk. Taking a quick detour that way, he leaned into his friend's cubicle.

"Hey, thanks for the breakfast sandwich this morning, buddy. You get everything handled? Any news?"

Ben shook his head. "They haven't caught him yet. The PI seems hopeful, though. He'll be in touch with me again later today."

"Sorry. Fair warning, we might be having dinner with my parents this weekend. Mom just called."

Ben leaned back in his chair and stared at him. "Huh?"

Jake grinned. "Hey, sorry, I forgot to mention this, but one of the conditions of you moving in is that you help me survive dinner with my 'rents."

That finally won him a smile. "You know they don't like me."

"That's just a bonus," Jake said. "I'm sorry, but I *am* a sadist. You knew that when you moved in."

Ben's smile widened. "They didn't consent."

"I don't care. They've been sadistic to me in their own ways throughout the years. Time for a little payback."

"You tell them about Allison?"

"Yeah."

"You tell them I'm living there now?"

He grinned. "Ooooh, yeah."

"I'm guessing from your grin that your mom wasn't happy about that."

He shrugged. "SSDD. And I still don't care what they think."

Chapter Ten

Ben

Wednesday and Thursday, they drove in to work together. Ben had managed to not repeat his voyeuristic adventure of Monday night.

He'd also moved from organizing the garage to organizing the spare bedroom.

And Jake's implement bag.

Thursday evening, he received a text from Tilly.

Lunch, Friday? My treat. Just you.

He sat on the edge of his bed. He and Jake really hadn't discussed lunch plans for tomorrow, although Jake would be driving himself because he had to stop at the mechanic on his way in to work. His car was acting up again and Ben was prepared to drive Jake home from work if they couldn't make the repairs by the end of the work day.

Okay. Where?

I'll pick you up. Text me your work address.

What about Jake?

Just you. Want to talk to you alone. No offense. He knows he's getting a private chat of his own later.

Ben's face heated even though he wasn't feeling the force of the Domme's gaze laying heavy upon him.

Yes, ma'am.

Honestly? No other reply to her felt right.

:) Good boy, but you don't have to call me that if you don't want to. I'll pick you at noon.

Thank you.

He texted her his work address and then went to tell Jake, who lay stretched out on the sofa and watching TV.

"I guess I have a solo lunch date with Tilly tomorrow."

"You do?"

He showed Jake the text exchange, and while Ben had wondered if he'd be upset, Jake surprised him by laughing. "So that's why she texted me asking if I could have lunch with her alone tomorrow. I'm dining with her on Tuesday."

"Huh?"

He pulled out his phone and showed Ben. Jake had told her he wasn't sure how his day would go, it would depend on if his car was ready or not, or if he'd have to go talk to the mechanic at lunch time.

"Oh. I'll leave you my car keys in case you need mine," Ben offered.

"Thanks." Jake set his phone on the coffee table. "By the way, I saw the progress you've made in the spare bedroom."

Ben was glad the only light in the living room came from the TV. "Yeah?"

"Looks good." Jake stared up at him. "Saw you've been working on the implement bag, too. Good job. Garage looks great, too."

"Thank you."

Sir. Sir. Sir. Sir.

SIR.

Jake

Jake was dying to tell Ben he was a good boy, but knew that was pushing too hard.

Get through playing at the party first, see where things go from there.

Hell, see what Tilly wanted to talk to each of them about. He could use her as a trusted sounding board, if nothing else. Maybe she'd suss out something from Ben at their lunch tomorrow to help Jake confirm or deny if Ben was even attracted to him.

Maybe, with Cris being bi, she'd have advice for Jake on how to handle talking to Ben.

The next day, he was sitting at his desk when Tilly and Ben appeared in the entry to his cubicle.

"There he is," she said.

Ben handed off his keys to Jake so he could drive his car to go talk to the mechanic. Jake wasn't even sure how much money he wanted to put into the car right now.

"Can I bring you anything back?" Ben asked him.

"Nope, I'm good. I'll grab something while I'm out."

Tilly turned and handed her keys to Ben. "Go ahead and start my car, please. You'll be driving. I'll be along in a minute."

Ben's eyes widened. "Uh, no offense, ma'am, but are you sure?"

Tilly looked at Jake and hooked her left thumb at Ben. "He a good driver?"

"Yeah."

"Then I'm sure. I scare myself enough driving with a bum arm. Don't want to scare the crap out of you, too. I'll be right there." Once they were alone again, she stepped closer and dropped her voice. "Guess you two compared notes about today's lunch date?"

"I'm assuming it's our private ass-chewing?"

"You're good. Quick on the uptake. I like that. I'll give you the same warning I'm going to give him. If there's stuff you want kept confidential from each other, that's fine, but tell me that before you tell me." She stuck her head up and glanced around before leaning in close again and dropping her voice to a whisper. "Between you and me and the fence post, dude. You're into him, right?"

Jake felt his face redden, but he nodded. "He doesn't know I'm bi. I don't want to tell him right now. It's too soon. I don't want him to think I'm being a douche after all he's been through with Mort. He thinks I'm straight."

"Score another victory for Landry and his spookily accurate bi-dar senses. Did you break up with the sandspur on accident, on purpose, or just coincidental timing?"

"It was already going to happen, even before I asked Ben to move in. So coincidental. I was tired of her bullshit and this was the perfect catalyst."

Tilly nodded, straightening and patting his shoulder with her good hand. "Thank you for the honesty. That's why I wanted to have lunch with *you* first, but oh well. I won't break his trust, but I'll try to get enough intel I can give you a thumbs up or down, cool?"

He held up his fist for a bump from her, which she returned. "Cool. Thanks."

She headed out, leaving him staring at Ben's keys on his desk. He reached over and picked them up, finding them still warm from having been in the man's pocket. He'd never really taken a good look at them before. On them, Ben had a small round enamel keychain with the Steely Dan logo on it.

Ben's favorite band.

A keyring Jake had given Ben at least five or six years ago for his birthday. Just one of a couple of small things, the kind of inexpensive gifts friends gave each other but didn't think about them after.

He stared at it for a long moment before pressing his lips to the warm emblem and then putting the keys in his pocket.

Ben

Ben sat hunched up behind the steering wheel while waiting for Tilly to emerge from the building.

Honestly? He was scared to adjust anything, and her legs were shorter than his.

When she finally walked out, she confidently strode across the blacktop parking lot and slid into the passenger side. "Let's—what are you doing?"

"Um…waiting, ma'am?"

She did the eyebrow arch. *Must be a Dominant thing.*

"Seriously?" she finally asked. "Adjust the damn seat and mirrors and stuff. You'll kill us like that."

"Sorry. I didn't want to mess up your settings."

She laughed. "I'm not going to hurt you in the bad ways, I promise. Plus, I have a preset I can use." She pointed to a button on the dash he hadn't been able to decipher, one which now made perfect sense to him.

After he had everything adjusted so he could comfortably drive, he looked at her. "Where to, ma'am?"

She'd slipped sunglasses on. "The Columbia on St. Armands. I'm in the mood for picadillo and deviled crab cakes. Can't get a decent version of either out in LA. Or a real Cuban sandwich. *Oooh*, Cuban sandwich. *Hmm*. Decisions, decisions. Definitely flan in my future, for sure."

He knew where the Columbia was, but he'd never eaten there before. "Yes, ma'am."

"You're a good nut, Charlie Brown." She smiled at him. "My friend the PI said he's working on your case."

"Thank you for that. I really appreciate it."

She waved the comment away. "I like helping. I like being help*ful*. I don't always get to be helpful for my friends and family. Sometimes life steps in and fucks shit up beyond all recognition before I can unfuck it for everyone."

She stared out the windshield for a moment, and if it wasn't for the sunglasses, he suspected she might actually be…melancholy. "So. How are things with you and Jake? Ready to kill each other yet?"

"No, ma'am. It's good. We worked out chores and everything."

"He won't let you do as much as you want, will he?"

Ben didn't take his focus off the road. "How'd you know that?"

She pointed at her head with her left hand. "Switch. *Duh*. Slave for years first. Wanting to serve is kind of baked into the hard-wiring, you know."

"Yes, ma'am."

She tilted her head as she studied him. "You are shitting-your-pants terrified of me, aren't you?"

"No offense? But yes, ma'am."

"Why is everyone scared of me? I'm a sweetheart." She reached down inside the top of her cast with a finger, trying to scratch an itch.

He finally let out a laugh. "You have a reputation, ma'am."

She glanced at the cast. "Hey, he's the first one I actually hit, and he deserved it." She frowned. "Well, okay, so Terrie set me up by not telling me they were getting married and he was sufficiently sorry, but that's beside the point." Her tone softened. "What we talk about today is between us. I won't even tell Landry and Cris. Anything you want held in confidence, it is. Talk to me about what happened with Mort. And I don't mean the financial stuff, buddy."

It caught him off-guard, the tenderness in her voice. Maybe it was her accidentally using the same term of endearment for him that Jake frequently used, but he found himself spilling his guts to her, to the point that he was nearly in tears by the time they arrived at the restaurant and he found them a parking spot. Not just about Mort, either, but about his romantic failures all leading up to and including Mort.

She'd reached over with her left hand while he drove and rested it on his thigh. Calming, reassuring, and not like she was hitting on him or anything.

Like a big sister.

He shifted the car into park and sat there. After sucking in a deep breath, he said, "I feel like a fucking idiot. I feel like you and Jake and everyone else saw what a fucking asshole he was. If I was that blind, how do I ever trust my instincts again? I mean, I ignored the red flags. How do I not let someone else fucking use me the way he used me?"

"Do you trust me?" Tilly asked.

"Yes, ma'am."

"Do you trust Jake?"

"With my life, ma'am. We're hopefully going to play at your party."

She patted his leg again. "So, hear me out. I think maybe you need to separate these two parts of your life." She held her hands in front of her, slowly spreading them apart. "Kinky from dating."

"I need a kinky partner, ma'am. I'm not vanilla. Vanilla doesn't work for me."

"No, you need a partner who *gets* that you're kinky. If you and Jake are going to play together, that part's handled for now, right?"

"Yes, ma'am."

"And you said you trust him."

He nodded.

"Then instead of thinking you need to settle with one person, just…go out. Date. Not even sex. Meet friends. Right now, most of your friends are kinky, yes?"

"Yes, ma'am."

"You are *really* making me feel old calling me that, but I'll allow it because you're so fricking adorable." She smiled. "Spend time with *Ben*. Date. Or if you don't want to date, *do* something. Join a damn bowling league, or save sea turtle nests. I don't care. Get a hobby outside of your current sphere of friends and meet people. Let Ben learn to wear his skin comfortably again, see what it feels like, before you decide you're going to be with anyone."

He stared at a group of seagulls pecking at something in the parking lot. "Separate the two," he said.

She nodded. "Separate the two. Let Jake beat your ass. It's easier to date than it is to find someone you can trust not to violate your limits in a scene."

"But—" His mouth snapped shut.

She took off her sunglasses. "But what?"

"Between us? Promise?"

She nodded. "I promise."

"I don't know if I can date anyone else."

"Why not?"

"Because I *really* like Jake. Which is dumb, I know, because he's straight. But what if I'm falling for my best friend? If he was gay and into me, hell, I'd probably already be sleeping with him. If I play with him…"

Tilly slowly nodded her head. "As long as I've known the two of you, I don't think I'm out of line in saying what I'm about to say. I've never seen or heard of anyone talking about Jake violating a boundary or a trust. Play together at least once. Then…talk about it. Be honest with him what you're feeling."

"I don't want to freak him out."

"Dude, he *knows* you're gay. If he had a problem with that, you wouldn't be living in his house, and he wouldn't have offered to play with you in the first place. You wouldn't even be friends, most likely. Talk things out with him. Give him some credit. Whatever you do, don't make a sudden decision about *anything* without letting some time work on it first. You might think you're falling in love with him, but then as the NRE wears off of *you*, you settle into a comfortable zone where you can compartmentalize those two parts of your life. And think of that as an extra safety barrier."

"Ma'am?"

"If you're 'bonding' with Jake like that, as his submissive or whatever you two work out, it means you're less likely to jump into the wrong thing with someone else, right? Hell, go online and chat with guys. Go out to dinner. Maybe even work something out with Jake where you ask him as your Dominant to set a boundary that before you can actually sleep with a guy, he needs to give you permission. Take things uber-slow with anyone. If they're worth it, they'll understand, so there's a benchmark right there for ya."

His finger traced the stitching around the steering wheel. "You think Jake might be okay with that? I trust his judgment a hell of a lot more than I trust mine at this point."

"You want me to outright ask him when I have lunch with him on Tuesday?"

He considered it. "I guess I really should ask him that myself."

"Or, I'm just sayin', I could suss things out for you, you know?

Kind of roundabout work on him. Not outright. Sneaky like." She smiled.

Shit. Why the hell not? He hadn't leaned on his friends before, and look how fucked up his life had become for not doing it. "Yes, ma'am. Thank you. I'd appreciate that."

She patted his thigh again. "Good. Now let's go eat. We can continue this conversation inside. I'm starving, and you'll have to get back to work."

Chapter Eleven

Jake

Jake tried to concentrate on what the mechanic was telling him, but his gaze kept focusing on the keys in his hand.

Specifically, on the small enameled keyring with the Steely Dan logo, which he kept running his finger over.

What were Ben and Tilly talking about at lunch? What would Ben feel like revealing to him later?

What would Tilly be able to tell him?

Anyways, another four hundred dollars dropped into his car. He had to do it, because if he didn't, it would affect the resale or trade-in value when he did buy a new one. And he hadn't planned on buying a new car for a couple of months yet. He had other things he'd wanted to put that extra money into, like a new mower.

"Go ahead and do it. When will it be ready?"

"This afternoon. We'll call you." The mechanic had him sign the estimate and Jake headed back to work after stopping for a take-out sub on the way.

His mind immediately went to Ben.

He was pulling into the parking lot when he spotted Tilly's car approaching from the other direction, Ben behind the wheel. Ben parked right next to where Jake had parked Ben's car. Tilly got out and hugged Jake.

"Just take it slow and steady, dude," she whispered in his ear. As she stepped back, she smiled and gave him a thumbs-up that Ben couldn't see from that angle as he rounded the front of her car.

"Thank you for lunch, Tilly." Ben hugged her. "And the talk."

"You're quite welcome, buddy." She poked Jake in the chest. "You get me next week, you lucky bastard."

He couldn't help but laugh. "Lucky me." He returned Ben's keys to him.

Had life's timing worked out just a little different, Jake knew he and Tilly might have ended up dating. But he'd been with someone when Cris left her, and then she had her recovery and pro-Domme period where they all knew she wasn't up to dating again. When he found himself single, Landry and Cris had entered—or re-entered, in Cris' case—her life, and the chance passed.

Considering current events, maybe that was for the best all around.

Tilly drove off as the two men walked toward the building. "Good talk?" Jake asked him.

Ben nodded. "Yeah."

"She's not so scary."

They both stopped walking, looked at each other, and burst into laughter.

"I can't believe you said that with a straight face," Ben finally said.

"Me, either." They started walking again, Jake leading the way.

Ben

That afternoon, Tilly sent Ben an e-mail with a couple of links to safer sites and apps that Ben could use to possibly meet guys locally.

Just remember—don't do anything without talking to someone first. And be safe. –T.

He checked out a couple of the apps on his phone and downloaded them. No time to set up profiles right then.

Besides, he wanted to make sure…

Make sure what?

That Jake was okay with him doing that?

Maybe I shouldn't do it at all. Just let things gel for a while. Settle into a long-term rhythm with Jake and then go from there.

Except…

He'd never ask Jake not to date, and he didn't expect Jake to put his life on hold for him, either. The guy was single now, and Ben knew it'd be likely no more than a couple of months before Jake was dating again.

And he didn't expect his friend, no matter what kind of D/s relationship they had, to sit around at home with him, or drag him around everywhere as a third wheel like Sheldon to Jake's Leonard and some-yet-to-be-named Penny.

That wasn't fair to the guy.

After work, as he drove Jake to the mechanic's, Ben asked, "We still on for dinner with your 'rents on Sunday?"

Jake groaned and laid his head back against the seat rest, closing his eyes. "Don't remind me. But yeah."

"I don't have to go if it'll cause you more trouble."

"Oh, no, you don't. You're not getting out of this one. I'm stuck having dinner with them, so are you. I go to dinner with you at your parents' house all the time."

"Yeah, but they love you. Oh, fair warning, I think Mom wants to try to fix us up together. I told her you're straight, but if someone's single and has a penis, she wants to hook me up with them."

"I gotta say, I love your parents." Jake opened his eyes. "Think they'd adopt me?"

"I think it's a little late for that, if you meant officially."

"Yeah, that's what I was afraid of." He ran a hand through his brown hair. "Did you want to go hang out at Venture tomorrow night? My treat. Scrye and Kel are doing a suspension class."

Maybe if they went, Jake could talk to people, hang out, maybe even meet someone. "Sure. That sounds like fun, thanks."

"So…Tilly. Any idea what I can expect from her next week?"

"I don't know. She warned me to go slow."

"That's sage advice."

"She told me I should get out more and just meet people."

Jake

Jake felt an uncomfortable creeping sensation along his spine. "Meet people how?"

"Just…not a relationship. Dating, but nothing serious. To avoid sex for now."

The creeping sensation eased, and while relief settled in, Jake damn well knew he'd need to examine that reaction more in-depth. He was *not* a jealous guy, never had been.

Weird.

But that had definitely been jealousy.

"Did she now?" Jake asked.

"Yeah. She sent me an e-mail this afternoon with links to some apps and websites."

He fought the urge to growl. "That was…helpful. Nice of her, I mean."

Ben glanced his way. "Yeah. But I really get what she's saying." He cleared his throat. "I'd like to play with you next weekend and then see how we feel."

Jake couldn't help but focus on Ben's face. "How so?"

"Kind of like what we've started talking about already. Maybe you and me playing, and if that goes okay, for now, any relationship I might have in the future would be separate from that. Safety. Checks and balances."

Jake relaxed a little. "I have no problem talking about that. I know I'm going to take my time and go slow in the future."

"I know you said you wanted to wait to have our limits talk next week, and I'm good with that. But I've seen you play before, and I've never seen you play in a way I'd object to. Just...please don't let anyone else touch me while we're playing."

Now Ben had his undivided attention. "No problem. But...I watched Mort bring others in to touch you and play with you during scenes."

Ben wouldn't even glance his way. The hard set of his jaw betrayed the tension coursing through him. "Yeah," he quietly said.

Jake reeeally wanted to take a swing at that fucker, Mort. "You didn't want him to, but he did it anyway."

"He always did it in the middle of a scene, and he always twisted it around to make me feel like shit, and then he'd end it with some backward statement about how I really didn't want to safeword and be a pussy, or words to that effect. Then at the end he'd be like, see, you liked it. Stop whining. So eventually I stopped saying anything because it was easier to put up with it."

"What an asshole. Buddy, I swear, when we're playing, *no one* touches you but me. The only time I'd allow it was if there was an emergency and I needed medical help for you, or help getting you free in a hurry."

Ben's face relaxed. "An emergency's different. That's okay. I would want you to then. Or if we pre-negotiated something, like Nate fire cupping me. As long as you were there with me."

"Since we're talking, any other points you'd like to bring up now? We're still having our talk about hard limits next week."

Ben took a moment to say it. "Are you okay with aftercare?"

"What do you mean?" Jake asked.

"Doing aftercare for me?"

"Why wouldn't I be okay with that? You've seen me do aftercare."

"I meant…I'm a guy. I'd like to…cuddle."

"So? I'm okay with that."

He didn't miss how Ben quickly wiped at his eyes.

"Wait." Jake took a moment to breathe through another wave of rage. "That fucker never did aftercare with you. Did he?"

Ben shook his head.

Jake took a long, deep breath before speaking. Railing about Mort wouldn't make Ben feel any better about the situation.

"Presuming we play, when we finish our scene, I've got a fleece throw I'll bring with me. We'll find a quiet couch or corner some-where, and we'll sit there and snuggle for as long as you want to. Understand?"

Ben quickly nodded. "Thank you." His voice barely sounded louder than a whisper.

Jake couldn't help it. He reached over and patted Ben's thigh. "Buddy," he gently said, "if I'm topping you, I'm taking care of you. Whatever you need, that's what we do. It's no fun for me if I'm worried that you're not getting what you need out of it. *That's* how I play. That's *why* I play. And that's a reason me and Allison hadn't played in months. I don't want someone to just go along with me. Like one of those Venn diagrams. There's me, and you, and the fun spot is in the middle where we overlap. We can skate around the edges of either side of that middle part, but the most fun is had squarely in the middle."

"I want you to have fun, too," Ben said.

"Oh, I'll have fun, believe me. So answer me this. I've seen you…play hard." Jake resisted the urge to say the man's name. "Is that how you really like to play?"

"I do. I need heavy play. But I need to be warmed up and worked into the heavy part of it, not slammed right into heavy play."

"Good, see? That's information I need. Tell me about your ideal scene, without thinking about me. You tell me what would be a perfect scene for *you*."

Ben opened up and did just that, and by the time they reached the mechanic's shop, Jake was glad he had his travel mug in his hand to hold in front of him as they walked inside, because he was hard as iron, his cock straining his jeans.

Ben detailed a scene that could have come straight from Jake's own imagination.

Game on.

***

Ben

Ben followed Jake home from the mechanic. Already he felt a lot lighter in spirit. Just being able to unburden himself like that to Jake, and know that his friend was not only okay with scening like that, but looking forward to it…

Tilly was right.

Of *course* Tilly was right. Sun rises in the east, sets in the west, and Tilly.

Is.

Right.

Ben quickly warmed leftovers for them and cleaned the kitchen before starting a load of laundry. Jake had headed outside to do laps in the pool, leaving his bedroom door open so Ben could go in and dust.

Yes, while Ben was in there he sneakily tidied up Jake's bathroom, stopping short of scrubbing the shower and toilet.

He'd get himself caught doing that.

Finally, he joined Jake out in the pool, following his friend's lead of wrapping a towel around him and dropping it just before jumping in.

Now they were both paddling around out there, naked, but…

It was okay.

Ben was able to relax.

Tilly was right.

Jake was right, too, and to be honest, he'd said it to Ben first.

Ben knew he could do this now. He could scene with Jake, maybe more than once if they both enjoyed how it went, and take his time working his way toward a dating life again.

He'd brought his cell phone out, too, leaving it on the table, the timer set to let him know when the laundry would be ready to transfer from the washer to the dryer.

Jake finished his laps and flipped onto his back, floating. "Feeling better after our talk?"

Ben had been floating but stood up, feet firmly on the pool bottom. "Yeah. Thank you."

Jake's eyes were closed. "Communication. That's all this is. Communication and trust. I trust you, and hopefully I don't fuck up your trust in me. You have to talk to me and communicate. Trust flows two ways. If you don't tell me something for fear I'll freak out, and I do something to harm you, I'll be scared to scene with you again."

He opened his eyes and craned his head back so he could see Ben. "As your friend and as your Top, no topic is off-limits. Especially pertaining to us scening."

"Thanks." Ben finally found the courage to say it himself. "Tilly might hint around at this for me, but I guess I should ask it myself. If…if I do start to date and want to get serious about someone, can we work out some sort of permissions between you and me?"

"What did you have in mind?"

"Exactly what we joked about, only seriously. If I meet someone, and after I get to know them, if I decide maybe I want to sleep with them or something, I have to come to you and talk to you and have you sign off on them first."

He wasn't sure if Jake was going to answer him at first. "If that's something you really want me to do, then after we scene at Tilly's party, let's sit down and talk about it. That's not a no, either. I'm not against that, if you really want it that way. Like everything else, we'll need to negotiate it."

More relief filled Ben. "Thanks." He had a thought. "If you wanted to play before then, I'd be okay with that, too."

Jake finally stood so he could turn and face Ben. "I appreciate that, but I'd rather our first time be somewhere not alone. I know that might be stupid considering we live together, but you've been through a lot. It doesn't hurt to delay a little and do things right. Builds up the anticipation. And playing here at home, alone, is something we could work up to if things go well."

Ben's initial disappointment was quickly tempered by relief. Of *course* that was the smart thing to do.

Duh.

And, of course, that was why he trusted Jake so damn much. "You're right." He was saved from himself by his phone's timer going off on the table. "Oh, laundry's ready."

"I'm doing mine tomorrow." Jake went back to floating again. "Since *someone* probably snuck in and cleaned most of my bathroom for me already."

Ben froze as he was climbing out of the pool. "Busted, huh?"

"Educated guess based on how long you were in there alone. Thank you. I appreciate it. Stubborn subby." But he smiled.

"Pushy Dom." He climbed out, enjoying the sound of Jake's laughter over the sound of his phone going off. He dried off and wrapped the towel around him before walking over to silence the alarm. As he went inside, he realized that calling Jake pushy was way more than the ironic joke he'd intended it in the beginning.

He hadn't been kidding when he told Tilly he trusted Jake with his life.

And the last thing the guy was, in reality, was pushy.

Thank god he's not like Mort.

Jake

As darkness fell, Jake switched from the pool to the hot tub, grabbing his towel along the way. He hadn't turned on any of the outside lights when he came out, so once again he was cloaked in darkness.

He didn't like the return of the feeling he'd had when Ben had asked him about signing off on guys he wanted to date.

Don't be a fucking idiot.

Didn't matter what the thumbs-up from Tilly had meant, he didn't know what the future held for him and Ben.

The last thing he wanted to do was screw up their friendship. Hell, he'd known Ben longer than any woman he'd been with.

Sure, he'd love to bend Ben over a bench in the spare bedroom right now, beat his ass, cuddle with him, and then see what they could do together in bed…

But that wouldn't be smart. Not if Jake wanted something to last between them. Ben still had a lot of healing to do. He needed breathing room.

Slapping a collar around Ben's neck and laying down rules for him wasn't healthy. Jake instinctively knew that.

Joking that they were playing Dom/sub housekeeping was one thing.

Inserting play into the mix—which as far as Jake was concerned was every bit as intimate as sex in many ways—was something totally different.

He knew he could be intense, and he knew Ben was very laid back, literally to a point that he was detrimental to himself in some ways.

Jake had to help the guy build himself up, regain his self-confidence.

Anyone could take the easy road and command submission from someone who'd been through the wringer.

Jake was never interested in taking.

He wanted submission to be freely offered by someone strong-willed.

That had been one of the things that attracted him to Allison early on. She hadn't been "bratty" back then, she'd had a backbone and he'd liked that. Wanted that. It was after he discovered that she only had one note to that song that he'd realized she wasn't who he thought she was. That'd been a year in, and he'd been determined to see if a little time and maturity would help.

It didn't.

If anything, feeling secure in her position with him had made her worse, since she knew he wasn't some abusive asshole.

Tilly was right. She was a sandspur.

Alone in the dark, Jake slowly started stroking his cock under the warm water, imagining what it'd feel like having Ben naked and tied to a bench. If they were at a place in their relationship where he could top him—naked—and finish their scene by fucking the other man's mouth…

Or maybe that tight ass.

Jake's eyes fell closed as he stroked harder, faster, knowing it wouldn't take long. It never did take long when he thought about Ben. And as his balls tightened and emptied, his orgasm coursing through his nerve endings, he choked back the groan of satisfaction trying to escape him.

Lying there catching his breath, he chuckled.

Poor Ben might never want to get in this hot tub again if he knew how many times I've jerked off in it this week while thinking about him.

Ben

Once Ben transferred the clothes to the dryer, he took a shower and rubbed one while out thinking about Jake. With that tension eased, he stretched out on his bed to await the dryer finishing its cycle.

Staring at his phone, he picked it up and opened one of the apps he'd downloaded earlier.

Why the hell not?

Tilly would never steer him wrong, and neither would Jake.

He went ahead and created a profile for himself, using the same e-mail address he used for his FetLife account so it wouldn't be traced back to any of his other social media accounts.

No more fucking Morts.

He'd do this the safe way.

Jake might not be in his cards romantically, but Ben already felt somewhat better knowing his best friend had his back and would help him make good decisions when he didn't trust himself any more.

Chapter Twelve

Jake

Saturday night, Ben was talking with Tony and Shayla over on the far side of Venture's social area when Tilly walked over to the table Jake was sitting at and plopped down into the chair next to him.

"Hiya."

Jake glanced around to make sure Ben was out of hearing distance before he draped an arm around Tilly's shoulders and pulled her in close.

Whispering in her ear, he said, "Gee, *thank* you for being *sooo* helpful and sending the guy I'm really into links to gay meet-up sites."

"You're welcome. Oh, wait, that was sarcasm. *Wow,* been so long since I heard some I didn't recognize it." She lifted an eyebrow at him. "Dude, sloooow. I bought you some tiiiime."

"He said you might hint around about seeing if I'm okay with signing off on people he gets serious with."

"*Oooh,* he brought that up? That's good."

"*How* is that good?"

She patted him on the cheek. "You're fricking adorable, you know that? See, if you'd not played a stupid het guy for years, you'd understand my evil plan." She also checked on Ben's location to make sure they weren't being overheard. "He trusts you. He's really into you and worried that, after you play, he might not be able to date anyone because he'll be in love with you."

That pulled him up short. "Really?"

"Yeah, *duh*. So play next weekend, huh? Enjoy yourselves and see where the conversation takes you after. Take the opening and admit to him you're bi."

"But it's too soon. I don't want him to think I'm a douche."

"Oh, maybe you should wait then...until *after* he fucking marries some other dude and you're his best man. I've heard last-minute protests at weddings are always a fun time. Nut the fuck up, you dom-dom, and yes that was meant as a punny insult. I can only do so much to help true love along. Asshole."

She kissed him on the cheek before bouncing out of the chair to go catch up with someone else and talk to them.

Herding her little ducklings around.

He settled into his chair to watch Scrye's demo.

Ben

Sunday evening, Ben was glad Jake opted to drive. Being around Jake's parents always made him feel nervous and tongue-tied. Like they viewed him as gum on the bottom of their shoes or something.

Usually, when he had contact with them, it was while at Jake's residence and with other people around, but it'd been a couple of years since he'd last seen them, when he'd helped Jake move into the house.

"I appreciate you wanting to include me tonight," Ben said, "but I'd be okay going off on my own. There's an Olive Garden in that same complex. I can walk over there and eat by myself."

"Ha! Nice try. Like I said, consider it sadism on my part. I hate to suffer alone. Besides, you're my best friend. Who better to have there with me tonight?"

"They don't like me."

"They hated Allison."

"I thought they liked Allison?"

"I think they like Allison *now*, since she's gone, but all I ever heard from my mom and dad when Allison wasn't with me was how much they hated her."

"Oh."

"Yeah. I'm used to it. They're not easy-going like your parents are."

"You say that now. Wait until Mom starts trying to measure you for a tux to marry us off. She's not subtle."

Jake smiled. "Maybe I'll let her. Let you film it. Show my parents and induce heart failure."

"You don't mean that. You love your parents."

"Loving them and liking them can be mutually exclusive. Your dad didn't run you ragged every summer vacation and weekend in high school working at his damn print shops for minimum wage while telling you how lucky you were. All I wanted to do was be a freaking kid, but nope. And he was three times as hard on me as he was anyone else because I was his son. He burned me out on that place and him before my senior year of high school."

"Sorry."

"It's a good thing Mom was a teacher. If she'd had to work with him all these years, she probably would have divorced his ass by now."

"How'd she manage to get out of doing that?"

"She confessed this to me long after my sweat-shop days, but one weekend after they got married he took her there to try to teach her stuff and talk her into quitting teaching. She deliberately screwed up as many expensive things as possible, while making it look accidental, that Grandpa practically ordered Dad to get her out of the shop and never let her behind the counter again."

"No!"

"Yep. Dad still doesn't know that."

"Why'd she let you work there as a kid then?"

"She didn't realize how bad he was. She never really saw that side of him before. Not for long periods of time. And she was used to teaching rowdy sixth graders, so she pretty much kept him in line at home. She also thought because I was a guy that maybe he wouldn't try that nonsense with me."

They pulled into the parking lot. Ben hoped he didn't accidentally say or do anything to piss his friend off or embarrass him in front of his parents. He liked living with Jake, and was looking forward to whatever their D/s dynamic might evolve into.

He didn't want to ruin a good thing. In the week he'd been living with Jake, he'd felt more relaxed than he had in a couple of years. He didn't resent doing chores, because Jake pulled his weight. On the contrary, he *wanted* to do more than Jake let him.

Mainly because he wanted to show Jake how much he appreciated letting him move in.

Okay, maybe he was trying to give Jake a preview of how easy it'd be for the two of them to slip into a formal D/s dynamic at home. That he could be a good submissive…unlike Allison.

Ed and Joyce Murray acknowledged Ben's presence, but they directed all the conversation and their comments at Jake once the initial unpleasantries were over.

Ben sat there and kept his mouth shut, smiling and nodding and trying not to let his stomach knot into a ball.

They were waiting on the check, which Ed Murray had said he'd pick up, when Jake's mom finally fired a warning shot over Ben's bow.

"So how long do you plan on staying at Jake's before you get your own place?"

Ben had asked Jake not to get into the particulars about Mort and that whole nasty business with his parents. Ben wanted as few people as possible to know the details.

He felt embarrassed enough as it was.

Before Ben could answer, Jake spoke up. "I've already told him he's welcomed to live with me as long as he wants. We have a lease." Jake offered his mom a wide, beaming smile that Ben fully recognized as Dom-tude, but his mom wouldn't. "I'd rather have Ben living with me and helping out for the foreseeable future. Makes my life a lot easier."

Both elder Murrays frowned, but it was Jake's mom who finally broke the uncomfortable silence. "Doesn't that...limit your personal life, dear?"

"Not at all. Ben and I are completely comfortable around each other. Neither of us mind if the other brings someone home. Right?" He'd directed that at Ben.

Ben nodded, hoping his smile looked natural and not forced. "Right."

The four of them walked out together after the bill was paid. Parting ways at the restaurant's front door, Jake hugged his parents while Ben once again smiled. They shook his hand, but he got the distinct impression it was only to be polite.

Jake let out a sigh of relief once they were safely in his car. "Well. That went better than I hoped."

Ben nearly choked. "Better? *Seriously?*"

Jake started the car. "Yeah. Not once did they try to get preachy with me or ask when I was going to come to church with them." He started backing out.

"They do that?"

"Every couple of times I see them, yeah. I always tell them nope, but it doesn't stop them from asking. That's why I love your parents. I know they go to church, but they never try to get us to go to church with them."

"They're Unitarians," Ben said. "They're pretty liberal. They were Methodists before that, then we moved and it was too far to drive. They found the church they're at now and really liked it."

"Anyway, I respect your parents a lot more for that. Mine spend time talking about others behind their backs and not exactly embodying what they claim they believe. It wasn't church I couldn't stand so much as it was the way my parents soured me on it, you know? I get it, that not everyone is like them. But Dad is so hot to put on a good impression and stuff. That's not me, you know that. I could give a shit what people think about me. I'm just...me."

Yes, that was one of the things Ben loved about his friend. As long as he'd known him, Jake had never cared what people thought of him. He wasn't "out there," or showy, or bragging, but he just...was.

"Thank you for being you," Ben said. "Thanks for being there for me."

Jake sent him *that* smile.

The one that always hardened Ben's cock. "You're welcome, buddy. You're my best friend. Of course I'll be there for you."

***

Jake

On Tuesday afternoon, Tilly picked Jake up for lunch and handed her keys to him. "Onward, my trusty driver."

Ben was, fortunately, immersed in a project and stayed at his desk to work through lunch. They'd driven separately today because Ben knew he might stay late to work on it.

"Bring you back something, buddy?" Jake asked.

"I brought lunch today, thanks."

Jake loved his smile, his blue eyes—

Tilly smacked Jake's shoulder. "I said onward, driver."

"Lucky I love you." He held out his right arm for her to hook her left through and escorted her out to the parking lot. "And lucky for you I'm a Dom with manners."

"Better manners than your boy. He didn't hold his arm out for me."

"He didn't, huh?"

She grinned, pointing at him. "Ahhh! Ah-*HA!*"

"What?" He helped her into the passenger seat.

"I called him 'your boy' and you didn't argue with me!"

Jake closed the door on her gleeful cackling and walked around to slide behind the steering wheel. He hoped by the time he got his knees unwedged from under his chin after sliding the seat back that he'd not be red in the face anymore.

"We're not official, yet. Don't jinx it. We still need to have a negotiation session about Saturday night." He figured out how to start the car. "Where to, wench?"

"Not many people I'd let call me that, you know. You and Gilo and a couple of others."

"*Ooh,* I'm honored."

"You should be." She slipped on her sunglasses. "Columbia on St. Armands."

"That's where you took Ben."

"Yeah? So? I love their picadillo. Trying to stock up on it before I have to go back to LA in a couple of weeks."

He headed in that direction. "You want to give me the carrot or stick first? If I get a choice, I'll take the ass-chewing before the friendly advice and encouragement."

"*Hmm.* Usually, I'd say sadist's choice, but since *you're* a sadist, I'll let it go. So yeah, Allison was a bitch, and you were a dumb fuck for never telling your best friend you're bi."

"It never came up."

"That's what she said. But what *I'm* saying is that you're an *idiot.*"

Bantering with Tilly was like trying to watch a sitcom where every character had mainlined Red Bull and gorged themselves on chocolate-covered coffee beans after doing three lines of coke and a pound of meth.

Jake took a deep breath to mentally regroup. "What'd Allison do to piss off Loren, Leah, and Shayla?"

She snorted. "Let's start with Shayla. This happened at a private party at Tony and Shayla's last year. The sandspur asked Shayla if Tony ever played with anyone else, and Shayla, of course, told her no, just the rare demo situation. Then the sandspur balls-out asked if that was negotiable, or if Shayla was just being jealous and controlling, followed by a ha-ha, just kidding kind of laugh when Shayla apparently channeled Zuul for a moment and gave the sandspur a death glare. So also sayeth Loren, who was standing right there and witnessed the whole damn thing with her own eyes and ears."

They were stopped at a red light. Jake groaned and dropped his head to the steering wheel. "Ooohhh, no. Why didn't Tony ever say anything to me?"

"Tony doesn't *know.* Which is probably for the best, because if he had known, he likely would have hunted the sandspur down and thrown her out on her ass for disrespecting Shayla, and you for being there with her. You think *I'm* fucking scary? I'm a damn pussycat compared to him. It just takes a lot longer to wind him up to a different wavelength than me. I'm the loud and noisy one. He's quiet. You ever get *him* fucking wound up, then god help ya, because nobody else fucking can or will."

The car behind them honked. Jake lifted his head, saw the light had turned green, and hit the gas. "They never told Tony?"

"They never told *any* of the guys, not Ross, not Seth, not Tony. If they had, you wouldn't have even been allowed in the club again, much less a private party. The women pretty much make up the party lists for their own homes, subject, of course, to their men signing off on them. People drop off and are added to the lists all the time."

"Why didn't they come to *me* and tell me then?"

She didn't answer at first. When he glanced at her, she was staring at him like he'd just sprouted a foreskin on his forehead.

"What?" he asked.

"You really are a fricking stupid guy, you know that? *Duh*, none of them are going to talk to *you* about something like that. They talked to *me*. Hello? Terminator Tilly."

She sighed. "Unfortunately, shit got busy in my life." Her tone softened, the snark disappearing. "When you go through what we did, it kind of takes priority over some little twatwaffle showing her ass at a party. Then we had KC to take care of. I'm sorry, it slipped my mind to talk to you. I'm talking to you *now*. I was going to try to talk to you before now, but I hadn't run into you at the club without the sandspur there, or when I could actually talk to you."

"So something else happened between Allison and Loren?"

"Yeah, at a different party, at Ross and Loren's. Similar comment, similar deal, the ha-ha just kidding response when Loren stepped forward with a butcher's knife in her hand that she'd been using to cut cheese with."

"She cuts cheese with a butcher's knife? Isn't that overkill?"

"Dude, *focus*! And ditto Leah, except Leah and Seth teach classes. Allison asked Leah about classes, then asked her about private sessions, got snarky, and that's when Leah told her to go fuck herself."

"*Our* Leah said that?"

"Our Leah is a territorial piranha. Don't let her fool you."

"And that explains why my private party invitations went *poof*," he quietly said.

"Bingo." Tilly let the silence settle for a moment. "The good news is, now you're with Ben, and—"

"I'm not *with* him yet."

She waved it off. "You know what I mean. *Anyhoo*, Loren, Shayla, and Leah are tickled to death you and Ben are *potentially* an item."

"You didn't tell them that, did you?"

"Of *course* I didn't fricking tell them that. I didn't *have* to. They're women, *duh*. They *did* the *fucking* math, unlike you stupid men. I told them you're best friends for ten years, he just moved in, him sub, you Dom, him gay, you straight but veeerrrry laid back about it, and they started placing bets on the pool sheet. Leah's the outsider at four months or longer. I have twenty on three wee—"

"*Tilly!*"

She blinked, all wide-eyed innocence. "What!"

He gritted his teeth. "It's probably a damn good thing you and I didn't ever date because I would have been spanking you every time I fucking turned around!"

She grinned. "And that's a bad thing…why?"

He grunted in irritation.

"You're so fricking cute when you get wound up. *Anyway*. Like I was *saying*. You're back on the private party lists, now that the sandspur is out of the picture. We all think you and Ben are adorable together as a couple. Just don't wait too long to make your move or he might slide right out of your hands and into someone else's."

"How do I break that news to him without sounding like I'm a douche who planned everything this way? I mean, I was already going to break up with Allison. She just happened to push me too far the weekend he moved in, and it made it easier to face the confrontation."

"Who says you have to get all freaked out about it? How about after you guys scene you tell him you're bi, want to do more, and negotiate the fuck out of it? Simple."

"It's not that simple."

"It *is* that simple. The problem is, you men want to fuck everything up and complicate it."

———

THURSDAY NIGHT AFTER DINNER, the two men sat down to discuss the Saturday night play party. Jake wanted to nail this down now so Ben would have time to think it through before Saturday night and make any necessary adjustments.

"Let's talk hard limits," Jake said. "Do you have a list?"

Ben nodded. "Nobody but you touches me. No scat or watersports or anything like that."

He didn't continue.

"What else? There have to be more than that. Marks?"

"Nothing I can't hide at work. No needles or branding or cutting."

Jake realized he'd have to draw his friend out. Ben's years under Mort's thumb had obviously taken a toll on his negotiation skills. "Knife play for sensation?"

Jake loved the way Ben shivered in the good way. "I'm okay with that."

"Let's back up then and start with the basics. Impact play?"

That smile of Ben's was going to harden Jake's cock. "Yes, please."

"Implements?"

"Everything in your bag."

"Everything?"

He loved the way Ben's throat worked as he nervously swallowed. "Everything."

Jake had already taken a peek. Ben hadn't removed any of the implements from Jake's bag. They were all neatly stowed in there.

"Play naked?"

"I would prefer that, if you're okay with it."

"I'm okay with that. So let's talk touching."

Ben's blue gaze nailed him, unwavering. "You can touch me anywhere."

"Anywhere?"

Ben nodded. "Anywhere you're comfortable touching me. I have no limits about where you touch me."

Jake's cock felt like a hard piece of iron straining against his jeans. "Restraints?"

"Yes, please. And a blindfold and gag."

What Jake hadn't told Ben was that he'd ordered a set of cuffs and a matching collar especially for him. Even if they didn't play, he was still going to give them to Ben as a present, so he'd at least have a set that had no connection to Mort whatsoever. They'd arrived on Tuesday and were waiting when Jake got home.

Since Ben had driven separately, Jake had been able to hide them in his room before Ben arrived home as a surprise for Saturday.

They spent over an hour talking, side-tracking, and going over more than Jake thought they would. And in the end, Jake felt confident that Ben was good with what they'd set up for Saturday night.

Now if it would just hurry up and *get* there.

Because he was *really* looking forward to it.

Chapter Thirteen

Nervous excitement coursed through Ben Saturday afternoon as he anticipated the party that night. Part of him kept his emotions firmly grounded with the likely possibility that Jake might not even be able to go through with scening with him. That was still a possibility.

Ben refused to act pissy about it, either, if that turned out to be the case.

Even if Jake couldn't do it, he knew there'd be a couple of other Tops in attendance he trusted who might be willing to step in and give him the beating he so desperately needed.

Like Tilly.

It didn't hurt that Jake wasn't objecting to the things Ben had been doing for him around the house, either. Maybe they didn't have an official D/s relationship, but it was nice to be helpful, and to have that helpfulness appreciated.

Allison can suck it.

Actually, from some of the things Jake had implied, Ben

suspected Allison hadn't been sucking anything there toward the end of their relationship. At least, nothing attached to Jake's body. That had likely been part of their final round of conflict culminating in the massive blow-up.

He still felt a little guilty about the knowledge he held regarding Allison's online activities, but why take a whack at that hornet's nest when she hadn't tried to contact Jake since their blowup two weeks earlier?

Jake had spent most of the morning outside working in the backyard mowing and doing other chores out there, while Ben had spent his time cleaning the inside of the house top to bottom with Jake out of his way.

Including washing and folding Jake's laundry and leaving it neatly stacked on Jake's bed.

Ben had been in the shower when Jake returned to the house. When Ben emerged from his bathroom and headed out to the kitchen with a towel draped around his hips, Jake called out to him as he walked past Jake's open bedroom door.

Ben stopped and turned. "Yeah?"

"Thanks for doing my laundry. You didn't have to do that."

Ben shrugged, forcing himself not to grin. "No problem. I like being helpful."

Jake walked over. "You know, I meant it when I said don't be in a hurry to move out. I don't have a problem with you living here. You couldn't find an apartment as good as this place for the same money, and you know it."

Ben choked back the hope wanting to make him break into a happy dance. Praying he looked and sounded nonchalant, he said, "Well, I don't want to overstay my welcome."

"You're *not*. If you were, I'd tell you." Jake stuck out his hand. "I'd appreciate you staying, if *you* don't mind. I don't want to take advantage of you, but you've made my life a hella lot easier by being here. In more ways than one."

Ben smiled and shook with him. "Thanks. I appreciate that. I enjoy living here with you."

"See? Even more proof this is right for both of us. Two happy bachelors."

Ben hoped his smile didn't slip. "Yeah. Two happy, single guys."

Jake

"Oh, just leave the implement bag inside the door to the spare room," Jake said. "I'll grab it when we leave." He wanted to sneak the set of cuffs and collar into it without Ben seeing. "If it's by the front door, we'll be tripping over it."

"Sure thing. I'm going to start the casserole."

"Thanks." Jake watched as Ben continued his walk down the hall toward the kitchen. He hoped he wouldn't let his friend down tonight.

He really wanted to scene with Ben. Jake knew his friend needed a good, hard scene. It was the least he could do for the guy after how he'd been busting his ass around the house. Right?

Right.

He couldn't have asked for a better roommate than Ben. Even Allison hadn't been as agreeable, much less as proactive, at helping out despite spending a lot of her time there with him.

She'd damn sure never been as proactive doing chores despite what she'd agreed to. Just getting her to load the dishwasher practically took an act of Congress. Although when it came time to spend money, she'd been right at the front of the line with her hand out, happy to let him do that for her and reluctant to chip in her fair share.

Jake hadn't played with anyone except Allison since they'd started dating. Hell, he hadn't topped Allison in several months before breaking up with her. She hadn't felt up to playing, and he wouldn't force her. He wasn't *that* guy.

He refused to be *that* guy. But it didn't mean he didn't have the desire to play.

It'd been more proof to him that the two of them weren't meant to be together. And look what it potentially led to.

I need to do this.

Being honest with himself, he wanted to do it, to top Ben. Ben could take a lot heavier impact play than Allison could. Ben also *wanted* a heavy scene. Jake sure as hell was in the mood to give someone a good beating.

So he'd never topped Ben before. He'd topped guys before he'd dated Allison. It wouldn't be weird, right? That they were friends and roommates and not romantically involved?

Yet.

Not like any of their friends would care. It was a private party, so not like he gave a shit what anyone thought, or that they would care what happened between them as long as Jake didn't violate Ben's safeword.

Truth be told, scening with Ben at a private party would be a lot safer than at the club. No chance of Allison showing up, interrupting them, and causing trouble.

Jake closed his bedroom door and headed for the shower. In the back of his mind, he couldn't help but think about their earlier conversation regarding Ben's ideal scene.

He also knew he'd need to work up the courage to admit to his friend that he was bi and hope the guy didn't get weirded out or feel betrayed.

After they played. Playing would allow a natural progression to another level of conversations between them when they talked on Sunday about whatever happened tonight.

Then Jake could ease his way into telling Ben the truth about himself and hope he didn't get shot down in the process.

Ben

Ben made sure he was ready to go early, while at the same time not saying anything to Jake about the time. Jake hadn't told him to keep track of that. If he was going to bottom to the man—and hopefully open the door to doing more of that in the future—he needed to act the part of the good submissive. Not top from the bottom.

He trusted Jake with his ass. Hell, he trusted the man with his *life*.

He damn sure needed to trust him with something as basic as time management.

Unless, of course, Jake put that responsibility on him.

He'd packed a couple of towels, a leather jock, a swimsuit, spare clothes, his ball gag and blindfold, and his own leather wrist and ankle cuffs in a backpack to take with them. He wasn't sure what Jake might have planned, but he wanted to be prepared.

He'd long since thrown away the leather collar he'd had, a cheap one that Mort had given him. The wrist and ankle cuffs he'd purchased himself before Mort.

With the casserole he'd made for their contribution to the potluck wrapped up and ready to transport, Ben headed to the living room. There, he turned on the TV and aimlessly channel-surfed.

When Jake left his room, Ben heard him head straight for the spare bedroom, where Ben had left the implement bag by the door as ordered.

Jake left the door open and Ben resisted the urge to get up and go help him.

If he needs me, he'll call for me.

When Jake emerged from the hallway a few minutes later, he

carried the implement bag and left it sitting in the entryway by the front door.

That's a good sign. Ben sat up a little straighter, watching.

Waiting.

He'd be a good boy, even if that wasn't exactly the stipulated dynamic between them for tonight. He'd show Jake how good he could be for him as a submissive. That it didn't have to be a gay or straight thing.

That it could be a full-time thing between them, even without sharing a bed.

Jake walked over and sat in the chair at the end of the coffee table. "I want to talk one more time before we leave. About tonight."

Ben nodded and kept his mouth shut.

"Any changes to your hard limits?"

"No, Sir. We've covered them. No marks that'll show at work. Nothing harmful. No blood drawn on purpose. No scat, no watersports. Don't share me with someone without asking me first if it's okay if they top me. No one else touches me except in emergencies."

"Red, yellow, green for safewords."

"Yes, Sir." Ben glanced at Jake's brown eyes when he realized what he'd been saying. "Sorry. I know we haven't discussed that. It just kind of came out."

"It's okay. I'd feel a little…weird if you called me that at work or something. In this context, I'm fine with it." And he gave Ben *that* smile, the one that threatened to harden Ben's cock every time he saw it.

Why can't he be bi?

Jake

Hell, Allison hadn't called him Sir most of the time, even when playing.

When she did, it was frequently tinged with more than a little sarcasm. Usually enough sarcasm to kill what enthusiasm he'd managed to muster to play with her.

The word seemed to fall naturally from Ben's mouth and sounded right to Jake's ear.

"Do you have a blindfold and ball gag, or do you want me to use mine?"

"I have those, Sir."

"I bought a little surprise for you that I'll show you when we get there."

"A surprise?"

He couldn't hold back his smile. "Yep. You'll find out when we get there. So here are our protocols for tonight. I *really* like you calling me Sir, so keep doing that. I'm going to refer to you as my boy. Okay?"

Ben nodded. "Yes, Sir." It broke Jake's heart just how eager Ben looked.

I need to tell him.

"I'll decide when we play, but if you feel you can't, you call red. Understand?"

"Yes, Sir."

"So do not pester me to play. I'll decide the how and where and when, as long as you haven't safeworded. When we finish, we'll find a spot for your aftercare."

More eager nodding.

"When I ask you for a color, regardless of when or what we're doing, I expect a green, yellow, or red from you immediately, even if we aren't playing. If you don't respond, everything stops as if you safeworded."

"Yes, Sir."

"Our protocols for tonight will be you ask for permission to leave my side or to go get something to eat or drink. You'll serve me first, when I request it. You may speak to others without permission, and you may hug friends or shake hands, unless it's someone you don't know or don't want to. If it's someone you don't want to, you look at me and give me a quick shake of your head, and I'll tell them no for you. Got it?"

Ben's whole body seemed to relax. "Yes, Sir."

Jake's cock ached, throbbing, and he needed a moment to breathe through it. Hell, by now, Allison would have been protesting the rules.

Ben thrived on them.

"From the moment we're done with this talk, even before we leave, I expect you to be in protocols unless you safeword. And let me repeat—you can *always* safeword, at *any* time, for *anything*. Understood?"

"Yes, Sir."

"Any time I snap my fingers and point at the floor, I expect you to kneel in front of me immediately."

"Yes, Sir."

"Any questions, comments, concerns, or adjustments you wish to make?"

"No, Sir."

"What's in the backpack?"

Ben told him, and Jake barely held back his grin. He wanted the cuffs and collar to be a surprise for him. Jake stared into Ben's eyes for a moment and then softly snapped his fingers before pointing at the floor in front of the chair he occupied.

Without hesitation, Ben rose from the couch and practically levitated into position in front of him, waiting.

Jake smiled down at him and stroked his head. "*Such* a good boy," he softly said. "That's *exactly* what I wanted to see."

He thought a soft moan escaped Ben.

Ben

Ben struggled not to sink deep into subspace. This was so unlike anything he'd experienced before. Mort always had trouble dropping him into subspace, and that was usually only after he'd started scening with Ben.

And it never felt like *this*.

That Jake could already have him spinning down that rabbit hole just from *talking*?

Holy shit.

Jake crooked his finger at Ben, indicating for him to rest his head against Jake's leg. He did, his eyes falling closed at the feel of Jake's fingers tenderly stroking his hair. "Who's going to be my good boy tonight?"

"Me, Sir."

"Who's going to do everything I tell him to?"

"Me, Sir."

Ben gasped when Jake's voice whispered in his ear, his cock now throbbing, aching from the Dom's tone. "Whose ass is going to bear *my* marks by the time we return home tonight?"

"Your boy's ass, Sir."

Jake chuckled, his hand pausing on Ben's head. "That's right. I'm going to take my time and warm you up nice and slow so you can take the hard strokes I know you need." Another stroke of Jake's hand in his hair.

It was all Ben could do not to wrap his arms around Jake's legs and nuzzle his face against his jeans. "Thank you, Sir." He couldn't believe how perfect this felt, and hell, Jake wasn't even gay!

I couldn't ask for a better friend than him.

"Tomorrow, we're going to have a long talk about what happens tonight. That's when we can get into the other discussions we've talked about. I want you to have a taste of what I'm like in full-on Dom mode before going there, though. All right?"

"Yes, Sir."

"Good boy." He patted Ben on the head. "Let's get going. I don't want to waste a moment of tonight."

Chapter Fourteen

Jake

They took Jake's car and he drove. If Ben wasn't already well on the way to subspace, Jake needed to turn in his Dom card, because Ben sure acted like he was.

When they arrived at Tilly's house and made it through the secure gate to the parking area, there were already four other cars parked out front. Jake had Ben grab his backpack and the casserole while Jake took charge of the implement bag. Jake had never been to Tilly's new house, the triad and their baby daughter moving in just a few months prior.

Ben shadowed Jake as they made their way up to the door and Jake rang the bell.

Tilly opened the door a moment later, broadly smiling when she saw them there. "Excellent!" She hugged him, then paused, obviously waiting for Jake to okay her hugging Ben.

"He's free to hug any friends he wants to tonight," Jake said.

She carefully did before taking the casserole dish from him.

"Follow me and I'll show you where you can dump your stuff and then show you around."

"Where's the little one tonight?" Jake asked.

"Leigh's got her over at their place." Tilly tipped her head to the left. "A few properties over that way." They ended up in the large eat-in kitchen, where food was already spread out over one counter. She left the dish there, then proceeded with the tour.

The large house had five bedrooms and five and a half baths, a large dining room, a huge living room area, a separate family room, and a home office, in addition to a separate pool house apartment on the back side of the lanai. The pool was even larger than the one at Jake's house, and they had a hot tub as well.

Jake didn't miss how strategically placed plants on the outside of the pool cage helped hide activities from view, as did a couple of temporary folding screens that had been placed inside the two doors leading outside from the ends of the lanai. Looking up, Jake realized he couldn't see stars.

"What's up there?"

Tilly looked. "Oh, a folding frame holding camouflage netting to prevent any drones from getting a peek. We pull it back during the day when we don't need it. Ingenious. Leigh's house has one, too."

The living and family rooms had been turned into play rooms for the night, and a couple of benches were already set up. More equipment was located in the pool house, and a portable suspension frame, complete with MMA mats under it, had been assembled on the lanai. There was also a large frame in the dining room. One of the bedrooms, which held a fold-out Murphy bed that was currently stowed, had been turned into a playroom. One of the bedrooms at the far end of the hall had a chair placed directly in front of the door and blocking entry, as did another bedroom.

"That's our room down there, and KC's room. For obvious reasons, those are off-limits tonight."

"You could have your own club night here," Jake noted.

"I know, right? You can stash your stuff here, if you want." She pointed to a corner in the home office.

Thus unburdened, they followed Tilly back to the main area, where Landry and Cris greeted them. They already knew Ross and Loren, of course, and Scrye and June. After exchanging greetings and hugs with them, Tilly introduced them to the other people they hadn't formally met before, two triads, Susan, Grant, and Darryl, and Rebecca, Toby, and Logan.

Rebecca's name, however, clicked with Jake. "Oh! You make the chainmaille jewelry."

She smiled. "Guilty."

Jake would stow that away for future reference. He'd already found his imagination straying far ahead of reality to what kind of day collar he'd like to buy for Ben, still vacillating between a necklace or a bracelet.

Something custom-made for him would be even better.

More people arrived, and as Jake had Ben fetch him a drink, or appetizers, Jake couldn't help but mentally make the obvious comparisons between Ben and Allison.

In the beginning, of course, she'd been eager to do things. As life wore on and she realized he wanted that from her all the time, basic, simple protocols like getting him a drink when he asked, or waiting to eat when they were together, she stopped doing it. Still, even in the eager days, she wasn't a plug-and-play submissive. Everything had to be told to her, coaxed from her.

Ben anticipated, almost to a spooky level. When Jake's cup of soda ran low, Ben would touch the hand Jake held it in, silently point to it, and then take it when given to get a refill.

Without asking.

Jake even had to remember to tell Ben he could get his own drink and food, because Ben patiently waited. The only time he asked for something for himself was when he needed to use the bathroom about an hour after they arrived.

That's when Jake retrieved the collar from his implement bag.

When Ben emerged from the bathroom, Jake stood there, waiting, and pointed at the floor.

He thought Ben might be close to happy tears when Jake buckled the collar around the man's neck.

He leaned in to whisper in Ben's ear. "I have a surprise for my boy," he said. "I ordered you a play collar and set of cuffs to be yours, brand new, never worn. That's your reward for being such a good boy for me the past couple of weeks."

"Thank you, Sir!"

He ruffled Ben's hair. "Good boys always get rewards. Let's get back to the party."

At one point Jake stood talking with Tony and Shayla and had, without even thinking about it, snapped and pointed at the floor. Ben smoothly dropped to his knees, his head resting against Jake's leg where Jake could play with his hair.

And it felt like the most natural thing in the world. By now, if they were going to play, Allison would have been bugging the crap out of him to do it and get it over with.

I need to stop thinking about her, dammit.

Still, everything pointed to Jake having made the right decision to break up with her.

Now all he had to do was nut up and confess his feelings to Ben.

Ben

Ben struggled not to burst into happy tears when Jake buckled the collar around his neck. Jake had bought him a collar and cuffs?

That had to be good, right?

Jake had a set of cuffs and a couple of different play collars in his bag. Ben had seen them there while arranging it.

This collar, however, hadn't been in there, and neither had any new cuffs.

Less than two hours after their arrival the party was in full swing. It was great to catch up with friends he either hadn't seen in a while, or hadn't been able to converse with while with Mort because of the guy's jealous, controlling ways. Unlike Mort, Jake let Ben talk with friends, as long as Ben stayed wherever Jake had put him, either on the floor or by his side.

He preferred the floor, because then Jake stroked his hair.

He felt cherished.

A good boy.

I'm a desperate fuck, all right.

Even more reason to agree with Tilly about taking his life slowly, and ceding control of some things to Jake, if Jake wanted to do that for him.

Jake wouldn't let him get fucked over.

He could trust Jake.

It seemed that Jake had a certain bench in mind that he wanted to play on, because he kept looking that way. Currently, a couple was using it, a man and a woman Ben wasn't familiar with. He had her tied down to it and was going after her with a cane and a Hitachi, forced orgasm torture mixed with pain that made Ben's cock twitch in envy.

At the private parties, house rules ruled. The invite for this party stated that, like Venture, the house safeword was red. Other than a few hard limits that were already hard limits for Jake and Ben both, full-on sex and sexy play were allowed.

In fact, one guy was sitting in a chair on the far side of the living room and was currently getting a blowjob from his submissive. She was bound, naked except for a rope harness that trapped her hands behind her, and he was torturing her nipples by tugging on her piercings while she serviced him.

Ben's cock throbbed. It was too damn easy to envision himself at Jake's feet, bound much in that same way, the man torturing his nipples while Ben blew him. He didn't have piercings, but if Jake ever told him to get them, he would. In a heartbeat.

Finally, the couple on the bench were wrapping up. Jake turned to him. "Get your backpack. Go use the bathroom and strip. Meet me out here, naked, except for your collar."

The good kind of fear raced through him. "Yes, Sir!" He almost tripped he turned so fast, and he knew he didn't imagine Jake's amused chuckle.

Five minutes later, he made his way out to the bench, keeping his backpack in front of him to hide his raging erection.

But he had his orders, and he wouldn't safeword for that.

***

Jake

God, he's adorable.

Jake waited until Ben was in the bathroom to go get his implement bag. Once the couple using the bench cleared out, Jake started laying out his implements, starting with the wrist and ankle cuffs, putting them on the bench where Ben would be sure to see them immediately upon his return.

Ben reappeared, the backpack held in front of him, hiding his cock from Jake.

Ben had emphasized during their negotiations that nothing was off-limits in terms of Jake touching him. Even if he wanted to do some mild CBT on him.

Jake wasn't sure how far he wanted to push boundaries tonight with Ben, but if that door already lay open, he'd definitely think about walking through it.

"Get one of your towels, and the blindfold and gag," Jake told him.

Ben did, turning and setting the backpack down to do it and giving Jake a prime view of the man's ass.

Holy…fuck.

It was sooo tempting to imagine grabbing Ben's hips and grinding the front of his jeans, where his erection strained against his zipper, against the man's gorgeous ass.

He shook himself out of that daydream when Ben turned with the items in hand. Jake took them from him, glancing down at Ben's cock as he did.

Yep, hard.

Nice.

He picked up the wrist cuffs from the bench. "Hands."

Ben's gaze focused on Jake's as Jake buckled the cuffs around Ben's wrists. Then Jake spread the towel over the bench and patted it. "Up."

Ben climbed into position, the kneeler comfortable enough to use for a while, and Jake buckled the ankle cuffs on him. Then he retrieved snap clips from his bag and hooked Ben to the bench.

"Good?" Jake asked.

"Yes, Sir."

Jake held the ball gag and blindfold in his hand as he knelt in front of the kneeler, eye-to-eye with Ben. "Color, boy."

"Green, Sir."

"Submit or safeword, boy?"

"I submit, Sir."

Jake held Ben's chin. "Any last-minute changes to our limits?"

Ben shook his head. "No, Sir."

Jake leaned in and kissed his forehead. "Good boy." He loved the way Ben's eyes widened in surprise, but he popped the ball gag in and buckled it around his head, followed by the blindfold.

"Color?" he whispered in Ben's ear.

"Green, Sir," Ben mumbled around the gag.

"You're going to get me so hot and bothered with that gagspeak I'll be rubbing one out later when we get home, you know that?"

It had the desired effect. From the way Ben's shoulders shook, Jake knew he was laughing. "Sorry, Sir," he mumbled.

Jake patted him on the head and then took a deep breath as he stared at the man's bare back and ass before him.

Fuck. Me.

This was like a dream come true. He wasn't even sure where to start.

Chapter Fifteen

Ben

Nervous tension raced through Ben's body. The kiss on his forehead, innocent and yet electric, searing Ben's nerves and making his already aching cock throb even more.

Obviously, Jake wasn't weirded out by that, so he'd stop worrying about it.

Should make future pool time more interesting.

Hell, he'd walk around naked unless Jake stopped him from doing it. The guy might be straight, but if he didn't mind Ben being naked, Ben could fantasize Jake was watching him.

Hey, a fantasy like that might keep him from jumping too quickly into something stupid with another asshole.

Stop thinking about Mort.

His Sir deserved all of his attention, here and now.

And the thought of Jake wanting to rub one out when they returned home was another nice visual.

Maybe I can talk him into letting me help him.

That could be part of their discussion on the way home tonight.

He sensed Jake's presence next to him, the heat from his body even though they weren't touching. Being restrained like this, even though he knew he could easily free himself, felt intoxicating.

Then…

Oh, then firm, stroking, warm hands starting at his shoulders and slowly, torturously slow working their way down either side of his spine, fingers digging into muscle, as much a massage as an opening stroke of what promised to be the hottest scene of Ben's life. It didn't take him long to realize what the other man was doing, either, as his hands roamed Ben's back, across his shoulders and down his arms, over his ass and down the outsides of his thighs.

Jake was exploring, locating muscles, bones, tendons. Planning his attack, taking measure of Ben's body.

Behind his blindfold, Ben closed his eyes, his head on the padded kneeler, trying not to hyperventilate or let his cock explode under him. He was afraid the slightest bit of friction might make him go off at that point.

Jake's thumbs dug into the muscles at either side of the top of Ben's spine, at the base of his neck, and pressed down hard as he dragged them down Ben's spine all the way to his tailbone.

A moan escaped him, the pleasure-pain a tantalizing precursor to what Ben knew was coming.

After several more passes like that, Jake started in with bare-handed spanking, along Ben's ass and thighs, up and down. Light strokes at first that didn't even sting as much as they warmed his flesh, building in strength until Ben balled his fists and bit down on the ballgag to endure.

When they suddenly stopped, Ben gasped, inhaling.

Jake's voice in his right ear startled him. "Color, boy."

"Green, Sir."

"Submit or safeword?"

"I submit, Sir."

"Good boy."

Next came floggers, a couple of different ones. Jake warmed up his back, shoulders, ass, thighs. At one point in a pause in the flogging, Jake's hand cupped Ben's sac from behind, squeezing, almost but not quite to the point of pain before he released him.

Before that, Ben had spiraled farther down into subspace than he'd ever gone before. Not so far he couldn't have immediately safeworded.

He didn't *want* to.

This time, it was his left ear Jake spoke into. "Color, boy."

"Green, Sir."

"Submit or safeword?"

"I submit, Sir."

Time disappeared. The noises of the party disappeared. Everything disappeared except the bench under him and the feel of Jake's hands and implements. True to his word, Jake took his time warming Ben up before doling out the first stingy impact from what Ben imagined was the lightweight acrylic paddle in Jake's bag.

He'd spent hours sitting on the floor of the spare bedroom, lovingly running his hands over every implement, eyes closed, memorizing their feel, their texture, even taking test swats against his own thighs or upper arms to see how they'd feel.

Nothing and everything in Jake's bag terrified him. In Mort's hands, he wouldn't have trusted a fur flogger at this point.

Jake could have had a bag full of Dexter kill tools and stupidly or not, Ben would have trusted him not to harm him or violate their agreed-upon limits. Especially since he felt Jake frequently checking his hands, his feet, feeling for temperature, sometimes having him squeeze his hand during a check.

During one pause, Jake set something dense but small, warm but metallic on Ben's ass.

He froze, not wanting it to fall, even though he'd been given no such order to hold still.

It felt like Jake was kneeling in front of him. "Knife play, boy. Submit, or safeword?"

"I submit, Sir."

Then the press of Jake's lips against his forehead again. Ben moaned against the ballgag, wishing Jake would kiss him on the mouth.

"Color, boy."

"Green, Sir."

"Hold very, very still."

Jake disappeared for a moment, Ben tracking his movements by the feel of the air around him, anticipating when Jake picked up the knife again. Even though Ben knew in his logical brain that knife play was more about the mindfuck than it was about actual danger, he froze as he felt the point start to lightly trace patterns along his back.

The hand returned to his scrotum, holding, slowly squeezing and making Ben moan with need, exquisite agony, and he fought the urge to hump Jake's hand. Jake slowly released the pressure on Ben's balls as he traced the knife up and down Ben's spine, once again starting to squeeze and pulling more moans from him.

"Submit or safeword?" Jake's voice had dropped, dark, commanding.

"I submit, Sir. Green."

"Good boy."

The pattern continued for a few minutes or infinity, Ben wasn't even sure, until both the knife and hand disappeared.

He moaned in disappointment for the loss of both, but especially Jake's hand on his balls. He hadn't quite reached the bad pain level with CBT yet, but had come close.

Next followed more implements—paddles, slappers, crops, canes, and others. Jake built up and stepped down, each crescendo a little higher and more painful than the previous, to the point Ben never wanted him to stop. It appeared Jake was trying to work up to, but not cross, the line of making him call yellow. Ben felt the way Jake paused between impacts every time he stepped it up, giving Ben time to process and even lovingly stroking his hands over the marks he left on Ben's flesh.

His hands.

His Sir's hands.

Owning him, checking him, stroking him, implements of soothing and torture and Ben couldn't even remember hearing Jake speak to anyone but him during the whole time.

The final explosion was a heavy cane Ben suspected was the dense black one of some sort of synthetic material, Delrin or fiberglass, Ben wasn't sure and didn't care. Hard single strokes, pauses between each impact, methodically working up and down Ben's ass and thighs, every stroke harder than the previous one.

His ass felt like it was on fire, and he knew sitting down for the next few days would leave him with a raging erection from the pain he'd feel each time he did.

The *good* kind of pain.

Tears rolled down his cheeks as he clenched his teeth around the ballgag and held on for dear life. He didn't want Jake to stop or pull back. Jake had brought him beautifully close to the precipice and Ben knew he wouldn't let him fall over.

Would always catch him if he did.

Just when Ben wasn't sure he could take any more, Jake stopped, laid the cane across Ben's back, and stroked the welts in his flesh. Now Jake's hands felt soothingly cool compared to his own burning flesh. He gasped around the ballgag, sucking in breaths and trying to process the pain.

Then Jake unclipped his ankles. Ben didn't move at first, even though he heard Jake putting away the implements, including taking the one he'd left on his back.

Jake unclipped Ben's wrists and removed the ballgag, then the blindfold. Ben didn't want to open his eyes at first and worked his mouth, jaw, feeling it pop from having bit down so hard during the scene.

It was the touch of Jake's hand against his cheek, palming him, that finally made Ben open his eyes. The man knelt there, inches away, his brown gaze dark and intently focused on him.

"Color, boy."

Ben wanted to heave himself forward and kiss him, tackle him, make love to him.

"Green, Sir," he whispered.

Jake smiled, and it was then Ben knew he was completely and utterly fucked.

He was already in love with this guy.

"My *very* good boy. You made me so proud."

"Thank you, Sir."

Jake put everything away before helping Ben sit up.

That's when he nearly burst into tears, because Jake hugged him, holding him as Ben sat there and got his bearings.

"Ready to go snuggle?"

"Yes, Sir," Ben mumbled against Jake's stomach. He inhaled, the familiar scent of laundry detergent and fabric softener, under-laid by *Jake*.

Jake helped him stand and handed him the towel. "Wait." Jake pulled a leash from his implement bag and left it on top after zipping the bag.

Ben stood there, waiting, ass throbbing and raw and endor-phins coursing through his veins.

He'd stand there all night waiting.

Until his Sir told him otherwise.

Chapter Sixteen

Jake

After wiping down the bench, Jake snapped the leash to Ben's collar, grabbed his bag and Ben's backpack, and led him away from the bench. The couches were full, but there was a quiet corner along one of the walls where they could sit on the floor and chill out for Ben's aftercare.

He led Ben there. Setting their bags down, he unzipped his toybag and grabbed the fleece throw from it. After settling in the corner, able to lean against the wall, he spread his legs and patted the floor in front of him for Ben to crouch before Jake draped the throw over Ben's back, completely covering him.

Ben settled between Jake's legs, his head resting against Jake's left thigh.

Jake reached under the throw and stroked Ben's hair. "Good boy," he softly said, glancing around and realizing no one was paying the slightest bit of attention to them. "Such a good boy."

Jake's cock ached, and he realized he'd conditioned himself over the years. Whenever he'd scene with Allison in private, it nearly always finished at some point with him making her come before busting his own nut.

Even before Allison, when he was in a relationship with someone, that's what he did. Or he'd go home and rub one out after he played.

However, tonight he'd be going home with Ben, although they didn't share a bed.

Ben wasn't just sitting there with his face touching Jake's thigh, he was nuzzling him. So Jake reached under the throw with his other hand and stroked Ben's cheek.

Jake's cock painfully hardened like steel when Ben's warm mouth closed around his fingers and started sucking.

Holy. Shit.

No, they hadn't talked about this. Not at all. Still, he couldn't bring himself to pull his fingers from Ben's mouth. It wasn't like he'd *made* him suck his fingers, right?

Right.

And they were only fingers.

Except right now, Jake's fingers felt like they were connected directly to his cock, and every sweep of Ben's tongue up and down them might as well be along his shaft and not his hand.

Jake leaned his head back against the wall, the hand on Ben's head stroking, slowing, fisting a handful of hair and holding on. Ben's responding moan vibrated not just through Jake's fingers in the man's mouth, but through Jake's thigh, too, where Ben's cheek was still pressed.

Ben inched farther up between Jake's thighs without Jake tugging to urge him in that direction. Closer, closer still, until his nose brushed against the front of Jake's jeans, along the zipper where his cock painfully pressed against it through his briefs.

This was getting…

Jake wasn't sure what it was getting. Getting him harder than he ever remembered being in his life, for sure.

Especially once Ben's nose brushed along the length of Jake's cock through his jeans. Nuzzling, sucking Jake's fingers harder as Ben gained confidence when he realized Jake wasn't stopping him.

Wait, why am I not stopping him?

Because in all honesty, Jake didn't *want* to stop him.

It felt like the rest of the party disappeared around them, the world shrinking, drawing in, until it was just the two of them in their private-ish corner, and all Jake felt was Ben there with him.

Ben grew bolder, nuzzling harder, making it obvious what he wanted to do, rubbing his nose up and down Jake's bulge, zeroing in on the head before traveling down his shaft again.

Jake wasn't inclined to interrupt him.

Ben's fingers had curled around Jake's hand, the one he was currently sucking. When Jake slipped his fingers out of Ben's mouth and reached for his zipper, at first Ben resisted a little, trying to keep Jake's fingers in his mouth, until he sussed what was going on.

Then, Ben released Jake's hand and took over, pushing Jake's fingers out of the way and sliding his fingers along Jake's zipper, finding the tab, slowly easing it down, even as his mouth sought and recaptured Jake's fingers.

All this taking place under the throw, out of view. Not that anyone would honestly care with, among other sexy activities currently going on, Scrye fucking June's brains out on the lanai, where he had her strung up on a portable suspension frame. Or with Sean and Cali tag-teaming Max in the family room, said man securely fastened to one of their new prototype bondage frames and spread wide open while being speared at one end by Sean's cock, and at the other by Cali and her strap-on.

Ben's fingers walked up the outline of Jake's cock and located his belt, working the buckle loose and free, opening it, then the button on his fly.

The fingers Jake had buried in Ben's hair tightened as Ben slowly brushed his fingers over the outline of Jake's cock through his briefs. Meeting no resistance, Ben started nuzzling Jake's cock through his briefs with his nose, even as he still sucked Jake's fingers.

It was all Jake could do not to start humping the other man's face. Ben's slow explorations were no longer tentative. They were sure, sadistically so, as if the other man savored this moment.

Hell, Allison hated going down on him and only did it if he worked her up first. Here was Ben, eager to oblige.

Fuck it.

No, they hadn't specifically talked about this, or negotiated it. Jake was beyond caring, though. He slowly pulled his fingers from Ben's mouth and they joined his other hand on Ben's head. Careful not to pull, not to force, he just rested them there.

"That's my good boy," Jake softly said, letting Ben make the next move. "If you want to, go for it. It's up to you. Your decision."

Jake knew this was taking things farther than they ever had before. If they did this, it meant he needed to admit to Ben he was bi, that this wasn't just a random fluke, and that he was attracted to Ben as way more than just a friend.

Jake wasn't prepared for how fast the other man could move. Still hidden by the blanket, Ben worked Jake's briefs down and exposed his cock, burying it in his mouth before Jake could even blink. Jake glanced down but all he could see was the outline of the other man under the blanket, his head now slowly bobbing up and down as he proceeded to give Jake the best blow job he'd ever had.

No. Shit.

Closing his eyes again, he rested his head against the wall and stroked Ben's hair. Hot, wet heat engulfed his cock as Ben's tongue slipped around his head and flicked along the slit before going deep again.

At this rate, he'd be blowing quickly. Ben must have sensed it, because he circled his fingers around the base of Jake's cock, pressing against the underside and helping Jake hold back his climax as Ben slowed his strokes.

Yeah…

Of course, he hadn't considered this as a likely possibility for tonight when he'd suggested topping Ben. They were friends and roomies. Jake had hoped tonight would open the doors to them talking about exploring options at some future point.

Not…this.

But there was no denying the man was good at giving a blow job.

Damn good.

Even with Ben slowing down and trying to prolong it, Jake felt his impending release draw close. "I'm gonna blow," he hoarsely said.

Instead of pulling back and off, like Jake had honestly expected Ben to do, Ben deep-throated him, his tongue brushing against the top of Jake's sac as it drew up tight and shot his load down his best friend's throat.

And there Ben froze, waiting, holding Jake's softening cock in his mouth and making no move to release it. All the while, Jake was trying to catch his breath and recover from what was the most earth-shattering orgasm he'd had in…

In…

Holy shit.

That hadn't just been the best blow job he'd *ever* had.

That had been the best *orgasm* he'd ever had.

He finally, gently tapped Ben on the top of his head. "Okay, buddy," he said. "Put your toy away."

Ben carefully, lovingly tucked Jake's cock back into his briefs after one final, tender lick and kiss on the head. Then he eased up the zipper, fastened the button, and took care of his belt before snuggling in, his cheek pressed against the front of Jake's jeans.

Jake felt himself basking in the afterglow of a good, hard climax and let one arm slip around Ben's shoulders as the man tightly cuddled against him.

Still not sure what the protocol was for this, Jake was happy to lie there for a while longer. Ben seemed in no hurry to move, either, but based on the hard-on the guy'd had following their scene, Jake knew he had to be wanting to bust a nut of his own.

Opening his eyes about twenty minutes later, Jake glanced around and had a clear view of the full bath just off the hall, and it was vacant. He tapped Ben on the head. "Sit up," he said.

Ben did, the glazed look still in his eyes as he pulled the throw around him.

Yep, Jake spotted his erection.

The least he could do under the circumstances was give him a helping hand. He wouldn't be an asshole and get his own nut off and leave the guy hanging.

Jake stood, grabbed the implement bag and Ben's backpack, and the end of the leash. Leading Ben into the bathroom, Jake set their bags down and locked the door while Ben wordlessly watched.

Jake turned him around to face the mirror over the vanity. "Hands on the counter. Lean forward. Feet apart."

Without a word, Ben immediately complied. Jake pulled the throw off him and dropped it onto his bag. Standing behind him, he nudged Ben's feet farther apart. He reached his left hand around Ben and cupped the front of his throat, pulling his head back.

"Look at me," Jake hoarsely rasped in his right ear. "Don't close your eyes. Keep your hands on the counter."

"Yes, Sir," Ben whispered, sounding deep in subspace.

"Submit or safeword?"

"I submit, Sir."

Jake reached around with his right hand and closed his fingers over Ben's cock. It wasn't quite as long as his own, but it was a little thicker. A soft, sexy groan escaped Ben, his blue eyes completely glazed and pleading for release as he stared at Jake in the mirror.

Jake explored, before tonight never having touched a cock other than his own. Not a real one, not counting various sex toys.

Not quite eight inches, Ben was cut, hot, hard, similar and yet different than his own cock. Jake felt slick pre-cum pearling at the slit and slowly started working it along the man's shaft for lubrication. He took his time, milking more pre-cum from Ben's cock as he slowly jacked the other man. It fascinated him. Even with his raw ass, Ben rubbed it against the front of Jake's jeans, grinding, trying to fuck the hand around his shaft.

Jake closed his left hand around Ben's throat a little more tightly, not enough to choke him out, but to hold him still. "Behave," Jake whispered in his ear. "Be my good boy."

The soft, needy whine escaping Ben stirred Jake's cock again, but the man fell still.

He'd deal with round two for himself later. For now, he wanted to reciprocate. They could cover this in their talk tomorrow.

His gaze never leaving Ben's, he slowly pumped, down, even lightly squeezing Ben's balls before sliding up again.

The man in his arms was totally, willingly under his control.

Something deep and instinctive inside Jake knew whatever had happened tonight had shifted his world on its axis. They weren't just friends anymore.

Being *just* friends with Ben wasn't going to be possible. Jake wanted more.

A lot more.

He wanted Ben. All of him.

He just had to take his time and figure out how to tell him and not fuck *them* up in the process.

Ben

Ben could barely breathe, much less think. Never in his wildest dreams did he ever imagine he'd have a serious shot at blowing Jake.

And now…this?

Oh…fuck.

The good kind of *oh, fuck.*

Hell, had Jake pulled out a condom and wanted to plow him right there, he'd happily lean forward and hold his ass cheeks open for him.

He didn't care.

He wanted this man, as much as Jake would give him.

More importantly, he wanted to be Jake's good boy.

He could tell Jake was still trying to get used to this, to Ben's anatomy, but he didn't dare break the order given him by Jake not to move his hands from the counter.

"Do you want to come for me?" Jake whispered in his ear.

"Yes, Sir. Please."

"Who's my good boy?"

"I'm your good boy, Sir."

Jake squeezed, pulling another moan from Ben, now enough natural lubrication for Jake's hand to really start sliding up and down the length of Ben's cock.

"You can come, but you have to clean up any mess you make."

"Yes, Sir."

Jake's hand sped up, different than it felt when he jerked himself off, and even better because it was beyond his control.

Sooo much better.

Pulse pounding, lungs burning from trying not to hyperventilate over the overwhelming sensations washing through his body, Ben held on to that counter for dear life. His climax quickly built in his balls, tightening, spiraling up and coiling until he struggled to keep his eyes open as it finally broke free.

Jake's hand sped up. "Good boy." All friction eased as his cum coated Jake's hand along his shaft and he slowed, lightly squeezing and milking every last drop from him.

When Jake held his hand up to Ben's mouth, Ben opened immediately, without prompting, and lovingly started licking every drop off him. The hand around his throat disappeared, his fingers hooking into Ben's collar and holding him like that.

"*Good* boy," Jake whispered. "*My* good boy. So good. *Such* a good boy for me."

Ben moaned, still not letting go of the counter but wanting to wrap his hands around Jake's and hold it there in his mouth, lovingly lick every square inch of his flesh.

So good. Soo, sooo good.

Nothing about this night had been even remotely like scening with Mort or hell, any other guy who'd ever topped him.

This had been, by far, the best scene, the best night, *ever*. Even before he got to cuddle with Jake and blow him.

Even before Jake gave him a handjob.

Because Jake had called him *his* good boy.

His.

Good boy.

Mort had been stingy on the praise, usually saving the best of it to get laid. He'd heard more good boys from Jake tonight than he had in the last year he'd been with Mort.

Eventually, Jake tugged on his collar, urging Ben down to his knees. "You can let go of the counter."

Ben did, seeing now where some cum had splashed against the cabinet. Jake guided him. "Lick it up. Every drop."

Without hesitation his tongue swiped along the surface, letting Jake guide him to a few other spots.

Then Jake stroked his hair and Ben couldn't help but lean against his leg, nuzzling his thigh. "Good boy," Jake said. "Very good."

Ben's eyes fell closed as he knelt there, the warmth of Jake's body washing through the fabric of his jeans and into Ben's cheek.

Perfection.

He didn't want this moment, or the night, to end.

"Are you okay?" Jake asked.

"Yes, Sir."

"You sure?"

"Absolutely, Sir."

"I...don't know what this means," Jake said.

"It's okay, Sir." Ben wasn't going to be stupid and press for something Jake wasn't yet ready for. "If this was only for our scene, I understand."

"You wouldn't mind playing like this again?"

A laugh escaped him. "*Hell*, no, I don't mind, Sir."

"I don't know what I'm going to want to do for now. I mean, beyond playing. Playing I'm good with. Obviously, it got me hot. I won't even try to deny it. I *really* don't want to fuck things up between us."

Ben finally tipped his head back so he could look up into Jake's brown gaze. "We can talk about it later, Sir. We don't need to analyze it now. I'm *okay*, I swear."

"I *really* don't want to bork our friendship."

"I won't let that happen, Sir."

Jake finally nodded, placing one last, gentle pat on Ben's head and motioning for him to stand. Ben fought the urge to cry as Jake unsnapped the leash from his collar and then removed the collar, tucking them away in his bag. He folded the throw and put it away, too, before handing Ben his backpack.

"Here you go. Take off your cuffs and get dressed. Oh." He pointed at the cabinet. "Please wipe it down."

Ben found a container of wipes under the sink and thoroughly wiped down the cabinet and the floor just in front of it, washing his hands before quickly dressing. Reluctantly, he handed the cuffs back to Jake.

"Thank you, Sir," Ben said. "I enjoyed that. A lot."

"I did, too. You sure we're okay?"

"I was worried you might get upset at me when I got pushy out in the living room."

Jake stared at the leather cuffs in his hands. "No, definitely not upset. It felt too damn good. But I never thought about something like that happening with you tonight, or I would have discussed it with you first. I'm sorry."

Ben laughed. "You do *not* owe me an apology, Jake. I was happy to do it."

"I was the Top. I crossed a boundary."

"We never defined that." *Crap.* He hoped Jake wasn't regretting what they did on his account.

"Exactly my point," Jake said.

Ben reached out and touched Jake's shoulder, making sure to look into his eyes. "I am *glad* it happened. You didn't push or force me. I knew damn well what was happening, and I fully consented to it. If I didn't want to do it, even in deep subspace I'm still perfectly able to sit up and safeword. I never get so deep I don't know what's going on. So never worry about that, okay? You play with me how *you* want to play with me, and if I need to stop you, I will. If anything, I owe you an apology for it. I gave you permission to touch me anywhere. I didn't get that same permission from you first."

Jake finally nodded and stowed the cuffs. After washing their hands they unlocked the door and emerged, Ben glancing around and noting that not a single person was paying any attention to them or what they'd been doing.

That relieved him. Not for his sake, but for Jake's.

There would be a lot of conversations between them in the coming days and weeks, no doubt.

Now if I can just convince him I'd practically kill for a chance to do this full-time with him.

Even if Jake wanted to date someone and play with him, Ben

would be fine with that. *Especially* if their play was like this. Hell, even if it reverted to some one-sided status, where Jake got him off and didn't let Ben repeat what he'd done, he'd be okay with that.

He wouldn't need anyone else, not really.

Just being Jake's boy would be...*amazing*.

What they'd done...nothing had ever felt so *right* before. Like he'd finally found exactly where he belonged.

Like he'd finally come home at last.

Chapter Seventeen

Jake

Despite what Ben said, Jake still worried he'd crossed a line. As he drove them home that night, he fought the urge to confess to Ben everything he was feeling.

To confess that he was bi and *really* had the hots for him.

But hadn't that been one of the things Ben emphasized? That he was glad he didn't have to worry about any pressure from Jake about…stuff? That he trusted Jake? Hell, after talking with Tilly, the emphasis on taking things slow and using Jake as his backup for judgment calls.

How would Ben ever trust anything he said if he dumped this onto him right now without a solid foundation between them?

If he revealed everything to him, wouldn't he be putting exactly the same kinds of pressure on Ben that Mort had? Making him no better than that asshole?

Worse, even, because he knew the emotional toll that part of the fiasco had taken on his friend, not even counting the financial crimes against him.

And he had Ben's *trust*.

Ben broke the silence first. "That was...tonight was incredible, Sir. Thank you."

"Thank *you*, buddy. Any time you want to play like that again, I would like that very much."

Ben let out a sigh. "Me, too, Sir." Silence descended again for a few moments, until Ben spoke. "I wouldn't mind being called your submissive, Sir. If you're okay with that."

Now's your chance...now's your chance...

Still, Jake chickened out. "I thought you wanted to explore dating."

"I...do. I can. We could still play and...I could date. If that was okay with you. Besides, I'm not ready to sleep with anyone right now, even if I had someone. Tilly was right that I need to wait and take things slow and get to know myself again. Right now the only thing I'm willing to commit to is being your submissive, because I trust you."

Jake's fingers tightened around his steering wheel. This was not exactly a problem he'd ever had before. He'd played with people outside of being in a relationship with them, sure. But they were people he liked well enough to play with, but not want more from them.

Especially if he—or they—were already in a relationship. He was *not* poly.

Ben...he wanted more. He wanted *all* of him.

Except Ben didn't know that.

But telling Ben, when he still felt so raw over Mort's betrayal, meant risking alienating his friend. Wouldn't it be better to go slow? Ease his way into it?

No matter what Tilly thought, just because Ben enjoyed playing with him didn't mean Ben was "into" him as more than a friend and play partner. Hell, Jake knew plenty of people who engaged in sexy play, or sexual play, who weren't in a "relationship" with each other.

Jake realized Ben was still waiting for a reply from him. "I don't want to stand in the way of your healing and what you need to do. I don't want to do anything that will hold you back." *I'm an asshole.* "And I don't want us to do anything to ruin our friendship." *I'm a fucking asshole.* "We'll talk tomorrow and see where you feel like going from here." *Oh, I'm such a fucking asshole.* "I'm good with what happened tonight. I had a lot of fun with our scene and with…the aftercare. All of it." He reached over and patted Ben's thigh, leaving his hand there. "There's no rush."

I'm a lying fucking asshole.

"Yes, Sir." Ben's hand came to rest over his, tentatively at first, then his fingers curling around Jake's as he realized Jake wasn't going to pull his hand away.

W HEN THEY GOT HOME, Jake put the implement bag in the spare room but noticed Ben didn't make any move to go into his bedroom.

"You okay, buddy?"

"You said earlier…you said you'd be rubbing one out at home. I…I don't mind helping you, Sir."

Jake breathed through the urge to shove Ben into his own bedroom, onto his bed, and claim him right there.

Too…

Soon…

"I appreciate that. But let's have our talk tomorrow first. I don't want to do something I can't take back."

He hated how disappointed Ben looked. "Yes, Sir." But he didn't move.

He got the feeling Ben had more to say.

"Did you need to ask something else?"

"Yes, Sir." Ben licked his lips and Jake imagined sucking on them, kissing the man until they were puffy and pink and moaning his name. "May I... Do I have permission to make myself come?"

Poor Ben was still deep in subspace. On the one hand, Jake didn't want to push.

On the other, he didn't want to do something to ruin the guy's night and crash him into dropping.

He walked down the hall, until Ben had to look up into his eyes. "Is my boy still horny?" he quietly asked.

"Yes, Sir."

He reached over and turned the knob to Ben's bedroom, pushing the door open. "Go in, strip, and wait for me." He walked to the spare room and retrieved the collar from his bag, taking it back to Ben's room.

The man was already naked, standing, waiting. Even in the dim light, the marks Jake had left on him showed against Ben's skin.

Hoping this wasn't a mistake, Jake buckled the collar around Ben's neck and then pulled the covers back. "On your back."

Ben dove into the bed while Jake kicked off his sneakers and tossed them out into the hallway. Still fully dressed, he stretched out next to Ben, on Ben's right, Ben's head cradled in the crook of Jake's left arm. Ben's cock stood straight, rigid, already leaking pre-cum from the slit.

"Does my boy want a reward for being so good tonight?"

"Please, Sir!"

"Stroke your cock and show me how you make yourself come. Don't come until I give you permission, though."

Ben reached down with his right hand and fisted his cock, slowly stroking. His left cupped his balls, massaging them.

Soft, warm balls Jake had enjoyed torturing earlier.

Jake hooked his left hand around Ben's neck, snagging the D-ring on the front of the collar with a finger. He reached over with his right and started tweaking Ben's right nipple, then the left, back and forth.

"Stroke your cock for your Sir and show him what a good boy you are to obey."

Ben moaned and the frantic, agonized tone made Jake's cock throb and beg for attention.

Jake breathed in Ben's scent, his sweat, his sweet undertone of lavender from the clothes soap, his mango shampoo, the sharp tang of pre-cum. Fascinated, he watched Ben stroke himself, keeping himself just before the edge, obeying, struggling to hold back as ordered.

"After I let you come, what are you going to do?"

"Clean up my mess like Sir's good boy should."

Holy *fuck*, he was a fast learner. "That's right. Are you close?"

"Yes, Sir."

"I'm going to count backward. You come when I say *one*. If you come too soon, that's a hard cane stroke for every number you didn't wait. If you don't come on one, you have to stop and hold it until tomorrow."

No, Jake wouldn't make Ben hold it. He'd figure out something to do now, maybe let him beg or trade cane strokes or something, so he could bust his nut.

Jake was almost hoping for an early blast off to give him an excuse to run his hands over that gorgeous ass again.

"Twenty…"

Ben groaned, moaning his way through Jake's tortuously slow count, Ben's breath gasping as Jake reached five and slowed even more, tormenting him, now even more proud of the man for managing it.

"Two…*one*."

Ben's hands sped up, ropes of hot cum landing on Ben's abs and coating his hand as a final, loud moan rolled out of him and finally died in a gasping breath while his eyes fell closed.

"Good boy."

Without opening his eyes, Ben lifted his hands to his mouth, licking his cum from them, scooping every bit from his skin and sucking it down, finally opening his eyes to look and see if he'd missed any before falling still.

Jake nuzzled the top of his head. "Go to sleep, my good boy."

"Yes, Sir…"

Seconds later, Ben was softly snoring.

Jake fought the urge to laugh. Ben was.

Fucking.

Adorable.

Moving slowly, so as not to awaken him, Jake extricated himself from the other man's bed and pulled the covers over him. Quietly closing the bedroom door behind him, he grabbed his shoes and carried them into his bedroom. There, he stripped and grabbed a towel before heading to the hot tub.

He got the first one out of the way immediately, wishing it was once again Ben's mouth swallowing his cock. Compared to that orgasm, what his own hand gave him paled in comparison.

As he replayed the night's events in his mind, including just before in Ben's room, his cock hardened again.

Holy crap, a hat trick.

Hell, two in one night had been rare for him lately, much less three. He couldn't remember the last time he did three pops in one day, much less in the space of a few hours.

Finally sated, he lay there and stared up at the stars.

It would be so much better if Ben were tucked there against his side, staring up with him.

Maybe one day soon.

He finally headed for bed.

Chapter Eighteen

Ben

Ben awoke the next morning disoriented, but as soon as he rolled over, the pain in his ass triggered his morning woody to go full on hard-core concrete.

And it allll came back to him.

Shit.

He'd been so deep in subspace when they returned home he would have done anything, begged anything of Jake, not to say goodnight to him.

And the man had…

He reached up and felt the collar still around his neck.

His Sir's collar.

He winced in pain as he sat up and climbed out of bed. It took him a few minutes to get his boner soft enough he could take a piss, and then as he washed his hands, he stared at himself in the mirror.

The collar.

The collar Jake had bought just for him.

His boy.

But it's just for play, right? He said we'd talk. Yes, he's amazingly cool with this, but he's not gay.

He'd always had a close relationship with Jake, except for when Mort had interfered. That was the bottom line, right? Mort had likely sensed Jake and Ben were close, and that might have threatened Mort's hold on him.

Hell, he still had the keyring Jake had given him six years earlier for his birthday, the Steely Dan keyring. A thoughtful gesture from his best friend.

Jake was always like that.

Turning, he looked at the marks on his ass and thighs in the mirror. Jake had left some really good ones on him that would probably last the better part of a week.

Yay!

Yet...uncertainty filled him. Where did they go from here? He didn't want to back Jake into a corner where the man felt responsible for him. He didn't want to stand in the way of Jake pursuing a relationship with anyone.

On the other hand, the thought of some woman blowing Jake made Ben...

Jealous.

Talk. We have to talk.

Getting dressed didn't feel right, but he wasn't sure if Jake would want him naked, either. So he grabbed a pair of shorts and carried them out to the kitchen with him and left them on one of the barstools at the counter while he started their coffee.

Collar on.

He'd let Jake take it off him.

It was a little after ten in the morning, and his phone hadn't charged despite plugging it into the charger. When he wiggled the connection, it finally showed the charging symbol.

I'll need to watch that.

He set it down when he heard Jake's bedroom door open.

The man emerged, wearing a pair of shorts and nothing else.

Ben nervously smiled as he got Jake's coffee ready for him and handed it to him. "Good morning, Sir."

Jake smirked over the top of his mug as he blew over it, then took a sip. "Good morning, boy. How's the ass?"

Ben thought his heart might explode. He turned so Jake could see.

"Nice marks. How do you feel this morning?"

"Good, Sir."

Another sleepy smile. "I don't mind that around here, but just between us. And for now, it's *not* a requirement, unless we're playing and I've told you there are protocols. Okay?"

Ben wasn't sure if that should make him happy or sad, so he opted to take it as a win. "Yes, Sir. Thank you."

Jake slid onto one of the stools and set his mug down in front of him, both hands cupped around it. "Did I go too far last night? With anything?"

"No, Sir. It was perfect. Everything." Something struck him. "That talk we had. About my perfect scene. That was…that was pretty much it, wasn't it?"

Jake's sleepy smile widened. "*Duh.* And yes, I had fun, too. A lot of fun. I'm open to repeating any or all of that at any time in the future."

"Does that mean playing here at the house?"

"Maybe." He took another sip of his coffee. "But not right now."

Ben reined in his disappointment. "Why not?"

"Because your ass needs at least a week to heal, maybe longer. There's probably some deep tissue bruising from that big finish that'll take a day or so to come out."

Disappointment disintegrated. "Oh. Oh!" He smiled. "Sure. And thank you for last night when we got home. That was unexpected. I really enjoyed it."

"I enjoyed it, too. I can't exactly do forced orgasm torture on you like I can a woman, so that was like the next best thing."

Ben tried not to let disappointment attempt to regain a foothold. Jake *was* a sadist. And yes, Ben knew how much his friend enjoyed that kind of play with his female partners.

"I know we talked health stuff before we played," Jake said, "but did you want a fresh round of testing from me right now?"

"No, Sir. I trust you. Mine all came back neg, and I have another round coming up."

"Okay." Jake sat back and seemed to study him. "Here are my thoughts. For now, if you want to *unofficially* consider me your Dominant, and you my submissive, you can. But for the purposes of FetLife, you can list yourself as under my protection. All right?"

"Yes, Sir."

"I'll list you that way on my profile. I don't want there to be any confusion right now for you." He seemed to need a moment to form his thoughts, so Ben didn't interrupt. "I think Tilly's idea of you taking some time to emotionally rebuild and meet people is a good one. As long as you don't jump into a serious relationship with someone you barely know."

"Yes, Sir."

"I think the 'under protection' designation on FetLife will be helpful for now with that. It'll give the average Dom pause and direct them to talk to me. Anyone else, I trust you can either refer them to me or you can tell them to go fuck themselves."

Ben nodded.

"Any problems with that so far?"

"No, Sir."

"We're still Jake and Ben. For the purposes of real-life, for our jobs, our responsibilities, that doesn't change. It can't right now. Not with everything else you've gone through. And I need time to breathe, too. Maybe Tilly's advice applies to me as much as it does to you. Maybe taking some time off from a 'relationship' with someone will be helpful."

Jake sipped his coffee. "Do you still want me to sign off on you sleeping with anyone?"

"Yes, Sir."

"How do you explain that to them?"

"If I get to that point with someone, they're going to know about us playing together. To be honest, I really liked what we did. If you want to incorporate orgasm play into our play on a regular basis, I'm seriously good with that."

Jake smiled, and Ben wanted to walk over and kiss him but held himself back.

"I was good with it, too. I just want to be careful."

"Careful?" Disappointment beat against his mental door, tears threatening to prickle his eyes.

"I don't want to do anything that would hurt our friendship. I don't want to mess up this new D/s thing we have, either. Baby steps. But Tilly's right that I don't want you to... I don't want to stand in the way of you being happy. I'm trying to make this not sound wrong."

* * *

Jake

What Jake was really trying to do was not make it sound like he had no interest in Ben, so that Ben wouldn't later think he was a damned dirty liar.

"I understand."

"You do? Good, because could you say it back to me so I know I didn't sound like an asshole?" Jake tempered his comment with humor, but it still tasted acidic and harsh going down.

"I know that I need to meet people. It'd be unhealthy of me to have a crush on you when you're going to be trying to meet people, too."

Jake swallowed. "Yeah," he said, hoping he sounded reasonably normal. "That."

Ben walked over. Jake turned and pulled him in for a hug. "I liked the aftercare," Jake told him.

"I did, too, Sir."

"Not just the sexy part," Jake said. "I enjoyed cuddling. I wouldn't want to cuddle a random stranger, but it was safe, and it was fun, and it was a nice way to unwind."

Ben relaxed in his arms, strengthening his grip around Jake. "Me, too. Either. Both. You know what I mean."

"I do." He took a deep breath. "Have you been chatting with anyone on those apps yet?"

Ben's answer sliced like a knife through Jake's gut. "A couple of guys. There might be one or two I want to have dinner with, but that's all for now."

"Okay." He sat back and Ben took that as his cue to step away. "I'm not going to have rules for you at this time about controlling your orgasms, even though I suspect you'd enjoy that."

Ben's cock twitched in response, making Jake smile as the men's gazes met. "Yeah, *that*. We'll play things by ear when we decide to scene. But if you want to make this an unofficial guideline for now, don't masturbate without permission the day of us planning to scene."

Ben's cock was fully inflated now. "Yes, Sir."

Baby steps. "I should warn you that I have been jerking off in the hot tub."

"Would you ever mind if I…joined you?"

Baby fucking steps. "I wouldn't mind at all. I wouldn't feel right asking you to help me out though if we hadn't been scening beforehand."

"I wouldn't mind."

"I appreciate that. Maybe we can even fall into a pattern of scening and then engaging in orgasm play to finish off the evening."

"Thank you, Sir."

Damn, he is so cute. "You can wear the collar around here, or at the club, obviously. If you feel like it. If you want to be naked, that's up to you, no rule about it, though. Just sit on a towel. Doesn't make me uncomfortable."

Ben smiled. "Yes, Sir."

"Outside of a scene, I'm won't have any formal protocols for you right now. If there are things you want to do that make you feel comfortable or safe, I won't stop you unless it makes me uncomfortable."

"Like what?"

"How you serve our dinner, or if you decide one night you want to sit on the floor next to me instead of on the couch. Just, whatever. But I *have* to know that this isn't going to screw us up as friends."

"It won't, Sir."

"Good." He sighed. "You really like it when I say *good boy*, don't you?"

"Yes, Sir."

"Okay. I'll make a point to do more of that. We'll let this roll for a while the way it is. Maybe next Saturday we can play again at Venture if I think your ass is up to it. But if you're serious about working up to a formal D/s arrangement between us, you need to see what I'm like and what I would expect out of you. I might decide we aren't going to play, and that means that's it, you don't get upset about it. And you're welcomed to safeword, always. About anything. That's sacrosanct. But if we eventually end up formal, you will have punishments if you don't follow a rule. Understand?"

"Yes, Sir."

"For now, whether it's your bedroom door or mine, if someone's behind a closed door, assume they're off the clock, so to speak. Unless you need something or have to ask a question. Then you can knock or text me. Does that make sense?"

"Yes, Sir."

Jake studied him. "You want the wrist and ankle cuffs, don't you?"

He eagerly nodded.

"Fine, you can put them on and wear them, but that's for you to choose to do, just like the collar. The only time I'll tell you to wear them is if we're playing. Understand?"

"Yes, Sir."

"You can keep them in your room, but if we go somewhere to play, you're responsible for bringing them."

"Thank you, Sir."

"Anything else?" Jake asked.

Ben seemed to think about it. "I just wanted to thank you again for this. For everything. I really appreciate it. Letting me live here, being so cool about...*this*. Thank you."

"You're very welcome."

Ben

Ben felt like a literal weight had lifted from his shoulders. As he went about his day doing chores and checking in on the conversations he was having online, he realized something.

This is...normal.

Okay, not normal-normal, but kinky normal.

Healthy.

This was how it was supposed to feel when two healthy adults had a relationship.

Why can't he be gay?

He cut off that line of thinking. Jake wasn't gay. And Ben knew he was incredibly damn lucky to have such a cool friend as Jake, willing to do things with him like that.

He'd just finished vacuuming his bedroom when he looked at

his phone again. Sitting on his bed, he opened one of the conversations he'd been having with a guy, Ian, from Sarasota. He wasn't bad-looking, and he seemed nice. He was currently online, too.

I need to meet people. Jake's putting forth a huge effort. The least I can do is get my emotional shit together and adult.

He sent Ian a chat request.

AS THE WEEK progressed and it looked like Ben would end up eating dinner with Ian on Friday, he was having second and third and fourth thoughts. He and Jake had settled into a nice routine around the house, but there hadn't been any hot tub sessions for either of them.

Despite Jake being clear with Ben, the events of the party confused Ben, in his mind...emotionally. On the one hand, he wanted to devote himself totally to Jake.

On the other hand, the man himself kept telling him it was okay for him to go out, to seek out dates.

And Jake wasn't gay, events of the party notwithstanding.

Right?

All he could do was take Jake at his word. Which was exactly what Jake had told him to do. He trusted Jake, and if Jake told him it was okay to date...well, that's what he'd do.

Even if it wasn't what he really wanted to do.

Thursday afternoon they were having lunch at Subway when Ben broached the subject. "I've been chatting online with that one guy, Ian."

Jake

Jake froze. "Yeah?"

Be a friend, be a friend, be a friend and not an asshole douche!

"He suggested getting together for dinner tomorrow night. Would that be okay?"

Breathe, asshole. "Sure, I guess. We've got plenty of leftovers. I'll be fine."

"I just… I wanted to make sure you were okay with it."

"Why wouldn't I be okay with you going out to dinner with someone?"

"Am I moving too fast?"

"Is it just dinner?" *Please oh please oh please!*

"He just broke up with a guy a few weeks ago and says he's only looking to meet people right now, too."

Jake's gut, which had painfully clenched, tried to loosen a little. "Then that sounds perfect, right?"

"I guess. Can we still go to the club Saturday night?" Ben asked.

Ben's ass had healed up well enough from last Saturday, and he was eager to play again.

"If you feel up to it, sure." Jake had kept his wank sessions confined to his own bed or bathroom, behind closed doors.

It was too tempting, he knew, to do more with Ben right now.

"Okay. Thanks."

"You don't have to thank me, buddy."

"It's just that I trust you. Maybe it sounds silly but I need to make sure you're okay with this. I don't want to upset you."

Liar, liar, do the lying liar pants on fire dance… "I'm okay. I promise you, if I have a problem, I'll speak up." *Liar.*

Ben finally smiled. "Thanks." At least the guy had remembered not to call him Sir at work. He didn't even do it all the time at home, usually only at meal time, when Ben insisted on serving Jake.

Jake was happy to let him do it, especially since it made Ben smile.

On the way home, Ben brought it up before Jake could. "Would you mind if I drove in alone tomorrow? Then I can leave as soon as I'm finished with work and come home to get ready."

"That's fine. I was going to stay late and finish a few projects anyway. Plus I wanted to go grocery shopping."

"Okay. Cool. I'll make sure I leave you some money and the list."

"Sounds good." Jake loosened his grip on the steering wheel when he realized he was trying to strangle it. "And text me if you need me as a safe call to get out of it early or something."

"I will. Darn."

"What?" Jake glanced at him.

"I could have sworn I plugged my phone in at my desk today. I guess I didn't. Maybe my charger's going bad." He held it up, showing the screen to Jake. "It's almost dead."

"Try my car charger."

Ben plugged it in. "There it goes. Thanks." He set it down.

Which was fine with Jake, because he suspected Ben had been texting with Ian. Jake had heard a new text tone around the house the past few days and deduced the guy had Ben's phone number.

It now felt like an invisible clock ticking in Jake's brain.

Maybe I need to talk to Tilly again.

Chapter Nineteen

Ben

Ben raced home immediately after work Friday to grab another shower and shave. Now he nervously stared at himself in the mirror as he prepped for his date with Ian. Something about this didn't feel...right.

Sure, Jake and Tilly had encouraged him to go out, to date. Ben wasn't even sure what it was that he and Jake had beyond friendship, D/s, and something close to but not quite friends with bennies within the context of their D/s play.

Still...

Ben wanted to be going out on a date with *Jake*. Even if just as friends.

He'd feel a lot better about this if Jake was home so he could talk to him about it, but he wasn't. This wasn't exactly something they could talk about at the office, and they didn't ride in together that morning because of Ben's date tonight. Jake had stayed behind to finish some stuff at work, barely looking up from his computer as Ben offered him a friendly smile and wave when he'd sought him out to tell him he was leaving.

Jake hadn't left orders for him to text or call him during his date, either, other than Jake said he'd keep his phone on and nearby in case Ben needed him.

Ben froze in front of his mirror. *What am I doing?*

Not counting the night of the party at Tilly's, Jake hadn't expressed an interest in pushing the boundaries beyond what they'd already agreed. Jake had *told* Ben he was okay with him going out, dating. And that he'd stop him if he thought Ben was moving too quickly.

Ben didn't want to be alone for the rest of his life. He could be play partners with Jake and still have a relationship besides him. Right? Lots of people did that, gay and straight.

Maybe this was even better, because he never had to worry about Jake being an asshole and taking advantage of him. He'd already proven that much, beyond any shadow of a doubt. Of all the people in his life, he could *absolutely* trust Jake.

Having these two parts of his life kept separate might be safest.

Ben was still picking up the pieces of what had happened to him the last time he'd merged the two. The PI Tilly had hired hadn't yet located Mort, although he had leads he was working on.

Grabbing his keys from the dresser, Ben headed out to the living room.

Dammit, phone.

He turned back to grab it from where he'd left it on the charger. No texts from Jake.

Crap. It hadn't charged at all, and now it was down to under twenty percent, even though he thought he had it plugged in all the way. *I'll charge it in the car.*

Looking at the time, he realized he needed to get moving or risk being late with traffic. After one last glance behind him at the house, he locked the front door and headed out.

Jake

Jake wasted as much time as he could at work before heading out. Publix first, where he slowly cruised up and down every aisle at least twice before eventually making his way toward the checkout lines. He'd stalled as long as he could. He hadn't wanted to get home before Ben left for fear he might try to talk Ben out of going.

Stupid.

Why should he care if Ben went out on a dinner date with some guy? It wasn't like he and Ben were sleeping together.

Technically.

Yet.

That thought—or was it wishful thinking?—had sneakily slipped through.

Jake closed his eyes as another memory from last Saturday swept through him. How...*fucking*...hot it'd been.

Fuck.

He couldn't get the memory of the feel of Ben's mouth around his cock out of his head. Hell, just standing there in the grocery store check-out line, it was all he could do not to start tugging at the front of his jeans, which had suddenly grown uncomfortably snug in the crotch region.

When Jake arrived home, he struggled against the wash of feelings trying to assail him when he saw the empty driveway and Ben's car not parked in its usual spot.

Ben was a single guy. He had every right to go out on a date with someone.

Dammit.

After schlepping the groceries inside and putting them away, he walked out to the pool and stripped, diving into the deep end and swimming the entire length before coming up for air in the shallows.

Rolling onto his back, he floated and stared up at the pool cage as he wondered why he was feeling…jealous.

Because he could try to bullshit himself all he wanted, but jealousy was the only thing that fit.

But that would mean…

Fuck.

I'm in love with him. He's my best friend, and I'm head over heels in love with him.

Never before in his life had Jake ever run up against this. Appreciate a guy's body? Sure. Although before now he'd never met a guy who'd made him want to flip that way.

Before Ben.

He was lusting after *Ben. Specifically* Ben. It was the whole package. The friendship, the D/s, the relationship—everything. Not merely what was between the guy's legs.

It was what was between Ben's *ears* that had Jake hot and bothered. His body was a bonus.

The way Ben had seamlessly fallen into a perfectly synchronized dance with Jake when he'd moved in with him. How he'd gone far above and beyond anything Jake had expected of him as a roommate or even as a friend.

He'd been…

Jake let out a groan.

He's been the perfect submissive.

Scratch that, what Ben had been had far surpassed submissive.

He'd been Jake's slave in everything but formal title.

And I'm a stupid fuck who not only gave him permission to go out on a date, I practically shoved him out the door and into another guy's arms.

Jake was beginning to think that maybe he deserved to be alone if he couldn't figure this shit out and get it right. He'd been attracted to guys before, but more in a bromance kind of way, not an in-his-pants kind of way. But since it'd always been women he'd dated up to this point, he'd claimed the label of het for the sake of simplicity, even though he wouldn't deny, if asked, that he was bi.

It was far easier to claim heterosexual around his parents, who didn't get the countless shades of sexual grey between gay and straight. Not that they'd ever asked, they'd just assumed he was straight.

Which, considering their narrow-minded view of the world, he'd been happy to let them assume.

This wasn't just attraction, though.

This was love, and Jake knew it.

Now *what am I going to do?*

It would be a long damn night until Ben got home.

He swam over to the side and dug his phone out of the pocket of his jeans.

Any idea on an ETA tonight? Just curious.

He hit *send* before his balls completely fell off. Before he could set the phone down, Ben had texted him back.

Around 10. I'll try to be quiet when I
come in.

Jake debated letting it go at that, but then his stupid fingers found they had a mind of their own and replied.

No worries. I'll probably still be up.

Instead of setting the phone down, he held on to it and waited. Ben replied a moment later.

:)

Jake finally set the phone down and pushed away from the wall. If he wasn't an asshole, he probably should have added a *have fun,* or something equally innocuous.

Except...he couldn't bring himself to do it.

Being completely honest with himself, he didn't *want* Ben to have fun. Jake wanted their date to bomb so Ben didn't see the guy again and…

And *then* what?

It wasn't like the guy Ben was seeing tonight was a Dom. Ben flat-out said he was vanilla. Ben had been open and honest with the guy that Jake was his Dom and they'd be scening together in the future. So they'd still be able to play together and do…whatever it was they were doing together.

Even though Jake still wasn't exactly sure *what* the hell it was they were doing together.

Likely, though, whatever they did in the future wouldn't be of a sexual nature, if Ben got involved with someone else. Jake couldn't imagine someone else being okay with it, because *he* wouldn't be okay with it if the positions were reversed. He knew people who were poly or swingers.

It just wasn't *his* thing.

He didn't share well.

With anyone.

Not sexually.

Not someone who was *his*.

And even though it might risk nuking their friendship, he knew he had to be honest with Ben about his feelings for him.

He swam a few laps before checking his phone again.

No new texts, and now it was nearly eight o'clock. Unless he wanted to be a total douchebag and keep interrupting Ben's date, he needed to let it go.

Unfortunately, that was the last thing he wanted to do.

Ben

Ben realized after replying to Jake's texts that his phone's battery was even more depleted now than it had been upon leaving home, despite being on the charger in his car.

Shoot.

Apparently, he'd need to get it looked at. That meant he couldn't even sit there and pass the time checking his e-mail or surfing the Internet as he fought the urge to pace outside the restaurant. He was nervous enough and didn't need to work up a sweat in the muggy evening air. Ian arrived right on time and walked up to him.

"Ben?"

"Hey, nice to finally meet you." Ben stuck out his hand and they shook without the awkward hug-shake dance.

The guy wasn't bad-looking, either. A little better in real life than he appeared in his pics online, although Ian was also a bit beefier in build than Ben normally would be attracted to. Not obese or anything, but...

He's not Jake.

Wasn't that the *real* issue? That he would be measuring *every* guy he dated against Jake?

I need to not think about him tonight.

"Ready to eat?" Ian had a nice smile, sweet green eyes, and neatly styled brown hair. He was a year younger than Ben, at thirty-four, and was gainfully employed as a paralegal in Sarasota.

"Yeah." Ben offered him a smile in return. "Let's go eat."

Jake

Jake swam for a while longer before climbing out of the pool. He refused to look at his phone as he gathered everything and took it inside, dripping water all the way through the living room and down the hall to his bathroom, where he rinsed off.

He was hungry, but he wasn't in the mood to eat.

To eat *alone*.

To not have Ben already pressing him to eat what he'd made him for dinner, eagerly serving him, collar on and using real plates and silverware and not the paper plates…

Shit.

Jake pulled on a pair of shorts and glanced at his phone, which was a mistake.

No new texts.

He made sure the ringer on his phone was turned all the way up and carried it out to the kitchen, where he stared into the fridge for a few minutes. He could heat up leftovers.

Leftovers made by Ben.

Slamming the fridge door shut, he stood there, pressing his forehead against its cool surface.

Fuck.

What the hell is wrong with me? He's my friend. I want him to be happy.

He still didn't move.

He's not my friend, he's mine. *And how the hell is he supposed to know I'm into him if he thinks I'm straight?*

This was *not* a problem he was used to having. Despite the not-sharing thing, he wasn't a jealous, possessive guy. Never had been. Any girl he'd dated, he'd never checked up on her, or hounded her, or isolated her from friends. She could go out to dinner with them, or see a movie. He was independent and wanted anyone he dated to be that way, too.

He felt that if he couldn't trust someone enough to believe they were where they said they were, doing what they said they were doing, then he shouldn't be with them. He'd never been *that* asshole, the one who constantly checked up on his girl, or even cared who she was out with.

He never *had* been.

Until now.

Until *Ben*.

Ben, who was only having dinner with a guy he'd just met. A guy he'd been texting with.

He finally yanked the fridge open again and grabbed the first container of leftovers he put his hands on. After dumping some onto a paper plate and nuking it, he took it out to the living room and sat on the couch to channel surf and eat.

Even this didn't feel right anymore. He'd been fine on the nights when he ate home alone while he was dating Allison.

So why wasn't he fine being alone *now*?

Because I want Ben here.

With me.

This was ridiculous. Why the hell would Ben be interested in more with him anyway, outside of D/s? They were friends.

Not exactly.

More. *Way* more. Ben had all but outright said he wanted to do more with him, and that likely remained unsaid only because Ben assumed Jake was straight and the way Jake had presented things to him.

Why the *fuck* was he feeling like this about Ben? Like he wanted to find out where they were, crash their date, drag him out of there, and...

And what, exactly?

For the first time in his life, Jake didn't have an easy, ready, sure answer to something bothering him emotionally.

And *that* bothered him.

It wouldn't be fair to Ben to tell him he couldn't date anyone, right? Just like Ben wouldn't be acting all boiled bunny over him going out with a woman.

Except...

There *wasn't* any woman in Jake's life. None he was even interested in chatting with online, much less dating.

Especially not since last Saturday at the party, when everything changed.

When *he* changed.

No, changed wasn't right, exactly, because he'd been attracted to guys before. Ben, however, was the first guy he'd ever been attracted to enough to pursue. The first guy he'd fallen in love with.

And even before the party, if Jake was completely honest with himself, he knew he was in love with Ben.

I'm being stupid. I don't know how he feels about me.

That was bullshit, too, wasn't it?

From day one of living there, Ben had been awesome, amazing.

It felt *right* living with him. Like he had a home at last, not just a house to rattle around in.

Everything they'd done before and since the night of the party felt *right*. Easy. Seamless.

Perfect.

Why was he fighting this again?

Yeah, I'm an idiot.

After eating, he tossed the paper plate and started to throw the fork into the sink for Ben to wash later, then stopped, reversed, rinsed it, and stuck it in the dishwasher.

I'm a Dom, not an asshole.

***

Ben

As Ben relaxed and their evening progressed, he realized he really liked Ian. The more time he spent with Ian, the more the other man's personality started to shine and they both loosened up, chatting, laughing. They had a lot in common, shared interests in TV shows and books, music, film—everything.

An easy thread of physical attraction seemed to connect them, too.

So why the hell do I feel guilty?

After their entrees and salads, Ian finally addressed the elephant in the middle of the table while they were waiting for their main course to be delivered. Ben had wondered how long it'd take him to get to it.

"So…you're into BDSM?" Ian asked.

The restaurant was busy, noisy, and they sat in a booth along the wall with dividers between them and the booths on either side. Ben still felt the need to glance around first.

"Yeah."

"*Ah.*" Ian played with the paper wrapper from his straw. "So… what's that like? I mean, what do you do?"

Ben knew the only way through this conversation was through it, and he'd better get used to having it again. It was one of the drawbacks of not fishing in the BDSM dating pond, so to speak.

"I like impact play, bondage, strict domination, and discipline. A variety of things."

Ian didn't look up from where his fingers folded and unfolded the paper. "But…what does that *mean?*"

"You want specific details?"

"I really don't know anything about BDSM. Other than that book. Which my sister told me about. I haven't read it."

"Well, I haven't read it either." Ben offered him a smile, which Ian returned.

Then Ben launched into an example of exactly what he liked.

Minus a retelling of what had happened between him and Jake at the party last weekend. And then later, at home.

That would only…confuse things.

No reason to throw in complications this soon. If things continued progressing, of course he'd include that as disclosure to Ian. But they were nowhere near that point yet.

Hell, he wasn't even sure if anything other than friendship

would develop between him and Ian. Why muddy those waters before it was absolutely necessary?

Ben paused while the waitress brought their entrees and set their plates in front of them. When they were alone again, he leaned in. "It's okay if you don't understand it, or don't want to do it."

Ian poked at his baked potato with his fork. "I'd need to know more about it, I guess. I'm not into being spanked, or doing the spanking. I'm not really comfortable bossing around someone I'm dating."

"See, it's not exactly like that. But that's okay. You don't have to be into it, as long as you don't mind if I do it with someone else."

Jake. Specifically *doing it with Jake.*

Again, he could narrow that focus later.

Ian's brow furrowed. "But is that…sex?"

"For some people, yes. For some people, no. For me, it depends on my partner." He tossed it out there. "If I was dating someone who wasn't into BDSM, but they were okay with me playing, then sex wouldn't be a part of my play. Might not be a part of it, anyway, if I'm not doing sexy play with whoever it is topping me."

"Okay. That makes sense. I was wondering, when you said your roommate's straight. Sounds like a nice guy, if he's being that cool."

Ben felt a little guilty for not telling the whole truth. "Like anything else, everyone has their own comfort level. Some people only top someone they're in an intimate relationship with. Some can top people they know casually."

"I think I'd be okay with that." He glanced in Ben's direction. "I mean, as long as it's not a no-go for you that I'm not into it."

"Not at all. But it is something I need."

Ian slowly nodded. "Okay. I guess that's something we don't need to get too detailed about tonight if it's not a deal-breaker. That's a future conversation."

Ben smiled. "Cool." The fact that Ian didn't have a problem with it, and seemed to still want to see where things went between them, was promising.

Those were his two big personal bombs—BDSM, and his ex and sorting out that legal situation.

If Ian was okay with both of those…maybe there was a chance things might work out between them. Ben had hinted that the reason he was living with Jake was due to a bad situation with his ex, including being ripped off by him.

That was as far as he'd admitted, but Ian had seemed okay with that, too.

Ben forced himself not to think about what Jake might be doing tonight, opting to enjoy his evening with Ian.

If Jake was going out with a woman, Ben would be happy for him.

Although he would be lying if he didn't admit to at least a little bit of envy. At least Jake wouldn't be going out with another guy, the thought of him doing that dragging the green monster from the depths of Ben's soul with a raging passion. Share Jake with a girl?

Yeah. Grudgingly.

Share him with another *guy?*

No fucking way.

Out in the parking lot, they stood, talking.

"You know," Ian said, "I feel like walking some of this meal off. Want to join me over on Siesta Key? Go to the beach?"

Ben didn't have to give that a second thought. "Sure. It's still early."

They drove—separately—over to the beach and spent more time talking as they walked. They weren't the only ones on the beach, and Ben was having such a good time he really didn't want the evening to end.

He wasn't foolish enough to go home with the guy tonight, though. Or invite him back to his place to talk more. Not without talking to Jake first. He'd heard too many horror stories to do the first thing without knowing the guy better, not to mention he felt a little gun-shy after what he went through with Mort.

And out of respect for his friend—and Dominant—he'd ask Jake before doing the second.

By the time they made it back to their cars, Ben went to check the time and realized his phone was completely dead. "What time is it?"

Ian pulled his phone from his pocket. "After midnight."

"*Wow*, I had no idea it was that late."

After a long hug that was definitely more than friendly, Ben hopped in his car and headed home. Trying to plug his phone into the car charger didn't work, either, so apparently the battery was fried.

I hope Jake's not worried.

Chapter Twenty

Jake

The longer the evening dragged on, the more Jake realized something.

I'm a fucking idiot.

He'd been scared to...what? Admit he'd finally met a guy who turned his crank?

A guy who perfectly matched him in what was quickly becoming obvious were the most important ways.

Ways he'd never really thought about before, because he'd never had a submissive—a *slave*—as perfect for him as Ben.

A guy he didn't just love, but was *in* love with.

As the clock ticked closer to ten, Jake swore he wouldn't be an asshole when Ben got home. That he wouldn't question him.

That he wouldn't do something stupid like drive him off by acting crazy.

Then ten o'clock hit.

No Ben.

Grabbing his phone, Jake spent a good five minutes staring at it, willing himself not to text.

Losing *that* battle miserably.

Finally, he sent it.

> Not to be a jackass but it's after 10. Just checking in.

And he waited.

And waited.

And waited.

By 10:30, he sent another text.

By 10:00, he was texting Ben every ten minutes.

At 11:00, every five minutes.

It was nearly one in the morning when Jake spotted headlights sweeping across the front of the house and pull into the drive. Ben's car. His relief that Ben was home warred with his anger over worrying about him.

Had Ben been ignoring him?

No, they didn't have anything formally laid out about tonight, but come on, common courtesy. Especially when Ben told him ten o'clock.

Ben hesitated when he walked through the door and saw Jake standing there.

"Sorry I'm late, Sir, but—"

Jake snapped his fingers and pointed at the floor in front of him.

Ben barely got the door closed before he hurried over and dropped to his knees.

"Where…*were*…you?" Jake kept his voice low simply to help mask his anger…and his shaky relief that Ben was home safe.

"I'm sorry, Sir. My phone isn't charging, and—"

"*Answer* my question." He was almost afraid to hear it.

"After dinner we both drove to Siesta Key and walked and talked for a while. I lost track of time. I'm sorry, Sir."

"I've been *worried* about you. You told me ten o'clock." But relief filled him that Ben hadn't been doing...*more* with the guy.

Now confusion entered Ben's tone. "I'm sorry, Sir. I didn't mean to worry you."

"So *all* you did with him was have dinner and talk? That's *it*?"

"Well, we walked on the beach, Sir. That's why we went over to Siesta Key."

Jake didn't know if he wanted to let out a triumphant crow, a relieved sigh, or an irritated growl at being made to worry. He leaned down and grabbed the back of Ben's neck, hard. "You will submit, or you will safeword."

"Sir?"

"Submit or safeword!"

"I subm—"

Jake barely gave Ben time to scramble to his feet before dragging him, his hand fisting the back of Ben's shirt collar, down the hallway to Jake's room, where he threw Ben down over the end of his bed.

Ben tried to sit up. "Sir, I—"

"Submit or safeword!" Jake screamed as he shoved him down again, this time pinning him by the back of the neck. "Pick!"

Jake was almost afraid of the answer, knew he was dangerously close to the edge of losing control, and maybe this wasn't the wisest of ideas.

"I submit, Sir," Ben whispered.

"*Stay!*" Jake tore out of his bedroom, across the hallway to the spare bedroom, and grabbed his implement bag. He brought it back and dropped it onto the floor, digging through it and pulling out the first thing his fingers wrapped around, a riding crop.

"Pants down!" Jake ordered. "Bare ass."

Ben had barely cleared his ass with his jeans before Jake was on him, pinning him down with his left hand while savagely going after him with the crop.

"Don't you *ever* fucking scare me like that again, do you understand me? Don't *ever* make me worry about you like that again!" Each stroke left an angry red welt across Ben's flesh.

Ben let out a cry with each strike, his hands fisting the covers, but making no move to escape, or stop Jake, or fight back, or cover himself.

After about twenty hard strokes, Jake reined himself in. "Submit or safeword!" He realized he was still screaming, the adrenaline hit finally starting to recede. It might leave him shaky and feeling sick on the other end of it, but at least his boy was home safe.

His boy.

"I submit, Sir."

Ben

There was a conscious part of Ben's brain which thought maybe he should be safewording instead of submitting, especially when he heard the shrill, frightened thread running through Jake's tone.

The rest of him refused to safeword.

He *absolutely* would submit. This was his Sir.

His owner, in Ben's mind.

When Jake paused and asked him that, tears of pain rolled down Ben's cheeks, but like *hell* would he tap out.

Not now.

Not ever.

Wasn't *this* what he'd always wanted? For Jake to take him in hand?

Ben heard the riding crop hit the floor and the feel of the mattress dip as Jake climbed onto the bed.

Jake rolled him onto his back, cupping Ben's face in his hands. What Jake did next almost shocked Ben into safewording.

Jake kissed him.

Not a simple, hey, how ya doin' kiss, either.

No, this was hard and deep, possessive, his lips slanted over Ben's and the stubble on Jake's cheeks scratchy against his face.

Jake grabbed Ben's hands and shoved them over his head, pinning him in place as he straddled him without breaking their kiss. It even shocked Ben so much—in the good way—that he momentarily forgot the pain throbbing in the flesh of his ass and upper thighs. Jake wasn't just holding his hands, but had a tight, nearly painful grip on Ben's wrists.

Finally, Jake lifted his lips from Ben's. "Don't you *ever* fucking scare me like that again, boy," he hoarsely rasped. "Guess I need to show my boy who he belongs to so he doesn't forget."

And then Jake kissed him again.

Okay, forget the fucking pain in his ass. Now Ben tried to grind his hips up against Jake, Ben's erection cradled in the V of Jake's thighs, against his shorts.

Jake transferred both of Ben's wrists into his left hand, and then reached down with his right to grab Ben's chin, hard, and hold his head still.

"Who do you belong to, boy?"

"You, Sir. I belong to you." He stared up into Jake's brown eyes, how intense and dark they looked.

He knew he was utterly fucked, because he loved this man. Was *in* love with this man.

"Whose ass is this?"

"Your ass, Sir."

Jake released his chin and then—raising the shock bar even higher—he grabbed Ben's cock and squeezed. "Whose cock is this?"

"Your cock, Sir."

No other answer felt even remotely right.

Jake leaned in, still holding on to Ben's cock, his lips just over Ben's. "Submit, or safeword," he whispered, his warm breath brushing over Ben's lips.

"I submit to you, Sir. Always."

Jake hesitated, their gazes locked. Then he released Ben's wrists as he sat up, his other hand still gripping Ben's cock. "FYI, I should have admitted I'm bi when you moved in. I *definitely* should have admitted it to you the night of the party when you blew me. I'm sorry I didn't say so earlier. I didn't want to scare you off."

Ben blinked, staring. "You're...bi?"

Jake arched an eyebrow. "Bi."

"I didn't know that."

"You never asked. You are, however, the first guy I've ever been with. But I'm monogamous, so my orientation's never been an issue before. I don't fuck around. You good with that?"

"Yes, Sir." Ben's brain swirled, trying to process that information on top of the fact that he was now being taken in hand, his dreams come true.

"New rules, boy," he said.

Ben nodded.

"You don't date *anyone*. You can go out with friends, but you don't *date*. You want someone? You have *me*."

"Yes, Sir." Ben refused to answer any other way.

Jake slowly pumped Ben's cock once. "I own this cock, and I own this ass, and I own your orgasms. You want to come? You ask me first and get permission from me. There might be times I don't give you permission, or I might make you do things to earn them. You disobey me over that, you'll find yourself permanently locked in a chastity cage."

Ben's cock twitched, and it was all he could do not to come over that declaration. "Yes, Sir."

"You're *my* boy. I don't share *my* boy with anyone. Understand?"

"Yes, Sir."

Jake let go of his cock. "Stay."

Ben didn't move a muscle.

Jake climbed off him, shoved his shorts down and off, and then climbed back onto the bed and straddled Ben again. Jake's cock jutted out, a thin trail of dark hair leading south from his navel to his trimmed bush around the base.

He knelt over Ben's face. "Don't make me come yet. Worship my cock."

Ben had already started opening his mouth, even before the order. Jake stared down at him. "Look at me while you worship my cock."

He kept his eyes open, staring up into Jake's face as Jake slowly slid the head of his cock into Ben's mouth. Ben let out a soft moan as he closed his lips around it, the tip of his tongue automatically seeking out the slit, wanting a taste of Jake's pre-cum. Ben hadn't been able to forget it from the night of the party, had longed for more.

"In case you were wondering, boy, I will be letting you come tonight. But don't come before I tell you, or I'll make what I just gave you look tame."

He mumbled, "Yes, Sir," around Jake's cock as best he could.

Jake smiled down at him. "That's my *very* good boy."

Jake

Jake prayed Ben didn't hate him in the morning, that he'd let him apologize for blowing his top like this.

He didn't like himself very much for it, but now that Ben was home, and safe—and multiple times had opted not to safeword— he wasn't about to let him go. Not yet.

He suspected if he stopped now it might even upset Ben.

The feel of Ben's lips around his cock...the night of the party wasn't a fluke. He was really *that* good.

Why have I been fighting this?

"*Such* a very good boy," Jake whispered, reaching down to stroke the man's hair.

Ben moaned and redoubled his efforts and Jake knew if he wasn't careful, Ben would be sucking his balls dry before he knew it.

And that's not where he wanted to empty them.

He wanted to claim his boy.

Finally, he pulled his cock from between Ben's lips and worked his way down Ben's body, straddling the man's hips. He felt Ben's cock rubbing against his ass as he reached down and started unbuttoning Ben's shirt.

Ben still kept his hands over his head, where Jake had put them and ordered them to stay.

He was a *very* good boy.

When Ben's shirt lay open, Jake parted the fabric so he could reach down and grab Ben's nipples.

He felt the man's cock twitch against his ass even as a moan escaped Ben.

"Mine," Jake whispered. Then he leaned in, sucking first on the right, then the left, ending each suck with a nipping bite that drew more deliciously eager sounds from Ben.

"Where's your collar and cuffs, boy?" he asked.

"In…in my tall dresser, Sir. Top drawer."

Jake climbed off him. "Stay. Do not move."

He padded down the hall and found them exactly where Ben had said they'd be. On his way back, he stopped by the spare bedroom and found the condoms and lube, along with nitrile gloves, that he kept in the side table that had formerly occupied Ben's room.

Back to his bedroom, where he grabbed a towel from the bathroom and then returned to the bed.

Ben hadn't moved an inch, as far as Jake could tell.

He pulled Ben's shoes and socks off him, finished yanking down his jeans and briefs, and dropped them to the floor. Then he buckled the collar and ankle and wrist cuffs on him, still not letting him move and not bothering to pull his shirt off him.

He grabbed a couple of snap clips from the implement bag before he returned to bed. Shoving Ben's legs up, he clipped each ankle cuff to the wrist cuff on the same side and pushed his legs wide apart, leaving him exposed.

"Color?"

"Green, Sir!" Ben's gorgeous blue eyes were wide.

"Good boy." He shoved the towel under Ben's ass, then pulled on the glove and started working lube into Ben's ass.

Ben moaned, slowly rocking his hips in time with Jake's movements.

"How's that feel?"

"Yes…Sir!"

"That's not an answer, boy."

"Good, Sir!"

Jake, personally, loved anal. Allison usually enjoyed it when he had her pussy stuffed with a vibrator and he fucked her at the same time, but Ben didn't have that anatomy.

So after stripping off the glove inside out and dropping it to the floor, he rolled a condom onto his shaft, lubed it, and used the left-over lube to slowly jack Ben's cock for him.

"Don't come until I tell you to, boy," he ordered.

Ben eagerly nodded, helpless. "Yes, Sir!"

He slowly jacked Ben's cock with one hand, while with the other he lined up his cock with Ben's ass and pressed the head against his rim.

"Last chance, boy. I do this, you become *mine*. Period."

"Please do it, Sir!"

Gritting his teeth to maintain control, Jake slowly pressed forward.

Chapter Twenty-One

Ben

Ben breathed through it, the familiar, achingly good stretching burn of a cock sliding through his rim, made so, so much sweeter by the feel of Jake's lubed hand stroking his cock.

He wasn't going to think. He wasn't going to question.

Ben was going to pray to whatever deities there might or might not be that his friend wasn't drunk and that he wouldn't forget a damn second in the morning.

He wanted to be Jake's.

And if this was what Ben hoped it was, he'd fight tooth and nail to keep it going.

Hogtied the way he was, Ben tried rocking his hips back for a better angle, to urge him faster, but Jake wouldn't be rushed. It was only after he felt Jake's pubes brushing against his ass that the man released Ben's cock, grabbed his thighs, and pushed back, rolling his ass up a little for a better angle.

They both moaned.

"Yeah," Jake gasped. He leaned in, pressing Ben's knees into his chest as he kissed him, fucking his mouth with his tongue.

Then he started moving.

Ben focused on not coming, being Jake's good boy, following orders. But it felt sooo…fucking…good!

The man was perfect, the head of his cock sliding across Ben's gland with every slow thrust.

"Look at me," Jake whispered.

Ben forced his eyes open.

"Mine, boy. Hear me? You belong to *me.* I'll keep you well fucked and keep your ass well beaten, but you are *mine.* Understand?"

"Yes, Sir."

"Nobody touches this ass, inside or out, except my hands and my cock. Got it?"

"Yes, Sir."

"You sleep in my bed every night, and when you're home, that collar better be on your neck and that ass bare for me to look at."

"Yes, Sir." Hell, just what Jake was *saying* was about to make Ben nut, much less the man's perfect cock fucking him.

Fucking him!

Jake's fucking me!

Jake kissed him again, slowing his strokes and allowing Ben a chance to pull back from the edge. "I need to get a lock for that collar. It's got the buckle for it." Another deep, slow kiss. "And the next time I come in that hot tub, it's going to be while fucking your ass with you bent over the edge."

"I have a confession, Sir."

Jake froze. "What?"

"I accidentally spied on you in the hot tub one night."

"Huh?"

Ben told him, watching Jake's expression turn from confusion to interest to playful sadistic glee. "Oh, reeeeally? And how did you enjoy watching me wank?"

"I rubbed one out watching you, Sir."

Jake's smile transformed into a grin. "What should Sir's naughty boy get for doing that, *hmm?*"

Ben knew damn well from Jake's tone that he was teasing, but then he took a hard stroke, distracting him. "What-whatever Sir says."

"Whatever?" Another hard, driving stroke.

"Yes, Sir!"

"*Hmm.* I think after we're done here, we're going to take a shower and Sir's going to have some fun with his boy."

Jake

Jake started long-stroking, a slow, steady rhythm he suspected would be hard for Ben to avoid exploding from. And if he did manage to hold it? Good for him.

His boy would learn, and Jake would have fun exploring all the possibilities with him.

Fucking Ben's ass was hot, tight, and threatening to make him explode with every stroke. He had so many fantasies, of fucking him doggy style, make Ben straddle him and fuck himself onto Jake's cock, getting a sex sling, hot tub, pool—but this first time, this very first time, he wanted to look Ben in the eyes while they both came.

He wanted his boy to know he meant every word he said.

That Ben was *his*.

If tomorrow morning Ben didn't wake up hating his ass for losing his shit.

He leaned in and hooked his hands under Ben's shoulders, holding on, Ben's cock rubbing between them. He was close, so damn close, and he felt Ben's pre-cum leaking, slicking their skin.

"Are you close, boy?"

"Yes, Sir."

He looked borderline desperate.

With their lips just inches apart, and staring into Ben's eyes, Jake said, "Then come for me, boy. Give it to me."

He started fucking him harder, faster. Ben let out a cry as Jake felt the man's ass contracting around his cock.

Holy fuck!

That triggered Jake's explosion, and he crushed his mouth over Ben's, swallowing the other man's moans as between them Ben's cum grew slick and Jake's balls emptied into the condom.

Breathing heavily, Jake slowed, stopped, not breaking his kiss with Ben. Wanting to freeze this most perfect of moments in time.

"Love you, boy," he whispered.

A sated, gorgeous smile filled Ben's face. "Love you, too, Sir."

After several minutes, Jake finally forced himself to move, unclipping Ben's cuffs and removing them. Then he led him into the bathroom, where Jake disposed of the condom before starting the shower.

"Oh, your collar." He took it off and laid it on the counter, noting Ben's almost sad gaze as he stared at it.

Cupping a hand around Ben's neck, he pulled him in for a kiss. "Buddy, you get it wet, you'll ruin it. I'll get you a day collar you can wear all the time."

"You will?"

"Of course I will." He spied the glove on the bedroom floor. "Oh, gotta grab that." He slapped Ben on the ass. "Get in the shower. I'll be right there." He went to retrieve the glove and grabbed the tube of lube while he was at it.

If they were going to be in the shower, he was going to see if he could get one more out of his boy.

Jake shoved him back against the wall, kissing him, pinning his hands over his head and working down the side of Ben's neck. He nipped and bit and sucked, loving the moans the shorter man made.

Lacing fingers with Ben, he squeezed his hands. "Sir wants to play with his boy's ass some more."

Ben nodded. "Yes, Sir."

Impossibly, Jake felt his own cock twitching. Maybe there'd be a shower blow job for him, too.

Releasing Ben's hands, he turned him around and bent him over, braced against the wall. Then he used the lube and started playing with Ben's ass, one finger, then two, loving the way Ben started fucking his hand as he played with him.

Reaching under Ben with his other hand, he found Ben was already hard again.

Jake slowed his motions, turning his hand and feeling around, noting when Ben gasped with pleasure. "Right there? That your button?"

"Yes, Sir!"

Now that he had him, Jake played with him, stroking his fingers over Ben's prostate, the hand on Ben's cock holding still and using it more as a way to keep him in position.

"Can you come for me like this, boy?"

"I...I don't know, Sir. I've never tried." Jake had read about prostate milking before, but never had a chance to try it as a giver or receiver. Now that he had his chance he refused to waste it.

"Try. You have permission to come, if you can."

Slowly, he teased him, rubbing him, occasionally stroking Ben's cock. The man's moans grew louder, more intense, until he felt Ben's cock harden just before it exploded. Jake started stroking, trying to intensify the feeling for him, Ben's entire body undulating under Jake's hands until, finally, he gasped.

"Yellow!"

Jake immediately released Ben's cock and withdrew his fingers from the man's ass. Ben was slow to move, at first.

Then he started laughing.

Jake used soap to wash off. "What's so funny?"

He finally straightened. "It took sex to make me yellow, Sir."

Jake grinned. "Not the first partner I've had that happen to." He pulled him in for a kiss, then snapped his fingers and pointed at the floor.

Ben dropped to his knees, which put him at the perfect position to suck Jake's cock, which was hard and ready after that fun.

"You know what to do, boy."

Ben eagerly swallowed him, holding on to the backs of Jake's legs while Jake cradled Ben's head in his hands. Eventually, as Ben worked him closer, Jake took over, now fucking Ben's face.

Even in this the man was fantastic, taking every bit and eager for more as Jake closed in. "Get ready to swallow, boy."

Ben let out a happy sounding moan and Jake didn't even have to pull his head onto his cock for Ben to deep-throat him as he came. Jake held on to Ben's head more for balance at that point as the force of his climax nearly took his knees out from under him.

Finally, breathing heavy, he stroked Ben's wet hair, tapping him on the forehead.

Ben tipped his head back but didn't release Jake's cock.

"Up."

Ben mumbled something, but the shake of his head around Jake's cock was obviously a negatory.

Jake sighed. "You won't suck a third out of me tonight, as tired as I am now. Let go of the toy."

Ben practically pouted as he slowly let Jake's cock slide from his mouth, then placed a final kiss on it.

Jake hauled him to his feet, holding him. "Let's rinse off and go to sleep, boy. You wore my old ass out."

Ben

Ben didn't want to stop, especially now that his ass was aching so nicely inside and out, but he let Jake hand him a towel and lead him back to his bed.

He'd never had an orgasm as intense as that one, with Jake rubbing his prostate and milking it from him while jerking him off. He'd heard about that, but had never believed it was so much stronger.

Ha!

As he curled up in bed, draped over Jake's chest, his leg hooked around one of Jake's, he pressed his face against his flesh and inhaled.

His Sir.

His!

"Go to sleep, boy," Jake mumbled, already sounding like he was falling asleep.

"Yes, Sir."

Still, even after the sound of Jake's breathing slowed and deepened in the dark next to him, Ben lay awake, happy, thinking.

Yes, his ass hurt, but it also felt damned *good.*

The fear in Jake's expression, in his voice...

It sickened Ben that he'd worried the man so much, unintentionally or not.

Tomorrow they'd be talking, of course. And if he knew Jake, he suspected the man would feel horrible for losing control.

Ben *got* it, though.

If Jake had been having those feelings for a while and was scared to tell him...

Everything made sense now when looked at in that context.

So had Tilly encouraged him to date because she thought he needed to...or to scare Jake into finally admitting his feelings?

Hmm.

He wouldn't put it past that sneaky Domme to engineer a faster hookup between them.

Finally, he yawned and closed his eyes, relief that he was finally with his Sir pulling him into sleep.

Chapter Twenty-Two

Jake

Saturday morning, Jake awakened spooned against Ben's back, his arm possessively draped around Ben's waist, and he mentally groaned.

He owed Ben a huge-ass apology for losing his shit the way he had the night before. As he lay there and stared at the back of Ben's head, the man stirred, stretching before glancing back at him with a sleepy smile.

Jake decided sooner was better than later for that apology. "Hey. I—"

Ben kissed him, long and sweetly and—okay, better than Allison had ever kissed him.

Kissed him so well, in fact, that Jake's cock started stirring.

"Good morning, Sir. Thank you for last night."

"I'm sorry."

Ben's brow furrowed. "For what?"

"For going crazy."

"I'm sorry I scared you. I should have kept better track of time when I realized my phone was dying. I should have told you my phone was dying."

"No, that's *not* the point. The point is, I was *way* out of line. I was a fucking asshole. I went berserk on you even though we didn't have a set agree—"

Ben kissed him again, this time while lodging one thigh perfectly between Jake's thighs, which finished hardening his cock in the process.

"Do you want to apologize, Sir, or would you rather your boy give you a good-morning blowjob?"

"Ben—"

Ben pressed the tips of his fingers against Jake's lips. "*Please* don't take it back," Ben whispered, looking nearly heartsick. "*Please,* don't take *any* of it back, not a second of it, and *please* don't tell me you didn't mean it. I meant *everything* I said and did last night. I want to be your boy. I'm *proud* to be your boy. I don't want you to share me with anyone, and I don't want to share you with anyone."

Jake stared into Ben's eyes.

Those big, blue eyes.

He grabbed Ben and kissed him again, a fist in Ben's hair as he did. "Then get down there and suck your Sir's cock, *boy,*" he rumbled.

Jake released him and rolled onto his back as Ben threw off the sheet covering them so he could scramble into position. Moans escaped both men as Ben sucked Jake's cock into his mouth, taking him to the root.

Okay, they still needed a rational, non-naked discussion about this.

But…later.

Once he'd busted a nut and got Ben off at least once, too. Because after what Ben had gone through last night, the man had definitely proved that he was a very good boy.

And Jake was proud to call him *his.*

Ben

Ben's momentary panic that Jake was going to take it all back quickly blew away like dead leaves in a hurricane as he sucked the other man's cock deep into his mouth, his nose rubbing against the soft down of Jake's pubes.

He softly moaned again when Jake's hands settled on his head, twining in his hair. "Don't forget my balls, boy."

With a hand curled around Jake's cock, Ben dove to it. He laved his tongue over the man's sac as Jake drew his knees up and spread his legs wide to give him better access.

He took one, then the other ball into his mouth, back and forth, alternating that between licking and sucking Jake's shaft and slowly fisting his cock. He swirled his tongue around the cut head, tracing the ridge, over his glans, back down again. Even tracing his taint but not quite going as far as his ass.

His Sir hadn't told him to do that yet, and he didn't want to push the man too far, too fast. Meanwhile, he'd enjoy getting to learn every inch of his Sir's body, and what the man enjoyed most.

Although the mental image of being tied up while Jake lowered his ass over Ben's eager mouth for him to rim him nearly made Ben come just from the thought. His own well-fucked ass, pleasantly aching from last night's fun, clenched in anticipation.

He'd never ask his Sir to do something he wasn't ready for or didn't want to do.

But that fantasy would also burrow deep in his mind, he knew. The thought of maybe his Sir one day wanting to do *that* to him.

For now, he was more than happy to settle for whatever Sir wanted to do.

And he wasn't even Jake in his mind anymore. Remembering not to call him Sir at work would be difficult.

Now he had the freedom to call him Sir all the time at home, without hesitation or second-guessing or worrying that it might wig Jake out.

Sir's nails raked over Ben's scalp, not pressing, not guiding, just...*there*. Ben didn't even know how long he lay there worshipping his Sir's cock and balls, the delicious haze of subspace spinning Ben deeply into that wonderful place he hadn't spent nearly enough time in lately.

"Good boy," Sir hoarsely said. "Finish me off."

Ben gladly complied, using his hands and mouth, sucking and stroking his cock, fondling his balls, eagerly anticipating swallowing a mouthful of his cum. He wanted to spend a lot of time getting to know him like this, every subtle cue his body telegraphed, the way his cock hardened, grew hotter, the way his balls tightened.

Finally, the man's body tensed as his grip on Ben's head tightened. "Yes!" Sir gasped.

He went deep, both men moaning, Sir with release and Ben happy to have brought him pleasure.

Ben didn't release his Sir's cock, falling still and holding the softening member in his mouth as Sir stroked his head.

"Good boy," he softly said. "*My* good boy."

Ben's eyes fell closed as he laid his cheek against the other man's thigh and held still, waiting.

Patiently awaiting his Sir's next order.

Jake

Jake lay there, his eyes closed, the feel of Ben's hair running through his fingers quickly becoming a familiar, welcomed sensation.

This.

This felt...*right.*

Peaceful.

Like he was where he was supposed to be.

For the first time in a long time, a sense of the world being *right* slipped over him, a feeling he'd never had while with Allison or any of the women he'd dated before her once realizing he was kinky and embracing the BDSM lifestyle and his Dominant side.

It didn't hurt that he'd just received a chart-topping blowjob, and the only ones close to it in quality had also been given to him by Ben the night before, as well as the one at the party. The delicious sensation of Ben holding his cock in his mouth didn't hurt any, either.

Finally, he patted Ben's head. "Come back up here."

Ben released his cock after placing a kiss on the head of it before he crawled up the bed and snuggled in Jake's arms, Jake draping a leg over Ben's and holding him in place.

Jake nuzzled his face against Ben's hair. "I'm going to need patience from you. I don't want to lose you."

Ben met his gaze, those sweet eyes staring into his as he smiled. "It's okay, Sir. I have more than enough patience for both of us."

"You're not a woman. I know you're not a woman and I'm not trying to treat you like one. But that's my practical frame of reference for my past relationships. I might be bi, but I've never been with a guy before. I might treat you like a girl. It doesn't freak me out that we've reached this point, beyond I don't want to fuck *us* up. So I need communication from you."

"Sir, I don't know any other way to say this, but I can't have a vanilla relationship with you if we're going to do this. I *want* you to decide things and be in total control."

"I can't micromanage you. I don't have time or energy for that."

"I don't mean that. I mean that we obviously talk and set our boundaries and protocols and rules, and once we do that, that's *it*. I want *you* to be the final authority. I *need* that from you."

"Last night—"

"Was *fantastic*."

Jake stroked Ben's jaw, stubble rasping against the pad of Jake's thumb. "Please don't interrupt me." He took a deep breath. "I lost control. And I'm sorry. I promise to do better. I *want* you to call me out when I fuck up. I'm making that an order. That you cannot submit, you *must* safeword, if I ever get out of control like that again. I promise you, I will *never* punish you for safewording. There will never be any retribution for safewording. But your first rule, the most important rule you have above all other rules, is that you *always* protect yourself and keep yourself safe, in all ways, even if it's from *me*. Understand?"

"Yes, Sir."

"However…" He lightly tapped Ben on the chin. "We *are* going to work up to where you will have punishment for breaking rules. That's different."

"Yes, Sir."

"Can you accept that?"

"I prefer it, Sir."

"Why?"

Ben tipped his head enough he could kiss Jake's thumb. "Because I'll feel safer that way."

"Safer?"

"More secure. With our relationship. That you're paying attention."

"You realize the goal is to *not* earn punishment, right? I'm a sadist. You want to be beaten, all you have to do is ask. I only have fun beating a willing ass, not one suffering punishment. I *hate* doling out punishment."

Ben smiled. "Yes, Sir. I mean…" He thought about it for a moment. "It means you care."

"I *do* care." Jake's thumb stilled. "I wanted to speak up when you said you were going out and thought I was just being an asshole. So I kept my mouth shut. It wasn't until I got home and knew you were out on your date that I realized how badly I fucked up by letting you go. I should have told you sooner. Hell, I should have admitted to you from the start that I was bi. Then you didn't come home or reply to my texts and it scared the crap out of me. I didn't know if you were okay or in some guy's bed or in a hospital somewhere. I know that's crazy, but it's what my brain was doing. I needed that massive kick in the balls to realize I might be losing the best thing I ever had."

Ben kissed his thumb again. "I'm sorry I scared you, Sir. I guess the battery's fried in my phone or something. Or the charging port is bad. I need to go by the phone store today."

Jake arched an eyebrow at him. "Yes, you do. Because one of our rules is if you aren't home when you say you're going to be, and I can't get hold of you, there better be an emergency involved or you'll get strokes."

"Can I ask something, Sir?"

"You can ask anything. I'm not a dictator."

"Does this mean I'm your boyfriend?"

Jake rolled on top of him and kissed him, long, slow, deep. Tenderly, tracing Ben's lips with the tip of his tongue and savoring every bit of his mouth.

"Means more than that, buddy," he said when he finally lifted his lips from Ben's. "To me, at least. If that's what you want to call it, then I'm your boyfriend, and you're mine."

Ben's arms settled around Jake, his hands resting on Jake's ass, and Jake thought it was the second best sensation in the world.

"Yes, Sir. It's what I want. I want to be your slave, and you my Master."

"Let's start with Dom and sub and go from there." Jake kissed him again, relishing it. He felt Ben's hard cock pinned between their bodies twitch as Jake slowly explored and tasted, tracing Ben's lips with the tip of his tongue again. "Let's build something strong, that's going to last."

Ben's smile warmed places inside Jake he wasn't expecting. "Yes, Sir."

"Dude, you can*not* call me that at work."

Ben's smile grew. "Yes, Sir."

Jake laughed as he sat up and stared down at the other man. "You are going to be a little bratty, aren't you?"

Ben grinned as he held up his thumb and forefinger, just a little bit apart. "Tiny bit. On occasion. *Just* to be playful. I know you don't like bratting."

"Just remember, if you brat too much for punishment, you might not like the punishment I dole out."

"Yes, Sir."

"Now then." He rested his palms against Ben's chest. "I need my first lesson."

"In what?"

Jake slid down Ben's body, climbing between his legs and pushing his thighs apart. Ben's erect cock lay against his abs. "I've never sucked a cock before."

"But Sir, you don't have to, if you don't want to."

"I appreciate that. While I'll admit I'd never met a guy before you who gave me the desire to do it, I do like the way you moan when you come. I never had a problem going down on a girl. I need a Bi-Guy 101 lesson. I'm assuming the trick is to do what I like and go from there?"

He loved how Ben swallowed hard and nodded, apparently speechless.

"Okay, then." Jake wrapped the fingers of his right hand around the base of Ben's cock, enjoying the noises the man made as he did. Slowly, making sure to tease him, he reached out his tongue and licked at the tip of his cock, loving the way it twitched in his hand.

Warm, smooth, what he'd imagined his own might taste like could he contort himself into enough of a ball that he could lick his own junk.

There is a damn good reason men usually cannot suck their own dicks. We'd never leave the house.

He started out exploring it like he might a popsicle, licking it up and down, around, working his lips over the shaft without actually swallowing it. Ben didn't seem to mind his technique. Every time Jake looked up Ben's body, he spotted his wide-eyes staring back at him.

Finally, while their gazes were locked, Jake took the plunge. He raised his head and started at the tip, slowly sliding Ben's cock between his lips, over his tongue. He'd tasted his own pre-cum before, so he wasn't shocked or surprised by the taste of Ben's. Salty, slightly tangy, before more of Ben's cock slid over his tongue as far back as Jake could take him before gagging.

I'll have to work on that.

It'd be a point of pride that he couldn't have his slave doing something like that better than he could.

He backed off, until just the tip was still between his lips, before slowly long-stroking again. He was able to get a little more of Ben's cock into his throat, but not all the way to the balls like Ben could. So he took up the extra with his fingers and used them to help stroke him, until seconds later, he felt Ben's shaft harden, grow hot, and then—

Ben's long, low moan of pleasure arrived about the same time his load did. Jake went deep again, swallowing, not stopping to think about the ramifications of what he was doing, that this was his first load of cum swallowed that originated from another man's balls.

Yeah, he'd tasted his own before, no big.

Ben gasped for air, jaw gaping, as Jake sat up. He smiled and stretched out on his side next to Ben, propped up on one arm.

"How was that for my first time?"

Ben stared at him, slack-jawed, before he started laughing.

"I hope that's good laughter."

Ben nuzzled in close, adorable. "Yes, Sir. *Very* good laughter."

Jake tried cuddling with him again. Ben was three inches shorter than him, built slimmer, even though bulkier than Allison.

No rounded curves on him like she'd had, either, meaning he fit even more perfectly against Jake's side.

Jake found himself nuzzling the top of Ben's head, loving the feel of Ben's hair against his cheek. "Think you can help me improve my technique?"

"There wasn't anything wrong with your technique that time."

"I need to go deeper."

He felt Ben's fingers trail along his side, down his abs. "Thank you, Sir," he softly said.

"For what?"

"For that. I know that was a big deal."

"Not really. I mean, okay, yeah, in terms of being my first time with all of *this*, maybe. But seriously, I like to reciprocate. I *enjoy* doing that. Is it TMI to admit I loved tying Allison up and doing oral for forced orgasm play with her?" He kissed the top of Ben's head. "Just wait until I'm feeling more confident and I start doing tease and denial on you, boy."

"Is there anything you don't want me to do to you, Sir?"

His implication was clear. Jake thought about it. Yes, there was, for now. Something he'd like to try one day. "Give me a little time to settle in and get used to things. I don't mind a little exploration down there, if you want."

Ben tipped his head back, their lips almost touching. "That's fine, Sir. I don't mind even if you never let me do that. This is *way* more than I ever hoped for."

Jake lost himself in kissing Ben, exploring, finding out Ben liked it when he got a little rough, nipping and sucking his lips and tongue.

He'd have to remember that. It'd been over three years since he'd had a new lover, and he'd have to not only get used to Ben, but Ben's anatomy.

Sliding a hand up Ben's abs, he found a nipple and started teasing it, pulling another moan from him.

"*Ooh*, Sir likey. I can see there will be nipple clamps in your future. Maybe nipple rings at some point."

"Yes, Sir."

He cupped Ben's cheek. "Look at me." Ben's eyes fluttered open again. "Okay, so here's the thing. Don't wholesale agree to stuff just because you're in subspace. If this is going to last, don't let me burn you out because you want to obey. We need to have limits."

Ben seemed to consider it. "No watersports, no scat. That still applies. Preferably no bruises or marks I can't hide at work." He smiled. "No sharing me." Then his smile faded. "That applies to you, too, right?"

"Oh, you're going to keep my hands full, no worries. My sexuality might be fluid, but my relationship status ain't. I'm hard-core monogamous, and expect you to be, too."

Some of the tension drained from his body. "Thank you, Sir."

"I'm not a sharer. My problem was, in the past, I could play with someone and not get attached to them. I got attached *to* you before I played *with* you. I was just too stupid to admit it to you."

Now came the playful, sexy smile, the little half-quirk of Ben's lips that hardened Jake's cock.

Jake continued. "Because I'm attached to you, I'm too fucking possessive to watch you date and sleep with someone else. I think we've proved that. I'm too possessive to share you with someone romantically, and in all honesty, I have no desire to date anyone else, much less sleep with them or play with them."

"I didn't move in meaning for things to happen like this."

"I know you didn't. Neither did I. Just another sign this was meant to happen, though, right?"

"Right."

"Anything else?"

Ben licked his lips, and the gesture was so cute Jake wanted to kiss him for it.

So he did.

"I really liked you fucking me last night, Sir. But again, if it's not something you're comfortable with—"

"I *loved* fucking your ass. That was hot."

"Thank you, Sir."

"Okay, I know I said I might put you in chastity, and I might. For limited times. For a scene. But I *enjoy* making you come. The only rule is that any time you come, it's under *my* terms. I want there to be pleasure in this for you, too, not just for me."

Ben nuzzled his head against Jake's chest again. "Thank you, Sir."

"Buddy, we'll figure this out. I'll try to be patient, you try to be patient, and don't hesitate to call me out. All right?"

"Yes, Sir."

"Now. We need showers, we need breakfast, and we need to figure out what the hell's up with your phone. So how about you go start the coffee and come meet me in the shower?"

Ben looked up at him again. "You want to shower with me?"

"Uh, *yeah*. We did it last night. Did I not make it clear that I'm kind of wanting to have a relationship with you?"

Ben finally smiled. "Sorry. Bad memories from…never mind."

Jake frowned. "Mort?"

His voice sounded quiet. "Yeah."

"Did that fucker what, use you in more than one way?"

"Kind of. It…it doesn't matter. He's gone."

Jake held him closer. "D/s is only part of what we do. We're already friends. We're now lovers. We're boyfriends. We're also people and partners, and maybe you want me to be Sir all the time. I get that. But there will be times I need to be Jake, and if you want me to be Sir, you're going to have to carry the burden of it in your head. Just like if you're not in the mood to be boy, I'm not going to force you to be all subby and whatever. We're *real* people."

Ben hooked a leg around Jake's. "Thank you, Jake," he whispered.

Point understood.

Jake leaned in and kissed him again, sliding a hand up his back to fist Ben's hair. "And even if we're not actively Sir and boy, we still *are* Sir and boy. In my heart and my head, that will always be there, just like you're always my boyfriend."

"Keep saying that, please."

"What?"

"*That.* Boyfriend."

Jake nuzzled his nose against Ben's. "Boyfriend," he whispered. "*My* boyfriend."

Ben's eyes fell closed, a happy sigh escaping him.

"Something else Mort never said?"

"No, Sir. I was only property to him. He made that perfectly clear."

"You're my property, too." Ben's eyes opened. "My most precious property, which I plan on guarding and nurturing and taking *very* good care of."

Chapter Twenty-Three

Ben

Jake headed for the bathroom while Ben went to the kitchen to make their coffee. It wasn't bullshit to say Ben felt lighter in spirit than he had in months, ever since the shit with Mort started falling apart.

Hell, even before then, Mort had never made him feel like this.

Talks like they'd just had never happened with Mort. He commanded and expected Ben to obey. That was okay in the context of a scene, but it didn't make for the best relationship.

Then again, what they'd had wasn't a relationship as much as it had been a parasitic condition on Mort's part.

Even more than Ben ever realized.

He'd just been too blind to see it at the time, too caught up in the role of daily life, working, taking care of their place and doing all the chores because that had been beneath Mort.

The bathroom was already steamy when Ben walked in and stepped into the shower. He wasn't expecting it when Jake pulled him into his arms and kissed him before he started soaping up Ben with his bare hands.

Including spending a lot of time on Ben's cock.

Which produced a fairly predictable result.

Jake laughed. "Now you get to wait until tonight for some relief, buddy."

Ben fought the urge to pout. "Tonight?"

"Oh, I plan on keeping you worked up in a frenzy all day." He leaned in and kissed Ben. "And no underwear today. Commando."

Ben swallowed hard. "Yes, Sir." That would feel interesting against his ass.

Which Jake was currently running his hands over. "Still feel like going to the club tonight? We get out of here early enough, we could hit Sigalo's with Tilly and the gang."

"Yes, Sir."

Jake

An hour later, they were at the mall but there was a line in the phone store. It'd be at least a thirty-minute wait until Ben's turn.

"If you want to go look around, Sir, I'll stay here."

"You sure?"

"I don't mind."

Jake leaned in and brushed a kiss across his lips. "Thanks, babe." He ambled through the mall, opting to give a wide berth to the store where Allison worked. Even though it was a large department store, one of the mall's anchor stores, and there was little chance of him actually running into her, he opted not to press his luck.

She'd sent him a couple of text messages the first week after they'd broken up, texts that he'd deleted without response, but he hadn't heard from her since then.

While he'd expected more push-back from her early on, and had nervously been waiting for an ugly blow-up from her, the longer he went without hearing anything the more he relaxed.

He'd emerged from one store after making a quick purchase when he heard a woman's voice.

"Jake?"

Ann, Allison's roommate, walked toward him.

Shit. "Hello."

"What are you doing here?"

"It's a mall. I'm shopping."

"So where's your roommate?"

"What do you care?"

"Because you broke up with my friend, that's why. And when I looked on FetLife last night, I happened to see you and Mort's boy-toy had changed your statuses to you're protecting him."

"Do you have a point?" He really didn't want to get into this conversation with her. Allison hardly ever went onto FetLife. In fact, when he'd looked at her profile when he'd changed stuff with Ben, it looked like she hadn't been active on the site in a couple of months.

"No." She looked him up and down. "I keep telling her you did her a favor."

"Then what's the problem?"

She smirked. "No problem. Just funny how all of a sudden, you and Ben are all over each other's feeds."

He made a mental note to block Ann from his profile when he got home. "Funny how?"

"Just…curious." She started walking away. "Very curious."

"What business is it of yours?"

She turned. "None whatsoever." She smiled. "Just curious."

He watched her walk away, toward the store where she worked with Allison.

Dammit.

Fortunately, the cell phone store was at the other end of the mall. He waited until Ann was out of sight to make a beeline for the phone store. They'd parked at an entrance close to it, so the chances of them running into Allison, as long as they headed straight to the car when they finished, were slim to none.

He hoped.

Ben was still waiting. "You all right, Sir?"

"Fine. Just ran into Ann. Allison's roommate. They work here."

A mask seemed to drop over Ben's face. "Oh."

"No worries. I just want to get this done and get back home."

"Yes, Sir."

Jake didn't want to let this go like that. He lowered his voice and stepped in close. "She's history. She texted me a few times that first week but I deleted them. I'll even block her number, if you want me to."

He seemed to be considering it before he finally shook his head. "No, Sir. I trust you."

He smiled. "Good boy."

Ben

They were back home by one that afternoon with a new phone for Ben. And Ben was ready to change into something more comfortable.

Like being full-on naked.

"Oh, got something for you while you were in the phone store." Jake pulled a tiny padlock out of his pocket and snapped it onto the collar's buckle, locking it on him.

"Where'd you get that?"

He grinned. "From that luggage store." He handed one key to Ben. "Put that on your keyring, please. I'll put the other one on mine."

Ben stared at it for a moment before throwing his arms around Jake and kissing him. "Thank you, Sir!"

Jake grinned. "You love that, wait'll I get a matching set and lock your collar and your cuffs on you at the same time."

Ben shivered. "Yes, Sir. Thank you!"

Ben went to put the key on his keyring. He was hoping they'd actually fool around some that afternoon, but then Jake returned from outside.

"I forgot to get pool chemicals. I need to run out again and get them before they close. The place I use isn't open on Sundays."

"Oh. Want me to go with you?"

Jake pulled him in for a kiss. "No, you have chores to finish. I want tomorrow to be a totally us day, no chores other than dishes. Okay?"

"Yes, Sir."

"Be my good boy. Don't play with yourself."

"I'll be good, Sir."

Jake left. Ben busied himself doing laundry and cleaning the floors when he heard a car return. Thinking it was Jake, he peeked through the viewfinder on the front door.

Ben didn't recognize the car that had pulled into the driveway, but he'd managed to yank a pair of shorts on before the doors opened and Jake's parents emerged.

Crap.

He snagged a T-shirt off the back of the couch and was pulling it on over his head when he realized he was still wearing his leather collar.

Crap!

He bolted down the hallway to Jake's bedroom, where he'd left his keys, and retrieved them from the dresser just as the doorbell rang. It took him two tries and looking in the mirror to get the key into the lock and get it opened and the collar unbuckled and off his neck. He left it sitting on the dresser and ran back down the hall toward the living room, taking a deep breath before answering the door.

Ed Murray almost seemed taken aback to see Ben standing there.

"Hey, Mr. Murray. Mrs. Murray. How you doing?"

"We dropped by to see Jake."

Ben stepped aside. "He's not here, but you're welcomed to come in, if you'd like."

There was something...odd about the expression on the older man's face. "Where is he?"

"Out running errands. He probably won't be back for at least an hour, or longer. You can call him, if you'd like."

Joyce Murray looked like she'd rather lick a public toilet than step inside the house with him there. "He didn't say he was going to be out today. I texted him and told him we were thinking about dropping by."

Dammit. Ben didn't want to get into any kind of pissing contest with his guy's parents, but he also knew he had to be careful not to appear to be anything other than a friend for now, until Jake had a talk with them and broke the news to them about them being together. That was Jake's news to reveal, not his. Out of respect for his lover and Master, if nothing else, he'd keep the peace.

"I'm sorry. I remember he said something about that, but honestly, I don't keep track of his schedule." *Liar.* "I only knew about the errands because he asked if I needed anything from the store." *Liar.* "But feel free to come in and wait. I'm sure he'll be happy to see you." *Pants not just on fire, but* flamingly *explosive.*

Joyce hugged her purse a little more tightly against her body but didn't step forward. "You don't know how long he'll be?"

Not quick enough, apparently. "Sorry, no. He didn't say." And hopefully they wouldn't want to hang around so long it would bork their plans to go to Sigalo's and the club.

"Never mind," Ed Murray said. "We'll try to call him later."

They had been gone about ten minutes when Jake returned.

Ben pulled on shorts, but left his collar on—which had gone back on his neck as soon as he saw the Murrays' car pull out of their driveway—as he walked out to help him.

"Did your parents call you?" Ben asked.

"They've texted me a few times." He pulled his phone out of his back pocket. "Oh, I guess I did miss a call from them. Why?"

"They showed up here."

Jake groaned. "Sorry, buddy. What happened?"

Ben filled him in as he helped Jake tote the containers of pool chemicals around back to the lanai.

"Sorry about that. I'll call them in a little while." He pulled Ben into his arms. "And now that I'm home, you can get naked again."

Ben felt his cock already inflating. "Yes, Sir."

Jake grinned. "I'm sooo teasing you until tonight."

Jake

Jake noticed when they walked into Sigalo's that night holding hands, Tilly was the first to spot them. She jumped up with a huge, ear-splitting *squee* and ran to hug both of them.

"*Yes!* That's twenty you each owe me," she called over her shoulder to where Leah, Loren, and Shayla sat with their respective men toward one end of the table.

Rebecca was supposed to be at the club tonight. Jake wanted to talk to her about making a custom day collar for Ben, because he wanted to collar him next Saturday night at the club.

Like hell he'd wait. Might not be a wedding, but he wanted a tangible reminder on his boy *now* to remind Ben who owned and loved him until they had their wedding and he put a ring on that man's hand.

Which led him to thinking about how he wanted to propose. But the collaring first, to make sure his guy was happy with him.

Then a wedding.

At one point, after Ben asked for permission to leave to use the restroom, Tilly stood and rounded the table so she could lean in and speak into Jake's ear.

"Good job, you. Finally got off your damn ass and claimed him."

His face heated. She wouldn't be so proud of him if she knew the exact circumstances. "Yeah. I want to collar him next Saturday night at the club, but I want it to be a surprise."

"We can do that. Leave it to me. Lucky for you, we had a scheduling change and I don't have to work full-time in LA for a couple of months. Loren and I will handle it."

"Thanks."

"You just have him there at five. We'll do dinner and everything right there. E-mail me a guest list."

"*Wow*. Thanks."

She grinned. "You thank me *now*. I'll hire Kel and Mal to take pics. *You* get to pay them." She kissed his cheek before bouncing around the table to retake her seat.

Landry arched an eyebrow at him. "Welcome to the Scheming Female Zone." He lifted his glass of iced tea in a toast.

Jake returned it, smiling.

Chapter Twenty-Four

Ben

Over the next week, they managed to not fuck themselves into exhaustion, somehow.

Not that Ben was complaining.

He knew they were going to Venture early on Saturday night, and while Jake wouldn't tell him why, Ben suspected based on some of their deep conversations over the past several days that he *knew* why.

But if Jake wanted it to be a surprise, it'd be a surprise.

Plus he didn't want to get his hopes up just to be wrong, even though on Thursday Jake had run out at lunch time, alone, on an errand he wouldn't tell Ben about.

Ben lay draped over Jake in bed early Saturday morning when his cell phone started vibrating on the bedside table.

"I should beat you for that," Jake mumbled from his side of the bed.

"Sorry, Sir." He grabbed it and couldn't process the number at first. A local number, vaguely familiar, then he realized who it was.

"Ben Hodges," he answered.

"Mr. Hodges, this is Detective Lorne Jacobs from the Sarasota County Sheriff's Office."

"Yes?"

"This is a courtesy call to let you know we arrested Mortimer Grimes last night. We've already notified the state attorney's office that he's in custody, so you might want to get in touch with your contact there to keep tabs on this case."

Relief flowed through him. "They caught the sonofabitch?"

"Yes, sir. He's currently being held without bond because he's a flight risk. You are not his only victim."

When Ben got off the phone with him twenty minutes later, Jake was sitting up, watching him, patiently waiting for the details. After Ben finished going through it with him, Jake hugged him.

"Congratulations! Now we can talk to Ed and have him follow the case for you."

"I don't know if I can afford that."

Jake cupped Ben's chin in his hands. "*We* can afford it together," he said.

"But what about getting you a new car?"

"This is more important."

"But...I can't ask you to do that."

Jake gently shook him. "You're not asking me. I'm *telling* you. You're my guy, and this is what's happening."

How ironic the differences, the vast gulf between Mort and Jake. Mort had been a selfish user, taking all he could, even more than Ben had been willing to give. At first, he'd thought it was sexy and hot...until he realized that was the only facet to the guy.

Jake "used" him, too, but only in the ways Ben loved, the ways that melted his knees and which were mutually satisfying.

"You all right?" Jake asked.

"Yes, Sir. Just realizing something."

"What's that, buddy?"

"That all these years we've been friends, I never dreamed we'd be where we are right now. And I can't imagine *not* being here with you."

"Well, that's better, right? I mean, not that Mort screwed you over. I mean we grew and matured and were best friends first. We both know what we do and don't want in a relationship. No stupid games. No bullshit."

"Yes, Sir." He realized something. "Oh! I need to get our coffee. Sorry, Sir." He started to get out of bed when Jake caught his hand.

"Bring back an implement with you. Any implement. Your choice."

"Sir?"

Jake grinned. "I think it's time someone needs to begin our weekend mornings with spankings. To wake up and start the day right. Just a few swats."

Ben's cock swelled, throbbing at the thought. "Yes, Sir. Thank you." This had been part of their discussions, a plan Ben was wholly on board with.

Because he knew it would make him horny, and he'd start his Saturday and Sunday mornings focused on his Master and deep in the headspace he loved and craved.

No way in hell would he say no to *that*.

* * *

FOR THEIR TRIP to Venture that night, Jake told Ben what to wear and had him leave the house wearing his leather collar, but without the lock on it. Jake had him hand over his wrist and ankle cuffs, and Jake stowed them in his implement bag.

Even though it was early, there were quite a few cars parked in the Venture lot already. Before shutting off the car, Jake turned to Ben.

"Serious question, Jake to Ben. Are you happy with what we have?"

Ben nodded. "Yes, Sir."

He watched Jake try not to laugh. "I said Jake to Ben, not Sir and boy."

"Sorry, Sir."

"Okay, dude, now you're just bratting."

"No! I mean—" He struggled for a way to say it that would make sense. "This *feels* right. Calling you Sir feels like the way things *should* be. I know you said we're Dom and sub, Sir and boy, but honestly? In my heart, and in my mind, you're my Master, and I'm your slave. You told me last week that sometimes I'd have to carry the burden of that in my head. So I do. And I carry it like that."

Jake stroked Ben's cheek before he leaned in and kissed him. "Master and slave, *hmm?*"

"Yes, Sir. Even if we're Jake and Ben, you're my Master, and I'm your slave."

Jake smiled. "Okay, then. That answers my question. Let's go on in. I think you already have an idea what's going to happen."

Ben's heart raced as Jake led him inside. No one was in the office, they were all inside and when the two of them walked through the door, cheers and applause broke out.

Ben struggled not to start crying, happy he had guessed right.

Jake left the implement bag by one of the benches on the old side and led Ben to the front of the room, where he snapped his fingers and pointed at the floor in front of him.

Loren walked over, smiling, a small satin bag in her hands. And, Ben noticed, Kel and Mal were there, taking pictures and filming from an angle that only captured the three of them.

Loren handed the bag to Jake, who didn't open it at first. Everyone settled, quieting as Loren started to speak.

"You all know why we're here today, so let's get going so we can get to the grub and fun."

"That sounds like a bad name for a sex toy store," Gilo called out from the back of the audience.

From the other side of the room, Tilly started laughing. "Sorry, buddy," she called back. "My gimpy hand won't let me chase you today."

"That's okay, sweetie. I'll take a rain check."

She blew him a kiss.

Everyone roared with laughter, Ben cracking up because even though Jake's gaze never left his, he, too, was smiling.

When the obligatory Gilo-induced laughter subsided, Loren continued. "These guys have been friends for a long time, and it took them a few side-trips and detours to finally find the right path. I'm honored to be here to witness these two men taking this step to demonstrate their love and commitment for each other. Jake?"

Jake took a deep breath. "There's part of me that wishes I hadn't wasted so many of our years as friends not seeing what was in front of me the whole time. Then there's another part of me who knows that things had to happen the way they did for me to really see *you*. All of you, and how what we have together, and who we are together, fits together.

"No great shocker, everyone thought I was straight all these years. Didn't really care people didn't know I was bi. It didn't matter. Until it did matter. Because I was terrified that I was going to screw up and lose you, when I never even realized I had you, at first.

"I love you, Ben. I love you in a way and more deeply than I've ever loved anyone before in my life. I love you, I'm in love with you, and I want to not just be your friend or your lover or you boyfriend. I want to be your Master. I want to protect you and own you and be there, by your side. I want you to call me out if I screw up, and I want the strength of your love behind me on those days when I feel like I don't have any of my own.

"I promise, in front of these people, friends I respect, that I'll never cheat on you, I'll never share you, I'll never leave you, and I'll cherish and take care of you as the most precious thing in my life, because that's what you are. You are the most precious, and I don't want to see what life would be like without you. And I'll always be there, as long as you want to be my lover, my boy, my partner—my slave. You already own my heart and my love. Will you please allow me the honor of owning you?"

Ben nodded, tears welling in his eyes and grateful that Loren ducked in to press a tissue into his hand.

"Ben," Loren said. "What would you like to say?"

It took him a moment to compose himself, and even then, he still felt the tears rolling down his cheeks. "I love you, Sir. I trust you. I can't imagine life not being like this between us. I spent a lot of years bouncing around, but I guess that had to happen for this to happen. I can't imagine any greater honor than to be your slave. I want you to own me. I want you to be the man I call Master, because for years I've called you friend. And I only want you."

Loren spoke up. "Jake, are you asking this man to be your slave?"

"I am."

"Ben, are you asking to give yourself to this man as your Master?"

"I am."

"And Ben, are you asking this of your own free will?"

Ben stared up at Jake. "Of my own free will, I'm asking you, Jake, to please be my Master and collar me as your slave."

Jake finally opened the satin bag he'd been holding. From it, he withdrew a chainmaille bracelet, and now Ben knew why Jake had been so eager to talk to Rebecca the week before. It was made from stainless steel rings, a heavy weave, except for one green ring near one end.

Jake studied it for a moment before he spoke. "I asked Rebecca to make this for you, not sure if I would be collaring you tonight as my submissive or my slave, because I wanted to know from you before I did it what you wanted. She does beautiful work, and it's perfect. I asked for her to include one ring that was different."

Jake

Jake struggled not to cry as he shoved away memories that nearly made him ill, of him losing control.

Of him coming very close to ruining what they had before they even had it.

Of him not being very "masterly."

"I asked for one ring to be different because I always want to be reminded that I am not perfect. When I look at this bracelet that you willingly wear as a symbol of our commitment, I want to see that one ring and be reminded that I have been given the greatest gift on the face of the planet. I want to be reminded why I always have to try to do better, to always put you first in my life.

"I also wanted *you* reminded of our rule above all others—that your first priority is to always take care of yourself, protect yourself, and keep yourself safe, even if that means keeping yourself safe and protected from *me*. I want that one little ring to always be a reminder that you are my slave, but you have an obligation by taking this collar to call me out and safeword if at any time I do something to violate that rule.

"By accepting this, it means we are committed to each other, and it means from this point forward, outside of any circumstance that violates our main rule, you accept my word as law in our home."

"Yes, Sir. I want that."

"Right wrist."

Ben held it up and Jake hoped his fingers weren't trembling as he fastened it around Ben's wrist. Then he leaned in and kissed him, hard, fisting Ben's hair and showing him publicly in a way he didn't often get to that he meant every damn word.

"Love you," he whispered.

Ben's face beamed. "Love you, too, Sir."

Chapter Twenty-Five

Jake

From their Sunday morning spanking, and then the rest of the week that followed, Jake knew he'd never been happier in his life than he was at that point. Six days after the collaring, and one day short of five weeks after Ben had moved in, and Jake *knew*.

Ben had been his friend for ten *years*.

He'd agreed to be his slave.

Now it was time to make it for life.

Jake still wasn't exactly sure how to spring the proposal. He'd been tossing around various ideas, and decided to play it by ear, even as he took Ben out to dinner Friday night after work.

Any time they were alone together like this, Jake noticed how Ben frequently touched his bracelet, which he wore whenever he didn't have his leather cuffs on. At home, it was the leather cuffs and collar. Out in the real-world, it was the bracelet.

As good in Jake's mind as a wedding ring.

As he imagined matching bands on their left ring fingers, he felt his cock twitch in his pants.

This man was *his*. Fuck going slow, he wanted to make sure he didn't let him get away. If he didn't know him well enough in ten years, he was never going to know him.

Throughout dinner, he'd thought about popping the question, but it didn't feel…right. The restaurant was busy, and while they were both in a good mood, Jake realized he wanted to be alone when he asked his guy.

An idea formed.

Why not *show* Ben tonight how much he was ready to make this for life?

He didn't have a ring for him, because he wanted Ben to help him pick out their wedding bands. He wanted them to match, to be a public statement of their love and commitment, one that vanillas and kinksters could understand and interpret.

When they returned home and Jake locked the front door behind them, he stopped Ben before he could leave the entryway.

"Hold up."

"Sir?"

"I know it's barely five weeks since you moved in, but I'm not going to wait any longer." He pulled Ben close and kissed him. "Tonight, there's something I want you to do for me."

"Yes, Sir?"

Jake nuzzled noses with him. "Time for me to switch things up a little. I want my boy to show me what he's got."

<hr>

Ben

"What are you asking me to do, Sir?"

Jake stared down at him with those sweet brown eyes. "I've

always said that, as a Top, I wouldn't want to do something to someone that I wouldn't be willing to have done to me."

Ben swallowed hard. "I'm not a Top, Sir. Or a switch. You know that. Please don't ask me to do that." The thought of taking a cane or paddle to his Master's ass nearly made Ben sick to his stomach.

Receiving it? Sure, no problem.

Dishing it out?

Nope.

"I meant in bed." Jake rested his hands on Ben's shoulders, never looking away, never breaking eye contact. "If we're going to do this thing for life, and mean it, then there's something I want you to do for me."

Ben started to grok what he was asking. "You want to catch?"

Jake arched an eyebrow at him and nodded. "Fair's fair. I once offered to let Allison peg me if she wanted, because I was curious more than anything, but she said no." Jake pulled Ben in again, his hands dropping to Ben's waist, his lips just above Ben's. "I want to spend the rest of my life with you. That means I want to know what the hell I'm doing."

His words spun through Ben's brain. "Sir?" Ben struggled not to pass out as he contemplated the implications.

Jake's eyebrow arched. "Unless you don't want to marry me. But I kind of thought I had been putting out those vibes."

"Marry?"

Jake smirked, the corner of his mouth turning up in that playful way Ben loved. He leaned in and kissed him between every word he spoke. "Will...you...marry...me?"

Ben rose up and kissed him, hard, grabbing him and holding on tightly. "Yes, Sir. I want to marry you."

Jake's arms tightened around him. "You scared me for a minute there, buddy."

"I just...I mean..." He swallowed. "Yes. Yes, Sir. I'll Top you in bed."

"Not even sure I'll like playing the little spoon, but I want to do it at least once. Obviously, I want my first time to be with the guy I love and plan to spend the rest of my life with. I want to show you how serious I am about this."

Ben reached up and cupped his cheek. "I love you, too, Sir."

Jake grinned. "Think of it this way. If I turn out not to really care too much about you fucking me, but you have fun doing it, then I'll dangle that over your head as a special treat for you to earn from time to time for being my very…good…boy."

He leaned in and sucked on Ben's lower lip, nipping, making him moan. "I plan on keeping my boy on his toes and always wanting more."

"I'll always want more with you, Sir. But what about your parents?"

A cloud crossed Jake's features for a brief moment before passing. "Fuck 'em. If they don't like who I marry? That's their problem, not mine. I'm forty-one years old. I haven't been happier in my entire life than I've been over the past several weeks. When I weigh that information, it means I'd be an idiot not to put a ring on your finger."

"They're going to disown you. They'll think you're gay."

"I. Don't. Care. Gay, bi, pan—nuances about sexuality will be lost on them. Frankly, it's none of their business who I spend the rest of my life with. And I already told them I don't give a shit about an inheritance."

Jake reached down and cupped a hand over Ben's crotch, where his cock strained against the front of his jeans. Jake's gaze narrowed. "Maybe I'll put a ring through the end of your cock, too. Something to lead you around by."

Ben's breath rushed through his lungs. "Whatever Sir wants," he whispered, hornier than hell. "I belong to Sir."

Jake squeezed again, lowering his lips to Ben's for a long, deep kiss. "And that's the other thing," Jake finally said when he broke their kiss. "Even before we played the first time, you were *showing* me you wanted to be mine. When I look back, I compare what I had with Allison to what we have. I dated her, what, three years? Never did I feel for her what I feel for you. She never acted the way you do, either. Ever."

Jake's hand over Ben's crotch lightly squeezed him again. "I can't deny I need someone who *needs* to be submissive to me. I don't want to play it on the weekends as a game. You're not just a submissive—you're a slave. *My* slave. You've spoiled me. You showed me that I can't be a weekend Dominant. I *need* to be a Master full-time. It's who I am. I never had a partner before who brought that out in me and wanted that part of me. You have a cock. So what?"

Ben nodded, speechless.

Jake reached up with his other hand and scruffed the back of Ben's neck. "Do you want to be my full-time slave, boy? For the rest of our lives?"

"Yes, Sir. Please."

"Lucky timing on our part, too. Same-sex marriage is finally legal. No bullshit to go through to protect ourselves." Jake backed him against the wall, nipping his lower lip again. "Marry me, buddy. Marry me before I fuck this up and scare you off."

Ben reached up and pulled Jake's lips down onto his, grinding his hips against him as he did. "Yes, I'll marry you, Sir."

Jake braced his hands against the wall on either side of Ben's head, grinning down at him as he ground his hips back into Ben's, pressing his ass against the wall.

"My *husband*," Jake whispered, his lips just over Ben's. "That get you hard? If you loved it when I called you my boyfriend, think about what I can do to you when I introduce you to people as my *hus…band*."

He drew it out, Ben's low, long needy moan swallowed by Jake's lips crushing his again. How the hell was he supposed to pitch to his guy in bed when just the man's *voice* could melt his spine into the texture of warm Jell-O?

Then he had an idea. "Bedroom, Sir? Please? Before you make me nut right here in my jeans."

Jake grinned. "Is someone horny?"

"Someone's always fucking horny with you, Sir."

"Good boy." He pushed away from the wall and let Ben go first, leading the way to Jake's bedroom.

Officially *their* bedroom now.

They both stripped. Ben grabbed Jake and kissed him, leading him into the bathroom, into the shower. If they were going to do this, they'd do it all the way.

After showing Jake how to clean himself out—and after using up all the hot water with Ben then teasing him with his fingers—they were both hard and horny and eager to get to the fucking.

With Jake on his hands and knees on the bed, Ben took his time carefully lubing the other man's virgin hole, loving the way he could make Jake moan while playing with his gland and careful not to get him so worked up he busted a nut right there.

Once he knew Jake was ready, Ben sat against the headboard and handed Jake a condom. "Roll it on me, Sir," he hoarsely said.

Jake arched an eyebrow at him as he slowly ripped the pouch open. He leaned in and kissed the tip of Ben's cock before positioning the condom and slowly working it down his shaft.

Jake's gaze never left Ben's the entire time, smoky and hot and playful, all at the same time.

"Lube." Ben pointed at the tube he'd left on the bed. "Lots of it."

Knowing what this was doing to Ben, Jake slowly stroked Ben's cock after squirting a heaping dollop into his palm. He gave a deft twist at the top of each stroke, around the head, before going down again.

"Okay," Ben croaked.

Jake wiped off his hand on a towel. "How do you want me?"

"On top, Sir." He patted his thigh. "Straddle me."

Jake leaned in and kissed him first. "Are you okay?"

Ben nodded. "Just horny as hell. If you don't listen to me and do what I say, I won't give you much of a ride, either, because I'll be blowing too fast."

Jake threw a leg over Ben's hips, bracing himself against the headboard with his hands. "Now what?"

Ben took a deep breath and held his cock pointed up. "Slowly lower yourself onto me, and stop once you reach bottom. Go slow."

Jake's gaze bored into his as he did, Ben biting down on his lower lip and moaning as he felt Jake's rim press against the head of his cock.

Fuuuck...

Jake

Jake wasn't an idiot. Not about this, at least. His guy had no desire to "top" him. In any way. He wanted Jake in control, and Jake was fine with that. Just the fact that he'd positioned them both like this was more proof of that.

Still, *he* wanted this. So far, Ben had managed to work him up to a hungrily eager state of sexual arousal bordering on pain. As he felt the tip of Ben's cock press against his rim, he paused, meeting Ben's blue gaze.

Hell, the guy was close to subspace.

He slid his arms closer together, penning Ben in as he leaned in close. Moving slowly, Jake pressed down, having to bite on his own lower lip as the pinching burn of his hole being stretched threatened to outweigh the pleasure he knew he was about to feel as well as give.

Ben's other hand closed around Jake's cock, not stroking, just barely squeezing, but more than enough distraction to make Jake let out a gasp and bear down through the initial discomfort. The head of Ben's cock popped through the first ring of muscle, both men gasping as Jake paused, getting used to it. Tentatively, he started moving again, remembering how Ben did it, slowly rocking up and down, seating Ben's cock more deeply inside his channel with each stroke until he finally felt his ass press against Ben's thighs below him and he realized Ben had pulled his other hand free.

Ben blew out a breath. "Hold still, please," he whispered. "Please?"

Jake leaned in and kissed him, long, sweetly, while Ben's hand slowly stroked Jake's cock. "Such a good boy for me," Jake whispered.

An adorable squeak escaped him. "I won't last long, Sir. I'm sorry."

He was still getting used to the feel of the man's cock in his ass, but loved the way it pressed against his prostate, especially at this angle. Combined with the feel of Ben's hand stroking his cock, he suspected this wouldn't be the only time they did it like this. Might be Jake calling the shots, but this wasn't a bad position at all.

Jake flexed the muscles in his ass, noting with amusement how Ben's face contorted with ecstasy every time he did.

"Does my boy like that?"

"Yes, Sir!"

"Does my boy like fucking his Sir's ass?"

"Yes, Sir!"

He leaned in and nibbled along the side of Ben's throat, down to the curve where it met his left shoulder, and bit down, hard, until he drew a pained cry from Ben.

That should be enough to distract him temporarily.

He held his bite, even feeling Ben's hand reflexively tighten around his cock, for several long seconds. When he loosened his hold, he licked at the mark.

"Your Sir is enjoying torturing you like this, boy."

"Thank you, Sir." Ben's slurred voice told Jake yep, the man was in subspace.

Jake kissed his way over to Ben's right shoulder and repeated biting there, making a mental note to include being a well-fitting cock ring for Ben to help him hold back longer.

Yeah, this was turning Jake's crank in a really hot way. It wasn't something he'd do simply to reward Ben, or reciprocate.

He was enjoying the *hell* out of it.

Sitting back, he stared into Ben's eyes again and yep, definitely subspace. He reached down and started tweaking Ben's nipples. "Hold back and do not come until I tell you to, boy. But make me come."

Ben started stroking Jake's cock, slicking pre-cum up and down his shaft, reaching for Jake's balls with his other hand and quickly building his release as Jake slowly rode Ben's cock. He wanted to see if he could time it right, so that he came just before Ben did.

"How does it feel fucking your Sir's ass?"

"I love it, Sir!" Ben gasped.

Jake's balls tightened, his explosion imminent. "Make me come, boy."

Ben's hand sped up on his cock as Jake started slamming himself up and down onto Ben's cock. As he felt the first tight, spiraling pleasure begin, he said, "Now! Come, boy!"

Ben let out a cry as Jake's ass spasmed around Ben's cock and he tried to thrust up against Jake. Ropes of cum shot out the end of Jake's cock, all over Ben's abs, as he felt Ben's cock throbbing inside his ass. The man's expression contorted into the sexy, familiar O-face Jake had fallen head over heels in love with.

Finally falling still, Jake leaned forward and kissed him, hard, sucking Ben's tongue. "Good boy," he said, pressing his forehead against Ben's. "Such a very good boy. Love you."

"Love you, too, Sir."

Jake pulled him up, wrapping his arms around him as Ben did the same, his face pressed against Jake's chest and Jake's cum a sticky puddle gluing their abs together. As he felt Ben's cock growing soft in his ass, Jake rubbed his chin over the top of Ben's head.

"That was amazing, boy."

"Thank you, Sir. You were amazing, too."

He kissed the top of Ben's head. "Now we just have one question left to settle."

Ben didn't move, his arms still tightly clinging around Jake's body. "Yes, Sir?" he mumbled from where his lips were pressed against Jake's chest.

"Are you taking my last name, or are we hyphenating both of our last names?"

Ben started to chuckle, finally lifting his head to look him in the eye. "Really? *That's* your question right now?"

"*Mmm-hmm.*" Jake kissed him. "Are you going to be Ben Murray, or Ben Hodges-Murray?"

"Sir's choice."

"No, I asked you."

"Just Murray," Ben immediately said. "Ben Murray, husband to Jake Murray."

"Done. But why?"

"Because I want my husband's name." He nuzzled the base of Jake's throat. "I want my Sir and husband to own me in every way, including that way."

Yeah, everything was different with his relationship with Ben than it'd been with Allison.

Everything.

Everything was far more right. More perfect.

Even knowing it came with a huge responsibility to be not just a responsible spouse, but a responsible Owner and Master, it felt perfect.

It felt like he'd finally come home at last, everything clicking into place.

Chapter Twenty-Six

Ben

The next morning, Jake had left Ben home to finish chores while he ran to the grocery store. Jake had taken Ben's car, because when he'd gone to start his it made a weird noise and ran poorly, which meant another trip to the mechanic on Monday.

Tonight they would eat dinner with everyone, then on to Venture to play and to break the good news to their friends about their plans.

Jake wanted to talk to Loren about performing their wedding ceremony, since she'd performed their collaring.

Mort was in jail, he had the love of his life—who was also his Master—in bed every night...and this was like a dream come true.

His happily ever after.

Ben was folding their laundry in the living room when the doorbell rang.

Dammit.

He was naked, as ordered, his leather collar locked around his neck.

After running to the door to see who it was, he was more than a little confused to find Allison standing there when he looked through the viewfinder.

A jolt of jealousy mixed with righteous indignation shot through his gut, twisting it, followed immediately by a tsunami of satisfaction.

Jake was with *him*.

Was *his*. Wanted to be his for *life*.

Thanks to Allison being a fuckup of the first order in terms of relationship material.

It didn't matter that Jake was bi, because Jake was monogamous.

Allison wasn't a vanilla, so he felt no compunction whatsoever about leaving his collar on. He pulled on the pair of shorts he kept next to the front door for unexpected occasions and then opened it.

Her smile immediately froze, fading when she saw him standing there. "Oh, hi. Jake here?" She tried to peer around him when he sidestepped to prevent her from just walking inside like she obviously wanted to do.

"Nope, sorry."

Her gaze narrowed. "His car's here."

"He took mine. He had to go to the store, and his is acting up."

"Oh." Now she seemed to be at a loss. "Can I come in?"

"Why?" He was under no obligation to be nice to her. Especially after what he knew she'd done just before Jake broke up with her.

"I'd like to wait for him and talk to him."

"He's going to be gone for a while. He just left. Probably a few hours. Try calling him." He suspected Jake would forgive him the fib.

"I've been trying to call him. It just goes to voice mail."

That was news to Ben. Jake hadn't mentioned anything about her trying to call him. "He's not returning your messages?"

"Well, I mean I tried calling earlier today. I didn't want to leave a message."

That gave him a measure of relief. Jake hadn't been hiding that from him. "I don't know what to tell you, Allison. I'll tell him you stopped by and that you were trying to get in touch with him."

Her gaze focused on the collar around his neck. She didn't move at first, like she had something else she wanted to say.

Finally, she did. "So what's with *that*?"

If he had hackles, they'd be up over her tone. "It's my collar."

"I know *what* it is. *Whose* is it?"

Something felt completely wrong about this. "What difference does it make to you?"

"Is it Jake's?"

He braced one arm against the door, and the other against the frame. "We done here?"

"Why won't you answer my question?"

"Because, quite frankly, it's none of your damn business."

Something about the set of her jaw set him on edge even more. Her eyes narrowed. "He fucking collared *you*? *Why* would he do that? Ann said she heard he collared someone already, but not who. Three *fucking* years I dated that asshole and he never collared me!"

Apparently, she hadn't been on FetLife in a while, or she would have seen their status updates. "I don't owe you an answer."

"Is that why he moved you in here with him? Was he cheating on me? With *you*?"

"No, unlike you, Jake was faithful. He didn't have Internet lovers on the side the way you did. FYI, chatting with someone on the Internet *is* most definitely cheating, even if you've never slept with them."

She gasped, her eyes widening in shock. "How did you—"

"Buh-bye." He slammed the door in her face, throwing the deadbolt.

Sooo fucking satisfying.

Jake had changed the locks a couple of weeks earlier, just in case Allison had somehow snuck a copy of his key. But for good measure, Ben also latched the safety chain. Jake would use the garage to come in, anyway.

Watching through the viewfinder, he saw at first she looked like she wanted to pound on the door, but rethought that plan. She pulled out her cell phone and called someone as she walked down to her car. Voice mail must have picked up, because she hung up and got back into her car, slamming the door behind her.

Once she finally drove off, he retrieved his own cell phone and called Jake…who answered on the first ring.

"Hey, buddy. What's up?"

"Allison just showed up here."

"Fuck. What'd she want? I've been sending her calls to voice mail all morning, but she won't leave a message. She literally just called me again a few seconds ago."

More relief filled him. Jake would have likely told him about the calls when he'd returned home had she not shown up. "She said she wanted to talk to you." He didn't know why this next statement still stirred up a little dread. "She saw my collar and asked about it." He gave as verbatim a retelling of the conversation as he could.

Then he had to add the last bit that he'd held back. "There's something else you need to know."

"What?"

"I wasn't going to tell you this. A couple of days after I moved in, I went to the mall to pay my cell phone bill." He retold the story of overhearing Allison in the food court talking with Ann about Jake and the guy she'd been chatting with. "I didn't want to tell you. I figured it didn't matter since you'd already broken up with her, and she'd apparently not slept with anyone else. I'm sorry I didn't tell you sooner."

When Jake finally spoke again, he sounded murderous. "She thought that wasn't cheating, huh? Screw her. I'll text her a fuck-off message when we finish with this call."

"I have a bad feeling about this, Sir."

"Don't worry about it. What's she going to do? Out us? She'll make herself an outcast in the local community if she tries it, and it's not like our jobs will be at risk."

"I don't know, but you didn't see the look on her face."

"Go on FetLife and block her right now. And do me a favor, please, and log into my FetLife account, too, and block her there for me. My password list is tucked into the back of that book in the drawer of my nightstand."

Warm fuzzies fought for control over the dread trying to settle into his gut. His Sir trusted him to do that?

Even more importantly, it meant Jake had no reason to hide whatever might be in his account from Ben.

That, right there, helped calm him. "Yes, Sir. I'll do it right now."

"While you're at it, change both of our relationship statuses to add that we're engaged to each other, in addition to Owner and pet, and Master and slave. I like pet better than property."

The warm fuzzies exploded, his cock also throbbing. "Yes, Sir." It was like his guy could read his mind.

Then again, that's why he's my Sir.

"Good boy. I'll be home in a little while. I'm almost done at the grocery store. Love you."

That froze Ben's feet, in the good way. "Love you, too, Sir."

Even after the call ended, Ben stood there for a moment, smiling as he stared at his phone.

So much about this—hell, *everything* about this was different than what he'd had with Mort. Yes, Jake was his owner, his Sir. But Ben felt like a partner, not just property. It was rare that Jake didn't take Ben's opinion into consideration, even if Jake didn't decide in Ben's favor.

It was the very act of the consideration Jake adored.

Loved.

After removing his shorts again, he headed back to their bedroom to get the password list, and then to where his laptop was set up on the coffee table. It only took him a moment to do it. They'd both unfriended Allison already, even though they had several friends in common with her, Jake more than him.

Yes, they were adult men, Jake owned his home, and Ben was out to his parents.

Jake wasn't out to his parents, but it wasn't like he was beholden to them. He'd talked about coming out to them before the holidays, but he wasn't in a rush. It wasn't like he had everyday contact with them.

Their jobs were secure. Hell, one of the shop managers was gay and had married his husband the day after the same-sex marriage ban fell.

When Ben heard the garage door roll up, he pulled his shorts on again and stepped out into the garage to help Jake unload the groceries.

Jake was already on his way in with the first load, and he paused to brush a kiss across Ben's lips as he passed. "You block her?"

"Yes, Sir. From both our accounts."

"Good boy. Thank you." He headed for the inside garage door.

"Sir?"

Jake stopped and turned. "Yes?"

"I'm sorry I didn't tell you what I overheard sooner."

Jake walked back to him, tipping his head to stare into his eyes for a moment. When he spoke, it sounded soft, gentle. "It's all right. If she really didn't sleep with the guy, it didn't put you in danger. But I think we need to make appointments to get new rounds of testing done. Just in case."

"Sir?"

"I would hate myself if she did something that gave me an STI that put you at risk."

Ben couldn't help it. He threw his arms around Jake's neck, even though the man was laden with grocery bags, and kissed him, hard. "I love you, Sir."

Jake grinned. "Love you, too, buddy. But these groceries won't unload themselves. The sooner you help me, the sooner you can get inside and get naked again."

Ben flashed him a grin in reply before he turned and literally ran for the car.

Once it was unloaded and locked up, and the garage door rolled down, Ben helped Jake put the groceries away. With that done, Jake pulled him into his arms and stared down into his eyes.

"In the future," Jake said, "I want you to tell me anything like that you hear. It makes me sick to think she could have done something that would hurt you."

Damn, this was a universe apart not just from his relationship with Mort, but from any other relationship he'd ever had before. Jake might be his Owner, but Ben felt like he was the one put first, always, in every way.

"Yes, Sir. Do you want to punish me for that?"

Jake stared at him for a long, quiet moment. "Do you feel you need punishment?"

He knew Jake was laying this at his feet to decide.

"I feel I owe Sir at least five for not telling him."

Jake's hands slid down Ben's ass. "Are you ever going to hold back information from me again?" he quietly asked.

"No, Sir."

"Is there anything else you haven't told me?"

"No, Sir."

"Then go pick the implement, strip, and bring it here."

Ben ran to the spare bedroom, pulling his shorts off as he did, and grabbed the heaviest cane from the bag.

When he returned to the living room he dropped to his knees in front of Jake and held the cane up, presenting it to him.

"Good boy," he quietly said in a tone that Ben couldn't quite nail down. But when he looked, Jake wasn't smiling the way he usually did when they scened.

"Sir?"

"I told you, I don't like giving out punishment."

Ben swallowed hard. "Yes, Sir. I'm sorry."

"I'm only giving you this because you feel you need it. Understand?"

"Yes, Sir."

"Lean over the back of the couch."

Ben got into position, his ass exposed.

"These are going to be hard. I'll take them slow, and you need to count each one for me. Understand?"

"Yes, Sir." He already felt the tears trying to break free. The disappointment in Jake's voice gutted him.

"Good boy." He laid the cane across Ben's ass, but he didn't hold him down, no fist in Ben's hair or hand planted in the middle of his back. "I won't hold you down for punishment. You have to be willing to take them."

"Yes, Sir."

Ben closed his eyes and wasn't nearly prepared for the arc of pain that sliced into his flesh as Jake nailed him with the cane. He let out a cry and forced himself not to come up off the couch. "One, Sir."

Had he thought Jake was a heavy player before? Holy crap, he'd swung for the outfield with that hit.

The second wasn't any easier, and he was sobbing as he choked out, "Two, Sir."

By the time the last was delivered, he felt heartbroken, like a failure, that he'd disappointed his Sir by not telling him what he'd heard. Then he was wrapped in Jake's arms as he sank to the floor cradling Ben against him, soothing him.

"*Such* a good boy," Jake whispered, trailing kisses across his forehead. "My very, *very* good boy. I love you so much. Clean slate." Jake rocked Ben back and forth, sitting with him on the floor as he cried in his arms.

"I'm sorry, Sir. I'm sorry I disappointed you."

"It's all right, buddy. I love you. Nothing changes that. I wasn't going to punish you for it."

"But I didn't tell you."

"Clean slate. Forgiven and forgotten."

Still, Ben sat, sniffling, reluctant to move and it was obvious Jake wasn't going to make him move, either.

Eventually, he sat up and looked into Jake's face. His Sir wore a sad smile. "Better?"

"Thank you, Sir."

Jake cradled Ben's face in his hands and gently kissed him. "You're far harder on yourself than I am, buddy. You're my good boy. For future reference, I don't enjoy punishment beatings any more than you enjoy getting them. I think we need to find a different kind of punishment for cases like this. It reminds me too much of me losing control that night, and that still makes me sick to my stomach to think about. I love you. I don't want to harm you."

Ben hugged him. "I love you, too, Sir."

They sat locked together in their hug.

"You sure you're going to handle doing this with me for life?" Jake asked, but his voice had finally returned to *his* Jake, slightly playful, sounding more easy and relaxed.

Ben met his gaze. "Try and stop me, Sir. I'm a very stubborn subby."

Jake touched the end of Ben's nose with his finger. "That you are, buddy. And I wouldn't have you any other way."

Chapter Twenty-Seven

Jake

Jake ignored the way his phone vibrated on the bedside table late Sunday morning. He had no desire to open his eyes and look at it and see who was stupid enough to actually try calling him at that hour on a Sunday morning.

Couldn't be anyone who actually *knew* him very well.

Probably a telemarketer.

He had no interest in talking to anyone.

Especially not when Ben currently knelt between his legs, giving him a good-morning blow job.

Ben had quickly spoiled him with those. If Ben's nefarious plan had been to use daily good-morning blow jobs as a tool to convince Jake a relationship between them was the right call, Jake had news for him.

It worked.

Jake bent his knees at the legs and drew them up, giving Ben even better access. Access he quickly took advantage of, tracing a line with his tongue down Jake's taint and around his rim before working up to his sac. Back and forth, from cock to ass and back again, drawing it out the way Jake had quickly grown to love.

Had he taken this step with Ben before he ever met Allison, he knew damn well he'd be married to the man by now.

Not merely because of Ben's outstanding oral talents, but because Ben was the whole package. Slave, masochist, and eager slut for him in bed. Ready to serve in any manner asked of him, as long as his trust wasn't violated and he felt appreciated.

Two easy conditions for Jake to meet. He had no desire to play with anyone else, man or woman, despite Ben assuring Jake he was okay with non-sexy play.

That wasn't the point. Jake had no *desire* to play with someone besides Ben. Especially this soon into their relationship.

Jake enjoyed it, watching Ben go down on him, loving the eagerness in his lover's every move.

Jake had been with good lovers before, all women before this, of course. Allison had never, even in their early days, approached this level of eagerness to please him, a selfless submission that flowed through everything he did, and not just sexytime, either.

Reaching down, he stroked Ben's hair before his fingers settled on Ben's collar. "I'm close, boy. Get me off."

Ben set to it, increasing the speed of his strokes, his tongue knowing exactly where to flick and lick, how to suck, until a moment later when Jake's balls erupted, filling Ben's mouth.

Jake tugged on his hair, drawing Ben up the bed and into his arms to kiss him. "Good boy," he said. "Go get our coffee ready, and go pick out an implement for me. Somebody's getting their Sunday morning spanking before they're allowed to come."

Ben grinned. "Thank you, Sir." He planted one more kiss on Jake's mouth before bounding out of bed and disappearing down the hall.

This was heaven. He'd tried the weekend morning spankings with Allison before, but she clearly wasn't into them, even when orgasm play was the reward for taking them. To the point that he abandoned doing them since it was obvious she resented them.

Ben *loved* them.

How did he know that? Because despite only doing this for a couple of weeks, he could count on Ben returning with something stingy or painful, not fluffy bunny the way Allison always had. She'd grab a leather slapper that was barely able to do more than make a loud noise.

Ben grabbed the stingiest cane or heaviest paddle.

Why?

Because he knew it made Jake smile.

After getting up to use the bathroom, he returned to bed with a couple of items and waited. Ben soon reappeared with two mugs of coffee on the tray, and…

Yep. The heaviest paddle from the bag.

Ben knelt at the side of the bed and held the tray up, presenting it and the mugs. "Your coffee, Sir. And the implement."

Jake picked up the paddle first. "You realize I let *you* choose, right?"

"Yes, Sir."

"So why this one?"

"Because Sir likes the way it sounds when it hits my ass."

"That is true." He picked up his mug of coffee. Even in this simple ritual, Ben was perfect. Ben had invented it. Jake had never asked him to formally present the paddle like this, or to kneel and await further instructions, or anything.

Ben had come up with it, as if reaching into Jake's brain and finding the perfect fantasy to perform.

Jake smiled at him. "That's my good boy. You may get up and have some coffee." He sat against the headboard, sipping his own coffee, the paddle lying across his thighs. Heavy, thick, about four inches across and made of stained pine, it would not only make a noise, but would leave marks.

Ben stood and set the tray aside, sipping his coffee before setting it on the bedside table.

Jake handed him his mug to put there as well, then patted his lap with the paddle. "Assume the position."

Ben nearly threw himself across Jake's lap. This was another way the man was perfect. He wasn't reluctant in the slightest.

He was eager. Ben's stiff cock, as much as his actions, were testimony to that.

Not because he wanted pain so much as he wanted to please. Taking the pain, even pain he might not want, pleased him because he knew it pleased Jake.

Jake laid the paddle across Ben's back and stroked his ass. The marks from the night before still lay visible in his flesh. "How many strokes does my boy think he needs this morning?"

He felt Ben's cock twitch against his thighs. "At least twenty, Sir." Ben's voice already sounded a little slurred, fuzzy, subspacey.

Jake grabbed a handful of right ass cheek and dug his fingers in hard, squeezing. "Why so many?"

"Because Sir likes to train his boy."

"That's right. I do." He repeated it with the left ass cheek, loving the way Ben's body tensed over his lap. "I have fun training my boy. Especially when my boy is so eager." Jake's cock had also started hardening again, the way it predictably did when he was about to lay strokes across the other man's ass. Today, he'd fuck Ben's orgasm out of him instead of giving him the hand-job he no doubt expected.

"Thank you, Sir."

Jake picked up the paddle with his right hand and grabbed a fistful of Ben's hair with the left to hold him in place. "Ready?"

"Yes, Sir."

"Count."

He laid them on as hard as he could, stopping at ten. Then he knew from the sound of Ben's voice that he was subspacey.

"Hands and knees, boy. Don't forget where we're at in strokes."

Ben complied, no doubt confused at this change.

Jake knelt behind him, rolling the condom onto his stiff cock and slathering it with lube he'd brought from the bathroom. He also applied some to Ben's hole, wiping his hand on the towel.

"On your back," he ordered. "Legs up."

Ben flipped over, immediately complying.

Jake knelt between his legs, Ben's ankles over his shoulders, and pressed the head of his cock against Ben's rim. "Where were we, boy?"

"Ten, Sir."

Jake picked up the paddle and laid it against the outside of Ben's left thigh. "Count." He smacked him three times, hard, working his cock into Ben's ass as he did.

It was all he could do to hold back his own orgasm as his cock slid into Ben's tight channel. Who needed a pussy when he had this deliciously fantastic ass to tap on demand?

Bonus, the delicious ass belonged to a great guy he trusted and loved.

Jake switched the paddle to his other hand and smacked the outside of Ben's right thigh three more times. Back and forth, he alternated smacking him and fucking him, until all twenty strokes were issued.

Dropping the paddle to the bed, he leaned in, pressing Ben's knees against his chest as he kissed him, pinning Ben's arms over his head. "Come for me, boy." He knew at this angle his cock was perfectly sliding over Ben's prostate. It only took him a few strokes, combined with the friction of their bodies rubbing against Ben's cock, to make Ben come.

"Yes!" Jake took several hard strokes to finish with him, loving the feel of Ben's ass squeezing his cock as he came. He fell still there, Ben pinned like a pretzel below him, and sucked on Ben's lower lip. "Such a good boy."

"Thank you, Sir."

They both froze as the doorbell rang. "Who the fuck is that?"

Jake muttered, more than a little irritated that their morning post-fucking cuddle was being interrupted.

"Maybe they'll go away?" Ben whispered.

"You don't have to whisper," Jake said. "They can't hear us from there. Also, it's *our* house."

The doorbell rang again after another minute, making Jake grumble. "Okay. Fuck. Let me go see who it is. You, *stay*."

He planted a kiss on Ben's lips before he got up and went to dispose of the condom and wash his hands, pulling a robe on as he headed for the front door.

Whoever it was, he wasn't in the mood for bullshit. They were interrupting his fun, so they'd get him in a bathrobe.

He didn't even bother looking through the viewfinder before he threw the door open, just to find his parents standing there, both of them dressed up.

He bit back the angry, "What?" he'd planned on saying before it could leave his mouth. "Hey. What's up?"

"I *tried* to call you before we got here," his dad said. "I called you when we left church."

Well, that explained the phone call he hadn't even looked at on his phone. Also explained why they were dressed in their Sunday best. "We just woke up a little while ago." He realized *after* he'd said it what, exactly, he'd said.

Unfortunately, his father picked up on it. "*We?*" his father asked.

"Me and Ben. What's up?"

His mom looked confused. "You and…Ben?"

Fuck it. "Yes, me and Ben. He lives here, too, you know. *What* did you want?"

His father was apparently the designated ass-chewer that morning. "We ran into Allison at the mall last night and she had an interesting story to tell us. Frankly, we thought she was lying. We came by here but you weren't home."

"We were out."

"Out where?"

"None of your business. Now did you show up here to tell me what the woman I broke up with, who it turns out was cheating on me, said about me? Because seriously, you should have called first."

"I *tried*." His dad's face looked tight, like he was holding himself back, his tone accusatory, as if Jake should be waiting and expecting his call. "You didn't *answer*."

"Maybe because I was busy getting blown."

He honestly hadn't meant to say that out loud. And at first, for a split second, he was pretty sure he hadn't said it out loud.

Then identical expressions of shock filled his parents' faces. "What?" they both said.

Shit.

They were still standing out on his front porch, too.

"I'm *sooo* not having this conversation with you this morning," Jake grumbled.

"You *will* talk to us," his father said. "What is going on?"

Jake braced one hand on the door frame, the other on the door and hoped to salvage this conversation, even though he knew there wasn't much chance of that.

"I broke up with Allison after a lot of thought and realizing that she and I were not compatible. Also, she was pretty immature. Then it turns out she was having an online affair. So anything she says is suspect. She showed up here and gave Ben a ration of shit while I was out. She never liked Ben, because he was my friend before I even met her. So one last time—what'd she say?"

It gave Jake a little satisfaction to see his father looking unsure now. "She told us you and Ben were…together."

"You never told us she cheated on you," his mother said. It amazed Jake how she managed to sound accusatory.

"You never asked, not that it's any of your business."

His father tried to step forward. "I think we need to come in and discuss this with you."

Jake didn't move. "Uh, no. I haven't even had a full cup of coffee yet. Trust me, you do *not* want to discuss anything with me right now. It *will* get ugly."

"I'm your father, and you will let us into this house. This was my parents' house."

"Yes, and I'm forty-one years old, and the deed is in my name, and I pay all the bills for it, thank you very much."

"Look. I'm being considered to be elected as a deacon in our church. I know that doesn't mean a lot to you, but it does to me. What are people going to think if we have a gay son?"

"You don't have a gay son." Okay, so while that was the truth, they would take it a totally different way.

He felt zero guilt and gave even less fucks at that point.

Or was that fewer fucks?

Now they both looked confused. His mom spoke first. "But... what about Ben?"

Jake didn't move, but he called over his shoulder. "Boy, grab that other robe from my closet and come here. *Now.*"

"Boy?" they asked together.

Jake would swear that Ben was there less than two seconds later, bless his heart. He ran up behind Jake, holding the neck of the robe closed in such a way as to conceal his collar.

Jake turned to him. "Hands down."

Ben immediately complied despite his face growing red. Jake adjusted the neckline of Ben's robe to show the collar, then draped his arm around Ben's shoulders and pulled him against his side, giving him a kiss on the cheek just to complete the picture in case there was any doubt.

"Mom, I know damn well what kind of books you read, because I had to help you with your Kindle a couple of months back when you couldn't figure out what you'd done to it. *Fifty Shades?* Hello, we live it. Ben's my slave, I'm his Master. He's collared to me. Now, unless you plan on going to your church group or whatever they are and volunteering this information, we're certainly not making it public. I know you've never approved of Ben and I being friends because he's gay, but that's your problem, not mine. You want to disown me over this? Well, that's not very Christian of you, now, is it?"

His father went even redder in the face than Ben was. His mouth opened and closed a couple of times before he took a step back and stared at Jake's mom.

"What kind of books is he talking about?" he demanded. "What did he mean by that?"

Yep. Divide and conquer. His mom's turn to make gasping fish lips at her husband before she returned her focus to Jake. "I hope you're happy!"

Jake knew damn well how she'd meant it.

He simply was beyond caring.

He offered them both a wide smile. "Actually, I am happy, yes. Next time you show up asking incredibly rude questions about my personal life, make sure you actually *talk* to me before you show up. You might be interrupting a spanking session or something." He'd started to step back to close the door when his father found his voice again.

"I don't know exactly what's going on here, but don't make us disown you. I refuse to leave my inheritance to a gay son."

Jake had always thought seeing a red haze in anger was just a metaphorical thing in books.

Nope.

He saw red.

Literally.

"Don't worry," Jake said, keeping his tone low and steady so he didn't start screaming. "The truth about your son really doesn't matter to you, let's be honest about that. All you give a shit about is appearances, and that's the way this whole family's always been. You gave me a guilt trip when I finally was old enough to stop letting you drag me to church every Sunday. Ben's mom and dad go to church, too, and they love him exactly the way he is. They've never in their lives felt ashamed of him. They don't give a crap if he's gay and I'm not, and they love me for who I am and who I am to Ben."

He'd started to close the door when his father stepped forward again. "You're saying you're...*not* gay? Then what is this?"

If Jake wasn't so pissed off, he would have laughed. "It doesn't *matter* what I am, Dad, except *happy*. If you can't accept that your son is happy, then I'm certainly not going try to change your minds. If you ever want to have a rational conversation about this when I'm actually awake, I'll be glad to. But you don't get to judge me or how I live my life. Especially not when I'm an adult and you don't pay my bills."

Jake fought the urge to slam the door in their faces. Instead he closed it, firmly, and threw the deadbolt before also hooking the chain.

Standing there for a moment, he took a couple of ragged breaths before turning to Ben.

The man looked heartsick, sad.

Jake immediately regretted putting him through that. He pulled him into his arms. "Come here, buddy."

Ben's arms wrapped around him. "I'm sorry, Sir," he whispered, sounding on the verge of tears. "I never meant for—"

"*Shh.*" He kissed the top of his head, his forehead, working down to his lips. Outside, he heard his parents' car start up and pull out of the driveway. "You're my *very* good boy. You followed my orders exactly."

"But...but they—"

Another kiss to silence and distract Ben. "Do you honestly think I give a shit about an inheritance? I have a roof over my head, food in the fridge, and the love of my life in my bed. I have a job. I'm way luckier than a majority of the people on the face of this planet. Don't you dare feel sorry for me."

Ben stared up at him. "But what if they disown you?"

He knew Ben couldn't imagine his parents doing that to him.

His parents were the polar opposites of Jake's parents, bragging about him to their friends—including church friends—and never caring about anything other than his happiness and safety. Even to the point they were nearly obnoxiously loving to him. Ben was close to them.

"So?"

Ben didn't seem to have a response for that. Instead, he let Jake pull him in again for a long, strong hug.

"Here's the thing," Jake said. "Your parents love me. They accept me. I love my mom and dad, but honestly? They're the main reason I never came out as bi before. It was easier to let them and everyone else assume I was straight. I was in my freshman year of college before I realized bi was a thing and I wasn't just confused. They don't see shades of grey, regardless of my mom's reading habits, ironically enough."

Ben snorted. "She reads erotica, huh?"

"Holy crap, stuff to curl your eyebrows. Makes what we do in real-life look tame. Dad will flip if he logs in and sees some of those books. Ménages, gang-bangs—including gay and bi guys. I strongly suspect most of her love life happens on a Kindle screen. Which pisses me off even more, that she reads stuff like that and is still closed-minded."

"Then I feel kind of sorry for her."

"And that's one of the reasons I'm so in love with you." He started backing Ben down the hall and toward their bedroom. "Now, I think we need a shower, and I think *someone* needs another distraction."

"I thought we were going to work on the front yard today, Sir?"

"Changed my mind. Only bush I'm interested in trimming right now is yours, and that needs to be shaved."

Chapter Twenty-Eight

Ben

At least the rest of the week was calm as their wedding preparations started. Ben's parents were crazy about Jake and beyond happy that they were getting married.

Shoving the uncomfortable run-in with the Murrays out of his mind, Ben spent the week focused on work and their wedding plans. He wanted to do nothing but look forward. Mort was currently winding his way through the legal system. Based on what the prosecutor told Ben, because it was a grand theft level crime, Mort would be doing a couple of years.

Wouldn't make up for what Ben had been through, but at least he couldn't do it to someone else anytime soon.

Ben had just arrived home from work Friday evening and hadn't even had time to undress yet when the doorbell rang.

Returning to the front door, he was more than a little shocked to see Ed Murray standing on the front porch.

Shit.

This *couldn't* be good. Especially not when Ben factored in the pinched, dark glare the man wore.

Taking a deep breath, he opened the door. "Hello, Mr. Murray."

"Hello, Ben. Can I come in?"

"Jake's not here."

"I know. I didn't come to talk to Jake. I came to talk to you."

Despite the uneasy feeling congealing in his gut, Ben stepped aside to let him in. As Ed Murray walked past, Ben pulled his phone from his pocket and thumbed the controls to hit *record* on the video camera, holding it so the screen faced him and wouldn't reveal he was recording.

He shut the door and followed the man into the living room.

"What did you want to talk about?" Ben asked.

The older man turned. "How much would it take to get you to move out and forget about my son?"

Ben wasn't sure he heard him right at first. "Excuse me?" He gave thanks for thinking about recording this.

"You heard me. How much? I ran a background check on you. You're in horrible shape. If I give you money to take care of everything you owe people, how much will it take to make you go away and leave my son alone?"

"Uh, if you ran a background check on me, it wasn't a very good one. Did it show the police report and charges filed against the guy who committed identity theft on me? Did it show the fact that he's currently sitting in county jail awaiting trial? Or the credit protection service I'm paying for to prevent new cards and accounts from being opened without my permission?"

Ed frowned. "What?"

"Yeah. If you ran a background check on me, that must have come up, right?"

He didn't look nearly as sure of himself as he had before. Ben knew the guy was over eighty, even though he looked good for his age, at least ten years younger, and seemed to get around fine on his own. "Does my son even know all of that?"

"Of course he knows. He was one of the first people I told. That's one of the reasons why he asked me to move in, because until my attorney finishes fighting with the credit report companies to clear my name, I couldn't get an apartment complex to rent to me."

Apparently, that took more of the wind out of the man's sails. "So what would it take to get you to go away then? Jake wasn't gay until all this nonsense after you moved in."

Fuck showing the video to Jake as proof of what they'd discussed. Ben knew *he'd* need to watch it to make sure he didn't just have a psychotic break with reality or something.

"What?" This was way more than just a refusal to accept the facts. Maybe Jake's dad was starting to show signs of dementia due to his advanced age.

"Jake. You turned our son gay with that silly Master and slave nonsense!"

Ben wasn't sure who was more shocked when he burst out laughing, him or Ed Murray.

It took Ben a moment to compose himself. "For starters, your son's been kinky as long as I've known him. Even before. That's how we first met. That actually *predates* me. Allison? She was his submissive. And she wasn't the first one. Also, not that a guy like you gives a shit, but Jake isn't gay."

"Well, I *know* that. You turned him gay. Allison told us that."

"I didn't *turn* him anything. He's *bi*sexual. Always has been, but he never admitted it to you because of how judgmental and intolerant you are. Besides, it's none of your business. And, FYI, Allison is pissed off that Jake called her out on her bullshit because she was only using him for money, and she was cheating on him."

Ed selectively ignored the last part of Ben's statement. "We are *not* intolerant! We have friends who are Black. And I have Black employees, even Hispanic ones. I have *no* idea what you're talking about. Jake has *always* dated women. Until *you* moved in."

"This is some sort of a joke, right? You're just yanking my chain?"

"Just tell me how much money it'll take to make you go away."

They both turned as the front door opened and Jake walked in, looking puzzled. "Dad? What are you doing here?"

"I—"

Ben held up the cell phone. "I can *literally* replay it for you. Trying to tell you what he just said... *I* wouldn't believe it if I wasn't standing right here. I'm still not sure I believe what he just said."

Ed Murray's face went red. "*What?* What did you do?"

"I recorded the whole thing on video." Ben stopped the recording and immediately hit play, handing his phone to Jake.

His father tried to walk over and take the phone away from him, but Jake turned, blocking him, as Ben slid between them, glaring at the older man and forcing him back a couple of steps.

As the video played, the audio clearly repeated the conversation.

Jake stopped it where he'd walked in. He turned to face them.

Now Ed Murray's face had turned white. "Jake, son—"

"Get out."

"But—"

"Get. The *fuck*. Out of my house."

Ed puffed up. "This was *my* parents' house! How dare you try to—"

"Yeah?" Jake got in his face. "You keep trying to throw that in my face, but it means *nothing*! I don't want your business, I don't want your money, and I don't give a shit about any inheritance. Give it to your fucking church, for all I care. And wait until I show Mom this video."

"You wouldn't you dare!"

"Maybe I should post it on Facebook. Tag everyone in your goddamned church—"

"Stop it!" Ed Murray ran his hands through his hair and Ben

wasn't entirely sure that the man might not be close to a heart attack. His color still looked pale as he jabbed a finger in Ben's direction. "I just want this nonsense to stop!"

"This 'nonsense' is who I am, Dad. I'm bisexual, and the person I fell in love with and decided to spend the rest of my life with happens to have a penis. Deal with it. This is exactly why I never told you guys the full truth before. *This* kind of reaction, and that it wasn't any of *your* damn business. If you really loved me, you wouldn't care who I marry as long as I'm happy."

"But did you see his credit history?"

Jake shook his head, looked at Ben as if to confirm he'd just heard what he just heard, then turned back to his father again. "Unbelievable. I'm going to make sure Mom gets you tested for dementia."

Ed's eyes widened again. "What!"

Relief filled Ben that he and Jake were on the same page.

Jake turned to Ben, handing his phone back to him. "Upload that to Dropbox, babe. Right now. Make sure to share the link with me. I'm going to e-mail the link to Mom for her to watch."

"Yes, Sir." Fuck it, it was *their* house, and he'd damn sure talk to *his* Master the way he wanted to.

Before Ben could step away, Jake pulled him in and kissed him, hard, before turning back to his father. "His ex fucked him over and is in jail right now. I've known Ben for a *quarter* of my life. I know the kind of guy he is, and if you don't have enough love for me to respect my decisions, then you can get the hell out of *my* house."

"Don't you dare show that to your mother! It…it'll destroy her, hearing about you!"

Ben glanced up from his phone, where the file was currently uploading to Dropbox. Jake slowly shook his head. "Dad, seriously, you are *not* living in reality right now. I suspect even Mom will agree with me. Maybe she needs to go to court and get a power of attorney for you so she can force the sale of the business. We can play this as proof. Maybe you've finally cracked under years of stre—"

His father headed for the front door, yanking it open and slamming it hard behind him.

Ben watched Jake walk over and throw the deadbolt, his expression grim. "How's that upload coming, babe? I want to e-mail it to Mom and call her before he gets home."

"Almost done." That's when the shakes hit Ben.

Jake walked over and took the phone from him. With his other hand he tipped Ben's chin up to kiss him on the lips. "It's okay, babe," he gently said. "*We're* okay."

"I don't know why I thought to tape it, but I'm glad I did."

"Me, too."

"You wouldn't have belie—"

Jake kissed him again, silencing him. "You're wrong. I *would* have believed you. I'm glad you taped this so we can show it to my mom. She's always let him take control of things. I'm hoping from his reaction that she has no clue he's here."

"I think I read this in a romance book once. Seriously, I can*not* believe this just happened."

Jake let out a sad sigh. "Now you see why I never bothered to talk about being bi before."

"Are you sure you weren't switched at birth?"

Jake finally smiled. "Crazy, right?"

"Yeah. Crazy."

* * *

Jake

Jake forwarded the link to his mom in an e-mail and called her. When she answered, she didn't sound upset or nervous.

"Hi, sweetheart. What's up?"

"Mom, where's Dad right now?"

Now she sounded confused. "He should be at work. Probably getting ready to close for the day. I think he was at the Fruitville shop today. Why?"

"I'm at home. He just left here a few minutes ago, and if you'll check your e-mail, you'll see why. I sent you a link to a video. Call me back as soon as you watch it." He hung up on her.

He went to sit on the couch, patting it for Ben to curl up next to him. He held his cell phone in his hand, waiting.

Sure enough, less than ten minutes later, it rang.

This time, his mom sounded shaky, upset. "Jake? What is going on? What was that about?"

"If you watched the whole video, then it stands on its own. That literally just happened about fifteen minutes before I called you. Ben had the sense of mind to record it. Dad must have been waiting and watching the house. He pulled in right after Ben got home. You saw when I walked in."

"I-I had no idea. Honey, I'm so sorry. I—"

Jake didn't want to hear any excuses. "Here's *my* ultimatum—I love you both, but if you want to be a part of my life, you must accept that Ben is going to be my husband. At this point, I'm not even sure I *want* the two of you at our wedding. The ball is in your court, Mom. Get Dad under control, and show that to his doctor and get him tested for dementia. Good-bye."

He thumbed the end button and let out a deep breath before looking down where Ben's head lay in his lap. He stroked the man's hair. "You all right, buddy?"

"Yes, Sir."

He didn't sound all right.

"I'm sorry you had to go through that. Sorry I wasn't here."

"You showed up just in time."

Jake's hand came to rest on Ben's arm. "I hope this doesn't make you reconsider marrying me."

Ben opened his eyes and turned to look up at Jake. "No, Sir. Thank you for standing up for me."

"Why wouldn't I stand up for you?"

He didn't answer, finally giving a little shrug.

Jake knew Ben wasn't a girl, but it was hard for him not to feel protective of his guy. "Buddy, I'm always going to stand up for you. I'm always going to have your back, just like I know you'll always have mine. I wouldn't be marrying you if I didn't believe that."

"I never wanted to come between you and your parents."

"See, that's where you're wrong. *You* aren't. This is on them. I know you can't imagine not having a relationship with your parents, but my relationship with them has always been different than you and yours. I love them, but we're not…friendly like you guys are." He patted Ben's shoulder. "Get up. Get dressed. We're going out."

"Out?"

"Movies and dinner. We can decide what on the way."

"Yes, Sir."

Ben headed to the bedroom.

Jake thought about watching the video one more time, to see if it was really as bad as he'd thought it was, if he overreacted, and then decided not to.

It'd only piss him off.

He hadn't overreacted, although to be honest, yes, he would have worried had he heard this story from Ben.

He suspected Ben would have held back, not wanting to drive a deeper wedge between Jake and his parents.

My boy is too kind-hearted. That was exactly how an asshole like Mort took advantage of him.

Not that the fucker would get another chance.

And like *hell* would he let anyone come between him and Ben.

Chapter Twenty-Nine

Jake

Once they were in Ben's car and heading away from the house with Jake driving, Ben used his phone to look up movies and times.

"That new Avengers movie is playing. Did you want to see that, Sir?"

Jake reached over and patted his leg. "Your choice, buddy. What about dinner?"

"We could grab dinner before. It's playing downtown. There's that restaurant that you like right around the corner on the same block."

"Okay. Buy the tickets online."

"Yes, Sir."

They found a parking spot in the lot behind the theater, opting to walk to the restaurant.

They had a great dinner, and since there was still a couple of hours before they'd be in the car again, Jake even opted for a glass of wine.

Hell, after the day they'd had, he'd earned it.

After Jake paid their check and they headed toward the theater, he noticed Ben walking a little differently, looking alert. "What's wrong, buddy?" He pulled him in, brushing a quick kiss over his lips.

A quick one was all he got, because Ben stepped sideways before Jake could get more than a peck in.

"I'm fine, Sir. I just don't want us to be late." He had been speeding up, practically pulling Jake along with him.

"We'll be okay."

It was only once they were inside the theater and on their way to the right screen that Ben seemed to relax.

"Jake? Ben?"

They turned at the man's voice. Scrye and June were approaching, the tiny woman practically throwing herself at them for hugs. "Hey, how you guys doing?"

Jake shook with the man, who dwarfed him with his imposing bulk.

"What are you guys going to see?"

"Avengers," June said.

"So are we. Want to sit together?"

"Sure." Scrye and June led the way, and fortunately they were early enough to get good seats, right at the bottom of the upper section.

Jake noticed June looking around before they sat. "What's wrong?" he asked.

"Exits," June and Scrye said together, sharing a glance before they both laughed.

"Huh?"

"We always scope out all the exits before we sit down," Scrye said. "Safety first."

"I'm a safety whore," June added with a playful giggle.

Scrye leaned in and kissed her. "That she is."

Ben

Ben relaxed and was able to enjoy the movie. Maybe it was the wine Jake had, or his complete lack of experience dating a guy, but Jake acted clueless about the group of four college-aged guys Ben had heard running their mouths about them back at the restaurant, when Ben had headed for the bathroom. Guys who'd left just before them.

Fortunately, they were nowhere to be seen.

Paranoia had saved Ben's ass many times, and it was not lost on him that had some of that same paranoia filtered over to worrying about his intimate life, maybe it would have saved him the whole Mort experience.

They enjoyed the movie, the theater nearly full by the time it started, and once it ended the four of them sat there to watch for the mid- or end-credit scene these movies always had.

As did about half the remaining audience.

Finally, once they exited, June started bouncing. "Okay, excuse me, I have to use the ladies' room." She hugged Jake and Ben before darting away.

Scrye laughed. "She's not the only one." He shook with them both. "Thanks for watching with us. That was fun. We should get together and do this more often."

"I'd like that," Ben said.

"Me, too," Jake echoed.

Ben had tried to get Jake to hand over the keys to him. Not because he thought Jake couldn't drive, but he thought if he had the keys he could urge his Sir to walk faster.

Jake, however, wouldn't be rushed. He caught Ben's hand, and despite Ben not wanting to stroll through a fairly deserted parking lot at that time of night in downtown Sarasota, he wouldn't over-rule his Sir.

They hadn't parked in the parking garage, taking a spot in the lot behind the theater. As they headed that way, Ben heard voices and felt the skin on the back of his neck prickle in a really bad way.

Catcalls, kissy noises, and *that* word.

"Hey, faggots."

"Sir, *no*," Ben whispered. "*Don't* do it."

Jake came to a screeching halt. Ben tried to keep pulling him, with their car maybe fifty yards away, but Jake released his hand and spun around.

"What'd you say?"

Ben started after him, an adrenaline spike hitting him and nearly making him sick. "*Jake*," he said, low. "*Shut up* and *let* me handle this!"

"Yo, assholes," Jake called out to the four guys. "You got a problem?"

The four drunk guys from the restaurant started to amble in their direction. The one in front spoke up. "What'd you say?"

Ben grabbed his arm. "Jake! Shut *up* and let *me* handle this! Please!"

The guys were about twenty yards away, and from the way two of them were staggering, Ben knew they were likely all still drunk. Ben knew they could make the car if Jake would just turn and run, *now*.

"Jake, let's *go!*"

"No, I'm not going to let some assholes dis my guy."

"Oh, *your* guy, huh?" one of the drunks slurred. "Does he squeal for you when he takes it up the ass?"

If Ben hadn't been holding Jake back, throwing his entire body weight into it, Jake would have run into the group swinging.

"Jake! *Red!*"

Jake stopped trying to shake him off and stared at him. "*What?*"

"Red! I fucking said *red!*" He snatched the keys from Jake's hand and was about to grab his arm again when he heard Scrye's voice boom across the parking lot.

"Jake? Ben?" He ran over, June shadowing him. "You boys okay?"

Then it hit Ben who, exactly, these two people were.

June and Scrye stepped between Jake and Ben and the four drunk guys, facing the drunks. From that angle, Ben could see June had the back of her shirt pulled up, her right hand on the grip of a handgun holstered in her waistband. Scrye's black leather vest, as well as his enormous hand, hid whatever it was Scrye was currently gripping.

"Hello, boys," Scrye said as he stared down at the drunks. "Ben and Jake here are good friends of ours. Are we having a friendly chat, or what?" Scrye didn't look like a CPA. He looked—and sounded—like a fucking scary biker. "Be a damn shame if this wasn't friendly. But if it is unfriendly, I'd suggest you turn around and walk away right now, because we'll make it a *lot* more unfriendly. And it's not me you have to worry about as much as it is her. Because her aim's a lot better than mine."

Ben started dragging Jake back toward their car, terror that they were about to be caught in the crossfire filling him as the drunks took several steps away from Scrye and June.

June didn't speak, but she started easing her gun up and out of her holster. Ben had a second to wonder if it was the same gun she'd shot and killed the guy with on Manasota Key when she and Betsy had been attacked that time.

He *hated* guns—they absolutely *terrified* him.

But in this case, he'd allow his friends to possibly save their fucking asses, all because Jake wouldn't listen to him.

"Dude, no problem here," one of the guys said, holding his hands up. Apparently he was either sober enough to realize the numbers had shifted, or understood that the two newcomers to the party were armed and they weren't. "We're going."

June didn't look back. "Ben, you got your keys out?" she called.

"Yes, ma'am."

"Go to your car. *Now*. Text us when you get home. We'll stay here until you're gone and make sure they don't follow you out of the parking lot."

Ben ran, hoping Jake was behind him. His hands trembled as he yanked the door open and slid behind the wheel, taking him several tries to get the key into the ignition and get it started.

Jake didn't argue, dropping into the passenger seat. As they pulled out and sped away up US 41, he glanced back in the rear view mirror and spotted June and Scrye still standing there, watching the guys as they slowly retreated.

"*Shit!*" Ben didn't realize he'd screamed that out loud until he glanced at Jake and saw him staring at him in shock.

Jake started to speak but Ben cut him off. "*No,* Jake. Shut the *fuck* up."

Jake shut up.

The adrenaline dump was still coursing through him when they got home. After texting June that they made it home safe, Ben led the way inside, barely remembering to turn off the alarm. Once the door was locked, he turned and shoved Jake, hard, against the wall.

"What the *fuck* was that?" Ben screamed at him.

"I wasn't going to let them—"

"Let them *what?* Say mean things and tell me my mom dresses me funny?" He shoved Jake again when he tried to step away from the wall. "You almost got us into a fucking fight because some drunk assholes called us names. We could have been in the fucking car and out of the goddamned parking lot!"

Jake had tried to come off the wall again, but Ben shoved him once more, this time pinning him by the throat. "If June and Scrye hadn't fucking come along and saved our goddamned asses, do you have *any* idea how fucking *badly* that could have gone?"

"They had no right to say—"

Ben kissed him. It was either shut Jake the fuck up now, and figure some way to calm himself down, or they were going to have one hell of a fight he didn't want to have.

Briefly, the night Jake took him in hand came to mind through his fear, the sour, ugly taste coating the back of Ben's throat as a wide variety of all too realistic scenarios played through his mind about how many ways tonight could have gone badly. How scared Jake must have been waiting on him to return home that night.

Ben broke their kiss and grabbed Jake by the shirt, dragging him down the hall.

"What are we—"

"Bed. Now."

Jake

Jake comprehended that Ben was mad at him, but the worst of his own anger—and fear—had died out on the drive home.

It felt like Ben was still terrified.

And Jake… wasn't exactly sure… why.

Ben shoved him back onto their bed and climbed on top of him, leaning in to kiss him. When he sat up, he held up his right wrist. "You see this fucking collar? What's that one ring mean?"

It slammed into Jake. "Protect yourself, even from me."

"Fucking A, it does." Ben leaned in, nearly screaming. "And what did you force me to fucking do tonight?"

"Safeword."

"Do you *fucking* know why?"

"You were afraid—"

"Goddamn *right* I was afraid, you stupid asshole!" Ben kissed Jake, who, confused, went from trying to sort this out to realizing that angry sex was Ben's way of coping.

And he needed to take his boy in hand.

He needed to *re*take control.

Because the last thing Ben was feeling right now was the one thing Jake needed to give him.

Safety.

Jake pushed him off him and rolled them over so that he was on top. He grabbed Ben's hands and shoved them over his head, pinning them in place. Slanting his lips over Ben's, he kissed him, tongue-fucking him while grinding his hips against Ben's.

Only when Ben started grinding back against him did Jake sit up and start taking his shirt off. "Gonna fuck my good boy's ass." He unbuttoned a couple of buttons before yanking the shirt up and off over his head. Ben tried to reach up and help him with his belt, but Jake slapped his hands away. "Stay. You can watch."

He unfastened his belt, then reached down and did Ben's, opening his fly and fishing his cock out so he could suck him down his throat.

When Ben threw his head back and moaned, Jake knew he had his boy's attention. "Stay." He got up and stripped, yanking Ben's shoes and socks off before pulling his pants down and off him. Ben was still wearing his shirt when Jake flipped him over and slapped his ass, hard. "Hands and knees, boy."

Ben complied, his head dropping onto his hands as he waited, ass in the air.

Jake grabbed lube, a condom, and towel, and returned to the bed. After getting Ben lubed up, all the while playing with Ben's cock, Jake slapped his ass again. "On your back."

Even as he did, Ben was pulling his legs up, spread wide, hands behind his knees to hold them.

"Good boy." Jake rolled the condom on and nudged into position. "If you can come while I fuck you, you can come. Otherwise, you're going to hold it." He threw the man's legs over his shoulders and plowed him like he stole him. Staring down into Ben's eyes, which now bore a delicious subspacey glazed look, Jake tried to time it so he didn't blow before Ben.

He bent the man practically into a pretzel and he fucked him, slowing down, speeding up, fucking him deep and making sure to grind against him at the bottom of each thrust.

Then, he sensed it, the way Ben's breath gasped, rapid, trying to rock his hips with Jake until, finally, he exploded. As his cum splashed between them, some of it onto Ben's shirt, Jake sped up while Ben's ass deliciously contracted and squeezed his cock.

"There's...my...good...boy." He punctuated each word with a hard stroke until his own explosion surged through him, filling the condom and leaving him breathless.

He lowered Ben's legs from his shoulders and started unbuttoning the man's shirt. "Now we can go to sleep." He opened the man's shirt and leaned in, kissing him hard. "Love you, boy."

Ben pulled him back down for another kiss. "Love you, too, Sir."

Other than helping Jake by shrugging his shirt off, Ben barely moved, already nearly asleep as Jake went to the bathroom to clean up, then returned with a warm, wet washcloth for Ben.

Sated, and safe, he curled around his boy and fell into a hard, deep sleep.

Chapter Thirty

Jake

Saturday morning, Jake awoke and immediately snuggled tightly against Ben's back. He snaked an arm around Ben's waist and deeply inhaled, reassured Ben was there, and safe.

They were both safe.

Ben wiggled his ass against Jake. "Good morning, Sir."

"Once again, I find myself starting a Saturday morning apologizing. This is becoming a bad habit."

Ben rolled over, running his fingers through Jake's hair, fluffing it a little. Jake didn't interrupt him, because he could tell from the look in Ben's eyes that he was trying to figure out how and what to say.

It also slammed home that Ben wasn't wearing his collar, or his cuffs. In the emotional turmoil upon arriving home last night, he'd never put them on.

"I know you warned me about you not wanting to treat me like a girl," Ben finally said, "but what you did last night was down-right dangerous."

Ben's hand stroked Jake's cheek, palming it. "I've made it to thirty-five without getting my ass kicked by a bunch of half-drunk douchebros. You did the absolute *worst* thing last night. I hate that you forced me to safeword to finally get your attention because you weren't listening to me."

"I'm sorry."

"Don't be sorry. Be *observant*. If I step forward to take over, Sir, it's because I *know* it's important and you likely don't. Guys like them, they're homophobic assholes. If they'd had a gun on them, one or both of us could have ended up dead. Thank god Scrye and June followed us."

Fear sliced through him. "Maybe I need to get a—"

"*No*. I don't want you to get a gun. I want you to *listen* to me. If we're up in St. Pete or Tampa or something, somewhere it doesn't matter nearly as much, or with a large group of people, that's different. But if I'm not all PDA with you somewhere, trust me that it's not because I don't want to, but because I don't feel it's *safe* for us to."

"It's not fair I can't walk around with the guy I love and hold his hand or drape my arm around him."

"No, it's *not* fair. You're absolutely right. Welcome to *my* world. Welcome to the world of countless queers since *ever*." He stroked Jake's cheek again. "You've crossed into an alternate universe, babe. The world doesn't see you as bi. The world now sees you as gay."

"I don't give a shit what the world sees."

"Cool, but there will be assholes who care, even though what we do literally has zero impact in their world. And you *have* to learn how to deal with it without getting your ass killed. *Hello*, does Pulse ring a bell?"

Jake blanched, thinking about the horrible mass shooting at the nightclub. "Did you know someone who was there that night?"

He gave Jake "the look." "Yeeeaahh," Ben drawled. *"All* the gays *all* over Florida have each other on speed-dial. Babe, that's *not* the point. The point is I am a *guy.* The average person's interaction with me, they have no idea I'm gay and don't even care. Had you *let* me handle it last night like I *tried* to, I probably could have diffused it by laughing and saying, 'Yo, he's my buddy, and I took him out and got him wasted because his wife just cheated on him and he's angry and upset, have a little respect and let us be, huh?' I noticed them back at the restaurant. And if you'd followed my lead, chances are, they probably would have backed off because they were drunk, too. The goal in situations like that is *de*-escalation. What you did *escalated* it like a fucking express elevator."

Now Jake felt even worse. "You're right."

Ben

"Being my Master means trusting *me* as much as I trust *you.* If I say I can handle something, I'll handle it. Especially something like that. I will *never* step forward to take control without asking first, except in an extraordinary circumstance. You *told* me my first rule above all other rules was to protect myself and keep myself safe, even from you. You're my Master and forced me into safewording last night to obey that rule. Frankly, that hurt. I know you wanted to protect me, but it felt like you felt I wasn't capable of handling it, even though I spoke up and said *let* me handle it."

"I'm sorry. You're right."

Ben took a deep breath. "We need a new rule, Sir. Second on the list. If I ever speak up and say I'm taking over, Sir needs to listen, step back, and let me *do* it, even if Sir doesn't understand why at the time. We can always discuss it later, and if you feel under the circumstances it wasn't warranted, fine, I'll take punishment for it. But that goes hand-in-hand with rule one."

Jake still looked distraught, like the full ramifications of how badly last night could have ended were finally sinking in. Ben prayed their near-miss, on top of the bullshit with Jake's parents, wasn't making Jake have second thoughts about them as a couple.

"Can you do that?" Ben asked.

Jake nodded. "Sorry, buddy. Agreed. New rule in effect." The way his brow furrowed told Ben he was likely struggling with his anger again, and his next comment confirmed it. "I was just so… pissed off. On top of dealing with Dad. I wondered if this was the kind of shit my uncle had to go through when he was alive, and I damn sure didn't want them talking to you like that."

"I know, and goddamn, I love you for it. You have *no* idea how much. But sometimes, we have to hold back. And yeah, it sucks and it's not fair and it makes me angry. Maybe one day we'll hit a point in this world where assholes like that don't exist anymore. Until that day, we have to *survive*. We can't spend our lives constantly enraged over assholes, because then they're winning. We have to work where we can for change, how we can, but still live *our* lives and be happy. I refuse to live in fear, and I refuse to let human garbage dumps like them ruin my happiness."

Jake turned his head to kiss Ben's palm. "Marry me."

"We settled that. I already am."

"I mean right *now*. Let's go get married. Elope."

"Um, well, for starters, it's Saturday morning. Second, we don't have our marriage license yet so we can do that. And third, Tilly and my parents would kill us if we screw up the plans now."

Jake

"Oh. You and your logic." Jake pulled him close again and was about to say something when his cell phone vibrated on the bedside table. When he stretched and reached for it, picking it up, he realized it was his mom.

"Fuck."

Rather than putting this off, he answered it, untangling himself from Ben as he did so he could walk out to the living room to talk to her. "Yeah?"

She didn't even sound like herself. "It's Mom."

"I have caller ID. I know it's you. What do you want?"

"I wanted to apologize for yesterday."

Yeah, that was the other part of the shitshow that had fired up his emotions last night.

He took a deep breath to try to calm himself before he spoke. "You weren't there. That was Dad."

"I know. I love you, Jake. I *do* want you to be happy. Can we please have dinner and talk about this?"

He turned and spotted Ben standing in the entry to the hall-way, arms crossed and leaning against the wall, intently watching.

"When?"

"Whenever you want."

He couldn't pull his gaze from Ben's. "We'll meet you Thursday night, seven o'clock. The steakhouse we ate at last time, the one on Bee Ridge." He couldn't remember the name off the top of his head.

And it would take that long for him to talk Ben into going, *if* he could even get him to go.

Ben frowned but didn't speak.

"Okay. Thank you. We'll see you there. I promise there won't be any more foolishness like yesterday from your father, either."

"I hope not. Otherwise, you won't have a son anymore. I swear, I'll walk away from both of you without a look back."

"No, please. Just…just hear me out at dinner."

"I can't talk right now, Mom, sorry. We'll talk then."

"All right. I understand. Love you."

Another deep breath. "I love you, too, Mom. You and Dad both. I'm just really, *really* angry right now."

"I understand."

He thumbed the *end* button and sank down onto the couch.

"Do *not* tell me you just made dinner plans for us with your parents, Jake. *Not* after yesterday."

Jake knew he was walking on shaky ground with Ben and didn't blame him. "She apologized and—"

Ben turned and stormed down the hallway to the bedroom that had been his, slamming the door after him.

Jake sat there staring at his phone. He knew anything he tried to say to Ben right this minute wouldn't be right, wouldn't help, and might even push his guy over the edge. One thing at a time, maybe.

This on top of hashing out last night's near-disaster?

What the fuck am I doing? I have no right calling myself his Master. I'm a fuck-up.

Still naked, he finally stood and walked out to the kitchen. Of *course* at some point yesterday, Ben had reset the coffeemaker and all Jake had to do was hit the power button.

He pulled their mugs out of the cabinet, got the creamer and sugar ready.

By the time he had both their mugs prepared, Ben still hadn't emerged from the back bedroom.

Jake had a hard time thinking of it as Ben's room now, because it wasn't, not anymore, even though his clothes and things were still in there.

They shared a bedroom. It was *their* bedroom.

Their bed.

He found the tray Ben used to carry their coffee mugs to their bedroom in the mornings and set them on it. Balancing that, he walked down to the end of the hall, hearing loud music from behind the closed bedroom door.

Steely Dan.

Hoping he hadn't fucked up his relationship with Ben by agreeing to the dinner in the first place, he reached out and knocked.

For a moment, nothing happened, and he wasn't sure if Ben was ignoring him, or maybe hadn't heard him over the music. Just as he was reaching to knock again, the music shut off.

"What?"

Jake hated that he had put the anger, the fear in his guy's tone. "May I please come in?"

Another long pause before Ben replied. "Yeah, fine. Whatever."

No *yes, Sir*.

Fine.

Whatever.

The top two anger words of all anger words when dropped into a lovers' discussion.

He opened the door. Ben lay stretched out on top of the bed, his hands laced behind his head.

He'd even pulled on a pair of shorts.

Jake stopped at the end of the bed. "I made us coffee."

"Thanks."

Jake fought the urge to simply drop the tray, climb onto the bed, and beg Ben to forgive him.

This was the possible reaction that had terrified him from the start, when he agonized over telling him he was bi.

The betrayal, the pain in his guy's voice.

The distant gaze, the refusal to look into his eyes.

How badly had he damaged his boy's trust, and how did he earn it back?

He carried the tray over to the side table closest to the door, set the mugs there, and then hesitated.

Ben still stared at the ceiling. The way he lay, his legs crossed at the ankles, the hard set to his jaw, everything screamed pain.

Anger.

Jake set the tray aside and risked sitting on the edge of the bed. "Please, talk to me."

He didn't speak again, waiting.

It took Ben several long, agonizing minutes to finally break the chilly silence, his gaze still focused up on the old popcorn texture coating the ceiling.

"I can't believe you agreed to dinner with them after what happened yesterday. Without talking to me about it first."

Jake knew whatever he said next might make or break the rest of their lives together, so he took his time to think about it before speaking.

"I'm never going to have the rapport with them that you do with your parents. I don't expect them to magically wake up one morning and throw rainbow bumper stickers on their cars. But they are my parents, and I do love them. Before I completely cut them out of my life forever, I'm willing to give them one last chance. *Only* one. If they fuck it up, I can walk away with no second thoughts.

"I won't force you to go with me. I love you too much to do that. And I also won't hold it against you if you decide not to go with me. I can only hope you'll remember how you once told me you didn't want to come between me and them and frame this in that light and not be angry at me for wanting one last dinner with them. Because that might be what this is. It might be the night I walk away from them and never see them again. Ever. It depends on how they react."

He watched his guy, let the silence once again settle over them. It took a few minutes before Ben's body started to relax a little, even though he didn't actually move.

Ben didn't look at him, but at least he'd stopped staring at the ceiling. His gaze appeared to be fixed on Jake's left hand, which lay on the bed. It took several long, agonizing minutes for Ben to speak again.

"I can't promise you I'll go to dinner. Right now, it's a hard no for me. If you want to go, fine. But I'm too angry."

Jake nodded. "I understand."

Ben took a deep breath and let it out again. Slowly, his gaze traveled up Jake's body, until Jake found himself staring into his guy's sweet blue eyes.

Eyes filled with tears, and that broke Jake's heart.

"I'm sorry. I just…I *can't*. I'll gladly spend the rest of my life with you and obey you, but right now, this is one thing I cannot do."

Jake risked reaching out and stroking his arm. "It's okay, buddy. I understand. I don't fault you for it. And you're right. I should have talked to you first instead of agreeing for both of us. I'm sorry."

Ben finally pulled his hands from behind his head and Jake realized Ben did have his day collar on, the bracelet fastened around his right wrist. He brushed at his eyes before he rolled onto his side and laced fingers with Jake.

"I love you, Sir. If this is the worst thing we end up dealing with in our lives, I guess we're lucky. I just wasn't ready for it. I'm sorry I stormed off and slammed the door. If you want to punish me for that, or for last night after we got home, I'll take it."

Jake stretched out next to him, relief filling him. "No." He gathered Ben into his arms, holding him, their legs hooked around each other. "We're people first, buddy. Shit's gonna happen sometimes." He nuzzled the top of Ben's head. "Although…"

Ben finally looked up when he didn't continue. "Sir?"

"*Someone* put on shorts without permission. I think at the very least I should get a blow job out of that."

Ben finally smiled, kissing him. "I think *someone* should give *me* a blow job for agreeing to dinner without asking me first."

"*Hmm.* You know what? You're absolutely right. Sixty-nine it is. Move your ass, *boy*, get those damn shorts off, and get on top of me."

Ben's smile widened. "Yes, Sir."

Seconds later, Ben was straddling Jake's head. Jake reached up, grabbed him by the hips, and pulled him down onto his face so he could reach the man's cock. Ben let out a moan that still vibrated through his body as he lowered his mouth onto Jake's cock.

Jake lost himself in pleasuring the other man, sucking him, licking his balls, even rimming him. Everything he did drew delicious gasps and moans from Ben, echoed through Jake's cock as he slowly deep-throated his Master.

Jake had wanted to get Ben off first, but as they lay there, his boy was too damn good, his mouth too hot and talented, and Jake felt himself getting close. Playing dirty, he worked a finger between Ben's ass cheeks and pressed against his rim at the same time he sucked on his cock, hard and deep.

That did it, triggering Ben's orgasm, the man fucking Jake's face as his hot cum pumped into Jake's mouth.

Now Jake could let go, reciprocating, and soon Ben was sucking a load from Jake, as well.

Jake kept his hands on Ben's ass, holding him there, Ben's softening cock in his mouth.

He didn't want him to move, didn't want to spoil this perfection.

Eventually, Ben released Jake's soft member and lifted his head. "Sir, you have to let go of your toy."

"*Mm-mm*," he mumbled around Ben's cock.

Ben laughed. "Sir, our coffee's getting cold."

With an exaggerated sigh, Jake finally released him after one final suck. Ben turned around, still straddling him, and leaned in to kiss him.

"Are we okay?" Jake asked him.

Ben nodded. "We're okay, Sir."

"I love you, Ben."

"I love you, too, Jake, but *please* let me drink my damn coffee. I think I earned it."

Chapter Thirty-One

Thursday night, Jake hoped he was hiding his anxiety well from Ben. The man was nervous enough as it was, which was why Jake was doing the driving tonight.

He drove with his left hand, his right holding Ben's, their fingers entwined.

Ben stared out the window, not speaking.

"I know telling you to relax is kind of pointless," Jake said, "but please try to relax."

"I can't."

"I know. Try. For me." He squeezed Ben's hand. "Please?"

Ben took a deep breath and faced forward. "*Why* are we doing this, again?"

"Because I'm doing the adult thing by giving them one last chance to be a part of our lives, even if my dad acted like a complete and utter ass. My mom was appropriately horrified by what he did. I suspect my father's still sleeping on the couch."

"Do they know I'm coming with you?"

"I told Mom *we* would meet them for dinner. I shouldn't have to specify who I mean by *we* when I'm talking about my fiancé."

"They're going to blow up. *He* will, at least."

"Which is why we're doing this at a restaurant. Neutral territory. If they refuse to behave themselves, we can leave. And we *will* leave. I promise."

How different their two families were. From the moment Adam and Betty Hodges learned they were engaged, she'd gone into hyperdrive helping plan the celebration. Fortunately, Ben had talked her into coordinating plans with him and Tilly and Loren and Leah, so that even while it would technically be a vanilla wedding, his friends could help Ben and Jake incorporate subtle things into the ceremony and reception to satisfy their need for the subtext they wanted.

They were trying to avoid having the "Master/slave" dynamic convo with Ben's parents. Ben's parents were simply happy for them, and that was more than enough. Around them, Jake and Ben would be careful not to do anything overt that would expose them to their kinky lifestyle.

In typical guy fashion, Jake was happy to let Ben and his "bride team" plan everything. Jake hadn't planned on designating Ben the "bride," especially now with the fall-out from their near-miss. But based on how Betty happily threw herself into the planning, Ben playfully earned that designation by default, and had, fortunately, dubbed himself with it.

They'd worked out a modest budget for the festivities and both of them were contributing to the expenses. As long as Ben stuck to that budget, Jake honestly didn't care how it went down, as long as at the end of the day they both wore wedding rings on their hands and were legally married in the eyes of the State of Florida. There was only one point he would insist on, and that he'd handle privately with whoever was running their music for the reception after.

Ben's parents also insisted on chipping in some cash to pay for a few things Ben's mom wanted. Like the men wearing fancy tuxes, and a wedding cake that was far more elaborate than what Ben had planned.

Ben understandably hadn't wanted anything to do with Ed or Joyce Murray after the bizarre showdown. Ben had even safe-worded on Monday to break their protocols and put his foot down, asking Jake not to talk about them around him. Finally, the night before, Jake begged Ben one last time, as his fiancé and not as his Master, to please go to the dinner with him tonight.

Jake knew Ben thought he was crazy for agreeing to Jake's request, but Jake had broken out the secret weapon of calling Ben his fiancé while nibbling on the side of his neck, and Ben had finally melted like an ice cube in a microwave.

Lucky for Jake. Because even though he was Ben's Master, he refused to pull rank on him about something like this and force him to go. Not when his first order to Ben was to protect himself, in all ways, even from Jake.

Refusing to go was practicing mental self-care, and Jake couldn't fault him for that.

Ben had enough resistance in his spine against Jake's nibbling to stipulate two conditions of his own for coming tonight. The first being that he alone got to be the one to sign off on whether or not Jake's parents could attend their wedding. The second, that if he got up and walked out at any point in the evening, Jake would pay their check and follow him immediately, no questions asked, and no begging for patience or to go back inside.

Jake had agreed to both conditions without hesitation.

Then he'd proceeded to suck not one, but two hard orgasms out of Ben before letting Ben reciprocate and give him one. Then they'd collapsed and fallen asleep.

Jake spotted his parents' car in the parking lot when they arrived, so they headed inside, Jake holding Ben's hand. The hostess pointed them in the right direction, and Jake led the way, stroking Ben's hand with his thumb as Jake refused to let go of him even while they threaded their way around tables.

He'd already told Ben their usual protocols were suspended for the duration of the meal, things like Ben waiting to eat until he was given permission, and letting Jake order for him.

Jake's father had ended up sitting directly across the table from him. He bore a painfully constipated expression, especially so when Jake's mom got up and hesitantly hugged them both.

The waitress asked for their drink order before quickly disappearing again. Jake leveled a hard gaze at his father for a moment. The older man had the decency to look embarrassed, at least.

His mom, seated on his left, reached out and touched Jake's hand. "Thank you for coming to dinner, Jake, Ben. I really appreciate it."

"*You* appreciate it?" Jake glared across the table at his father. "Guess that's not a royal we, huh?"

His father didn't speak.

His mom patted his arm. "Honey, I know we haven't handled this well. But I'm your mother, and I love you."

She clasped her hands in her lap and stared down at them for a moment. "I won't deny that there was always this plan that you'd take over your dad's business, get married, start a family of your own. I tried for so long to have a baby, and we couldn't. When we finally had you, yes, I suppose I projected our ideals onto you."

She lifted her head and stared into his eyes. "We're not perfect. And despite your father's idiocy, we do love you. I want to be a part of your life. I don't want to miss your wedding. If Ben makes you happy, then I want to be able to see you be happy, together. Please?"

Jake let out the breath he hadn't realized he'd been holding and looked at Ben, who was seated on his right.

God love him, his guy nodded.

Jake reached over and covered Ben's hand on the table, curling his fingers around Ben's. "I don't expect you to understand or approve of our relationship. If it hadn't been for you two showing up on our front porch that morning, we never would have said anything about the…*other* stuff that we do."

His mother had the decency to redden in the face.

"But," Jake continued, "if you want to be a part of our lives, that means accepting Ben as my husband. I won't leave him behind just to make you comfortable. And for the absolute *last* time, I have *zero* interest in taking over Dad's business. I don't know how much more clearly I can say that. I keep telling him to sell it so you two can enjoy the money. I don't need you two to build up some inheritance for me. Sell out and enjoy it. Sell the other properties."

At this point, they were both pretty much pretending like Jake's dad wasn't even sitting there.

"We wanted you to not have to worry about the future."

"I don't. Ben and I have good jobs. I'm really lucky Grandma left me the house, but it needs work, and that's fine. We can handle it. I'm not living in my car and eating out of Dumpsters."

"Your grandfather started that business," his dad muttered, not meeting his gaze. "He put his entire life into it to leave his family a legacy. He grew up broke and worked hard for it. He asked me to not let it die."

"I *get* that, Dad, but it's not what *I* want to do. Just because you let Grandpa force you into taking over and running it doesn't mean I don't have a backbone. Sorry, not sorry. Sell the damn business. Grandpa's dead. Isn't it time you stop trying to make the man happy at the expense of your own happiness?"

"We *are* worried," his mom said, shooting her husband a dark glare, "that you're getting married so soon. I mean, Ben only moved in with you, what, five weeks ago? Six?"

Jake could understand *this* fear, at least. It was logical and rational. "Ben and I have known each other for over ten *years*. We've worked together, and we're best friends. If I'd just *met* him five weeks ago, yes, I'd wholeheartedly agree with you. But I *know* this man."

His father found his voice again. "Then why didn't you fall in love with him before?"

"Dad, it's complicated. When I'm in a relationship, that's it. I give one hundred percent to the person I'm with. I honestly don't think like that about other people while I'm with someone. I've always been attracted to guys *and* girls, but I never felt like that about Ben before because either he was taken, or I was. Once we were both single, then it was a different situation."

His father shook his head. "This doesn't make sense to me. How do you wake up and suddenly love a guy after being with women for years? I mean, Adam, he was—" He bit back whatever he was about to say. From the pained look on his face, Jake suspected there were conflicting emotions at play regarding his father's deceased older brother.

His only sibling.

Disowned by his parents just out of high school, and with whom he'd had little contact before the man's death ten years earlier.

His father spoke slowly, like he was trying to choose his words carefully. "I...I'm not understanding how this works. Help me understand."

Jake gave the man credit for that. He'd have to explain that nuance to Ben later. His father *was* trying, that much was obvious.

"I didn't just suddenly fall in love with Ben. This has built over ten years, and didn't come into focus for me until we were living together and both single at the same time. *That's* what you're not getting. You and Mom got married only six months after you met, right?"

Both of them reddened in the face.

"If you really want to parse this, Ben and I are being far more cautious than you two were." Jake glanced at Ben, who kept his gaze fixed firmly on their clasped hands.

"We came here tonight in good faith, despite what you did, to hear Mom out. From this night forward, there will be *no* discussion about our relationship, except in positive terms. We're getting married in a couple of weeks, and you are invited, as long as you don't disrupt the ceremony. You either accept it or you don't, but it's going to happen. End of story. Just because your parents were intolerant assholes doesn't mean you are required to be intolerant assholes."

His father had gone silent again, his gaze on the empty bread plate in front of him.

Jake's mom reached out again, touching Jake's arm. "We do want you to be happy. We just need time to get used to this."

Ben shocked Jake when he spoke. "Time is fine, Mrs. Murray. But I won't be disrespected, and I won't let either of you disrespect Jake. I honestly don't care if you like this, or me. I really don't. I love Jake, and I want to spend the rest of my life with him. I don't want to come between him and you two, but our lives come first.

"He's right that this wasn't sudden. I always thought he was straight, too, if that means anything. I didn't know he was bi. Which is another part of this equation—I never knew he might be into me because I didn't think he would. He's been my best friend for years. I think since both of us have been through a lot, had time to mature, it's better it happened like this. If you two can't at least show us common courtesy while we're together, then we won't be spending time with you."

Jake's mom, seated across from Ben, offered him a hesitant smile. "Your parents are really okay with this?"

"Yeah. When I came out to them years ago, they were like, so what? You're our son and we love you. The people we work for don't care. Our friends not only don't care, some of them have relationship dynamics that make us look like Puritanical fuddy-duddies. Just be glad it's only two of us and we're not a poly triad or something."

Jake didn't interrupt, watching his mom's face, seeing the way her smile slipped a little before she forced it back into place. "Are you all right with us coming to your wedding?"

Ben looked at Jake, then back to her. "I agree with Jake. If you want to attend and will be courteous and not disruptive, then yes. I'm fine with you attending. And don't worry, the wedding is totally vanilla. We're going to have friends and co-workers and even some of their kids there. It'll be like any other wedding."

Jake thought maybe Ben was done, but he wasn't. His next remark was pointed at Jake's dad.

"And FYI, if you think any amount of money could have made me walk away from Jake, you're wrong. Put a prenup in front of me to protect the precious 'inheritance' you want to leave him, and I'll prove it. I've been broke before. I survived and recovered. But what I wouldn't recover from is having my heart and soul ripped out if I lose this guy, because he's the love of my life."

Now Jake stepped in, gently squeezing Ben's hand. "You're not signing a prenup," he softly said. "I don't want one." He looked at his dad. "Well?"

His father deflated, visibly settling back in his chair. After a moment, he slowly nodded. "I'm sorry. Yes, I want to be at your wedding." He took his glasses off and wiped at his eyes. "You're my son and I love you."

Ben squeezed Jake's hand this time, his head snapping around and their gazes meeting. The tight, thin smile he gave Jake wasn't a huge victory, but Jake would take it.

Then the waitress showed up with a smile on her face as she set their drinks out. "Are we ready to order, or do we need a few more minutes?"

***

JAKE DIDN'T TRY to force conversation on the way home. Ben sat slumped in the passenger seat and stared out the window, lost in his thoughts. The rest of the dinner had been slightly tense, but bearable. His father had even made an attempt at conversation, sticking to safe topics, like helpful suggestions for Jake about what to look for when he finally replaced his car.

Huuuuge win, as far as Jake was concerned.

The only panicked moment Jake had was when Ben suddenly stood at one point, then paused, looking back to meet Jake's gaze. "Sorry. I'll be right back."

Jake nodded and nervously watched until he realized Ben was heading toward the restrooms.

Whew.

He thought maybe his parents would take that moment to pounce, jump at the opening to have him alone and start brow-beating him.

To their credit, they didn't.

Actually, his father's next comment took him completely off-guard. "You might want to look into replacing that old pool pump with a salt water system when you finally have to switch it out. A little more expensive at first, but you'll save money in the long run."

"Um, thanks. I'll look into that. The records Grandma left show it was replaced about ten years ago."

"The water heater's due to be replaced, too. I put that one in about fifteen years ago, not long after your grandfather died."

"I'll keep an eye on it."

"The A/C system will be getting long in the tooth. If you have major problems with it, seriously consider replacing the whole system. It'll save you a lot of money in electricity every month. They're much more efficient now."

Ben's voice from the passenger seat shook Jake out of his thoughts. "What'd your parents say when I went to the bathroom?"

"That's spooky."

"What?"

"I was just thinking about that." He told him.

"Seriously? You expect me to believe your dad talked about the house?"

"He did. I'm not going to lie to you."

Ben went quiet again. Jake hadn't specified they were returning to their usual protocols yet. He'd let Ben give him that signal.

Tonight was too fragile, too uncertain.

His guy needed to feel safe and Jake desperately didn't want to fuck it up.

They were nearly home before Ben spoke again. "Do you really think they'll behave themselves at the wedding?"

"They might not be the most talkative people, and they might not stay very long after the ceremony's over, but yes, I think they will be civil and behave themselves."

"I'll settle for civil."

When they pulled into the yard, Jake didn't shut the car off, at first. "Are we still okay?"

"We're still okay, Sir."

"You don't have to drop back into that right now if you don't feel up to it."

Ben patted him on the thigh. "I appreciate that, *Sir*. If *someone's* feeling a little guilty about tonight, your boy respectfully suggests that Sir's guilt can be alleviated by a long, slow fuck resulting in Sir's boy having a nice, hard orgasm."

Jake leaned in and kissed him. "You sick of me yet?"

Ben rewarded him with a grin and slid his hand between Jake's legs to cup his bulge. "Give me about thirty years, and then ask me that question."

Chapter Thirty-Two

Ben

"Oooh la la," Tilly said from the bedroom doorway, a Cheshire grin brightening her features. "Look at *that*."

Ben spun for her, the tails of the tux jacket flaring as he did. "Well?"

"I thought seeing your head hunk in a tux was amazeballs. You two are a pair, all right. Remember, we've got kidlets in the audience and this is a vanilla-friendly day. Try not to rip each other's clothes off after saying 'I do.'"

"Thanks for being my matron of honor. And for letting us have the wedding here."

She closed the door behind her before walking over to hug him. "Hey, I'm just glad the two of you got your act together and figured out you're happier together. There are a lot of people happy for you guys."

"Are Jake's parents here yet?"

"Yep."

"Oh, boy. Are they behaving?"

"Adolph and Eva look like they stapled their smiles into place, but your mom and dad are talking their ears off about how happy they are you two are together, sooo…" She shrugged. "I'm calling it good."

He laughed. "You're the good kind of evil."

She grinned as she adjusted his tie. "I need the horns to hold up my halo, dammit." She brushed a piece of lint off his shoulder. "Your dad is fricking *adorable*, by the way. He keeps telling everyone how he gets to walk you down the aisle and give you away."

Ben groaned. "I just want this day to be over."

Tilly gently poked him in the shoulder. "Don't take them for granted." Her smile faded. "Cris' dad threw him out when he was just a kid. Literally. Not even out of high school yet. Thought he was gay. His mom took the dad's side. That whole family was whacked. Cris' last memory of his dad is the guy screaming at him from a hospital bed, tossing him out of the room. I'm just sayin'. There's worse parents to have."

"Like Adolph and Eva?"

"Oh, fuck me, kiddo. Don't you dare tell your owner *I* called them that if you slip around him."

They both turned at the knock on the door. "Yes?" Tilly called out.

Leo's daughter, Laurel, bounced into the room. She was dressed in a gorgeous flower girl's dress picked by Ben's mom after Tilly volunteered Laurel for the gig. Ben couldn't remember how old she was. He thought she was eight or nine, but she was precocious beyond her years. She spent a lot of time around Tilly because her mom, Leo's ex-wife Eva, worked for Tilly, Leigh, Lucas, and Nick at their movie production offices there in Venice.

"Aunt Tilly, Aunt Loren sent me to ask if everyone's ready."

"Just about, sweetie. Are all the guests here?"

"I think so."

"Then I'll be out in a minute."

She first flounced over to hug Tilly, then Ben. "Thanks for letting me be your flower girl, Ben."

He hadn't quite yet earned "uncle" status in the girl's eyes, even though many of their friends in the Suncoast Society group had already been dubbed aunts and uncles by her.

"You're welcome, sweetie. Thank you for being our flower girl."

"I get paid in cake." She grinned. "*Corner* pieces. With extra flowers."

Tilly pointed at the door. "You go tell your Uncle John right now that he's in trouble with me for putting you up to that."

The girl giggled as she ran out the door, yanking it closed behind her.

Tilly shook her head.

"Uncle John?"

"Gilo. Damn SAM." Tilly made another adjustment to his tie. "You good?"

"I just want this over with. This is crazy. I would have been happy getting hitched at the courthouse."

"Yeah, not with this group. And you would have broken your parents' hearts."

"Was it your plan all along to give me the dating sites to force Jake's hand?"

A slow grin crossed her features. "Maaaaybe."

"You have the ring?"

His heart nearly stopped when she slipped her hand into her pocket, then froze, patting her pockets before grinning and coming up with the ring box.

"Don't scare me like that!"

She leaned in. "What part of 'sadist' do you not get, sweetie?" She pecked him on the cheek, used her thumb to wipe the lipstick mark off, then headed after Laurel. "Get ready to move. I'll send your dad in when it's time."

Alone again, he stared at the mirror over the dresser. There stood a grown-up-looking version of himself staring back. Thirty-five, and here in the space of a couple of months he went from being alone and homeless to being…home.

And owned.

Mind, body, heart, and soul.

He didn't feel like an adult, though, and wondered when that was supposed to kick in.

The feeling that he was all grown up and responsible.

SOMEHOW, the guest list had ballooned out of control. As Ben walked down the aisle, arm-in-arm with his dad—at his dad's insistence—Ben quit counting how many people were there. Several dozen, most of them friends from work, or from Venture and the Suncoast Society.

He focused on Jake standing there waiting for him, with Loren smiling at him as he walked down the aisle.

Tilly was there, too, as was Tony, who Jake had asked to be his best man. While the wedding party and Laurel were fancied up, as his mom called it, they'd specifically told the rest of the guests they could dress casually, shorts and sundresses in the late evening warmth of the outdoor wedding.

When Ben had joked about not just having Tony wear a tux, but making Tilly wear a tux, too, she'd immediately agreed to it with a playful grin, noting it'd hide her cast.

Loren, however, had opted for a pretty skirt and a light blue corset that matched the colors in their cummerbunds and the decorations and cake frosting accents.

His dad handed him off to Jake at the end of the aisle and went to join Ben's mom, and Jake's parents, in the front row.

Loren beamed. "Dearly beloved, we're gathered here this evening to join these two for life. If there's anyone who has a reason this shouldn't happen, speak now or forever hold your peace."

Ben had almost expected a noise from Ed Murray, but it was Gilo coughing in the back, standing there with a few other friends from the Suncoast Society who were broadly grinning, that triggered a titter of knowing laughter from some of the audience.

When Ben glanced at Tilly, she winked. Obviously, that had been arranged.

Loren smiled but managed not to crack up. "Join hands, you two."

Kel snapped pics as Mal filmed the ceremony for them, and Ben was desperately glad for that, because he wasn't sure if he'd remember anything but Jake's sweet brown eyes as he stared up at him.

* * *

Jake

I'm gonna kill Tilly and Gilo for nearly making me laugh. Jake caught her playful wink from behind Ben during that hat-tip to their kinky life and returned it.

No, not really. He loved them for working the familiar comedy act into the ceremony in a vanilla-safe way. He'd been to enough collarings and weddings with their group to have seen it play out before. Gilo cut up, and Tilly went after him, like they'd bantered at the collaring. It'd become a tradition with their group, people rarely asking them *not* to do it.

Of course when asked they didn't.

But again, that was rare. It'd become a running joke, and a beloved part of their group's treasured history. And he was glad to be a part of it.

As he stared down into Ben's eyes, he tried not to lose himself in his emotions and stay focused on what Loren was saying, but it was hard. Holding his guy's hands, being there with him, it was as if there weren't a yard full of people ready to celebrate with them.

Just the two of them, because at the end of the day, that's what mattered.

They'd said their vows during the collaring, and that was, to Jake, even more important than what they were doing now. So he'd asked Loren to keep it short and sweet and basic, and to keep the "love, honor, and obey" vows. Jake wanted it over with quickly so they could get the pictures out of the way, have their first dance, change into shorts, and then not sweat their balls off for the rest of the evening.

Tilly had even bought the four of them matching tuxedo T-shirts.

As they exchanged rings, Jake found himself blinking back tears, wishing his uncle had been able to do this. He'd never forget at the funeral, watching the man's partner of over twenty years sobbing as they'd buried him.

Not able to be legally married back then.

"Lucky" for the man, the family had disowned Adam and hadn't challenged his partner on anything.

"By the power vested in me by the State of Florida, I now pronounce you husband and husband. Lay one on him, buddy."

As Jake pulled Ben in for what they'd already agreed would be a tame kiss because of kids in the audience, Loren leaned in and whispered, "Congratulations, you lucky dudes." Jake kissed Ben, smiling down at him as Loren announced, "I present to you Misters Jake and Ben Murray."

The audience broke into applause and cheers as the two of them turned and walked back down the aisle together, arm and arm.

Fortunately, Kel and Mal were good at what they did and got the pictures over quickly, including shots with them with each set of parents.

Jake thought they might leave early, but they surprised him by settling in at a table with Ben's parents for the reception part of the festivities.

Tilly had arranged for a DJ, and as Jake and Ben were called up for their first dance, he smiled as Ben blinked away tears when he recognized the song.

"You didn't?" he whispered.

Jake arched an eyebrow. "I did."

They slowly danced as Steely Dan's *Home at Last* filled the air.

Ben rose up to kiss him. "Love you, Mr. Murray."

Jake grinned. "Love you, too, Mr. Murray."

Ben

They weren't going anywhere special for their honeymoon. Jake had mentioned getting a hotel room somewhere, but the only place Ben wanted to go was home.

Their home.

They were going to budget for a trip at some point, once they'd replaced Jake's car. They were thinking maybe Yellowstone, some place they could go hike and be alone.

Maybe check "make love in the woods" off their bucket lists.

Finally, at the end of the night, even after they'd changed into shorts and the tuxedo T-shirts and the last of the guests were helping tidy up, Jake's parents walked over to them to say good-bye, hugging them both.

"Congratulations," Ed said, handing Ben an envelope that looked like it held a card. "This is from us. We do want you to be happy, and we do want to be a part of your lives. It's obvious you guys have a lot of friends who are doing better by you than we have. I'm sorry about that. We're going to try to do better."

Ben didn't want to open the card right then, but he did give them both an extra hug. "Thank you for being a part of our day." If he couldn't show a little good will to them, he was not only being a sucky slave, he was being a sucky husband.

They'd requested no gifts, but in lieu of that people could make donations to one of four listed charities, three of them for LGBTQ causes and one of them the local animal shelter. Ben guessed the majority of the cards they'd received would either be just cards, or cards and a donation notation. He handed that card off to Tilly to pack in their car for them as they started to say their final good-byes to everyone.

"Thank you for everything you guys have done," Ben said to Tilly after another hug.

"No worries. Cris and Landry were happy to help, too." She grinned at her men. Cris currently held their daughter, who was now wearing just a diaper because Laurel had helpfully tried to help her eat a piece of cake and they'd ended up fingerpainting her and Laurel's baby brother with frosting.

Upon returning home, they unloaded the car and then Ben stripped, getting naked, except for his collar and wrist and ankle cuffs.

And his wedding ring.

He'd climbed onto the bed when Jake appeared in the doorway, wearing nothing but his tuxedo jacket and an evil grin. "Did someone save some energy for their *hus…band?*"

Ben snorted. "Dude, we get jizz all over that, they'll charge us an extra cleaning fee."

He stalked across the bedroom and climbed up onto the end of the bed. "I don't care." Straddling Ben, he laced fingers with him, pinning his hands over his head before leaning in and kissing him. "Ever fucked a guy in a tuxedo before?"

"I think technically you need more than just the jacket to consider it a tux."

Jake arched an eyebrow at him.

"Sir," Ben added.

"That's better." He kissed him again, hardening Ben's cock,

especially as Jake rubbed himself back and forth, his cock also hard and ready.

Jake reached over to the bedside table and grabbed a condom and the lube from the drawer. "I think I want to finish off the day with you inside me." He rolled a condom onto Ben and lubed him up. Then he perched with the head of Ben's cock just pressing against his rim. "Beg for it, baby."

"Please let me fuck you, Sir!"

Jake reached down and started playing with Ben's nipples, tugging on them. "You can beg better than that."

"Please let me fuck your ass, Sir!"

"Better."

"Sir, please let your boy fuck your gorgeous ass with this cock!"

"Closer, and damn sexy, but not exactly what I'm looking for."

Ben struggled against a growing frenzy of sexual frustration. "May I *please* fuck my husband's ass?"

Jake impaled himself, both of them groaning. "*There* you go, buddy. *That's* what I wanted to hear." He leaned forward, grabbing one of Ben's hands and putting it on his own cock before starting a slow, sexy grind on Ben's cock. "Don't pop before I tell you to."

Ben's groan was swallowed by Jake as he kissed him again. It was currently taking every ounce of control Ben had not to come. Jake's ass felt tight and hot and perfect and Jake knew how much he loved this. They'd fucked like this several times since that first time, and it was now always Jake in control of it, even when Ben was on top, especially since Jake realized that Ben enjoyed it that much more that way.

Jake rested his forehead against Ben's. "That's it, buddy. Stroke my cock and get me off. Make your hubby nut all over your hand so you can lick it up like the good boy you are."

Ben struggled to maintain control. Jake had apparently figured out devious ways to short-circuit Ben's nervous system. Ben had never come so hard, or so many times in his life, as he did with Jake. Part of it, he knew, was that their relationship was so fresh, but he also knew it was because things were just that *right* between them.

He felt Jake's cock getting harder, the way his ass twitched around Ben's cock.

"Almost there," Jake hoarsely said. "Get ready."

Ben jacked him faster, slicking Jake's pre-cum up and down his shaft, until, finally, Jake gasped. "Now."

It was a combination of things that pulled Ben's orgasm from him. The feel of Jake's ass squeezing his cock, the look in his husband's eyes as his cock exploded in Ben's hand, and the knowledge that this man was his for life slamming into him.

Jake grabbed Ben's cum-coated hand and removed it from his cock, pressing it to Ben's lips.

Automatically, Ben started licking, sucking, only a little surprised when he felt Jake's lips and tongue also running over his hand, tracing around his mouth, helping him.

When they were finally cleaned up and cuddled together in bed, Ben was nearly asleep when Jake spoke.

"Love you, boy."

Ben snuggled tightly against him. "Love you, Master."

***

Jake

Jake spooned along Ben's back, draping an arm around his waist as he nibbled at the back of the man's neck. "Morning, sleepyhead. *Mister* Murray."

"*Mmm.* Morning, Master." As Jake hoped he would, Ben wiggled his ass close, backing up against him as tightly as he could, which quickly coaxed Jake's morning wood into a full-blown, raging hard-on.

Jake wasted no time climbing on top of Ben in a sixty-nine, the two of them quickly making each other come before collapsing on the bed in a panting heap.

"Coffee?" Jake asked.

Ben leaned in and kissed him. "Yes, Sir. Morning spanking?"

"Afternoon spanking. I want to wake up first. Then I'm taking my *husband* out to breakfast."

Ben grinned. "Yes, Sir." Ben left their bed and stopped by the bathroom before heading out.

"Oh, bring the cards in with you," Jake called out as he headed for the bathroom. "Let's go through those this morning."

"Yes, Sir."

Ben returned a few minutes later with the cards and while a Sunday morning news program played on the TV, they started opening the cards as they sipped their coffee.

Jake had become interested in one of the news stories when Ben made a weird noise next to him.

"What?"

Ben had gone white. He held a card, staring at it with wide eyes.

"Babe, what?"

Ben slowly closed the card and passed it to him.

He opened it and the first thing he saw was the check.

For twenty-five *thousand* dollars.

Jake made the same noise Ben had just made as he double- and triple-checked that he was reading it correctly.

A check from the bank account of Ed and Joyce Murray, payable to Jake and Ben Murray.

Inside, the note on the wedding card was written in his father's hand, but his mom had also added a short, *We love you!* and signed it.

Dear Son,

I'm sorry that I haven't been the best father the past several months. And for the things I've done before that alienated you. We love you. Your mother broke out an old family album the other day and I stared at pictures I hadn't taken the time to look at in a while. Of you as a baby, of your high school graduation. And others. You do deserve to be happy, and I'm proud of you for being strong enough to find that happiness. Please use this to either replace your car, or do any work you need to the house, however you need to use it.

I love you,
Dad.

The words blurred as Jake realized he was crying.

Ben hugged him. "Holy shit, Sir," he said. "I think hell just froze over."

"I think maybe my Dad's heart finally defrosted," Jake said.

Chapter Thirty-Three

Ben

The Friday evening less than a week after their wedding, and both sets of parents were due at the men's house at eight for dinner.

Ben had invited all four of them.

He'd also taken the day off from work to prepare, making sure the house was clean top to bottom, and preparing a lavish dinner he hoped would woo Jake's parents.

He figured it was the least he could do after the wedding present they'd given them.

Most of which Jake was currently driving, after they'd gone out Sunday afternoon and went car shopping, closing the deal Monday morning after filing their marriage certificate. Jake now had a dark blue, two-year-old Honda CRV with less than ten thousand miles on it, and they'd paid cash for it. The trade-in they would have gotten for his car wasn't good so they opted to keep it and were planning on having it detailed and selling it themselves.

And they still had some funds left over to put into the house, or savings, or maybe even a vacation.

Jake arrived home a little after five, walking in and kissing Ben in the kitchen. Today, Ben wore shorts and his day collar with Jake's blessing, Jake knowing the stress he was already under by offering to do this and not wanting to pile more onto him.

"It smells great, babe."

"Let's hope they like it."

Ben's parents predictably arrived nearly forty-five minutes early, his mom eager to help despite Ben assuring her he didn't need any help.

When Jake's parents arrived at a quarter 'til, Ben was dressed in jeans and a short-sleeved button-up shirt, but barefoot. Jake had kept his work clothes on, slacks and a button-up shirt.

Ben had also asked Jake to let him answer the door for them. He hoped his smile looked right as he welcomed them inside, shocked when both Ed and Joyce gave him hugs.

"It smells lovely," Joyce said.

"Thank you."

He'd already thanked them over the phone for their wedding gift when he called Joyce and invited them to dinner.

He was willing to extend the olive branch to them.

As long as they didn't yank it out of his hand and whack him over the head with it.

* * *

Jake

Jake knew what a feat of bravery this was for Ben, so he let him completely call the shots, from the menu to how it went down.

He wasn't sure exactly what Ben hoped to accomplish with this dinner, but he would be happy if they got through it with his parents being polite and not leaving Ben upset by the time they left.

Once they were all seated at the table, his father even shocked Jake. "So tell us about your new car, son. Are you enjoying it? Did they give you a good deal?"

This he could handle. They got to talking about that, which relaxed everyone. The topics shifted back and forth, until Jake's mom asked Ben's mom about their church.

Jake and Ben, sitting at either end of the table, met each other's gazes and fell silent. Jake knew Ben's thoughts were probably mirroring his own.

W.

T.

F?

But Betty, bless her heart, plunged on, her husband happily adding his opinion, chatting away about their busy social life there, their friends, how happy they were with the minister, the volunteer projects and charities they helped out with.

Jake and Ben remained silent, frozen, watching.

Eventually, Jake's mom revealed her agenda.

And it shocked Jake so much he actually set his fork down to listen.

"Ed and I have been thinking about changing churches. Over the years, as we look back, we realize it's not the same church we started attending when we first got married. It was his parents' church, not mine, but I really didn't want to make waves with my new in-laws at the time. Would you mind if we attend your church with you this Sunday?"

"We'd be delighted to have you," Sam exclaimed with a beaming smile. "We can even go out for brunch after, if you'd like."

Ed nodded. "I'd like that," he quietly said. "That sounds nice."

When Jake met Ben's gaze again, the other man's jaw was, literally, dropped.

The two moms seemed to take up the bulk of the conversation. It wasn't until toward the end when Ed finally spoke again, picking up the tail end of a comfortable lull in the discussions.

"Jake, I wish you could have known your Uncle Adam. I'm sorry that I didn't stand up to my parents and build that bridge with him."

He glanced across the table to the Hodges. "He was my older brother. Three years older. When he left for college, he admitted to my parents that he was gay, and they completely disowned him. My father had been grooming him to take over and run their business after college."

He stared down at his plate, where he idly pushed a pea around with his fork. "I'd planned to study design. I wanted to build furniture, work on home interiors. When my parents cut Adam out of our lives, I was told in no uncertain terms that I was their only son, and that I'd study business in college and take over from my father."

A chill swept through Jake. He'd never heard this story before. "Why didn't you ever tell me that, Dad?" It would have put a lot of things into perspective.

It would have put *everything* his father did into perspective.

"Because I was busy trying to make a living and please your grandfather. Then I met your mom and wanted to raise a family with her. I swore I'd never do what my dad did...but then we didn't have kids, and I'd reached a point where I'd resigned myself not to doing that. And then we had you and fear took hold. Your grandfather still owned the business. I knew I had to stay there and do what he wanted. He kept talking about how he was so proud of me, and was proud of you, too. That you'd be continuing the legacy."

He set his fork down and took a deep breath. "I guess it's time I follow my son's lead and take a stand of my own against my dad. Your mom doesn't even know this yet, but I've decided to sell the business. I found a broker in Sarasota who handles things like this. And we're going to sell the other properties, too. You're right. Life is short. Your Uncle Adam escaped and went on to be happy. He sent me a letter after you were born and told me how much he missed me and how happy he was for us. I wish I'd reached out to him…but I didn't. And now I can't talk to him. He was my older brother, and I loved him so much. He was everything to me. He'd encouraged me to follow my dream to design furniture."

"And then your father threatened to cut you out of their life, too, if you didn't toe his line," Ben quietly said.

Ed nodded. "I won't lie to you two and say I agree with this. But I love my son, and I want him to be happy, and I don't want to cut him out of my life. So I know I need to set that aside and be happy for both of you. If we could start over again from that point, I would be very grateful to you both."

Ben was the one who got up first, rounded the table, and hugged the older man from behind. "Thanks, Mr. Murray. I agree. Clean slate."

"Call me Ed. Or Dad. Whichever you want."

Jake's mom was crying as she leaned over and hugged them both. "Thank you, Ed." Across the table, Betty and Sam both dabbed at their eyes with their napkins.

Jake got up and rounded the table to join the group hug. "Thanks, Dad."

The older man let out a sniffly laugh. "I'm going to pretend I've gained another son. We always wanted a large family. Well, I'd be an idiot to not look at this like we're gaining a son, right?"

"Right, Dad," Jake said.

Ben

Ben held it together until both sets of parents finally left. In the entryway, he clung to Jake as he burst into tears. "Oh, my *god*. Did that actually *happen?*"

Jake held him. "Yeah, buddy. It did. Good job, you." He kissed him, pulling him in again for another long hug.

"Your poor dad. Honestly? I went into tonight thinking if we could get through dinner and I didn't end up with an ulcer that it'd be a win. I never in my life would have imagined he'd open up like that."

"I didn't even know all that. I mean, I knew about my uncle, barely. I went to his funeral. My dad never talked about him when I was growing up. Uncle Adam would send me birthday and Christmas cards and stuff with money or gift cards in them, but I didn't know him. I'd always send thank you notes back to be polite."

"I promise I'll always try to remember *this* if your dad's ever an ass again. I'll try to always have patience with your dad, even if he acts like a jerk."

"Thank you. I appreciate that. I don't expect this is some miracle, though. Maybe he's really changed. I wouldn't be shocked if we get pushback from him at some point."

"Doesn't matter. Took a big man to admit what he did tonight. I'll focus on that."

Jake stared down into his blue eyes. "Any regrets, mister?"

Ben smiled up at him. "Not a single one, Master."

Jake swatted his ass. "Then get naked, and get that collar back on so we can do the dishes." He released Ben and headed toward the kitchen.

"But I'll do the dishes, Sir."

"I'm helping. The faster we get them done, the faster I can feel that sweet cock of yours fucking my ass." He glanced back to spot Ben's grin.

He was already unbuttoning his shirt. "My cock, Sir?"

"You heard me. Good boys get rewards."

"Thank you, Sir!" He raced off toward their bedroom to change and get his collar.

Jake chuckled to himself as he rolled up his sleeves even farther and started filling the sink with hot water so he could scrub the cooking pots.

Yep, situation normal.

Whatever *that* was.

A moment later, Jake heard Ben turn on the living room stereo and the tones of Steely Dan filled the house.

Jake grinned, truly happy. *Home at last, indeed.*

THE END

Keep reading for more information about my Suncoast Society series!

About the Suncoast Society Series

While most of the books in the Suncoast Society series are standalone works that can be read independently of the others, many characters in the series appear in multiple books.

For the reading order, related books, character information, trivia, and more, you can visit the series page on my website at:

http://www.SuncoastSociety.com

You can also sign up for my author newsletter, where I post info about both my Lesli Richardson and Tymber Dalton pen names, and never miss a new release or update:

https://tymberdalton.com/newsletter/

Other Titles

Sign up for my author newsletter, where I post info about both my Lesli Richardson and Tymber Dalton pen names, and never miss a new release or update:

https://tymberdalton.com/newsletter/

Writing as Lesli Richardson:

Maxim Colonies:
1) *Jailmates*
2) *Farborn*
3) *Saudade*

The Great Turning Series:
1) *The Great Turning*
2) *The Great Turning: Into the Turn*
3) *The Great Turning: Future Ages*

Governor Trilogy:
1) *Governor*

2) *Lieutenant*

3) *Chief*

4) *Yes, Governor*

5) *Pet*

Determination Trilogy:
(Set in the world of the Governor Trilogy.)

1) *Dignity*

2) *Diligence*

3) *Desire*

Devastation Trilogy:
(Set in the world of the Governor Trilogy.)

1) *Dirge*

2) *Solace*

3) *Release*

Inequitable Trilogy:
(Set in the world of the Governor Trilogy.)

1) *Indiscretion*

2) *Innocent*

3) *Incisive*

Devout Trilogy:
(Set in the world of the Governor Trilogy.)

1) *Sacred*

2) *Profane*

3) *Penance*

The Bleacke Shifter Series:
1) *Bleacke's Geek*
2) *Geek Chic*
3) *A Bleacke Wind*
4) *Bleacke Spirit*
5) *A Bleacke Christmas*
6) *Geek-Speak*
7) *Bleacke Expectations*
8) *Bleacke Moments*
9) *A Bleacke Outlook*
10) *Bleacke Blessings*
A Bleacke Meeting: A Bleacke Shifters Story

- *Of Boardwalks and Bison*
- *Cross Country Chaos*
- *Poly*
- *Her Vampire Obsession* (Midnight Doms Series)
- *"His Vampire Morsel"* (*All Souls' Night: A Midnight Doms Anthology*)
- *How Many Times Do I Have to Say I'm Sorry?* (Maudlin Falls 1)
- *Fierce Radiance* (Space Confederation 1)
- *Acquainted With the Night*
- *Whip Me, Beat Me, Make Me Write Hot Sex* (non-fiction)
- *Blow Sh*t Up!* (non-fiction)

Lesli Richardson is better known by her more prolific *USA Today* Bestselling Author Tymber Dalton pen name. Please visit her website for more info on all her titles under both pen names, including full book and series listings, trivia, character information, and more.

http://www.tymberdalton.com

About the Author

Author Lesli Richardson, who is better-known by her more prolific wild-child Tymber Dalton pen name, lives in the Tampa Bay region of Florida with too many pets of various species. She writes in a wide variety of heat levels and genres, from mainstream sci-fi all the way to scorching ménage.

The *USA Today* Bestselling Author (as Tymber) and two-time EPIC award winner is a part-time Viking shield-maiden in training who loves to shoot skeet and play D&D with her friends. She's also the author of over 250 books and counting, including *The Reluctant Dom*, *Cross Country Chaos*, *Her Vampire Obsession*, the Bleacke Shifters series, the Governor Trilogy series, and many others.

She lives in her own little world, but it's okay—they all know her there.

She loves to hear from readers! Please feel free to drop by her website and sign up for her newsletter to keep abreast of the latest news, snarkage, and releases.

Honest reviews are always welcomed. They help with a book's visibility and can boost its placement on book retailer sites. Even a few lines about what you felt reading the book will help. Thank you so much, it's greatly appreciated!

Newsletter: https://tymberdalton.com/newsletter/
http://www.tymberdalton.com